GALE $31.∞ 11/16

DR. KNOX

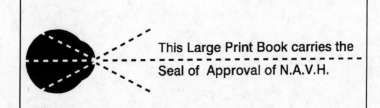
This Large Print Book carries the
Seal of Approval of N.A.V.H.

DR. KNOX

PETER SPIEGELMAN

THORNDIKE PRESS
A part of Gale, Cengage Learning

LP FIC SPIEGELMAN

Farmington Hills, Mich • San Francisco • New York • Waterville, Maine
Meriden, Conn • Mason, Ohio • Chicago

GALE
CENGAGE Learning·

LIBRARY OF CONGRESS CATALOGING-IN-PUBLICATION DATA

Names: Spiegelman, Peter, author.
Title: Dr. Knox / by Peter Spiegelman.
Description: Large print edition. | Waterville, Maine : Thorndike Press, 2016. | Series: Thorndike Press large print thriller
Identifiers: LCCN 2016030502 | ISBN 9781410494344 (hardcover) | ISBN 1410494349 (hardcover)
Subjects: LCSH: Large type books. | GSAFD: Suspense fiction.
Classification: LCC PS3619.P543 D7 2016b | DDC 813/.6—dc23
LC record available at https://lccn.loc.gov/2016030502

Published in 2016 by arrangement with Alfred A. Knopf, a division of Penguin Random House LLC

Printed in Mexico
1 2 3 4 5 6 7 20 19 18 17 16

For Alice, Adam, and Ben

They call me and I go.
It is a frozen road
past midnight, a dust
of snow caught
in the rigid wheeltracks.
The door opens.
I smile, enter and
shake off the cold.
William Carlos Williams,
"COMPLAINT"

CHAPTER 1

Mia should've been it for the day. She had bruised ribs and a slash down one long white leg, though not from shaving. She was worried about a scar, and that it might hurt business. She swung her dark hair over her shoulder and fluttered painted eyelids at me. " 'Course, for some guys it might be a draw," she said. Her voice was low and scratchy.

"Charge them extra," I suggested.

Her Adam's apple bobbed as she laughed. "You got a flair for marketing, Dr. Knox. Do I need stitches?"

"Just a tetanus shot and butterfly strips," I said. "Jerome do this?" Jerome was Mia's boyfriend, her pimp, and her alleged fiancé. He said they'd get married after she had the surgery, but I thought he was full of shit. I was pretty sure that — deep down — Mia thought the same.

She batted her eyes again. "He doesn't

mean anything by it."

"Jerome's an asshole."

"He was pissed 'cause Azul lost to Tigres last weekend, and he lost a bunch of money."

"So he's a degenerate gambler, a sore loser, *and* an asshole," I said as I ran an alcohol swab over her wiry arm. "The trifecta. One day you're going to get hurt for real."

Mia winked, and winced as I stuck the needle in. "*Ow!* You gonna take me away from all that?"

"I'm too old for you."

"You got mileage, sure, but you still got it goin' on. You got that lean, aging surfer thing working — or maybe it's an aging ski-bum thing. Either way, girls notice. Guys too."

"You've got the aging part right," I said, and pressed a Band-Aid over the injection site.

"Not to worry, baby," Mia said. "I got energy for two." She laughed deeply and waggled a finger. "And look — you're not too old to blush."

"I lead a sheltered life."

"Bullshit," she said, giggling. "You've got some crazy in you." She touched a fingertip to my tattoo — a tribal braid that ran

10

around my biceps, just below the short sleeve of my scrubs. "You get that in the library?"

"A momentary lapse in judgment. Keep the leg clean."

"I keep it all clean," Mia said, "every inch." Then she winked again and glided from the exam room.

I looked at my watch. Nearly 7:00 p.m. Nearly there.

Before Mia, there'd been Greggie, an ashen, greasy-haired wraith, shivering, mumbling, and shopping for 'scrips again. I'd offered him B12, a sandwich, and a rehab referral — which I did whenever he came in looking for drugs behind some bullshit symptoms — in response to which Greggie had rubbed his hands together over and over and finally said, *Fuck yerself.* Every two weeks, like clockwork with Greggie.

And before him, lined up since early morning, there had been the bleak parade of the homeless. Beneath sedimentary layers of rotting clothes, I'd found three pneumonias, a conjunctivitis, a diarrhea, four staph infections, two cases of lice, knife wounds, contusions, rat bites, and countless varieties of ulcerated skin crud — and each patient with a stench so earthy and power-

11

ful it was like a suffocating hand over my face.

Lydia Torres, my nurse and the manager of the clinic, called it *underpass disease.* I thought of it as *San Julian syndrome,* after the street not far from here whose doorways and curbsides were the closest things many of these folks had to an address. *San Julian syndrome:* the slow and not-so-slow decay of the luckless, the mad, the addicted, damaged, damned, and forgotten. TB and its complications, diabetes and its complications, hypertension, Hep C, HIV, bipolar disorder, schizophrenia, PTSD, and that most desperate diagnosis of all: poverty.

I'd seen many of today's homeless before, several under different names. There was no particular reason for the serial aliases, I'd learned — sometimes their old names just didn't suit anymore, or had been forgotten, or simply couldn't bear the weight of more history. And, really, who couldn't understand that.

I peeled off my gloves, tossed them in the can, and took a deep breath. The air in the exam room was used up — crowded with the smells of disinfectant, Mia's perfume, the lingering reek of street folks, and traces of my own sweat. I leaned over the steel sink and looked into the steel mirror. Angles,

12

planes, a web of lines about narrow, green eyes, and gray streaks in short, straw-colored hair. *Aging surfer, aging ski bum.* Aging right before my eyes. I ran the water and sluiced some on my face.

Not a bad day, all in all, and far from the worst. No screamers — not really loud ones, anyway — no violence to speak of, no sudden deaths, and, thank God, no kids. No great victories, but I'd stopped expecting those a week into my residency. Medicine was by definition a play for time, a holding action — skirmishes fought hand to hand or with small, inadequate armament. But always — no matter how long you dragged it out — the outcome was preordained. A rigged game.

I dried my hands and face and thought about the joint upstairs, on my kitchen table. A shower, a change of clothes, a six of Stella from the fridge, the lawn chair on the roof, the joint, and the May twilight over L.A. These private fiestas were something of a ritual on Friday evenings. On other evenings too, of late — perhaps on too many others. I closed my eyes and pictured the view from up there, the low, shabby skyline of the neighborhood — *Skid Row–adjacent,* one of our hilarious part-timers had called it — the downtown towers looming in the

13

west, and the sunset behind them, the sky banded in acid pinks and reds. I could almost feel the gritty wind.

I went down the hall to what passed for my office — a wood-paneled, windowless nook with a three-year-old Real Madrid calendar caught in perpetual February on the wall. The desk was a heap: perilous stacks of forms to be signed — state paper, federal paper, private insurance paper — all to chase reimbursements that didn't cover the rent; more bills to be paid, most on second notice, some on the third; and on top of it all another letter from my landlord, Tony Kashmarian.

This one was mostly the same as the several he'd sent recently: a reminder that the clinic's lease was up at the end of August — three months from now — and that, unless I wanted to exercise my right of first refusal, the building was going up for sale. This one, though, named a listing price — a seven-figure one.

I shook my head at the number — its size and lunar distance, the mockery it made of the down payment I'd been scraping together. How was I supposed to conjure a number like that, when every payroll was a scramble? Certainly no banker in his right mind would lend it to me, and lately they were all in their right minds when it came to mortgages. And if I didn't find the money, where was my little operation supposed to move? And where was I supposed to live? I'd been asking those questions for months, and knowing Kashmarian's price just put me further from the answers. I thought again about the joint in my kitchen and headed for the stairs.

I was at the stairwell door when I heard cries from the waiting room — a woman's voice, choked, high-pitched, animal — and then Lucho pounding down the hall.

Lucho — my greeter, my bouncer, officially my physician's assistant and the clinic's assistant manager — filled the corridor. He was pale and sweating. "It's a kid," he panted. "He's blue."

"Fuck," I whispered, and took a breath as if for a deep dive.

Not just a kid, but a little kid — no more than five. He wore navy shorts and a blue-and-white striped polo shirt, and he was thrashing and gasping and sliding off one of the plastic chairs. His mother — I assumed it was his mother: they had the same chestnut hair, and the panic in her eyes was a mother's panic — knelt beside the boy, slapping him on the back and speaking in a terrified voice. Arthur, Lucho's boyfriend and our IT consultant, stood behind her, frozen in mid-offer of a cup of water. I picked the boy up. He was maybe thirty-five pounds.

"Where's Lydia?" I said.

"Home by now," Lucho said.

Fuck.

I carried the boy to an exam room. The mother followed, talking and stifling sobs. I didn't understand a thing she said, but it sounded like Italian to me, though not quite. Great. And then my vision sharpened and narrowed, and I was pulled down the bright, rushing tunnel of emergency.

The boy's skin was clammy and white, tinged blue at the fingernails. His lips were cyanotic too, and swollen, and there were hives on his cheeks and neck. He flailed in my arms like a just-caught fish. His eyes darted, and he reached for his mother. There was wheezing and whistling in his chest — the sounds of an airway closing fast. The boy twisted again, nearly out of my grasp. *Shit.* The fight for breath was hard enough on the boy's heart, but panic and thrashing would add to the strain, and up the risk of cardiac arrest. If he didn't asphyxiate first.

I laid him on the table, laid a hand on his chest, tried to find a pulse in the small wrist.

The boy yanked his arm free, smacked me in the eye, in the mouth.

I grabbed both his arms, bent to his ear, and whispered, "It's all right, pal. We're gonna be fine." I put two fingers to the boy's neck and found a pulse. It was rapid and thready.

The woman pulled at my arm, saying something, yelling it. She raised her hand to her mouth, again and again. The boy made a rattling gasp that ran like an electric current through his mother.

"*Arahide,*" she said. "*Arahide!*"

"Something he ate?" I asked, and the woman nodded. "What? What did he eat?"

"*Arahide,*" she said again, and her brows came together. "Peanut!" she yelled.

Lucho was standing in the doorway of the exam room, and I waved him in. "Tilt the table," I said, "head down, feet up, and don't let him fall off." And then I ran down the hall.

I fumbled my keys, cursed, and got the med closet open. I scanned the metal shelves and grabbed EpiPens, an IV kit, a pediatric gauge needle, a bag of saline, a vial of IV Benadryl, an intubation kit, which I hoped I wouldn't need, and a trach kit, which I prayed I wouldn't. I ran back to the exam room, dumped the supplies on the

17

counter, and tore open an EpiPen. I took out the injector and popped the safety cap.

"Hold his leg," I told Lucho, and then I pressed the pen into the boy's bare thigh, and kept it there for a five count through his scream.

It took four minutes for the epinephrine to kick in, which passed like four hours. Finally, the boy's wheezing and whistling began to subside, and the blue tint faded from his lips. With easier breaths and more oxygen, his panic faded too, and so did his mother's. She combed her fingers through his hair, and cooed at him in what wasn't Italian. I waited five more minutes and hit him with half of another EpiPen.

Twenty minutes later, the boy's color was good, and so were his pulse and BP. Lucho hauled an oxygen bottle from the med closet, and I held the mask up for the boy to eye suspiciously before I slipped it over his nose and mouth. I'm good with an IV — accurate and fast, from lots of practice — and I had the line in and the tubing taped down before the boy could do more than yelp in surprise. I pushed Benadryl through the port, and between the antihistamine and exhaustion, sleep took him fast. I watched the boy's breathing and checked his pulse, and then I stepped away from the table.

I leaned against the wall. There was an adrenal tremor in my knees, and my scrub shirt was patched with sweat. Kids. I took slow, deep breaths to steady my pulse.

The woman tapped my shoulder and said something to me I didn't understand. I looked at Arthur and Lucho, who shrugged. "English?" I asked the woman. "Español? Français?"

She nodded slowly, and her brow wrinkled again. "The boy is good?" Her voice was soft, and her English heavily accented. Something eastern European.

"It was an allergic reaction — a pretty bad one — but he should be fine. We need to keep an eye on him, though — watch him for a while. And no more peanuts for him — ever." The woman let out a long, shaking breath and took my hands.

"You understand English?" I asked. She nodded, and I took a closer look at her.

She was young, not twenty-five, and just a shade over five feet tall. Her body, in jeans and a pink tank top, was slender but strong-looking — conditioned, trained for some-thing. Too slight for a swimmer — a gymnast perhaps, or a dancer, or an aerialist run off from the circus. Run from somewhere, I thought. Her skin was waxy and shining with sweat, and her hair, bound in a chestnut braid, was long unwashed. Her eyes were dark, wary buttons in an oval face, and her mouth was a downcast bow, sullen and perfectly shaped. A guarded face — barred and bolted — but pretty. More than pretty. And that was with all the bruises.

They were everywhere — under her left eye and along her jaw, on her neck and down her arms to her wrists. I could see the shapes of palms and thick fingers in some places, and divots where the fingers had worn rings. The damage wasn't fresh — a week old perhaps, and starting to heal. Beneath the bruises — despite them — something radiated from her: an insistent, thrumming sexiness. It was like an electric field that bristled the hairs on your arm as you passed, or a riptide that pulled at you even on dry land.

I snapped on a fresh pair of gloves and reached for one of her bruised arms. She jerked away, and her eyes flashed. Her fists were clenched and raised — ready.

I pointed at her arm and her cheek. "Those need looking at." She stepped back, shaking her head. "I won't hurt you," I said.

She wrestled down her impulse to fight and spoke again. "Is toilet?"

I pointed to the far end of the corridor, past the med room. "End of the hall, on the left. And then I want to look at those bruises."

She took my hands and stared down at them. "Thank you," she said softly. It came out as *tank you.* "I come back." Then she headed down the hall.

I went back to the exam room, and Lucho and Arthur followed. I checked the boy's pulse. Nice and steady.

"That was fucking scary," Lucho said.

"Kids always are," I said.

"He's really going to be okay?" Arthur asked.

"He should be. Either of you get a name for him or his mom?" They shook their heads. "You know what she's speaking?"

"Arabic?" Lucho offered.

Arthur shrugged. "Sounds like a neighbor lady we had when I was kid, and she was Romanian — but that's just a guess."

"Somebody went at her pretty good," Lucho said.

I nodded. "She'll be lucky if —" There was a metal shriek from down the hall, followed quickly by a solid *thunk.* I looked at Lucho. "Was that the — ?"

"Back door," Lucho said, and he sprinted down the hall. In a moment he returned, shaking his head. "She bolted, doc. Down the alley and gone."

"You're fucking *kidding* me," I said softly.

From his deep sleep the boy muttered something, but none of us could make out the words.

CHAPTER 2

"He is not a goddamn puppy, doctor," Lydia Torres said. Her voice was an angry whisper; her square face was dark and clenched, and her many smile lines were invisible. "You cannot keep him just because he wandered into your yard."

I looked from Lydia to Lucho, who said nothing, but stared at his shoes and backed slowly from the waiting room. I understood his caution. At five and a half feet tall, Lydia was built like a bull terrier — a solid cylinder of muscle and, just then, menace. Her hair, a thick, natural black despite her fifty-five years, was pulled in a tight bun, and her heavy brows were gathered in a squint. Her shoulders were squared for a fight. Still, I held my ground.

"I'm not suggesting anything permanent. I'm saying we look out for him until his mother comes back."

Lydia's face grew darker, and she counted

on rigid fingers. "First, you don't even know if this woman *was* his mother. Second, mother or not, you don't know she's coming back. And, third, don't be giving me this *we* crap — it's *me* you want looking out for him. We got to call the cops, doctor, them or DCFS."

"Child and Family Services? You can't be serious, Lyd — it's one shit storm after another with them. You remember that series in the *Times* last month? They can't find their asses with both hands. I wouldn't trust them to look after a cup of coffee."

"It's *their* job, doctor, not ours."

I shook my head. "And besides, she *is* his mother — they look alike, and you don't get that kind of scared unless you're a parent." I turned to Lucho. "You were there — tell her."

Lucho put his hands up and shook his head. "I learned young not to correct my *tía,* doc. I'm gonna check the kid."

"You've got your nephew intimidated," I said.

Lydia sighed. "Him, but not you. Piss-poor mother, if she is his mother — running out on a son like that."

"She said she'd be back."

"From the *bathroom,* doctor. And she said it right before she abandoned him."

"She didn't abandon him. She was afraid of something. I think she was on the run."

"And this you get from what — a few bruises?"

I had a professor my fourth year of med school, a white-haired internist who'd told me: *Your nurse sees more patients than you do, and spends more time with 'em. She talks to 'em about things you don't, and knows 'em in ways you can't. Not listening to your nurse is like watching TV with the sound off — you might figure out what's goin' on eventually — but chances are you'll miss something, and in the meantime somebody will die. So — you can listen to your nurse, or you can be an asshole. Try not to be an asshole.*

Even when I was twenty-six, and still very much an asshole, it had struck me as sound advice, and I'd tried to follow it. Certainly I listened to Lydia — she was smarter and more experienced than any nurse I'd worked with, had more clinical sense than most of the doctors I knew, and was tougher by far than any of them. I listened to her even when she spoke to me as if I were an errant child, and made *doctor* sound somehow ironic. I listened, but didn't always agree.

"It was more than a few bruises, but it's not just about those. Take a look." I beckoned, and she followed me to the file room,

25

a narrow space lined with metal cabinets. Arthur was sitting at a desk at the back, looking at a laptop. His tanned face went pale when he saw Lydia's expression.

"Play the security video again, will you?" I asked. Arthur nodded, tapped at the keyboard, and turned the laptop around for us to see. Two windows opened on the screen.

"This is from the front-door camera," Arthur said, pointing to the window on the right, "and this is from the one mounted on the second-floor corner."

The window on the left showed an image of an empty sidewalk and a storefront, viewed from above. The angle was oblique, but the clinic was plain — the big front windows, the glass door in between. Security grating aside, it still looked like the hardware store it once had been.

"See the time in the corner?" I said. "Seven-nineteen — that's when we were in the thick of it with the kid. Not five minutes after he and his mom came in."

Lydia interrupted. "You don't know that she's his mother."

"Just watch."

"I'm watching. All I see is —"

And then two men appeared on the screen, in the left-hand window, walking quickly. They looked big in their dark suits, and they moved in unison, with a precise, tight gait. They stopped in front of the clinic and scanned the street. Then they spoke to each other and stepped to the front-door vestibule. Their hard white faces and crew-cut scalps filled the right side of the screen. The men squinted, bent to the door glass, put meaty hands to meaty brows, and peered in. They tried the door, but found it locked. They didn't ring the bell, and after a while they walked away.

Arthur tapped keys and the two windows blinked, and displayed a live feed of the empty street and the empty doorway. Lydia looked at me. "Who were they?"

I shook my head. "Not the usual neighborhood types. And they seemed to be looking for someone."

"Those suits and the hair . . . They could be cops."

It was my turn to look skeptical. "You think so?"

"Some kind of cops," Lydia said. "La Migra, maybe — who knows? Anyway, how do you know they were looking for the woman?"

"I don't — not for sure. It's a guess based on observation, like a preliminary diagnosis."

"Don't patronize me, doctor."

"I'm not pat—"

"Sure you are. We should call the cops or DCFS, and you know it." Her mouth was firm, frowning. I sighed and closed my eyes.

A few years back — it seemed like a hundred sometimes, sometimes last week — in another life, quite far from here, I'd watched too many kids wake up on gurneys or stretchers, sick, maimed, always in pain, to find that everything they'd known — parents, siblings, homes, schools, villages, the ground beneath their feet — was gone. More than gone: hacked apart, scattered, annihilated. I'd never forget the vacant, blasted look in their eyes as the new facts of life beat against them like a horrible tide, and incomprehension, denial, and raw terror swept them away. I'd had little to offer any of them besides a hand to hold for a few minutes, some empty words, and sometimes space on a truck that would carry them into a mostly well-meaning, sporadically competent, and always overburdened refugee bureaucracy. I never knew where they wound up — a proper hospital, maybe — one with actual walls, or a camp or orphanage. The next wave was always coming in, and I never had time to find out. I didn't know what this kid's story was, but I didn't want to put him on a truck — and

especially not to DCFS. Not unless I had
to.

"The boy's going to wake up confused
and scared," I said. "He's going to want his
mom and she won't be around and he'll be
terrified. You want to turn him over to a
bunch of people he's never seen before?"

"*We* are a bunch of people he's never seen
before."

"You really want to hand him to Family
Services, Lyd? On a weekend? We won't
even get the A-list idiots on a weekend."

Lydia sighed massively. "You know the
shit we could land in?"

"All we're doing is waiting for his mother
to come back for him. She said she was
coming back —"

"From the bathroom."

"She said she was coming back, and
there's no crime in waiting. If she doesn't
turn up by Monday — if I can't find her by
then — we'll call whoever you want to call."

"*Find her?* You said she'd come back for
him — now you have to find her? You
moonlight as a detective now?"

"I'll ask around the neighborhood, see if
anyone's seen her."

"While I babysit."

"You had big plans this weekend?"

"Never mind my plans. You think 'cause

I'm a woman I don't mind taking care of kids?"

"It's not the gender thing so much as the fact that you raised Lucho and his sister up from babies, and you did it by yourself."

"Now you're blowing smoke at me, doctor. I'm supposed to take him home?"

"My place isn't child-friendly."

Lydia rolled her eyes. "God only knows what goes on up there. Does the kid even speak English? You weren't sure the mother did."

"She understood it."

Lydia shook her head and sighed. "Just till Monday."

"Tuesday the latest."

"You should pay me overtime for this," Lydia said. "Time-and-a-half at least." She looked at Arthur. "And don't think you two aren't gonna help. I'll make a list; you'll go to the market."

"Nothing with nuts," I said.

She nodded. "Yeah, I got —" And then her eyes flicked to Arthur's laptop and caught there. Her face hardened again. "Like we don't have enough trouble already. What's that pirate doing here?"

I looked at the screen and at the lean, whippy figure in it, standing by the front door, smiling lazily for the camera. Then I went through the waiting room and let Ben Sutter in.

"What do you say, brother?" Sutter drawled. "You up for a house call tonight?"

Chapter 3

The 101 was fucked, Sutter said, so we took surface streets north and west as the sky ripened from pink to purple, and lights came on all over town. San Pedro to First; First into Beverly; Beverly to Vermont to Franklin to Outpost and into the hills. Like everything about Sutter, his driving was fluid and nonchalant, and it was only on close inspection that you noticed the precision and speed.

He was thirty-five, five years younger than me, and at six feet tall, an inch shorter. His heritage was an elusive thing — African, Asian, Scots, Native American, maybe Hispanic too. Sutter himself claimed not to know the precise recipe, but, whatever the mix, the result was striking. His features were sharp and angular, as if chipped from coffee-colored stone, animated by a nimble intellect and a sometimes merciless wit, and softened by laugh lines around his mouth and pale eyes.

The rest was muscle. He was cobbled, plated, and wired together with it, and the first time I'd stitched him up it seemed amazing that anything could pierce that armor. But three bullets had, along with an ugly chunk of shrapnel. Even that torn up, he'd refused treatment until he saw that his wounded teammates and the children they had brought in — a boy and girl, both eight, pulled from the remains of a refugee encampment, and caked in ash and mud — were being looked after.

That was six years ago, at a Doctors Transglobal Rescue field station in the Central African Republic, halfway between Bangui and Berbérati. I was running the place — little more than a tin-roofed shed with tarps for doors — and Sutter, who'd cashed out of the Special Forces by then, and cashed into the private security business, was babysitting some German geologists. The geologists were unscathed but full of complaint over detours and delays, and before I'd started pulling bullets from him, Sutter had threatened to shoot them if they didn't shut up.

He took a left on Mulholland, ran the window down, and hung his elbow out. The evening air was soft, and smelled of eucalyptus and dust. I drummed my fingers on the dash, and Sutter looked over. His gray eyes were bright.

"Lydia seemed less happy to see me than usual," he said. "Something going on?"

I told him about the boy, his missing mother, and the men peering through the clinic's windows. He squinted, and I told him about Lydia's impulse to call child services and my desire not to.

He raised a skeptical eyebrow. "She's got a point."

I shrugged. "I don't want to hand him over to those clowns unless I have to."

Sutter smiled. "You want help looking for the mom?"

"I'll let you know."

We drove in silence for a while, along the twisting road. "Hard to believe she still doesn't like me," Sutter said. "After all these years."

"Lydia doesn't like me that much, and I sign her paycheck."

"Which makes you part of the oppressor class. But me — I'm a workingman. Plus, I've got a way with people."

"And modesty too."

I looked out the window, at the shadowed hillsides and canyons along Mulholland. Then I unzipped the black duffel at my feet.

34

It was an ER in a hockey bag: surgical kits, anesthetics, pain meds, tranquilizers, antibiotics, sterile gauze, splints, rolls of tape, packs of surgical gloves, IV kits, bags of Ringer's lactate, and bags of saline. I took another count of the surgical kits, then looked into the back seat. There was a matching duffel there, packed with a surgical stapler, a blood pressure cuff, a portable EKG, a portable sonogram, a laptop, and more gauze and gloves. Next to that was a small cooler filled with ice packs and three bags of O-negative blood. I opened them both and scanned their contents.

Sutter was watching me. "This makes four times you've taken inventory."

"I'm a nervous guy."

He snorted. "If only."

"Meaning what?"

"Meaning I served with nervous guys and with eager guys, and I know the difference. I'd feel better if you got less of a charge out of walking into a room full of guns."

I sighed. We'd had this conversation before over the years. "I didn't think tonight was that kind of gig."

"Any gig can turn into that kind of gig."

"Some rich-kid slacker in the Hollywood Hills — seriously?"

"*Any* gig."

"Usually, the patients don't shoot at me, because they need me."

"Until they don't."

"Isn't that where you come in — making sure I don't get shot, and that I get paid?"

"It's easier when you're less eager."

I shrugged.

I'd been working these night jobs with Sutter for more than three years, since I took over the clinic from the ancient Dr. Carmody and discovered after the first month that I could make payroll or make rent, but not both. Sutter, ever the entrepreneur, had an answer. The arrangement was simple: house calls for cash, paid up front, and no questions asked beyond the medical ones. No paper filed — with cops or anyone else — about gunshot wounds or drug overdoses or STDs or patients who might be persons-of-interest in connection with . . . whatever. And no names exchanged — not theirs, not ours, not ever.

Of course, for some people in the market for undocumented medical care, anonymity was impossible: their faces stared out from TV and movie screens, from magazine covers and billboards, from every corner of the Internet. What those patients wanted above all was silence, complete and absolute. After three years we had established a reputation for it among the lawyers, agents, PR flacks, crisis consultants, and the other breeds of handlers and fixers who rang in the middle of the night. Or Sutter had established a reputation for it. It was my fervent hope that I had established no reputation at all — that I was entirely unknown. With every one of these night calls, I bet my license on it.

"This lawyer didn't say anything about the wounds?" I asked.

"You got what I got: multiple GSWs. End of message."

My knee bounced up and down in four-four time. "But you actually know this guy — the patient?"

"Turns out I knew his pops. He's a director. He makes these crappy, basic-cable action flicks — commandos versus monsters or aliens or some shit. I was his tech adviser on a few of 'em. Wanted me to show his starlets how elite special operators would grease zombies."

"SEALs learn that?"

"Whole chapter on it in the counterinsurgency manual."

There were still cars in the dusty lot at the top of Runyon Canyon when we passed, and a couple of runners cooling down in the gathering dark. Five minutes later, Sutter turned the truck onto a brick drive that climbed around a hillside for fifty yards and then was interrupted by brick pillars, a wrought-iron gate, security cameras, and an intercom. We rolled to a stop by the metal box.

"You order the Korean fried chicken?" Sutter said to the speaker. There was no answer, but the gates swept open.

The drive curved upward some more, and ended in a brick plaza and a low-slung house of glass, red stone, and sharp edges. There were desert plantings around the house, and lights among them, and they cast jagged shadows over Sutter's truck, and on the yellow Turbo Carrera, the black Lexus, and the battered green Accord parked out front.

Sutter checked the load in his Sig Sauer, slipped it in a holster, and mostly covered it with his Ozomatli tee shirt. I hoisted the duffels from the truck, and he picked up the cooler, and we headed for the big front door. I stopped as I passed the Porsche and pointed my chin at dark splotches on the paving.

"Somebody's leaking," I said.

"And not oil."

The door opened before we reached it, and a pudgy young man with thin arms stepped out. He was short and flushed, with sweat in his thin blond hair and damp spots on his polo shirt. His khaki pants were too tight around his waist, and didn't quite reach the tops of his boat shoes. He spoke in a quavering voice.

"You're the doctor?" he asked Sutter.

"He is," Sutter answered.

The sweating man put out a tentative hand. "Doctor . . . ?"

"Dr. X," Sutter said. "You're not the guy who called."

"That was my boss. He . . . he couldn't be here. He's in court on Mon—"

Sutter cut him off. "You're what — an associate?"

The man nodded. "Second year. And you are . . . ?"

"The office manager. You have something for me?"

The man reached into his pocket and handed Sutter a white envelope. It was wrinkled and damp but the right thickness. Sutter tucked the cooler under his arm, and riffled a thumb through the cash. "Where's the patient?" he asked.

"He's in the den. I . . . I'm going to wait out here."

I nodded, and followed the blood trail through the door.

CHAPTER 4

There were acres of polished stone and wood in the house, and long runs of floor-to-ceiling glass, and everything smelled of lemons. The rooms were large and flowed one into another, and they all had wide, twinkling views of the city. I followed the blood and the sound of moaning. After a while, I heard voices.

"You've got to keep still," a young woman said.

"I can't keep still," a man whined. "I can't keep any fucking way that doesn't hurt like a — Oh, Jesus, look at this. I'm gonna puke again."

"Here, baby, I've got another towel — lift up a little."

"Ow! Son of a bitch, Astrid — that fucking *hurt*!"

"If you just stay still —"

"I can't!"

The den, when I finally got there, was not

a room full of guns. It was dominated by a massive window, and by a sectional sofa in fawn-colored leather and bloodstained towels. A woman in her late twenties hovered over the sectional. Her body was tanned and curved, with strong calves and arms, and her hair fell in stiff blond waves around a tanned, feline face. She wore cutoffs, a peasant blouse, and an expression of irritation mixed with anxiety as she looked down at the bleeding man. There were patches of dried blood on her arms and legs.

The man was younger, maybe twenty, and he lay on his side with his knees drawn up and his hands tucked between them. He was lumpy and pale, and his face was a sweating beige potato. His hair was dark and frizzy, and there were acne scars on his cheeks and beneath his underfed soul patch. His lips were chalky, his arms and elbows scraped and bleeding. He wore jeans that were wet from waist to knee with blood, and it looked as if a bear had bitten off his left rear pocket, along with a good-sized chunk of what was underneath.

I put the duffels down, unzipped both, squeezed antiseptic on my hands, and pulled on surgical gloves. The man and the woman turned to look at me, and relief

41

swept over their faces like wind across a pond.

I was relieved too. The man was conscious and alert enough to whine, so right there we were ahead of the game. And though he was bleeding, blood wasn't actually spurting out of him — at least not that I could see.

"You the doctor?" he asked. "I'm Teddy. This is Astrid."

"I don't need names."

The woman squinted. "You a real doctor?"

"That's what my diploma says," I answered. "The Web site I got it from even threw in some Latin."

Astrid looked alarmed, and so did Teddy. "That was a joke," I said. I pulled a blood pressure cuff and a stethoscope from one of the duffels, and an IV kit and a bag of fluids from the other. "Give me your right arm, and tell me where you were hit."

Teddy hesitated, and looked at Astrid. Then he put his arm out. "I was in the Valley, out by —"

"Where on your body."

Teddy swallowed hard. "My . . . my ass," he said. "My ass and my thigh."

I crouched by the sectional, and slid the blood pressure cuff over Teddy's arm. I put the stethoscope on and inflated the cuff.

"BP's low, but that's not surprising. You have any health problems? Diabetes? HIV? Asthma? Anything?"

"No . . . I . . . my doctor said I could lose a few pounds."

"You've made a good start. On any meds — prescription, recreational, anything?"

"No . . . nothing. Weed sometimes."

"Allergies?"

"Uh . . . I get hay fever. And cats — I'm allergic to cats."

"You weigh what . . . one ninety, one ninety-five?"

"One ninety-one."

I slipped the cuff off. "Left arm now."

Teddy shifted, and held out his other arm. I wrapped a tourniquet above his left elbow, and tapped for a vein. Then I swabbed the arm and tore open the IV kit. I glanced at Astrid, who had stepped back and was watching openmouthed, with wide eyes.

"You mind her being here?" I asked Teddy.

"Astrid? No, no . . . it's fine if she stays."

"And you?" I asked Astrid as I took out the catheter. "You're not going to faint on me?"

Her eyes narrowed. "I'm fine," she said.

"Great. Get me garbage bags."

"Like . . . plastic ones?"

"The bigger the better."

Astrid looked at Teddy. "In the kitchen," he said, "under the sink." She trotted from the room.

"You're shocky, so I'm giving you fluids. Then I'm going to stop your bleeding, patch what I can, and give you antibiotics and some pain meds. Sound good?"

"Can I have the pain meds first?"

"We'll get there," I said. "Now, this'll sting." I popped the cover off the catheter, pressed it against Teddy's inner arm below the elbow, pulled the skin, and slid the needle into the vein.

"Fuck!" he yelled. "That fucking *hurt.*"

"I bet," I said, and taped the tubing to Teddy's arm. Astrid returned with a fistful of white garbage bags. "Give me the bags," I said. I pointed at a brass floor lamp. "And bring that closer."

Astrid wrestled it to the sectional, and I hung the Ringer's lactate bag from it. Then I checked Teddy's pulse at his neck, his wrists, and his ankles.

"You're running fast."

"Is that bad?" Teddy asked.

I shrugged. "It's about par, all things considered. But your pulse is strong at your extremities, and that's good."

"My ass hurts something fierce," Teddy

whined.

I held up a syringe. "Got your ride waiting," I said, and I injected morphine sulfate into the IV port.

"How am I really?" Teddy said, a trace of sleepiness already in his voice. "Am I okay?"

"If your wallet was back there, it's KIA," I said. "Otherwise, you're not too bad." I looked at Astrid. "How about some music."

She looked confused. "What?"

"Music," I said, and pointed at a bookshelf, and an iPod mounted on little speakers there. "Something with a beat."

Astrid hesitated for a moment, and went to the shelf. In another moment Raphael Saadiq came on. "Heart Attack." I smiled. "Turn it up."

Line cooks must know the feeling — slicing, stirring, firing — assembling dish after dish from menus as familiar as nursery rhymes. Magicians must know it too, working one feint, one precise trick, after another — show after show, anticipating the gasps from the audience, and every round of applause. Certainly I'd known something like it back in college, when my soccer coaches had run us through endless three-man passing drills — against two, three, four, five defenders — moving in shifting triangles up and down the field. It was as much about

45

muscle memory as about conscious thought — maybe more so. And that's how it was as I worked on Teddy.

So on went the surgical mask, out came the bandage shears, the jeans were sliced away, the gunshot wounds — a messy but uncomplicated through-and-through of the left glute, and a deep furrow in the right quad — were flushed with saline. Coagulant powder went into the ass wound, then pressure, then dressings. The thigh wound got sutures. After that, a slug of prophylactic antibiotics — Ancef would do the trick — and then a tetanus booster.

All the while, the garbage bags filled up with the shreds of Teddy's pants, bandage wrappers, bloody gauze pads, bits of tape. The music played, I tapped my foot, and now and then paused to check Teddy's pulse and BP, which, along with his color, stabilized and then improved. And Teddy — with loopy morphine logic and a steadily thickening voice, and despite my insistence that I wasn't interested, that I really didn't want to know — talked and talked and talked. About how hard it was to get a business off the ground, about how much he hated the Valley, about what a cheap prick his father was, but mostly about his very bad day.

"You even know where Tujunga is? It's

past Pacoima, for fuck's sake. That's like the ass of nowhere. You drive farther east, you're in New York or something. Took me fucking forever to get there. And I'm at this . . . I don't know what the hell it was. One of those self-store things, where people keep the garbage the garbage man won't take. It's up on this hill, and I'm waiting for . . . for some people. I'm standing by my car, looking down at Foothill. There's a big-ass truck jackknifed across most of the street, and there's melons or something rolling around everywhere, and some insane backup, and then this dick in a Hummer — he leans on his horn, pulls out of the crowd, and drives up on the fucking sidewalk. Must be doing fifty at least, and people are waving and jumping out of the way. I take a couple of steps forward, 'cause I know there's gonna be a serious crunch and I wanna see, and then it's like somebody kicks me — and I mean fuckin' *hard* — right in the ass. I thought I was going down that hill, for chrissakes. And then there was another kick, and I was on the ground, and my pants were wet. And not in a good way."

Teddy thought this was funny, and he chuckled to himself, and noticed Sutter leaning in the doorway.

Sutter held up the little cooler full of

blood. "You gonna top off the tank?" he asked me.

"Not yet."

Teddy squinted at him for a while. "Who're you?"

"The nurse," Sutter said. Astrid smiled at that, and Sutter smiled back and winked at her.

Teddy scowled, but the morphine and the ebbing of his own terror were making him drowsier by the moment. He shook his head. "You sure? You don't look like a nurse." Sutter chuckled softly, and Teddy scowled more and went back to his story.

"Then I'm down on my belly, and I just want to get the hell out of there, so I drag myself to the car. I get in and get down to the street somehow. I couldn't feel anything then — my leg was practically numb — but by the time I get on 134 my ass is like on fire. I don't know how I made it back in one piece."

Sutter nodded sympathetically. "The holes I saw in your Porsche — you were lucky to make it out at all. What were you doin' there in the first place?"

Astrid shot Teddy a warning look, which he didn't recognize. "Doing?" Teddy said. "I was supposed to meet some people is what I was doing."

Another concerned nod. "Business meet?" Sutter asked.

"Should've been no trouble," Teddy said. "A simple swap. Now I don't know —"

Astrid coughed elaborately. "Teddy, babe, you should take it easy. Right, doc? Shouldn't he keep quiet?"

I didn't look up from my suturing. "That's never bad advice," I said.

Teddy yawned and looked at Sutter. "You're not really a nurse, are you?"

"What gave it away?"

"You —"

"Teddy!" Astrid said sharply. "You're fucking high on pain meds. How about you keep quiet, baby? Just rest."

I peeled off my gloves, tossed them in the garbage bag, and stood. I stretched my arms over my head. "That should do it."

"You're finished?" Astrid said. "Teddy's okay?"

I nodded. "He was lucky — the bullet didn't hit gut or bone. He should be all right if he takes it easy and gets some looking after."

"What kind of looking after?" Astrid said.

I began stowing gear in the black duffels. "He's going to need antibiotics for at least a week. I can leave you some, but he'll need more. And his ass needs maintenance. A

49

wound like that, there're always foreign bodies in it — bits of fabric, maybe bullet fragments, grit, who knows what. It needs to be drained, cleaned, and re-dressed periodically, watched for infection."

"Aren't you supposed to do that?"

"I've done what I can for now. As far as anything else, I'll tell you what I tell everyone I see in these circumstances: he should see a qualified health professional for follow-up care."

Astrid squinted and looked at Sutter. "What the fuck does that mean? Isn't that you?"

He smiled. "We get paid, we'll be here, hon."

Astrid shook her head. She said nothing, but her look was eloquent: *Assholes*.

On the way down the hill, I asked Sutter if he thought Astrid would call for follow-up care for Teddy. He laughed.

"He'll be lucky if she doesn't turn him into barbecue."

CHAPTER 5

I awoke with a bar of sunlight across my
eyes, tangled in a cotton blanket, sprawled
on Nora Roby's sofa. There was a shower
running somewhere, the smells of brewing
coffee, oranges, and toast, and music coming from speakers on the bookshelves behind me. I had fragmented memories of
calling Nora from Sutter's pickup the night
before as we rolled down from the hills, of
meeting her at a dim, noisy cave in Silver
Lake, of Nora's long hair — jet, shot with
gray — against the leopard-print upholstery
of a corner booth, of too many hipsters and
too much irony, of Nora driving me to her
house. The sound from the bookshelves
resolved into a song: acoustic surf music,
twangy, retro, and earnest.

I turned and fell off the sofa, tagged my
elbow on the coffee table, and upended one
of the empty wine bottles there. It spun
across the Persian rug and the tiled floor,

and came to rest against the French doors that led to the garden. I sat up and squinted in the light flooding through the Los Feliz cottage.

"Fuck," I said, rubbing my elbow. My throat was lined with steel wool.

The shower went off, and Nora called from her bedroom. Her voice was amber and smoky. "You talking to me?"

"Your sofa's too small," I said. "Also, your house has too much light." I wrapped the blanket around me and searched among the cushions for my clothes. I found my jeans and Nora's panties, but couldn't locate my own underwear.

She laughed. "That's what the listing said: *convenient to Hillhurst restaurants, and too much light for your hungover guests.* It's what sold me on the place."

Nora walked into the living room. She wore cutoffs and a sleeveless black tee shirt, and her arms and legs were long, firm, and graceful. She was tall — just a few inches shy of my height in bare feet — and her pale face was striking, if not television pretty. Her eyes were large, searching, and nearly black, her nose was strong, and her mouth generous — warm when she smiled, somber and daunting otherwise. At rest, it was an icon's face, a grave Madonna's, a scholar's, but in motion something mischievous was there, something wayward. She ran fingers through her damp hair and grinned, and looked a decade younger than her forty-two years.

I hitched the blanket up. "Also, your music's too loud."

"I think it's last night's Merlot you're hearing," she said.

"And you feel fine?"

"I didn't drink as much, and I already ran five miles this morning."

"Nobody likes smug," I said, and fished my boxers from behind a cushion. "Pediatricians don't need a bedside manner?"

"I didn't think you were a child, though maybe I got that wrong. For grown-ups, I prescribe a few milligrams of smug, plus a shower and coffee."

I'd met Nora a year ago, at a wedding extravaganza in Santa Monica, where I was a reluctant plus-one for a pediatric resident who'd been volunteering at the clinic. Nora supervised my date at UCLA Medical Center, along with both of the brides, and she'd come to the reception accompanied only by her considerable self-possession. She wore a gray gossamer dress, and smiled as she crossed the hotel terrace and introduced herself. She knew who I was, and had a champagne flute for me, and one of her own. We refilled them several times as the toasts kept coming, and left together before the cake.

I'd had more than a few relationships in the decade since my marriage had sputtered out, all brisk, friendly, but slightly chilly affairs, with sadly consistent contours: the company was amusing and bright, the sex vigorous, and the exit doors were always in plain sight, none further than a few months away. I told myself that that's what happened in war zones, but my relationships in L.A. hadn't been any different. Until Nora. I wasn't sure what accounted for how long things had lasted between us. Maybe it was her intelligence, or the warmth and kindness I saw whenever she volunteered at the clinic — the way the kids took to her. Or maybe it was because she was as suspicious of romantic entanglement as I was, and expected even less. Or maybe, after a long time alone, I was ready not to be.

Showered, shaved, and drinking coffee at the kitchen table, I felt slightly less fragile. I spread strawberry jam on a croissant and told Nora about the latest letter from my landlord.

"I get that he's serious about selling," I

said, "but he's delusional about the asking price."

She looked at me over the top of her iPad and smiled. Her teeth were very white. "Delusion is what L.A. real estate is about. He'll get his number, or something close — if not in August, then a few months later."

I drank some coffee. "What happened to the market being in the toilet? Underwater mortgages, abandonments — where did all that go?"

"Do you ever look at the business section? There's all this foreign money in town, looking for a place to park. An American safe-deposit box with a view — that's what the guy on *Bloomberg* called it."

"It's Skid Row, for chrissakes."

"That's authentic urban grit down there. Hipsters pay up for that — it makes the artisanal cheese taste better. And they're just the first wave; a few years from now your street will look like Melrose."

"You know, that building's in shit shape."

Nora laughed. "Don't try to understand it: it's Chinatown, Jake. The real question is: what are you going to do when he sells?"

I rubbed my jaw and felt tired again. "Find someplace else, I guess. There're other vacant storefronts in the neighborhood."

Nora shook her head. "You think other landlords will be different? Even if you find a place you can afford, you'll be going through the same thing in — what — a year or two? The tide's running against you there. You should check out the Valley. Over there you could find a place to live that's not above your office, and maybe then you'll finally unpack. How many years has it been, living out of a backpack? Four?"

"Three and a half — and I don't live out of a backpack. And screw the tide; screw the Valley too."

"Excellent wind-pissing," Nora said, laughing. "What's so bad about the Valley?"

"Besides being too hot, flat, and ugly?"

"And where you are now is such a garden spot? There are sick people in the Valley. Poor ones too."

"My ex said something like that before I went on my first gig with DTR."

"And?"

"I told her that there were doctors in New Haven to take care of them, if not as many as there should be. But where I was going, I might be the only doctor. If I didn't show up, no one else would."

Nora raised a graceful brow and smiled coolly. "That's heady stuff, Dr. Schweitzer — tough to compete with. What did the missus say?"

I shrugged. "As time went on, she minded less and less."

She chuckled. "I imagine. Still, there *are* other clinics downtown — good ones too, and better funded."

"My patients don't go to them."

"If you weren't there, maybe they would."

"Some of them would; some wouldn't. Anyway, there are plenty of doctors in the Valley."

Nora poured more coffee into her mug. "Plenty of doctors," she said, smiling, "and not so many lost causes."

"Don't mock my good works," I said. I drank some coffee and took some sections of an orange from a blue glass bowl.

"Speaking of lost things . . . ," I said, and between bites of the orange I told Nora about the vanishing woman, and the little boy she left behind.

Nora peeled another orange while I spoke, her long fingers pulling off the skin in a single curling ribbon. She listened without comment and was silent for a while after I finished. Then she sighed.

"Lydia's right — this is what DCFS is there for."

"Seriously? Am I the only one who thinks they're useless?"

57

"It's a bureaucracy, like any —"

"It's not just any bureaucracy. It's kids' lives they fuck around with."

"And is there any better excuse for getting into a little trouble than trying to help out a kid? I mean, who could blame you for that?"

I squinted at her. "Meaning what?"

"Meaning, I think sometimes you get bored, or restless, or something. Maybe the clinic work gets predictable, and then you want to stir it up — add some risk to the mix. Or do I have that wrong?"

"You studying for the psych boards?"

She smiled. "I'm a gifted amateur. Are you going to ignore my advice and go looking for this woman?"

"I am."

"Do you have some kind of plan, or are you going to put up fliers?"

"I thought I'd ask around the neighborhood. Maybe someone's seen her."

"Let me go on record that this is a bad idea."

I drank some more coffee. "I don't see why."

"You tell me you think this girl is on the run from somebody. So it follows that she might be hiding, and that this might make her hard to find — no? Not to mention the risk that you might cross paths with the guys who are already looking for her."

"Maybe they could tell me something."

Nora shook her head. "And maybe they'd have questions for you. Maybe you could end up looking like she did."

CHAPTER 6

It was ten when Nora dropped me at home, and eleven when I went out again. The marine layer had burned off by then, and it was brighter and hotter on the street. I squinted through my sunglasses, tucked the still photos from the clinic video into the pocket of my shorts, and locked the door behind me.

My neighborhood, a drunken trapezoid bounded roughly by the L.A. River in the east, Main Street in the west, and Fourth and Tenth Streets in the north and south — where the shiny new downtown faded into the warehouse district and Skid Row, and the main veins of gentrification dwindled to gritty, artsy capillaries — was an odd sort of small town, and definitely not of the Norman Rockwell variety. Not unless you accessorized his Main Street with coils of razor wire, security cameras, barred windows, and roll-down metal curtains, punctuated the blocks with trash-strewn lots and fire-gutted buildings, and for his rosy kids and smug burghers swapped battered working folks, streetwalkers, dopers, and dusty platoons of the homeless pushing mounded shopping carts or slumped in doorways. It was a decidedly unlovely place, as distant from the glossy Westside, or even from freshly scrubbed Pershing Square, as it was from Oslo or Mars. And there was nothing easy or secure in the lives of the townspeople, under siege as they were from a moribund economy, La Migra, dope-dealing street gangs and their clients, the relentless tide of gentrification, and their own diseases, demons, and bad, bad luck. But still they hung on. Some of the villagers recognized their local doctor; some even waved as I passed.

My first stop was Carmen's — a low cinder-block bunker around the corner from the clinic, and tucked between a sheet metal shop and a fabric wholesaler. It was painted in horizontal bands of yellow and parrot green, had two red metal doors, and a sign above advertising sandwiches, soda, beer, and an ATM. I stopped at the outdoor counter and spoke to Mateo through the service window.

Mateo owned the place, did the cooking,

and came to see me about his hypertension. Sometimes he brought his wife, who was diabetic, or his mother-in-law, Carmen, who was mildly asthmatic and awesomely mean. Mateo made a wicked iced coffee — pitch black, but smooth — and he poured it over plenty of ice in a tall plastic cup. He pushed a jar of sugar syrup through the window, along with my coffee and a straw.

"*¿Qué tal,* doc?" he said, and his heavy brown face creased into a smile.

"I'm all right, Mateo. How about you?"

Mateo nodded. "Still here."

"That's what it's all about. How's Ana, and her mom?"

"Ana's good — trying to get exercise and watch the diet, like you said. And Carmen . . ." Mateo shrugged.

I smiled at him and took the photos from my pocket. "Maybe you can help me out," I said. "I'm looking for a woman who came by the clinic yesterday. She left something behind, and I'm trying to get it back to her." I slid the photos of the woman and the boy across the counter.

Mateo pulled a pair of smudged half-glasses from his apron and perched them on his nose. He squinted. After a while he shook his head.

"How about these guys?" I asked, and

passed photos of the two crew cuts across the counter.

Mateo squinted harder. "Sorry, doc. Don't know *los soldados* either."

"You think they're soldiers?"

Another shrug. "The hair, the big necks, kinda mean-looking — that's what I think of."

I took back the prints and stared at the two men. *Los soldados.* I thanked Mateo and tried to pay for the coffee. He refused my money and refilled my cup, and I continued down the street.

The next few hours were much the same, except hotter and without free drinks. At soup kitchens, shelters, bodegas, check-cashing joints, building-supply yards, and wholesalers of fruits, vegetables, and candy, I exchanged greetings and small talk, heard about symptoms, looked in a few throats, palpated some necks, bellies, and limbs, and passed my pictures around. And people studied them, shook their heads, and said, "Sorry, doc," in many languages.

Under the relentless sun, the city was a baking brick: hard, brown, parched, and cracked. I bought a lime Jarritos at a bodega on Eighth Street and found some meager shade to stand in. I drank the soda and held the bottle to my neck and looked across the street. A line of the homeless, ten of them, genders obscured by layers of clothing, sheltered beneath the frayed awning of a boarded storefront. Some held signs, crudely scrawled on cardboard, that asserted past lives — *OIF veteran; Five kids; Fry cook* — advertised a willingness to work for food, or simply pleaded: *Need money food home NEED HELP.* At the end of the line, the smallest figure held the largest sign. It wasn't hand printed, but a collage of words and letters cut from newspapers and magazines. The text twisted this way and that, and finally wound into an illegible knot — an incoherent ransom note from a mind held hostage by itself.

I shook my head, then finished my soda and went back to the grocery. I returned my empty bottle and bought ten gallon-jugs of water. It took me two trips across Eighth Street to deliver them. It wasn't world-changing, I knew; improving the next few hours for them was the most I could hope for. Another holding action. Sometimes it was the only action to be had.

I sighed and pulled out my phone. I called Lydia and asked about the boy.

"Of course he's okay, doctor," Lydia said. Her voice was low, and I could hear television in the background. "What do you think — I wouldn't call if there was a problem? He awoke at eight last night, a little disoriented but with good vitals, and an appetite. I kept his diet bland, but let him have as much as he wanted. He went back to bed around ten-thirty, and slept till nine this morning."

"What did you tell him?"

"I said he'd gotten sick, and the lady he was with brought him to the clinic. I said we'd look out for him until she comes back."

"Did he say anything? Did he tell you his name?"

"He says his name is Alex."

"Just Alex?"

"That's all he says when you ask."

"So he speaks English."

"Yes, what little he says is in English."

"Did he say anything about the woman?"

"He calls her *mamá.*"

"I told you."

"But he doesn't say anything else about her — no name or anything — and he shuts down when you try to talk about her."

"And nothing about where he lives?"

Lydia sighed. "He's looking at cartoons now, doctor. I'm no detective like you, but I didn't think it was the time to interrogate him. If you want to come over . . ."

"I'm out trying to find his mother now."

Lydia sighed. "Try hard," she said. "The boy is not in a good way."

"You said he was doing okay."

"Physically he's fine, but there's something else going on. I'm pretty sure this isn't the first trouble he's had."

"Meaning what?"

"I'm talking about his reactions. The kid doesn't cry, he doesn't ask any questions, he does what he's told, but otherwise doesn't say a word. He pretends to watch the cartoons, but he doesn't laugh — he doesn't even smile. And the whole time he's really watching me — like, every move I make."

"Watchful, guarded, lack of affect . . ."

"You got it — the kid's seen hard times before. I don't know if it was neglect or abuse or what, but this isn't his first trauma. He needs help."

"Shit," I whispered.

"Exactly, doctor."

By two I hadn't found Alex's mother, or much else, and the heat and glare were like a vise as I jaywalked on Agatha Street. There was a knot of adolescent boys on the far corner, leaning against a pickup with a red metallic paint job — gang kids, on break from dealing rock and rolling addicts on the nearby blocks. The guy in the driver's seat, scarcely more than a kid himself, was their boss: the shot caller, the headman of the crossroads. Squads like this could be found at intersections around the neighborhood — legations from gangs across the city, all drawn by the endless supply of victims.

I knew some of the shot callers, though not this one. I could feel the weight of his gaze — the gauging of effort and payoff — as I crossed, and adrenaline bubbled in my veins. The kids watched me and laughed derisively. I didn't look, but I didn't look away. Psychosis wafted off them like cheap cologne as I passed, and I was reminded of child soldiers I'd seen years ago, driving by in trucks, in clouds of dust and madness. As I walked by, I thought of what Nora said about boredom, and what Sutter said about my fondness for rooms full of guns, and shook loose another memory.

It was of driving, with my mother. I was eleven, and it was summer and night — quite late — and my mother had only just returned from the hospital; my father was still there. My mother was restless and fidgety when she walked through the door, irritable and brusque as she paid the sitter, pacing the house afterward, from room to room, chain smoking. Finally, she picked up her keys and her purse and said that she needed air and was going for a drive. She paused at the door to ask if I wanted to go along. I didn't need to change out of my pajamas, she said, or even put on shoes.

It was a warm night, cloudless, with a moon, and the wind was deafening when she put all the windows down. The road was fresh-paved — still smelled of tar — and was like a black carpet as it unspooled, empty and smooth, through the Connecticut hills. There was one stretch, a mile or more long, of blind curves and quick rises and dips through pasture and woods; with the right touch on the gas and on the wheel, my mother said, we could fly. We drove its length dozens of times that night, laughing when we felt the tires lift, shrieking at the swoops and sudden drops, screaming and crying in elated terror when she put the headlights out and the fields and trees turned silver, and when she took her hands off the wheel.

Nora and Sutter weren't quite right: I wasn't chasing trouble, or chasing off boredom, but maybe, sometimes, I was chasing something else. I remembered the body rush of that ride — could still feel it sometimes — the hurtle and plunge, the crazy swing between thrill and panic. And sometimes I could smell her eucalyptus soap and her cigarettes. I let out a long breath as I left the gangbangers behind.

The photos in my pocket were damp and wrinkled, and so was I, and I was thinking about another iced coffee when I rounded the next corner and saw the slack-bellied silhouette of Gary Fleck in the doorway of his auto body shop. He was sucking on a cigarette, and when he saw me he took a last, furtive puff and flicked his smoke to the curb.

"Dr. Knox," Gary said. "I seen you marchin' around all day. You collectin' for somethin'?" His voice was raspy and, thanks to the emphysema, empty of force. He had sallow skin and blasted capillaries across his nose and cheeks. His khaki shirt had stains down the front, and someone else's name over the pocket. His thick, stained hands grasped each other nervously.

"Those things will kill you, Gary."

"So you keep tellin' me."

"But you keep on smoking."

"I know my limits, doc. I quit the smokes, I'm gonna pick up a bottle again — simple as that. Fifteen years sober won't mean shit. And the booze'll kill me quicker than the ciggies will, and maybe not just me."

Gary's face sagged with his sad insight,

and I knew a lecture was worse than point-less. I patted his arm. "I'm the one who needs help today," I said, and I took out my wilted photos.

Gary looked relieved, and took them. He squinted and brought each one almost to the tip of his nose. He shook his head. "They haven't been here, not when I've been around, but I was at jury duty most of last week. Lemme ask Scotty."

I remembered Scotty as the nervous kid whom Gary had dragged into the clinic a year back, with a suppurating puncture wound in his right calf. Gary pushed through the dirty glass door to his shop and I followed.

It was dim inside, but no cooler. An exhaust fan was working to little effect, and the smells of epoxy and paint were heavy in the air. There was a garage bay to the right, and Scotty was there, studying the crumpled door panel of a black Lincoln. Gary waved him over.

Scotty wiped his hands on a rag as he ap-proached. He was skinnier than I remem-bered, and the ink on his arms was new, but the big eyes, big ears, and bobbing Adam's apple were the same, as was the confounded expression.

"Check these out for Dr. Knox," Gary

said. "Tell him if you seen any of these people around."

Scotty didn't ask why, but took the stills and peered at them. And slowly nodded. "I seen her and the kid too, but not around here."

It took a moment for it to sink in. I wiped a hand across my damp forehead. "Where and when, Scotty?"

"A few days ago — must've been Wednesday. I noticed her 'cause of the kid, and 'cause she was all banged up — like she was in an accident. That why she came to see you?"

I shook my head. "Where did you see them?"

"That's the other reason I noticed: you don't see moms or kids coming out of that place."

"What place?"

"A couple blocks over — on Sixth, near Town. You know, that hotel place — the Harney it's called."

Gary laughed out loud. "Jesus, Scotty, the frickin' *Horney*? I wouldn't call that a hotel, boy — they rent their rooms by the quarter-hour."

Scotty blushed. "I know that — it's why I noticed 'em."

"Oh, he *knows,* doc," Gary said. "Kid

knows all about the girls over there. I told him, he's gonna catch something, he keeps going there, but he don't listen."

"You think the woman and her son were staying there?" I asked.

Scotty shrugged. "I saw them coming out, and then I saw them like an hour later, on the way back in. She was carrying a grocery bag, like from a bodega."

"Just the two of them?" I asked. "Nobody else with them?"

"Just them."

I tapped the pictures of the two men. *Los soldados.* "How about these guys? You see them around?"

Scotty shook his head. "Nah, these aren't them. I never seen these guys."

"What do you mean, *these aren't them?* *Them* who?"

"These aren't the guys who were here, asking about your girl."

Gary coughed, and his face reddened dangerously. He spit a slug of phlegm on the floor and glared at Scotty. "You didn't say anybody was in asking questions."

Scotty shuffled his feet. "They didn't come inside. I had the bay open and they were out in the street. They had a picture of her — but not like yours, doc. She was wearing a bikini top in theirs, and she wasn't all beat up."

"What did they want?" I asked

"Same as you — they asked if I'd seen her around. Said there was money in it."

"How much money?"

"I didn't like the way they looked, so I didn't ask," Scotty said. "Fucking creeps — I didn't tell 'em anything."

Gary grinned and clapped Scotty on the shoulder. "See, doc, kid may be dumb, but he ain't stupid." Scotty blushed again.

"Any idea who these guys were?"

"They didn't say and I didn't want to know. They gave me a piece of paper with a phone number to call if I saw this chick, but I tossed it."

"This was what day?"

"Thursday, in the afternoon."

"And you hadn't seen them around before?"

Scotty shook his head. "Not before or since. A good thing too — guys like them give the neighborhood a bad name."

Big and bigger, Scotty had said. And *ugly and uglier.* And *scary.*

I scanned the streets as I walked from Gary Fleck's shop to the Hotel Harney, and though I saw people who fit that general profile, I didn't see any that matched the specific descriptions Scotty had given, of a hulk with blond cornrows, and another with a tattoo of a heart with a dagger through it on his chin. It was hotter on the street, and there were large dark patches on my tee shirt by the time I made it to the hotel.

I didn't think the Harney had ever been much in the many decades of its existence — a backdrop to some crime-scene photos, maybe, and a not-infrequent stop for the EMTs or the coroner's van — but now it was even less: five stories of faded brick and bad karma, a boarded-up coffee shop on the ground floor, and a threadbare awning. It was a toss-up as to which would offer a more certain death — a fire, or the fire escape that was made mostly of bird shit and rust. There was a clutch of working girls wandering listlessly out front, but none that I recognized. I paused on the threshold and thought of bedbugs, drug-resistant staph, a smorgasbord of STDs, and wished I'd worn long pants and maybe a hazmat suit.

The lobby was small: a dim stairwell going up, a pay phone kiosk with wires where the phone used to hang, an elevator the size of a coffin, and the front desk, huddled behind a plate of wired glass that was smudged, chipped, and cracked in many places. The man behind the desk was smudged, chipped, and cracked too, and bony, grizzled, and red-faced from too much drink. He was topping off his tank when I came in.

The deskman looked up and put aside his Olde English forty-ounce. "You need somethin'?"

"A minute of your time."

"Don't bother tryin' to sell me anythin'."

"I'm not selling," I said.

The deskman drank again. "Then you're buyin'. People pay for time around here."

I took out my pictures. "I just want to know if you've seen these two — if they stayed here recently."

The man squinted at the photos, and tapped a slot in the glass. "Pass 'em through." I did, and the man looked at the stills for a while. "I don't know 'em," he said eventually. "But I'm not here all the time. You want, I could ask the other guy."

"Sure. Thanks."

The man held up a hand and rubbed his grimy thumb slowly against his grimy fingertips. His blue eyes were watery and sly. "Twenty," he said. I sighed and pulled my wallet out. I passed a twenty through the slot.

"Where's the fuckin' phone?" he grumbled, and dug through the debris before him. He came up with a cell, and fished a piece of paper from his back pocket. He swiveled in his chair and rolled away from the desk. I looked at his sunburned neck as he muttered into his hand, and counted the moles that might become malignant. Four, maybe five. Or maybe that last one was just dirt.

There were clacking footsteps behind me, and a blur of color — bleached blond, blue, pink, and yellow — and I turned to see Shelly go past. Shelly was a streetwalker who came into the clinic now and then — bladder infections and STD tests, mostly — and she stopped in the doorway and squinted at me before she stepped into the glare. When I looked at the deskman again, he was rolling back to the wired window.

"My pal says he don't know about a girl staying here with a kid," he said, returning my photos. "You want to leave a number, I could call if they turn up." He smiled and rubbed his thumb across his fingers again. I suppressed a shudder and took out a card and another bill. I fed them through the slot.

The deskman looked at the card. "This that clinic over by Carmen's?"

"That's it."

"Chick stiff you on a bill?"

"Something like that," I said, and walked out.

The heat was battering now, and I paused under the Harney's awning to put on my sunglasses. A figure waved from across the street, from the shade of a ratty sweet-gum tree. I crossed over, and Shelly nodded at me. She was somewhere in her twenties, small-boned, fair, and jumpy. Her peroxide hair was streaked blue in front, and her pink-and-yellow striped tube top was split at the seam. She looked at me over the top of massive white sunglasses.

"You're not buds with that prick Troop, are you, doc? You know he's a douche bag."

I shook my head. "I didn't even know his name till just now. I was asking him some questions. I'm looking for somebody."

"So I hear."

"Hear from who?"

She shrugged. "You know that guy'll say anything to scam a buck off you. Really, he sucks."

"I'm getting that impression. Maybe you've seen this girl around, or the little boy." I proffered the photos, but Shelly had stopped looking at me. I followed her gaze across the street to Troop, who stood in the doorway of the Harney, staring at us. Out from behind his desk, he was bigger than I would've guessed, with bowed legs and a jutting gut. He shaded his eyes with a meaty hand, and I turned back to Shelly in time to see her disappear around the corner.

CHAPTER 7

I was in front of the clinic, showered and wearing a clean tee shirt and jeans, when Sutter rolled up in a BMW convertible. It had racing wheels, white leather, and a paint job the color of a new penny — flawless but for what looked like a bullet hole in the passenger door. I threw my bags into the vestigial back seat.

"New ride?" I asked as we pulled from the curb.

Sutter tapped on a touch screen in the dash and music came on — something Brazilian and propulsive. "Got it today," he said. "Used."

I ran my finger around the edge of the bullet hole. "Not gently."

Sutter smiled. "Guy I did something for was short when it came time to settle up. He threw in the paper on this and we called it even."

"What kind of something?"

Sutter smiled wider. "The kind you don't want to know about. How'd your day go? You earn your missing-persons merit badge?"

We were eastbound on the 10, and warm air rushed over us. I pushed the seat back. The wind ran through my damp hair.

"She's still missing," I said, and told Sutter of my wanderings. As I spoke he frowned, and when I finished he shook his head.

"You look like you bit a lemon," I said.

"Walking around, showing her photo — that isn't the smartest tactic. Unless you want to be the goat."

"The goat?"

"The staked goat. Bait."

"I'm not —"

"You've got one, maybe two sets of guys looking for your young mom, and one set at least is walking around with pictures, offering cash money to people. You don't think somebody's going to mention to somebody that you're looking for her too?"

"Nora said the same."

"That's 'cause she's smart — except for hanging out with you. Have you thought about what you'll do if these guys come around?"

I shrugged. "Play it by ear."

Sutter shook his head some more. "From what I see, you've got no play, brother — but I think you know that. I think last night with Teddy was too tame for you, and you're looking for action." I said nothing, but watched the flow of traffic on the 10. Sutter laughed. "Well, maybe tonight will be more like it."

"Why? Are we headed for a room full of guns?"

Sutter shrugged. "The guy who called didn't say, but it definitely won't be the Hollywood Hills."

We stayed on the 10 until we crossed into San Bernardino County, and the San Gabriels were large and dark ahead of us and the land began to rise toward them. We got off in Ontario, at the Fourth Street exit. The airport wasn't far, and blue light from the runways shimmered in the sky. A FedEx jet flew low across our path, and dropped a curtain of exhaust over us.

Sutter drove the streets around the airport, watching his mirrors, until he was satisfied that we were alone. Then he headed west on Fourth Street and north on Campus. We angled north and west some more, until we were in Upland, in a quiet neighborhood of ranch houses from the 1960s. They were small and tidy, with brown yards, and SUVs

81

and pickups in the driveways. The hush on the streets, and the stillness and ordinariness of the houses were somehow ominous in the dusk, and it was easy to imagine bizarre and terrible things taking place inside the neat boxes. Easy for me, anyway. Sutter pulled to the curb and produced a phone.

"I'm supposed to call when we're close," he said to the phone. "We're close." Then he dropped the BMW into gear and drove away. We took a right at the end of the street, and drove into a cul-de-sac.

There were two houses in the little circle, both with overgrown yards and dark windows. We pulled into the drive of the one with a FOR SALE sign out front, and Sutter flashed the high-beams twice. They lit vertical gray siding, a gray front door, and the faded vinyl of an attached garage. Two men were in the front doorway, both big, both dressed in jeans and dark tee shirts, and both with handguns in their belts. Sutter chuckled.

We climbed from the BMW, and the bigger of the men walked out to meet us. The night was quiet but for the ticking of the car's engine and the crunch of gravel under his boots. He stopped and raised a hand.

"Right there," he said. "I gotta check

those." His voice was Texan. Under a blond crew cut, his face was wide, ruddy, and brutal.

"Look with your eyes," I said. "That stuff needs to stay clean." I put the duffels down and unzipped them. The guy looked back to his friend in the doorway, who nodded. "Back up," Tex said. He squatted, peered into the duffels, then opened the little cooler. He blanched when he saw the blood bags.

"We good?" Sutter asked.

"Seems like," the guy in the doorway said. "Come ahead." He was a handsome weasel, with black hair, olive skin, and a grin. He sounded like back east — New Jersey, maybe.

"Cash first," Sutter said.

"Up front — since when?"

Sutter sighed. "Since always. You guys should talk to whoever you talk to, and get the terms straight. That way you won't have this problem with the next doc who comes out. If you can find a next one." Sutter cocked his head, and I picked up the duffels and cooler and stepped toward the car.

Tex didn't like that. "What the fuck?" he said, and reached for his gun. And stopped midway when he saw Sutter's weapons, two

Sig Sauers, one pointed at him, the other at Jersey.

"Let's stay polite, fellas," Sutter said, smiling wider. "Otherwise, even my friend won't be able to help you."

Jersey put up his hands. "No need to get all pissy. I know the deal; I was just fuckin' with you. I got your cash here, if I can take it out of my pocket."

"If you'd done that to begin with," Sutter said, "you wouldn't need to ask permission."

Jersey reached back slowly with one hand and held up a brown paper bag, folded over on itself. He tossed it, and it landed between Sutter and me. I picked it up and took out the cash — banded packs of hundreds, new and sharp-edged. I showed them to Sutter, who nodded.

"We have to worry about these numbers being on a list somewhere?"

Jersey was indignant. "Shit, no. Now, you guys want to come look after —"

"We don't need names," I said.

Inside, the house was dark — gray carpets, dingy walls, heavy drapes across the windows — and too warm. The air was moist and close and smelled of sweat, cigarettes, burnt coffee, car exhaust, and the clotted reek of old fast food: the fragrance of flight.

84

Above it all was an odor unique unto itself — worse than a fish market gutter, or a landfill marinating in the August sun; worse than the ammoniac smell of the incontinent, or the sulfurous stench of a nicked intestine. It was the smell of old meat, when the sweetness has fled and only rot remains. The smell of a living body becoming a corpse.

It strengthened as I followed Tex's pointing finger past a kitchen, an empty bedroom, and a bathroom, to the end of the hallway. There was a blond girl there, reedy and wan, maybe twenty. Her long, straight hair was tied in a sloppy braid down her back, and her jeans were limp and slept in. Her eyes were shadowed from exhaustion and red from crying.

"You're the doctor?" she whispered. Another accent, deeper south. I nodded. "Thank fuckin' Jesus. He's in here." She turned to the door behind her and put a hand on the knob.

"Just a sec," I said. I put the duffels down, unzipped one, and took out disinfecting gel, surgical masks, and gloves. I washed, and slipped on gloves and a mask. "Hands," I said.

She squinted at me. "What for?" she said, but held them out anyway.

I squirted gel into her palms. "Wash," I

85

said. "Then gloves and a mask."

Her eyes widened. "What the hell? He hurt his leg is all. It's not like he's got embola."

"It's not Ebola I'm worried about," I said. She put on her mask and gloves and opened the door.

The smell rolled from the darkness in a noxious wave. I was ready for it, but still I gagged; the girl was used to it. We stepped inside. The only light was a dull-yellow wedge from the bathroom that fell on a side table, a wooden folding chair, and a double bed piled with blankets.

"Lemme get the lamp," the girl said, and she picked her way through the darkness. There was a click, and a dim light came through the singed shade of a standing lamp and lit the rest of the room. On the floor were backpacks, empty soda bottles, a nearly empty doughnut box, a sleeping bag, and a box of shotgun shells, but no shotgun.

"Karl told me not to open the curtain or the window," the girl said. She moved to the bed and pulled the blankets back from the unmoving form that lay beneath. When she did, the smell grew stronger.

The man on the bed moaned. Breathing was hard labor for him, and his chest rose and fell too fast. "Callie," he whispered.

"Hey, baby." His accent was like the girl's. He raised a hand. It took all he had.

"I'm here, Billy," she said. "And I got the doctor. He's gonna set you right, honey." The man muttered and closed his eyes, and Callie swallowed a sob. "He's in and out," she whispered. "Last day and a half, mostly out. Last couple of hours, he's worse than ever."

Under the bad light, under the sweat and gray pallor and shivering, it was hard to tell his age. Thirty, maybe. He was blond and bearded, thick with muscle, pierced several times in one ear, inked down both arms. He wore a tee shirt, soaked with sweat, and blue boxers that were stained and stretched tight around his right thigh, which was swollen and rotting from an infected, full-thickness burn.

It was a trench across the width of his thigh, six inches above his patella and down deep into the quadriceps. There was a black eschar — a thick, leathery crust — inside and around the wound, which was cracked in spots and oozed a rank green pus. Radiating out from the eschar, his leg was webbed with red streaks — the visible tendrils of a spreading infection. I sighed, slipped a blood pressure cuff on his arm, and pressed a strip thermometer to his forehead.

"What happened to him, and when?" I asked. Callie reddened, looked down, and stuttered. "I don't need to know what he was doing at the time," I said, "just what burned him, and how long ago."

"It was four — no — five days back now. It was a torch did it — an OA torch. Oxy-acetylene."

Billy groaned, and turned toward me. "Everything was good . . . and then, outta nowhere, this guard . . . Karl was supposed to . . ."

Callie put a hand on his cheek. "You don't gotta talk, baby. Doctor don't need to know that stuff." She looked at me. "He's burnin' up again."

She was right — the strip said 103. "How long has he been running a fever?"

"Three days, I guess. And last couple of days he says the leg is hurtin' all up and down."

"It's the infection."

"When it first happened, he said it didn't hurt at all."

"That's because the nerve endings were burnt away. Has he been passing water?" She looked puzzled. "Is he peeing?"

"Not for a day, maybe more." Callie looked down again and her shoulders shook. The BP cuff whirred and hissed and finished its work. I read the gauge: 80/70. *Shit.*

"I'm going to start an IV," I said. "You get some garbage bags. Then you might want to wait outside."

"Screw that," Callie said. "I'm not waitin'. I'm gonna help."

A tremor went through Billy and he grabbed my arm. His grip was desperate and hot. His voice was choked. "Callie's a good girl, doc — smarter than shit. Way smarter than me. I don't tell her enough."

"I'm right here, fool," she whispered.

I put my hand on Billy's and squeezed it gently. "You're a lucky guy," I said, "to have a girl like her. Now just lay back and relax, and let us fix you up."

Billy managed a smile, and then he sighed and sank deeper into the mattress.

It took a while for me to do what I could for him, though I knew from the start it wouldn't be enough.

CHAPTER 8

I carried the duffels down the hall; Callie
followed with the garbage bags. We stopped
in the kitchen, stripped off our masks and
gloves, and bagged them. My shirt was
damp with sweat, and my eyes were gritty
from working in bad light. I squirted disinfecting gel into her palms and my own.

Jersey was on the sofa, looking at his
phone. Tex was in a folding chair, drinking
beer, eating pistachios, and flicking the
shells halfway across the living room, at a
big glass ashtray on a card table. The ashtray
was overflowing with cigarette butts, and
the shells bounced onto the floor. Sutter
leaned by the curtained front window and
looked half asleep, though he wasn't. Tex
looked up and pointed at the girl and
laughed.

"Hey, Karl, check out Callie — she's
Nurse Jackie."

Karl shook his head and rose from the

sofa. "About time, doc. Guess we made you earn all that scratch. How's Billy boy doing?" The girl clenched her fists.

I stretched my arms and shook out my hands. "I couldn't debride the burn — it's too large and too deep, and, the shape he's in, he wouldn't survive it. But I cleaned it up as much as I could, put a drain in, dressed it, gave him fluids, and something for the pain. It was all I could do, and it'll make him more comfortable. But it won't change the course of things."

Karl squinted. "So you're sayin' what? Is he gonna be okay when we gotta boogie, or not?"

I looked at Callie, who was looking at her shoes. She'd heard it already, but was braced for the reprise. "He should've been in a hospital five days ago," I said. "Now it's too late. The infection is systemic, his kidneys have shut down, and his lungs are failing. Billy's in septic shock. He's dying."

Callie pointed at Karl. "You hear, Karl — *five days*! He needed help five days back but you said no. You fucked that up, fucked up the guards too — this is all on you!" The girl hiccupped and wiped an arm across her nose.

Karl shook his head. "That sucks, Cal. Billy's a good guy, a good box man."

91

"Now you care," she said. "Fuck you."

Karl flicked a dismissive hand at her. "How long's he got?"

I shrugged. "Twelve hours, maybe less. Once the kidneys quit . . ."

Karl pursed his lips and looked at Tex. "It's a problem if he goes twelve hours."

Tex flung another shell at the ashtray. "It's a problem if he goes more than eight — we got a plane coming."

"I don't know what to tell you. It's not a precise thing."

Tex snorted. "We can make it precise," he muttered.

"What the fuck's that mean, asshole?" Callie said. "And why's it matter to you, anyway? Y'all go on your way. I'll stay with Billy till . . . I'll stay with him."

He shook his head. "That's not gonna work. This place is good for another day, maybe, but then what? People are looking for us, remember? Where are you goin' alone?"

"That's my business."

Some more glances with Tex, and then Karl nodded slowly. "If that's really what you want. But your cut —"

"My cut is *mine,* Karl — I worked for that. And Billy's cut too — I'm the closest he's got to kin."

Tex reddened and stood. "The fuck you
—"

Karl put a hand up. "You're being a bitch,
Callie, you know that?"

"Then it's good we're goin' separate
ways."

"A world-class bitch . . . But out of respect
for Billy, sure, fine — your cut's yours. And
Billy's too." He looked at Tex some more,
and Tex sat.

Sutter cleared his throat and looked at
Karl. "You guys want new friends, go to
Facebook — 'cause we're really not interested. And we're especially not interested in
hearing about names, cuts, travel plans, or
anything about your family feud, okay?"

Karl smiled his sly smile and laughed.
"Don't get so wound up — we trust you. I
thought everybody out here was supposed
to be all chill."

Sutter sighed and shook his head. "Whatever, dude," he said. Then he pushed himself
off the wall, crossed the room, and headed
down the hall.

"Where you goin'?" Tex said.

Sutter kept walking. "To piss, maybe take
a dump. You want to watch?"

Tex started to rise again, but Karl stopped
him with a minute shake of his head. Sutter
called back to me as he stepped into the

hallway bathroom. "Then we're rolling, doc, so get your shit together."

I knelt and zipped up the duffels. Karl watched me and smiled some more. "You want a beer before you go, or something stronger?"

"No, thanks." I handed Callie a small envelope. "It's for pain, if he needs it. Give him one; if that doesn't do it, give him another." Callie took them, nodded, sniffled.

Karl chuckled. "If he's so far gone, why bother? I mean, why go through all the crap you did tonight, if you knew it wouldn't do any good?"

Tex snorted. "Probably afraid we wouldn't pay."

"You already paid," I said.

Karl's face tightened. "No shit, doc — why bother?" he asked. I looked at him and said nothing, and the already thick air thickened some more.

"You deaf now?" Tex said. "You didn't hear what the man asked?"

I looked at Tex. "I heard. I'm just not sure how to answer."

"Use small words," Callie said under her breath, but Tex caught it.

"Like you're some fuckin' genius."

Karl made a long-suffering sigh and looked at me. "Seriously, why do that stuff for him if he's just gonna die?"

"The short answer is that it's my job, to do what I can: not to hurt him; to save him if I'm able, or try my best to; to do something about his pain, if that's all that's left. Those are the rules."

Tex snorted. "What fuckin' rules?"

"When you're a doctor, douche bag," Karl said. "Like how they have to keep their mouths shut about their patients."

"So, what, he's like a priest?"

Karl sighed and looked at his watch. "What's with your pal — he fall asleep in there?"

As he spoke, the bathroom door opened and Sutter emerged, wiping his hands on his jeans. "You want to stay out of there for a while," he said. "Burritos for lunch." He looked at me. "You ready to hit it?" I nodded, picked up my bags, and moved to the door.

Tex stood up again. "Well, thanks for not much," Karl said, and moved toward the door too. "No fault of yours, I guess. You sure you don't want a beer before you book?" He looked at his cell as he spoke, and tapped out something on the screen.

"We're good," Sutter said, smiling, and then there was a pinging sound from the direction of his pocket. He smiled wider and reached back and tossed an iPhone to the floor. A text message glowed on the screen, and for a moment we all stared at it: *Comin out now. Lock n load.*

"I took it off your boy outside," Sutter said. "The wannabe sniper on the roof, with the AR and the crappy suppressor. He can't answer now, by the way."

Sutter had a Sig Sauer in each hand, pointed at Tex and at Karl, whose expressions blurred from confusion to shock to rage.

"One at a time," Sutter said. "Guns on the floor, two fingers only. You first, Karl."

Karl shook his head and gathered breath and forced a smile. "I gotta say: respect, man — *mad* respect. No shit. How —"

"The ashtray. A lot of butts, all the same brand, same bite mark on the filter. A heavy smoker filled that thing up, and the smell's still fresh in the air. But neither of you have touched a smoke since we've been here. So where's Smoky? Plus, your boy was all fidgety up there. Noisy. We can talk more when you're on the floor, Karl. Two fingers. Now."

Karl took the gun from his belt, knelt, and put it on the carpet. Sutter kicked it away as Karl stretched out on his belly, and then Tex lunged. And collapsed into a gasping, cursing heap, curled around his groin. Sutter plucked the gun from Tex's belt.

"You telegraph bad, pal," he said. "You should work on that."

"Screw —" Tex began, but ended with a scream when Sutter stomped on his ankle.

I turned to Callie. She was breathing hard and her face was lit with pleasure. "Did you know there was someone on the roof?" I asked.

She shook her head. "Who, Dub? I didn't know where the hell Dub went to. I figured Karl sent him out for somethin', or maybe he was in the garage. I wasn't mindin' that asshole; I was tryin' to take care of Billy. Besides, you never asked for no head count."

Sutter laughed and looked at Karl. "Your buddy's trussed up in the bathtub — still breathing too. I'm happy to treat you boys the same, despite what giant dicks you are, so long as you don't fuck around anymore. So I'm gonna take your weapons and put some zip ties on you, and then we'll be on our way. Callie can cut you loose when we're gone." Sutter looked at me.

"You want to grab the zip ties, doc? They're in the glove compartment."

"We can't leave her," I said.

"What?" Sutter said.

"We can't leave the girl here. They're go-

97

ing to kill her."

Callie inhaled sharply, and Sutter sighed. "You don't —" he started, but I pointed at Karl.

"You heard his bullshit. You know what they had planned for us. You know I'm right."

"What?" Callie said. "They're gonna *what*?"

"And?" Sutter asked. "I don't see how this is our problem."

"So we're supposed to leave her?"

Sutter shook his head. "This is *exactly* what I'm talking about. This shit is *not* our shit, and yet somehow you make it our shit."

"We're supposed to leave her — her and Billy both? Because, one way or another, he'll be dead too when they leave."

"You said he'd be dead in a few hours anyway."

"It's still not right."

Karl snickered, and it was too much for Callie. "You think it's funny, motherfucker?" she shouted. "You gonna shoot me and Billy and take our fuckin' money, and you think that's so fuckin' funny?"

He looked up at her and grinned. "It's nothing personal, Cal. Not *that* personal, anyways."

Then she kicked him twice, fast, in the

face. Karl yelped and wrapped his arms over his head, and Sutter looked resigned and disgusted. He tucked one of his guns into his armpit and caught Callie and lifted her, one-handed, still kicking, by her belt loops. He dropped her in front of me. "Maybe you could manage your girlfriend," he said, and turned to Karl. "And you, asshole — you and I are gonna renegotiate fees."

Billy died quietly, two hours later. Sutter frayed the plastic on Karl's zip tie before we left, enough so he could work himself loose with some effort. Callie wanted to kick him some more, but I pulled her away. Still, Karl was less than grateful when we walked out, and I could feel his glare on the back of my neck even as we drove west on the 10.

It was still warm, and we kept the top down; the wind carried off the smells of infection and death. No one spoke, but Callie sobbed and shook the whole way back. She hadn't decided what her next move would be, but thought Union Station was a place to start, and we dropped her near a hotel on Chavez that was walking distance to the trains. Callie climbed out, slung her backpack, nodded at Sutter, squeezed my hand, and disappeared.

Sutter turned onto Alameda going south,

and still we didn't speak. We stayed silent into Little Tokyo, and when we passed First Street, I couldn't take it anymore.

"It's not my fault those guys were morons," I said.

"It's not," he said after a while. His eyes never left the road.

"I didn't make them try to ambush us."

"Nope."

"And I had nothing to do with their plans to kill Callie and her boyfriend."

"No, you didn't."

"Then why —"

"You made her our problem."

"What would've happened to her was . . . wrong."

"Like that's rare? The world is full of all kinds of wrong — take five paces in any direction, you can't help but trip over it. Read a newspaper and you choke on it. You want to fix that shit, fine, but it's a full-time job, brother, the pay is lousy, and nobody's gonna thank you. No one's ever happy to find a missionary at the door."

"No one except people who need help."

"Somehow they're never the ones with the guns. Believe me, I get it — that itch to make things right. I had it myself, and I scratched it till it bled. It's why I signed on with Uncle in the first place, and why I signed off after seeing my work — work guys shed blood for — get turned to shit by dickheads looking to make a buck, or who couldn't keep their Predators in their pants. But I'm over it now. Now I fill the hours with simpler things: having some fun, making some bread, taking care of family, trying to get through the day without killing anybody, shit like that. You, brother, muddy up those waters."

"Tonight we did the right thing."

"It's great we're so awesome," Sutter said, sighing. "But I'm trying for simple, doc, and being your friend is sometimes the opposite of that." I nodded and said nothing, but watched the streets turn darker and more empty as we neared my home.

Sutter dropped me in the alley, by the clinic's back door, and drove off. The alley was quiet, and smelled of garbage, piss, and soot. My Honda was parked in the shadows. It was dusty, old, and in need of new tires, and I felt much the same. I put my baggage down and was rattling my keys when the car came around the corner.

It was a Land Rover, black with silver trim, neither dusty nor old, and its very large tires had an oily sheen in the sodium light. They squealed when the car swayed around the corner, and again when it rocked to a halt six inches from my knees.

CHAPTER 9

I recognized them from Scotty's description, as soon as they got out of the Rover. *Big and bigger. Ugly and uglier. Scary.*

The guy with blond cornrows was bigger, around six four, around 240 pounds. He wore black cowboy boots, black jeans, and a red tee shirt sprayed onto a chemically enhanced torso. His face was bony and pumpkin-colored under the lights, and when he smiled his teeth looked too large. His eyes were eager and darting, the pupils huge. Speeding. Maybe he thought the anabolic steroids didn't make him aggressive enough.

The other guy was definitely uglier. The tattoo on his chin was as Scotty had described — a black heart with a dagger through it — but Scotty hadn't mentioned the ink on his cheeks and neck — stars, elaborate crosses, Cyrillic letters — or the shaved head, or the expression of animal meanness on his meaty face and in his black eyes. He was about five ten and maybe two hundred pounds, and he wore gray pin-striped pants that were too long, and a pink shirt unbuttoned almost to his waist. His torso was like a steamer trunk, and there was thick hair on his chest, and more Russian ink. Wired wrong, I thought. Crazy.

"You the doctor?" Cornrows said. There was the trace of an accent in his voice, and he sounded like he was struggling not to laugh. I didn't answer, but thought about the scalpels in my bags, and that I'd never get to them in time. "You're him, right?" He looked at something in his hand. "Dr. Knox. And this is your clinic?"

My pulse spiked, and I tasted the tang of adrenaline on my tongue. I looked at my car, and the Dumpster alongside it. Nothing there.

"Who are you looking for?" I said, and took a step back.

"C'mon, you're him, right — the doctor?" Cornrows said, and smiled wider. Tats looked up and down the alley, and saw nothing that troubled him. He came toward me. Cornrows chuckled and said something in Russian; Tats stopped, though not happily.

"What do you want?" I asked. "Is somebody sick?"

Cornrows got a kick out of that, and the harder he laughed, the darker his face became. "Yeah — you. You're coming down with something serious any minute, so better to take care of yourself now."

I took another step back. I looked around the back door and along the building's back wall. Not a pipe or scrap of wood. I'd never seen the alley so fucking clean. I fingered my key ring, and slipped the longest and sharpest key between my middle two fingers and made a fist.

"What do you want?" I asked again.

"You know what we want, doc — we want same as you. We want to know where is she."

"Where who is?"

Tats spit, then muttered what sounded like a curse. Cornrows' sigh was weary and disappointed. He said something to Tats, who went to the Rover and pulled an aluminum bat from the rear seat. He came toward me.

I took a deep, shaky breath and let it out slowly. I looked at Tats' neck, at his trachea and suprasternal notch. I tightened my grip on the keys.

Cornrows shook his head. "She something to you, doc, you're gonna take a beating for her?"

"I don't know who *she* is. And, by the way, you're making no sense. If I'm supposed to be looking for her — whoever she is — then why do you think I know where she is?"

That stopped Cornrows for a moment, but Tats seemed not to hear, or to care. He took another step toward me and slapped the bat head in his palm. "You going to bullshit around, or you going to say why you want her?" His voice was like rocks in a bucket.

I shrugged. "She came in here."

"And she is what to you, huh? Your *bliad*?"

Cornrows smirked. "Means 'whore,' doc. He wants to know if Elena's your whore. Which would be a problem, right? Only one boss at a time."

Elena. I smiled.

Tats didn't know what to make of this, so he smiled too. It was not a pretty thing. His teeth were gray and oddly shaped, and many were missing. "You are doctor," he said. "You also woman? In my country, most doctors are woman."

"And most of the assholes are men," I said. This he understood. His face darkened and he brought the bat back. "I hear you're offering money," I said, and Tats paused again.

Cornrows smiled, like he'd run into an old friend. "Yeah? Well, you heard it right, doc. You got info, we got cash."

"How much?"

"Depends on what you got. Could be decent, though. Maybe couple of grand."

"That's not enough."

"Could be more — depends."

"Could be ten?"

Cornrows smiled wider. "Shit, doc, for ten you bring her gift-wrapped to my boss."

"Tell me who he is and where to find him, and I'll see what I can do."

He chuckled. "So ten's not really your number, yeah? You continue fucking with me."

I fought to control my breathing, and shrugged. "It's just how I am."

"You got balls, doc," Cornrows said, "for another couple seconds anyway." Then he nodded at Tats, who came on again.

I pointed up and behind him. "You guys realize you're on camera, right?"

They both turned and looked at the security camera, mounted high up on the wall and looking down on the back door. Cornrows said something in Russian, and Tats nodded and jumped onto the hood of the Rover, and then to its roof. He was quicker and more agile than I would've guessed. He swung the bat one-handed, and there was a loud metallic chime, and the camera and its metal housing came off the building. They bounced off the Dumpster with a hollow clang. Tats leapt from the Rover's roof and landed in a crouch by the front fender.

"Thanks, doc," Cornrows said, smiling. "You save us a pain in the ass." Tats smiled too, and came toward me again.

"Yeah, you saved me some trouble too," a voice called from behind them. "Now I can shoot you douche bags and not worry about it showing up on YouTube." Cornrows and Tats whirled as Sutter stepped into the cone of the sodium lights, and they froze when they saw his gun.

He held the Sig in a two-handed grip in front of him, and he sighted down the barrel as it swung in an easy arc between the Russians. Tats said something in Russian, in which *mudak* and *pizda* figured prominently. Sutter laughed and said something Russian in response. Cornrows and Tats were surprised and unhappy.

"You want to clear the line of fire, doc?" Sutter said, and jerked his head.

My thighs were like lead, and my chest was tight. "I want to talk to them."

"You can do that after I shoot 'em. Just in

the knees for starters."

Tats shuffled toward me and adjusted his grip on the bat. There was a flat crack, and Sutter buried a round between his feet. Tats froze. "I like you there, *da*?" Sutter said. "And roll that bat over to me."

Tats made a disgusted grunt and flung the bat into the darkness, where it clanged, banged, and rolled to a stop.

"Who's your boss?" I asked Cornrows.

He shook his head and smiled grimly. "You have your nigger shoot us now? Is that where we're going?"

Sutter chuckled from across the alley.

"What does your boss want with her?" I said.

"Fuck your cunt," Cornrows said. "We're leaving. You want to shoot, shoot. Just remember, he's not the only guy in town with guns." Tats glared at Sutter; then he and Cornrows climbed into the Rover and disappeared in a squeal of tires.

"I saw that movie," Sutter called after them. "Fucking Ivans — never anything original." He tucked the Sig behind him and crossed the alley. The smell of burnt rubber hung in the air. "I made them when I dropped you off. They were waiting down the block. Then I saw them pull into the alley. They didn't seem like regulars, so . . ."

"Thanks."

"They were looking for your girl?"

"Elena — they called her Elena."

Sutter nodded. "I hate to say *I told you so,* but I'm pretty sure I said that marching around with her photo wasn't the smartest move. How many people you talk to today? Anybody could've dimed you."

I knelt, and lifted a white rectangular scrap from the asphalt. "It wasn't just anybody," I said. "They had my card."

Sutter laughed ruefully. "See what I mean, brother? The opposite of simple."

CHAPTER 10

I'd left the shades up, and yellow light from the street fell on the bare brick walls and worn floorboards of my apartment and lit dust motes in the air. I dropped the duffels by the door, left the lights off, and tapped the thermostat. The A/C cycled up, and I walked through the big space that was living room, dining room, and kitchen, and grabbed a Stella from the fridge. It was icy on the back of my throat, and the cold ache spread through my sinuses and made a tiny dent in the mantle of fog around my brain.

I took slow, deep breaths between sips, trying for more oxygen. At the end of an endless day, I had all the post-call symptoms: I was wired, tired, jangly, underfed, overcaffeinated, and my attention span was flickering like a match at the beach. I drank some more beer and looked at the phone on the wall. The message light was blinking, but I couldn't bring myself to listen and wasn't sure I would comprehend it anyway. I kept moving, because to sit, I knew, was to sleep, and I wasn't ready for that.

My apartment spanned the floor, and there were windows and views all around, though the northern one was of the alley and the southern one of a potholed parking lot. To the west, glossy and glowing, were the towers of the ever-newer downtown, closer each time I looked. To the east, in daylight, I would've seen the cityscape flatten into warehouses, rail yards, and the concrete arroyo of the L.A. River. Now it was urban pointillism — yellow dots on black, picking out intersections, loading docks, the gated pens where trucks and buses slept. I walked to the bathroom and looked out the window into the alley below. There were no cars there but my own, and no people at all. I wondered which way Elena had run last Friday, and who'd been chasing her then — *los soldados* or the tattooed Russians. Maybe both.

I drank more beer and said her name aloud. My voice echoed, rebounding off the brick and boards and the few pieces of furniture I owned. A Formica table in the kitchen, a battered slab of maple that was more or less a desk, an armchair of synthetic suede, a doughy, slipcovered sofa, swaybacked bookshelves, a wrought-iron bed, and a clouded mirror with a chipped black frame — all bought at neighborhood secondhand stores that were gone now, or rebranded as *vintage*.

Here three-plus years, and it looks like you're expecting evac anytime. On the off chance no helo's coming, why don't you hang a picture, or put a rug down? Sutter had said that the last time he stopped by, but I didn't agree. I had dug in here — you just had to read closely to see it.

There were books on my shelves, and not just the rippled paperbacks that I'd picked up used at the bookstore on Spring Street. There were volumes older than I was, which had survived through med school, residency, marriage, a storage locker in New Haven while I was abroad, and then the trip west when I washed up in Los Angeles, with no plan of what to do and no idea of where else to go.

There was a copy of Guyton's *Textbook of Medical Physiology,* its cloth cover frayed and faded, that had been my father's when he was in med school, and a Mitchell-Nelson *Textbook of Pediatrics,* in even worse shape, that had been my grandfather's. By its side was my great-grandfather's Gray's *Anatomy.* It was much abused by time and humidity, stained with coffee, Scotch, and who knew what else, but his father's inscription was still legible in purple ink in front: *To the next Dr. Knox.*

I was, on my father's side, the latest in a long line of Drs. Knox, who had tended to the ill and injured of Litchfield County, Connecticut, since before the Revolution. Until I came along, anyway. I was the first Dr. Knox not to settle in Litchfield County, or in Connecticut, or maybe not anywhere at all. I was also the first to go west to medical school, the first to divorce, the first to work in Africa, the first to be relieved of that work. So many milestones . . . In fact, the aberrant behavior had started a generation earlier.

My father, Wilton Knox, was the first Dr. Knox to marry another physician — to marry any woman who worked outside the home — and the first Knox to marry a Jew. Which had no doubt set his Anglo-Saxon ancestors spinning in their Litchfield graves. His living relatives weren't thrilled either, nor were my mother's — though I imagine her parents were by then long past being surprised by anything she did.

Marilyn Berg was their youngest child. Their other children had joined the family's scrap metal business in Buffalo, married within the tribe, and dutifully produced the next generation, and Marilyn was expected to do her part — was all but promised, the story went, to a local dry-goods prince — but she'd had another future in mind, and it didn't involve being anyone's hausfrau. It did include a full ride to Vassar, though, and afterward to the Yale School of Medicine, and she'd dared her parents to stop her. They didn't try. She was the first in her family to go beyond high school, and she was never other than first in any of her classes.

I took a long pull of Stella and took the Guyton off the shelf. There used to be a picture in here. It was tucked in back, a black-and-white snapshot taken when she was in college, and I held it up to catch the streetlight. She was on a bench, and a Gothic spire loomed behind her. She wore a skirt like a pleated horse blanket, a white blouse, and the impatient scowl she donned for every photo. There was a pile of books beside her. Behind the sour look, she was eastern European lovely — small, dark-haired, pale, awkward, and insubordinate, her eyes full of intelligence and banked anger.

She'd met my father in New Haven. He was two years older, but a year behind her in med school. She made extra money tutoring; he was having trouble with bio-chem. They took their residencies — his in internal medicine, hers in emergency medicine — in Boston. They married when he passed his board exams and she finished a post-residency fellowship in critical care. She was three months pregnant at the time.

It was back to Litchfield County then, to a white house behind stone walls, and to the eighty-bed hospital nearby, where my mother ran the ER and my father was an attending, and where they practiced side by side — old-school doctors, true believers in a notion of medicine-as-religious-calling that was dated even then. They worked there, twelve hours a day or longer, six days a week, until just past four on a December morning a dozen years later, when my mother died. She was coming back from a call, the road was icy, the embankment steep, and the river running fast. It was a single-car accident, a week before my birth-day.

So went the family myth, anyway. But it was unreliable narrative, I knew: simplified, sanitized, improved for romance and tragedy — as if it needed any more. And, as family stories do, it left out the messy bits, the contradictions and cobwebs. So how to

116

reconcile their tireless devotion to patients, their skill and confidence as doctors, with their absolute bafflement as parents? How to explain that my presence seemed often to astonish them, as if I'd been left just that moment at the doorstep? What to make of the chaos inside our house — the chronically unmade beds, unwashed laundry, dust, and filthy dishes — the neglect so nicely camouflaged by white clapboards? What to make of my father's fondness for drink, of my mother's moods, which swung without warning from manic to polar and remote? What to make of the whispers after her death about a Dexedrine habit? Family: unknown, unknowable, the most commonplace and obstinate of mysteries. I laughed aloud at my own melodrama, and my voice sounded strange.

I raised my beer and found the bottle empty. I went to the fridge for another and downed half of it on my way back to the bookshelves.

I had more photos, in a box on a shelf. I drank more beer and lifted the lid. There was a picture of the two of them on top, from when they were residents, on a rare day off. They were in the Public Gardens, by an ornate willow, and they looked like refugees — thin and pale and exhausted.

There were other pictures, but I didn't want to look — they did nothing to patch my fractured memories of my parents into anything coherent. My closest approach to that came from the smell of a certain industrial disinfectant, a synthetic pine that was sweet and stinging — my madeleine.

The doctor's lounge at their little hospital was awash in the stuff. The room had a green vinyl sofa, a card table and folding chairs, tin ashtrays, and two vending machines: one that dispensed ossified candy, and another that hissed and burbled and spit something warm and brown and caffeinated into a paper cup. I rode with them on night calls until I was ten or so, and they would park me on that sofa and disappear through the swinging doors, down the hall to the ER. Besides the disinfectant, the lounge smelled of cigarettes and burnt coffee, and the overhead lights made a noise like angry bees. One night the boredom became too much and I followed them.

There was a nor'easter, and a drunk had driven a pickup into a station wagon. The woman in the wagon had a broken leg and had gone into labor six weeks too soon, and the fetus was in distress. The drunk, it turned out, had also eaten lots of Seconal. It took a minute or two for anyone to notice me there. That was long enough for me to see.

In the nearest bay, my mother was delivering the baby. It was by C-section, and there was screaming and blood on the floor, and her gloved hands and gowned arms were wet and red to the elbows. In the next bay, my father was wrestling with the drunk, who was the size of a boxcar and who roared and bucked, despite the nurses holding him, as my father snaked a tube down his throat.

It wasn't the violence of it that I remembered best — the blood and shouts and physical struggle — or the terrible intimacy, or the grotesque slapstick — a nurse sliding on her ass through a pool of vomit, the drunk's trumpet flatulence. Rather, it was my parents' composure through it all. They were the only fixed points in the reeling chaos, the steady drums and baseline, the poles around which the globe swung — calm, sure, commanding, and, to me, never more real. Never more parental.

My second beer was gone, but I'd brought along a third and didn't break stride. I returned the picture to the box and made the mistake of glancing inside as I did. Margot smiled up at me, and I shuddered and put the lid back on.

Margot — blue-eyed, flaxen-haired avatar

of Fairfield County privilege and entitlement — tall, slender, ever appraising. My ex-wife. I finished the third beer in a long swallow.

It was in San Francisco. I was in my last year of med school; she was working in venture capital. It was a drinks thing — a biopharma start-up looking to cultivate new doctors. I wasn't cultivatable, but I liked the view of the bay from the hotel lounge, and also the vodka tonics. Margot was sipping Stoli, neat. I don't know what I was thinking then — my father had died two months before, after a dozen years of steady drink and diminishment, and it's possible I wasn't thinking at all. I certainly wasn't seeing straight.

So I took in the dangerous cheekbones, the lanky grace, the wry line of her mouth, the knowing chuckle, the poise, and all the rest, and read it as cleverness, an irony that maybe masked a deeper wound, a generous heart, a love of beauty. I misread. Massively. What I thought cleverness was in fact a casual cruelty. The irony: no more than affectation. The warmth: practiced good manners. And the aesthetic sense: just a keen eye for everything that conferred status.

Gunfire punctured my beery musing, and I went to the kitchen window and took a look. There were just a few shots, widely spaced, and they weren't nearby. It wasn't a rare occurrence around here, and after the Central African Republic — the long bursts of full auto that would rip through the night — these pops were tame. I listened some more, but heard no shouts, no tires squealing, no sirens. A celebration, maybe, or somebody making a point.

I sighed and looked at the joint that had waited so patiently on the table. I reached for matches and struck one and opened a window. Warm air came in, and I lit up and took a hit. The smoke expanded, and I held it for a moment and coughed. The glowing ember lit the window orange, and made a jack-o'-lantern of my reflection. I laughed and found another Stella.

Margot had never pretended to be other than what she was; if I'd been fooled by anyone, it'd been by me. It had taken me the whole of my residency and longer to figure it out. In the meanwhile, we'd returned to Connecticut, I to work at Yale–New Haven, she at a private equity fund in Westport. We lived in Stratford, and I'd lost count of how many precious off-duty evenings I'd wasted watching boats on the Housatonic while her colleagues droned on about clients, bankers, real estate, golf handicaps, flying private, carried interest, private schools, and Republican fundraisers. When I wasn't bored, I pitied them. How they deluded themselves that all that crap meant something, that it was anything but comforting fiction, protective distraction from the realities of life: the nasty, brutish, and short parts, the horribly random parts, the parts where we're powerless to protect our loved ones from anything. I mostly thought they were fools and cowards. In darker moments, I envied them.

I took another hit, then washed the rawness from my throat with beer. Margot was spoiled and her values were toxic, but she was never stupid. She saw the arc of things before I did — from the time I took my first gig with Doctors Transglobal. I was three years out of my residency when I began, and my initial assignments were just a week or two long. I was packing to leave on the second one, to Brazil, and she watched from the doorway.

"I've never seen your ER empty," she said. "It's SRO whenever I've visited. So I guess this isn't about demand for health care suddenly collapsing in New Haven."

She was cross-legged on the bed while I packed for my next assignment, a project in Guatemala. "Always somebody to help,

122

huh? And always somewhere else. I thought a couple of trips would get those fantasies about saving the world out of your system. But they're in there deep, aren't they? Down in the bone."

Before my first trip to Africa, she'd said: "The more you go away, the less of you returns. One of these days, you won't come back at all."

She was right about that. The trip after that was an open-ended one, to the C.A.R. I was there three months when the divorce papers came and I signed them the same day.

A burning ash fell to the table and left another scorch mark.

Little remained of my marriage. Margot got the place in Stratford and most everything else. The one thing I still had from her sat atop a bookshelf: a leather-bound journal. She'd given it to me on my first trip, but it'd remained stubbornly blank until I got to the C.A.R. The medic I'd replaced there, the exhausted Dr. Demetrios, suggested that keeping a journal was useful, that writing had helped her avoid drinking too much. I don't know how lucid her entries were, but mine were mostly fragments — impressionistic, wandering, fevered, and lacking any coherent narrative.

Which made them entirely faithful to my experience there.

I looked, but couldn't see the journal in the darkness. Not that I would've touched it. I rarely opened it, not to the entries, not to the photos tucked in back — of Merry, one of my nurses there, and Mathieu, her son. She was twenty-five then, and would be no older. And Mathieu? Close to Alex's age back then. I touched my right flank above the hip, along the oblique, and then I touched my left quad. I could feel the ripples of scar tissue through the fabric of my jeans and tee shirt.

I exhaled a dusty breath and rubbed a hand across my eyes. The joint was gone, and the beer too, and soon the night. I needed sleep, but my bed was so far. I stood, listed to port, leaned against the window. The red light blinked on my phone.

"Fuck," I whispered, and pressed the message button. There was silence at first, then street noise — traffic and indistinct voices — then shallow, shuddering breaths, like someone fighting tears. I listened twice more, and took a breath of my own.

"Elena," I said aloud.

Chapter 11

Lydia's house was a white bungalow on Repton Street, in Highland Park — a neat, Spanish-style box on a street of similar boxes. It had a red tile roof, a narrow porch, a lawn in front that looked like a putting green, and a short chain-link fence all around. Her block was slow to wake on Sunday morning, empty but for a bleary-eyed woman and an old collie who struggled on the buckled sidewalk. I nodded at them as I opened Lydia's gate and went up the cement path. Before I made the porch steps, Lydia boiled through the front door. She wore a white tee shirt with no sleeves, and green scrub pants. Her hair was resting uneasily on her shoulders, and her hands were on her solid hips.

"We get one phone call, and that's it?" she said. "You forget we're here, maybe? You think I'm the fucking lost-and-found? You look like shit, by the way."

I held up a white bakery box. "Doughnuts from the Nickel," I said. She scowled some more, but her heart wasn't in it. "Got four maple bacon in here, and some red velvet."

She shook her head, but her face softened. "I've got coffee on."

Lydia's house smelled of coffee, wood soap, and cedar. Her kitchen had a red tiled floor, and yellow-and-red tiled counters, and it was cleaner than many places where I'd performed surgery. The appliances were old but gleaming, and the breakfast nook had a bay window and a flood of sunlight. The window looked onto the backyard, where there was a lemon tree, a profligate Chinese hibiscus, a stretch of lawn, and Alex, kicking a soccer ball with Arthur and Lucho. The kid wore gray gym shorts, a yellow Galaxy tee shirt, and — despite Arthur's and Lucho's best efforts — a look of concentration but not of enjoyment.

"He do okay last night?" I asked.

Lydia shook her head. "He ate fine, pretended to watch TV, and went to bed when I told him. I don't think he slept much, though, and he cried when he thought no one could hear."

I sighed. "You got him new clothes."

"*You* got him new clothes — the old ones needed washing. They were pricey, though, the old ones."

"Yeah?"

"That little striped shirt, those shorts, his sneakers, even his underwear — altogether they probably cost more than your car. They come from France, and Artie says only a few stores in town carry them — in Beverly Hills, Westwood, and Brentwood."

"Artie knew that?"

Lydia gave me a pitying look. "He knows how to read labels and use Google. You're not the only one who can play detective, doctor. And, talking about that — did you get anywhere finding the mother?"

I drank some coffee and took a deep breath. I didn't want to lie to Lydia, but the best I could do was to not lie completely. "I think her name is Elena. I found somebody who saw her and Alex together. Apparently, they were staying in the neighborhood."

"Staying where?"

I took a while clearing my throat. "The Harney," I said finally.

Lydia's brows leapt. "*¿Un burdel?*"

"That's the place."

"What the hell kind of woman brings her child to a whorehouse?"

"The kind that's in trouble, Lyd. The kind with people after her and no place else to go."

Lydia crossed her arms. "And what about those people? You find out something about those men on our security cameras?"

I shook my head and drank some more coffee.

"Elena, eh? Well, it's something, but not enough, doctor. Unless she shows up tomorrow, we got to call Family Services. The kid needs help."

I nodded vaguely, then refilled my coffee mug and put some doughnuts on a plate. "Let me talk to him," I said, and went out the back door.

Alex froze when I stepped into the yard. Arthur and Lucho looked at me and then at each other. Arthur juggled the soccer ball from one foot to the other, then flipped it deftly to Lucho, who trapped it.

"Hey — doughnuts!" Lucho said, straining for jolly. "You want one, Artie?"

"Sure. How about you, little man? You like doughnuts?"

Alex looked at me, at Lucho, at Arthur, at the doughnuts. He nodded slowly, his pale face empty of expression.

"All right," Lucho said. "How about some milk with that?" Another slow, careful nod. "C'mon, Artie, let's get milk." Arthur nodded and they both went inside.

Lydia had a tile-topped table in the yard,

and four wrought-iron chairs. I sat in one of them and put the doughnuts down. "Take your pick. I like the vanilla glazed myself, but they're all good. This one's got bacon on it. You like bacon?"

Alex approached warily, his eyes flicking from me to the plate.

"Have a seat," I said.

He sat. After a while his hand reached out for a maple frosted.

"Good choice," I said. "You're Alex, right? I'm Adam. I don't know if you remember me. I was there when your mom brought you in — when you weren't feeling well. After you ate the peanuts."

Alex looked at me some more. "I remember," he said. "You're the doctor." His voice was small and faraway, as if it had come from the bottom of a well.

"Yep. You can eat that doughnut, you know. No peanuts." He nodded slowly and took a bite. Color rose in his cheeks.

"Lydia told you your mom left you with us?" Alex locked his eyes on the tabletop. He nodded slowly. "We're trying to get in touch with her. Do you know how we can do that?"

"No."

"Were you and she staying at a place near my clinic? It's called the Harney — kind of an old place, made of brick? Lots of women stay there."

Alex nodded. "It . . . it was noisy in there, and it smelled bad. My mother didn't want me to touch anything."

"I bet. How long were you guys there?"

"I . . . I don't know. A few days."

"How'd you get there?" I asked. Alex looked up at me, puzzled. "Did you drive there?" He nodded. "Your mom had a car?" Another nod. "She drove you?" Again a nod. "Do you know where Elena is now, Alex? Any idea where we can find her?"

He sighed deeply at the mention of her name. His gaze shifted to the lemon tree, to a branch heavy with fruit. A tiny breeze sprang up, and I could smell lemons, dry lawn, the heat swelling in the air. Alex shook his head.

"Is there somebody else we could call? Somebody who takes care of you? Your dad, maybe, or an aunt or uncle? Your grandma or grandpa?"

Alex stiffened, and his eyes found a patch of earth beneath his feet. He shook his head. "I'll wait for my mother," he said softly.

"How about school?" I asked. "Is there someone we could talk to there?" This didn't merit even a head shake, and he sat still and silent until the back door opened and Lucho appeared with a glass of milk.

"Drink up, *mijo,*" Lucho said.

"He say anything?" Lydia asked when I returned to the kitchen. She filled my coffee mug and looked through the window, into the backyard.

"Not much. Not anything, really. His mother brought him to the Harney from somewhere — somewhere more luxurious, I guess, given his clothes. But, wherever that was, he doesn't seem to want to go back, or even to say a word about it. He just wants to wait for his mother."

Lydia shook her head. "Adam," she said. Her voice was quiet, and her eyes were sad.

"They'll grind him up, Lyd. With all the goodwill in the world, DCFS will grind him up."

She sat at the kitchen table and sighed. "You know, when they tossed me out of Palms, and I had Lucho and Linda to feed — they were little then, and their goddamn mother was still up in Chowchilla — I didn't know which way was up. I didn't know if I could even get another job."

I nodded, because I knew the story. For ten years, Lydia had been a scrub nurse in the cardiac unit at Palms-Pacific Hospital, one of the nation's leading medical centers.

131

She was at the top of the nursing food chain, and had assisted on angioplasties, bypasses, valve replacements, stent insertions — everything up to and including transplants — until she ran afoul of a surgeon with a gin problem. He'd walked into a catheter ablation stinking of it, and Lydia had walked out and filed a complaint. But the surgeon's father-in-law had a wing named for him at Palms, and a seat on the board of trustees, and so much for Lydia's career. Her next job, when she finally found one, was something of a step down: at the L.A. County Medical Center Jail Ward.

"Christ," she said, "I didn't know if I could put dinner on the table back then. But I got work, I kept my head down, and we got by. After a while, I even scraped together a down payment on this place. You didn't see it when we first moved in, doctor — it was a fucking mess."

"It looks great now, Lyd, but where are we going — ?"

She held up her hand. "It wasn't easy to put aside the money for it, or for Lucho's school things, or Linda's. It wasn't easy working in that jail for fifteen years — the place is a fucking shithole. I didn't like it, but I did it. I kept my head down and kept my mouth shut and did it. 'Cause I remembered what happened when I didn't do that — when I tried to do the right thing to the wrong people. And I remembered how they did me at Palms — trying to make me say I didn't see what I saw, getting other people to lie, the bullshit they made up about time sheets and missing meds and —"

"They were trying to scare you."

"And it worked too. I learned a lesson from that — about how fast you can lose things, how fast they can be taken. One wrong step . . ."

"You're overreacting, Lyd. What we've done is totally defensible. We thought the kid's mom was coming back, so we looked after him for a few days. Nobody's going to bust chops for that."

"Not if we call Family Services tomorrow. But I know what *a few days* means to you."

"You're —"

"I'm not your mother, you know — I had enough playing mother with Lucho and Linda. I don't want to be mad or lecture you or make you feel bad — but you scare me sometimes. You're a damn good doctor — and you know I don't say that easy. You're smart and you've got a good eye; you're a hell of a clinician. And you're very careful, at least when it comes to the patients. Never sloppy, never lazy — you care

133

about them, doctor, I know that. You got good medical sense, but it's the rest of your sense I worry about."

"My sense is fine."

Lydia shook her head. "I'm not a complete idiot, doctor. I don't know what you get up to with your pirate friend, but I notice what happens to the bank account after — those cash deposits. I don't know the details, and I don't want to — but I know bad judgment when I see it."

"I don't know what to tell you, Lyd. We —"

She held up a hand again. "I don't know how many more years I'm gonna do this, doctor. Tell the truth, I'm surprised I'm still doing it, after all the time at the jail. But Dr. Carmody — *dios mío,* he could talk — am I right? He had *pasión.* He talked me right into the clinic."

Lydia drank more coffee. "Junie's mother died six months ago," she said. Junie was a nurse from the jail hospital — her boyfriend, maybe, though she never said. "So he has her place in the desert now, way out there. He's fixing it up for retirement. He wants me to go with him, maybe. A few years, and I might. Until then, I don't need explanations from you. I just need peace and quiet."

134

I nodded at her and smiled, but could make no promises.

CHAPTER 12

According to the street girls Sutter shmoozed, Troop wouldn't show up at the Harney until two on Sunday afternoon, so we hid from the heat and ate tacos at a stand on Fifth Street. We could see into the kitchen from the counter, and a black-haired woman there was smiling at Sutter.

"I can talk to this guy myself," I said around my taco. "You don't have to be here."

Sutter laughed and drank his lemon ice. "Talking, you'll do fine. It's what comes after I'm worried about."

"The guy's an MI waiting to happen. I think I can manage."

"The trick is not to have to. Plus, Mr. Coronary has friends."

I shrugged. "You got more work coming up for me?"

"You know I can't predict. I get a call when I get a call, and then I call you." Sutter drank more of his lemon ice. "The wolf at the door?"

"Constantly. I'm not close to what I need for the building."

Sutter looked contemplative, as he did when opining on anything involving logistics, tactics, small arms, or real estate. "Downtown's too hot a market now."

"As I keep pointing out: it's not downtown, it's fucking Skid Row."

"It's just a matter of time before they rename it Downtown East or something. Check out the Valley, brother. I picked up a couple of short sales there — nice ranches — had them renoed and rented in no time."

"Your real estate empire grows ever larger."

"You should try it — putting down some roots. I'm closing on a little apartment complex in Chatsworth next week. I could set you up. It's got a pool and a nice laundry room."

"I don't think so."

"You moving in with Nora?"

"What?"

"Don't look so surprised. You spend a lot of time there, and she doesn't seem to mind."

"Houseguest is one thing, playing house is another."

"Who said anything about playing?"

"Nora's not interested in more than what we've got, and I've had my fill of marriage. One was more than enough."

Sutter reached the bottom of his lemon ice with a loud slurp. "That's it for you and love? One and done? Tapped out?"

I squinted at him. "You sound like an ad for a dating Web site."

"I'm a believer, brother — I'm all about the romance. My only problem with love is that there's just too much of it around. Some days, it's everywhere I look. For instance, another five minutes staring at that line cook back there, I may to have to propose. Check out those eyes. And that dexterity. I'm a sucker for a girl who knows how to work a knife."

Troop was a half-hour late for his shift at the Harney, and when his sour-looking colleague came out, Sutter and I went in.

Troop was locked in his wired glass bunker, studying a fresh bottle of Olde English. He looked up at Sutter and didn't like what he saw. He liked me less. His mouth opened before he knew what to say, and all that came out was an asthmatic wheeze.

I pointed at his chest. "That doesn't sound good. You a smoker, Mr. Troop?"

As if to answer my question, he dug in a shirt pocket for a cigarette. He plugged it in his mouth, lit it, and coughed. "What're you doing here? I told you I'd call if I heard anything about that chick. Did I call you and forget about it?"

"You didn't, but I wondered if that was because you didn't have my number anymore. Because you gave it to your Russians."

Troop's florid face grew redder. He made a flicking motion with his hand. "*My Russians?* I don't know what the fuck you're talking about."

"Plus, you owe me money. Forty bucks."

He laughed. "You're a funny guy, doc. Now, if you two want a room, I'll give you a break on the rate. Otherwise, fuck off."

"Who are the Russians?"

"*Who are the Russians?*" Troop repeated in a whiny schoolyard sneer, and he pantomimed jerking off. He grinned and puffed his cigarette, and in one fluid motion Sutter leapt to the countertop, vaulted the glass barrier, and lit on Troop's desk with barely a sound. Troop's mouth opened and he wheezed again; his cigarette fell into his lap.

I was surprised too, but I hid it better. I chuckled and pointed at Troop's smoldering crotch. "You'll want to do something about that. I think those pants are made of petrochemicals, and they'll fuse to your skin if they melt. It'll be ugly."

Troop looked down, horrified, and Sutter stepped easily from the desktop and poured Troop's bottle of malt liquor — the better part of forty ounces — into his lap.

"What the fuck!" Troop squealed, and jumped to his feet. He stumbled backward, slapping at his wet crotch. His rolling chair collided with a card table, knocking over a soda bottle, some paper cups, and two grease-stained bags from Sonic.

Sutter laughed. "This guy's a comedy show. Just like that English dude — Mr. Bean."

"Wha . . . what the fuck!" Troop said again, scuttling sideways into a filing cabinet, and sweeping an old cassette player to the floor. It shattered, and sent a tape and plastic shards across the linoleum.

Sutter shook his head. "Really, I can't add to this. He's leaving me with nothing to do."

"Who are the Russians, Mr. Troop," I said, "and what do they want with the girl?"

Troop swallowed hard. "I . . . they . . ."

"Sit down," I said, "before you fall down."

He did, and his chest heaved. "I don't know what Russians —"

Sutter leaned his hips on the desk and

rested one sneakered foot on Troop's chair, between his legs. Sutter sighed and pushed off slowly, rolling Troop to the far corner, where he stopped with a gentle bump.

"I get that you're scared of them," I said, "and I can see why — they seem like scary guys. But they're not here now, and we are. Whatever they might do to you is theoretical. What we do is . . . more concrete."

"Who are the Russians?" Sutter said quietly.

Troop looked down into his soaked lap. "They . . . they work for Rostov," Troop said, half swallowing the words.

"Who's Rostov?" I asked.

Sutter stood up straight and rubbed his chin. "Siggy Rostov," he said. "He runs whores, among other things. Whores, gambling, loan-sharking, the list goes on — but mainly whores. Probably half the girls who work out of here work for Siggy somewhere up the line. That right, Troop?"

"More than half."

"What's this Rostov want with her?" I asked.

"I don't know. It's not like those guys tell me shit."

"When did they come around?"

Troop wiped his brow. "They're always around here, but they started asking about her on Friday, middle of the day."

"She wasn't here?"

"She and the kid went out in the morning. They didn't come back."

"How long had they been staying here?"

"Since last Tuesday. Paid a week up front."

Sutter nodded. "Paid for a week, but didn't stay a week. She leave anything behind?"

Troop looked into his crotch again. "I . . . I don't think so."

"You want to try that again?" Sutter said.

"I . . . I found some stuff under the bed."

Sutter shook his head. "Going under a bed at this place — you're braver than you look. Let's see it."

Troop shifted in his seat. He pointed to his desk. "Bottom drawer, on the right — but there was next to nothing."

Sutter opened the drawer. He took out a white plastic grocery bag and looked inside. He picked through it and shrugged, then tossed it over the glass wall to me. "See what you make of it."

There wasn't much to see: two pairs of Alex-sized tee shirts, shorts, underpants, and socks, a pair of Alex-sized sandals that looked like leather but were actually plastic, two new toothbrushes, a tube of candy-flavored toothpaste with superheroes on the label, a bottle of chewable multivitamins shaped like funny cavemen, a granola bar, and, at the bottom, a wallet. It was leather, buttery and supple, a softly glowing black on the outside, and inside an arterial red. There was a logo embossed on an inside flap, a leaping horse, and a monogram — HM — in gold Helvetica letters above the credit card slots. Other than the lingering smell of money, it was empty.

I held it up for Troop to see. "You find it this way?"

He nodded, and looked at his crotch again. "I told you, next to nothing."

Sutter slapped the back of Troop's head. "Try not to be so full of shit," he said, smiling.

"What was in there?" I asked.

Troop reached into his back pocket. His own wallet was a nylon-and-Velcro affair, like a lumpy gray brick. He peeled it open and took out a thin stack of cards. "Some guy's business cards — that's all there was. I figured the chick took the credit cards and cash."

Sutter took the cards. "Hoover Mays. No address, just a 213 phone number. Who the fuck is named *Hoover*?"

"You planning to do something with the cards?" I asked.

"Thought maybe I could call the guy, sell his wallet back. Even empty it's worth something, and I wasn't gonna tell him it was empty."

Sutter slapped his head again. "Douche bag. So this was it — the shopping bag, the wallet — nothing else?"

Troop rubbed his head. "I swear."

Sutter looked at me. I shrugged, and he looked at Troop. "Here's your deal," Sutter said. "You talk about our visit with no one — including and especially Siggy Rostov and his monkeys — and we do the same, okay? You tell no one how you spilled your guts to us, and we tell no one, and everyone sleeps soundly at night. Am I transmitting clear?"

Troop nodded. "It's clear."

"Okay, then," Sutter said, and he pocketed Hoover May's calling cards, leapt to the top of Troop's desk, and vaulted the glass again with no more effort than a leaf in the wind.

CHAPTER 13

"So — your girl is probably a working girl," Sutter said. We were in my apartment, above the clinic, and he was tilted back in one of my kitchen chairs, drinking a Stella, his sneakers on a windowsill.

"How do you get there?"

"It's a short walk. Probably ninety-nine percent of the women Siggy Rostov knows are hookers — and a hundred percent of the eastern European women. Then there's the fact that he's sent his boys out hunting for her, which I'm pretty sure isn't so they can tell her about the sweepstakes she just won. If he's gone to that trouble, it's asset recovery."

"And she's the asset — his property?"

Sutter nodded. "Siggy's a slaver, with a pipeline of product from eastern Europe into L.A. He used to get his girls from traffickers, but then he figured out there was bigger profit in vertical integration, so he

145

cut out the middlemen and put his own people in place up and down the line, from the recruiters and wranglers to transpo. Most of the girls go into his brothels; the youngest, prettiest ones he sets up in apartments he has around town. In theory, they're working to pay off their passage. In fact, nothing ever gets paid off, and they work for him till they can't anymore."

I took a deep breath. "What a fucking pig."

Sutter drank some Stella. "Siggy in a nutshell."

"How do you know this guy?"

"He wanted to hire me once upon a time, not long after I got back to town."

"To do what?"

"Security, executive protection, that kind of thing. He was expanding at the time, bumping up against a Cambodian crew in Long Beach, and the Mexicans just about everywhere else, and he was nervous. He was right to be — that war got *muy caliente* for a while."

"You passed?"

He nodded. "Not enough soap and water in the world to get over working for a guy like Siggy. Plus, I never had trouble finding gigs."

I twisted the cap off my own bottle and drank some beer. Cold spread into my chest. I flipped the cap across the room, where it bounced and spun on the counter and finally landed in the kitchen sink.

"It doesn't make sense," I said. "Say Elena's a hooker, that she's an illegal, on the run from this Rostov — where does Alex fit in? He speaks English better than she does, with no accent, he's got these expensive clothes, he's well fed, and besides the peanut allergy he's in good health. Elena may be fresh off the boat, but Alex isn't."

"Sounds like he's been here in the golden West for a while. And not hanging out at places like the Harney."

"So where has he been hanging out? And what about those two guys on my security cameras — *los soldados*?"

Sutter nodded and drank more beer. "They do look like a couple of grunts, and definitely not out of Siggy's kennel."

"What do they want with her?"

"Maybe it's not her they want."

I sighed and picked up the white plastic bag we'd taken from Troop. I took out the wallet.

"Hoover Mays," I said. "His wallet is expensive."

Sutter laughed. "And he has the greatest name ever."

"If you can afford a wallet like that, maybe

you can afford expensive French clothes for your kids."

"You think he's the boy's father?"

I shook my head. "I have no clue."

Sutter tipped his chair back to level. He turned to look at me. "So fire up your laptop, brother. Let's drink more beer and gather some data."

We went to the living room and I turned on the Mac. While it cranked, Sutter wandered around, shaking his head. "Maybe curtains," he muttered. "I could fix you up."

"Here's Google," I said.

As it turned out, there was plenty about Hoover Mays online — much of it on various social networking sites, supplied by Mays's current wife, his ex-wife, his children, and Mays himself. It wasn't hard to find, and it wasn't hard to assemble from it a sketch of Hoover Mays's life.

So he was fifty-three years of age, born in Santa Barbara, to an old California family — which, I'd learned since moving here, could mean that they came with the Spanish or arrived last week. In the case of the Mays clan, it was the gold rush that drew them, real estate that made them money, and three successive generations of morons that pissed most of it away. Hoover seemed to be their last, best hope of getting some back.

He'd graduated from USC with a degree in marketing, attended B-school at Anderson, worked as a staffer for a Republican congressman from Santa Barbara for a couple of terms, and then became a lobbyist in D.C., first for mining interests and then for the firearms industry. He'd married in the eighties, had a son and a daughter soon thereafter, divorced when Clinton came in, and hit the mother lode in 1999, with a conversion to Catholicism and a second marriage to the daughter of a Brazilian beverage magnate.

Hoover returned to L.A. at the turn of the century, to look after his new father-in-law's California real estate, take positions on the boards of several cultural institutions, and have another couple of kids with his much younger new wife.

Sutter stood behind me as I clicked through pictures. "He married plenty of money," Sutter said. "But none of his kids look anything like Alex. And — Christ — check out the older kids. They could double for Barbie and Ken."

"Thinner versions of Hoover, with more hair."

I stood, and stretched my arms over my

head. "I see nothing to connect Hoover to Elena, or to Alex, or to Rostov, for that matter. And your theory about Rostov and Elena is still just a theory. And besides all that, I still have no fucking idea where Elena is."

Sutter laughed and went to the fridge. I heard the cap come off another beer. "Welcome to the wonderful world of intelligence, brother — of which, by the way, you have none."

"Thanks."

"Not that kind of intelligence. I mean intel — as in a story — a tale that connects the dots and makes the data make sense. Without the story, the dots are just dots."

I joined him in another beer. "Like symptoms but no diagnosis."

"Dots," he repeated, and drank from the bottle. "I'm thinking you need to let Lydia call Family Services."

I shook my head. "The hell I do. Elena left him with us because she saw that we'd take care of him, and he's waiting for her. I'll be damned if I'm turning him over to the fucking DMV. What I need is to talk to some people. Hoover Mays, maybe, or Siggy Rostov."

Sutter almost spit his beer. He coughed, took a deep breath, and looked me in the eye. "I can't be too clear on this point: the very last thing you want to do is talk to Siggy Rostov. About anything. At all. 'Cause chances are it would be the very last conversation you had. And why the fuck would you want to do it, anyway?"

"You said it yourself — I've got nothing but data points. I figure if I talk to Rostov some of them might make sense."

"Not if your brains are all over his carpet. Did they not cover that in med school?"

"So what would you do?"

Sutter looked at his watch. "Me? I'm meeting somebody in a while, up on the roof of the Standard — a red-haired girl from Calgary, who got herself a part in a cop show pilot and wants to celebrate. That's the only plan I've got."

"What would you do?" I said again.

He shrugged. "Hoover Mays looks approachable. Guy's got his whole life story — including his fucking calendar — up on Facebook, so he shouldn't be hard to find. And there're plenty of pictures of him online. You could show his pasty mug to the kid and see what he makes of it. Then of course there are those soldiers of yours — on your security cameras."

"What about them? I have no idea who they are."

"No idea now, but they'll be back. I guarantee it."

CHAPTER 14

They came back on Monday, which started early and messy.

Eduardo was there at 6:00 a.m., before I'd made it all the way downstairs. He was a day laborer, with abraded hands, a broken left wrist, and a right knee cut so badly that a flap of skin hung down over the head of his tibia and laid the patella bare. It looked like the unripe flesh of some exotic fruit, and Eduardo's hands, wrapped in newspaper, were like bloody fish. Eduardo himself looked like he'd been touring an abattoir. As he skirted the edges of shock, he explained in fluent English that he'd bounced from the back of an overcrowded contractor's pickup truck as it rode over a corner curb doing about forty.

"He didn't stop when I fell off, even though all the guys were yelling," Eduardo said, gasping. "He didn't even slow down."

I pushed up the security grate and led him

inside. He was lucky as far as nerve damage went, but there was a lot of blood, a lot of glass and grit to pick from the wounds, and a lot of slow, fine work with forceps and needles. Despite the local anesthetic, there was also a lot of yelling.

When Eduardo hobbled out at eight-forty-five, in a spare pair of scrubs, splinted, sutured, bandaged, and with prescriptions for antibiotics and pain meds, my fingers were sore, my eyes stung, and my waiting room was overflowing. Fractures, contusions, burns, abscesses of the arms, legs, and buttocks, poisonings, overdoses, chest pains, pneumonias, toothaches, dog bites, cat bites, and human bites — and that was just the first wave. It was a full house — a moaning, muttering, sometimes screaming circus — and not atypical for a Monday. Something to do with demand pent up over the weekend, and maybe the full moon on Saturday night.

Lucho and Neena, one of our part-time physician's assistants, were in the waiting room, in triage mode: assessing, prioritizing, and, for the most urgent cases, arranging transport to ERs at County-USC or Good Samaritan. Lydia and Katy, another part-timer, were in exam rooms, and so was I, except when one of them needed help, in

154

which case I ran around. I ran a lot that day.

But we found a rhythm in the chaos — a jazzy, bantering, urgent beat. Lucho kept the background music going, and kept the coffee coming too, and every now and then there was a doughnut or an apple or half of a chicken burrito to eat. I looked up and it was ten, then noon, then 4:00 p.m. The faces and the ailments, like the hours, went by in a blur.

A few times I caught a glimpse of Alex standing in the doorway of the file room, where Lydia had installed him for the day with picture books and crayons and drawing paper. His eyes were huge and locked on me. I caught Lydia looking at me too sometimes. Her gaze was dour, and I was pretty sure I knew what she was thinking. I was grateful that there was little time to talk.

By 6:00 p.m. we'd gotten through the worst of it. There was a guy from a loading dock around the corner with a long wooden splinter in his leg, a twenty-something woman with what looked like a fractured ring finger, and a fortyish woman with an earache, but besides them, the waiting room was empty. And then *los soldados* came in.

I heard them before I saw them.

"You're not Knox," a gravelly voice said

from the waiting room. "No, you gotta be . . . Luis Ortega, known as Lucho. Resides in unnatural sin with one Arthur Silva at 1531 1/2 North Hobart, in East Hollywood. Graduated Franklin High School, signed on with the army afterward, served a couple of tours in and around beautiful Fallujah with Operation Iraqi Shit Storm. No complaints heard from those quarters — so I guess nobody asked and nobody told, eh? Came back to L.A. and attended Dupree Technical Institute, whatever the fuck that is, for certificates as a medical assistant and a medical office manager. Which makes you — what — qualified to run a fax machine? No criminal record as a big boy, but juvie is another story. There we got assault beefs, a B&E, a GTA, a weapons collar, and all classified as gang-related. But only one conviction, on Assault Two, and for that you got off with probation and your record expunged if you kept your nose clean, which I guess you did. All of that means your auntie Lydia sprang for a decent lawyer, huh?"

"Who are you," Lucho said, "and what the fuck do you want?" I had never heard so much anger in his voice, or so much menace.

"It's not you I want, hero, it's your boss."

I came down the hall. Alex was in the file room. His eyes were wide and frightened. I put my finger to my lips, then pointed to the desk at the back of the room. He nodded and disappeared behind the swivel chair, and then Lydia pushed past me, on into the waiting room. I followed.

There were three of them. I recognized the two twenty-somethings from the security video: they wore khakis and polos today, and in person looked blockier and more angry. The third man was bigger and older, in his fifties, with white hair cut high and tight on a blocky head, skin like sunburned vinyl, and shiny scar tissue on his thick neck. His smile was large, hungry, and confident, like a shark's when it's about to feed. He was the guy in charge, and his large, scarred hands held a file folder.

Lydia, red-faced, brandished her cell phone like a can of Mace. "You want us to think you are cops or something? I'll call the real cops in a second, you don't get the hell out of here."

The older guy laughed and consulted his file. "And speak of the devil: it's Aunt Lydia. Another one with a past — guess the doc likes his help scuffed up. Got kicked to the curb after ten years at Palms-Pacific for running your mouth about your betters, and wound up emptying bedpans at the lockup. Ouch. Maybe not the best judgment, ratting out that lush, huh? Maybe good to think twice about who you're fucking with." He smiled wider and looked at me. Lydia's mouth opened and closed. I put a hand on her arm and stepped around her.

"You're looking for me." I said.

"At last," he said. "The *jefe* of this toilet." He cleared his throat and made a show of leafing through his file and reading from it as if from a prayer book. "Adam Knox, M.D. Born and raised in Lakeville, Connecticut, graduated from the Colebrook School — is that like finishing school or something? Went to fancy university in Providence, Rhode Island, played soccer for 'em till you screwed up your knee, went premed, then med school, then blah, blah, blah. Nothing much exciting till you start volunteering for Doctors Transglobal Rescue. Saw some of the armpits of the planet with that outfit, yeah? Busted up your marriage along the way — probably for the best, considering."

I forced a smile and interrupted. "Am I supposed to be freaked out that you can use Google and work a printer?"

He chuckled. "Be fair, doc — that wasn't all public-records shit. Your boy's juvie file, for instance — that took a little effort."

"I've known these people awhile. Your recital isn't news."

"Not to you, but maybe to your patients. And how well do these folks know you? For instance, do they know how you almost got yourself killed over on the dark continent?"

I glanced around the waiting room. The man with the splinter and the woman with the fracture looked scared. The woman with the earache was gone.

"You're upsetting my patients. If you keep interfering with our business —"

"This a business?" The shark grin widened. "Anyway, we're just talking. And don't these folks have a right to know how you got dragged outta the Central African Republic, shot up and bloody and in disgrace? Shouldn't they know about" — he looked at his file again — "Marie-Josée Lisle?"

He mangled the pronunciation and I corrected him. "Jo*say*. It's pronounced Jo*say*."

"Whatever — she was your nurse, right? *Was.* Dangerous thing, working for you. Surely these folks have a right to know that." He grinned some more. Lucho squared his shoulders, and the two young *soldados* stiffened and took a step toward him. I looked at Lucho and shook my head.

"Who are you?" I asked.

"Just a guy who wants information, doc. The more you provide, the more good you do for you and yours."

"Unless you people leave now, I'm going to call someone."

He laughed. "*Calling someone* doesn't work for you — my phone book's got a bigger dick than yours. For instance, even though little rat-turd clinics like this are barely regulated in this town, I bet I could find some people to come down and look around. Audit your controlled substances, maybe, or go over your Medi-Cal claims, or check out your wiring for code violations — that kind of shit. Maybe they wouldn't find anything, but maybe they'd shut you down for a week while they dug around."

I looked at Lucho. "Would you take these folks into the exam rooms?" He nodded and beckoned to the remaining patients, who all but ran to follow.

"What do you want?" I said.

"I told you — information. You had two people in last Friday afternoon — a woman with a boy. I want to know where they are."

I squinted at him and shook my head. "You're kidding, right?"

He shook his head. "Right. I drive all the way down to this fucking sewer 'cause I'm a big kidder, doc. I bring these ass kickers with me 'cause I'm kidding."

"You never heard of doctor-patient confidentiality? We don't discuss our patients — full-stop."

"I'm not asking what they came here for — I could care less. In fact, I could care less about the girl. I just want the kid."

I looked at Lydia, who was pale and stony-faced. "Call 911, please."

The shark put up his hands. "Doc, you don't want to go that way — I promise you — not with us. Remember my phone book? You bring cops in on this, who do you think has the credibility — you or us? I guarantee, it'll be us."

"Who's *us*?"

He shook his head again. "You want time to think on it — take some time. But not too much."

"Who are you?"

He reached into his pants pocket and took out a business card. There was a phone number on it and nothing else. "We lost something. We want it back. Save everybody heartache, doc — call the number." Then he turned and walked out the door. The two younger crew cuts waited until he was on the street; then they followed.

Lydia sputtered. "What the —"

161

"Check on Alex," I said, and ran to the window. The crew cuts were climbing into a black Suburban. The engine was already running, and when the doors shut, it pulled from the curb in a squealing U-turn. I found a pen in my scrubs, and as the SUV rolled past, I scrawled the plate number on the back of the shark's card.

CHAPTER 15

Ben Sutter's house was in Venice, on Horizon Avenue, a short walk from the beach. It was blue clapboard with white trim, tucked, shoulder to shoulder, in a row of vividly painted, wildly expensive cottages. It had a teak fence in front, draped in bougainvillea, and a porch with a bench. There were stone floors inside, a big steel-and-granite kitchen that opened to the dining and living rooms, and a wall of glass doors that looked onto a brick patio, more flowering shrubs, a fig tree, and a carport. There were two bedrooms upstairs, one of which Sutter was still refurbishing, as he had refurbished the rest of the house, by himself. It'd been mostly a shell when he bought it five years earlier, and not much more than that during the months I'd slept on the sofa. Now he routinely rejected unsolicited offers for the place that approached seven figures, and chuckled to himself every time.

The bougainvillea flowers were glowing red in the twilight as I drove past. There was never street parking in the neighborhood, and I pulled my Honda into the alley and into Sutter's carport. The streetlights were just coming on, and they buzzed irritably and made the air quiver. I recognized Sutter's truck, and the BMW with the bullet hole, but I didn't know the green Mini Cooper. The Mini's owner was inside, and I didn't know her either.

She was tall and Asian and deeply tanned, with a whippet body, a long black ponytail, and an elaborate tattoo of an ocean wave frothing around her left shoulder and running in a sleeve down her left arm. She wore a white spaghetti tee, black yoga pants, flip-flops, a silver ring on one of her toes, and a diamond chip in her nose. She was standing at the bottom of the open stairs, drinking kombucha from a bottle, and reading something on her phone. She looked up at me unsurprised, and smiled.

"You didn't block me, did you?" she asked.

"I don't think so."

She smiled wider. " 'Cause I've got to teach class in like — *yikes* — fifteen minutes. Gotta jump." She grabbed a clump of keys from the kitchen counter. "Tell him I'll catch him later," she said, and glided through the glass doors and across the patio. In a moment the Mini started up and pulled away.

It was always noisy in Venice — humming day and night — but it was quiet in Sutter's house. I heard ticking in the vents, water running upstairs, the ever-present ocean breeze moving foliage on the patio. Then there was a muffled pat, no louder than snow falling, and a flash of gray, and Sutter's cat was on the counter.

She was small and ash-colored, with a white blaze on her chest. She had wandered in one day while Sutter was fitting stones for his floors, and never left. Despite her size she had a rich, throaty purr, so he called her Eartha. She sniffed my hand, then bumped it with her head and licked a knuckle. Her tongue was like warm sandpaper.

"Hey," I whispered. She looked at me, tilted her head, then leapt off the counter and vanished in the shadows. I turned on more lights and took a bottle of water from Sutter's refrigerator. As I drank, I leaned on the kitchen counter. My neck and shoulders were still tense from this afternoon.

Lydia had found Alex under the desk, shaking and wide-eyed, but not crying. He hadn't seen any of the men, so he couldn't say if he'd seen them before. He might have recognized the shark's gravel voice, though he wouldn't or couldn't say from where, and none of us wanted to press him on it. Lucho sat with him while Lydia and I tended to our last patients. We worked in uncharacteristic silence, like the hush after an earthquake when you're not certain that it's over, or if another tremor might hit, or another dish might fall. When we'd seen our patients out, we spoke.

"What the *hell*?" Lucho said as he locked the doors. Lydia swore softly, in Spanish.

I looked at her. "They're after him, Lyd," I whispered.

"I got that, doctor."

"And they don't seem too worried if we call the authorities. Like they're connected —"

"I got that too."

"And they want us scared — scared that they'll fuck with us," Lucho said.

Lydia was silent, and her mouth was a hard, white line. "Shit," she whispered finally.

We'd waited a while before we took Alex out of the clinic, and when we did it was through the back. Lucho pulled his car up to the door and drove Alex not to Lydia's, or to his and Arthur's place, but over to

Echo Park, where Arthur's sister lived.

Eartha bumped my leg and threaded herself around my ankles. A light went on over the stairs, and Sutter came down. He wore cargo shorts and a faded red Moto Guzzi tee shirt. The scent of Dial soap followed him as he went to the refrigerator and took out a carton of orange juice.

"Your friend said she'd catch you later," I said.

"Tina?"

"I guess. She didn't look much like a redhead from Calgary."

Sutter smiled. "Janine. Janine is from Calgary, and she split after breakfast. Tina has a yoga studio in Marina del Rey."

"She seemed quite limber," I said, and I laid the shark's card on the counter.

Sutter picked it up. "What's this?"

I told him the story, and he listened without interrupting or moving. When I was through, he pursed his lips and nodded curtly.

"So . . . they're pros: the info they dug up on all of you says that. And they want you to know that they're pros, and to be freaked by that: the way they used the info says that. They also want you to know — or to believe — that they're wired in, that they or their clients have juice. It may or may not be true, but they want you to believe it. So . . . pros, but maybe not so good at the job."

"No? 'Cause they scared us pretty good."

"Yeah, but they were kind of heavy-handed about it. Not that there's a lot of subtlety in this business, but really — three guys? Threats of audits and building code violations? Maybe it's just me, but I think there're better ways. But those are just style points. The bigger problem is, they didn't take time to know their audience. If they had, they wouldn't have come on the way they did and push all the wrong buttons with you guys."

"They pissed us off."

"Exactly — they dug you in deeper, which is not the objective. Of course, their biggest problem was that they didn't know where the kid was. They certainly didn't know he was in the next room."

"No?"

"If they had, they would've grabbed him. So . . . pros, but not great ones. Or maybe they were just rushed."

"Good, bad, in a hurry, whatever — I didn't like it. Can you find out who the car belongs to?"

"The phone too," he said, and pocketed the shark's card. "And when I do, what are you going to do with that info?"

"I don't know. Talk to whoever it is? Ask him what he wants with the kid? Intimidate him?"

Sutter smiled. "Yeah, that'll work well."

"I'm supposed to let these dicks just take the kid?"

"You could hand him over to DCFS, or call the cops."

"And if these goons are as connected as they say?"

Sutter put up his hands. "You'd better figure out how far you want to take this."

I drank some more water. "I'm waiting for Elena. If it turns out she's not coming back, or can't, then we'll see."

Sutter looked at me and sighed. "All right, then. I guess the only thing is to read and react. We see who these guys are, who they work for, and hope they're stupid, or easy, or both."

"We?"

He smiled. "You're a payday, brother. Got to look after that." Sutter looked me up and down. "Why are you dressed so fancy?"

I was wearing a blue blazer, my newest jeans, loafers, and a blue-and-white striped shirt with a buttoned-down collar. "Hoover Mays. He says on Facebook that he's going to a fund-raiser tonight. A benefit for some new labs at the USC med school — like they need it. It's in Santa Monica, at the Brinkley. I figured I'd try to talk to him."

He looked me up and down. "You look like a tennis pro cruising for bored housewives."

"The Web site said the evening's theme was 'California clambake.' I didn't know what that meant."

He shrugged. "At the Brinkley it could mean black tie. But what the hell — it's all in the swagger. Just look like you belong." And then a muted burr came from Sutter's cargo shorts. He fished out three phones and tapped the one that glowed.

"Go ahead," he said. He squinted for a moment and shook his head. "Go slow — when did he call? And they're at his place? The one in Pacific Palisades? How did he sound? Okay, he's actually in front of me right now. Just hang for a second." Sutter muted the phone and looked at me, grinning.

"Timing is everything, brother," he said. "Want to make some cash?"

"You've got a call?" I asked, and Sutter nodded. "What — right now? I've got the thing at the Brinkley."

"What time?"

"Cocktails at seven-thirty, and then the

main event's supposed to start at eight-thirty."

"Which means nobody gets there till nine, and people won't be even a little lubricated till ten. You want Hoover nice and loose, right?"

I nodded. "I need all the help I can get."

"There you go — you've got plenty of time." I hesitated and Sutter spread his hands. "C'mon, brother, you said you wanted to raise money quick. Besides, you're going to want to take this."

"Yeah?"

"It's your wifty pal — Gable."

I was silent for a moment, and then I shook my head and laughed. "All right, but I need to borrow clothes from you. I've got to keep my Brinkley duds clean, and things with Will are always messy."

Sutter nodded and smiled and tapped his phone. "Tell your boy to sit tight and stay calm; help's on the way."

Before he was my patient, I'd known Will Gable the way everyone did, from his movie roles — the broody, romantic vampire, the broody, romantic hacker, the broody, romantic journalist, drug smuggler, spy — and from the inescapable tabloid coverage of his untidy love life, which always involved other young and pretty boldfaced names. I'd never sat through any of Gable's films, so my first sight of him beyond the Internet or the grocery checkout was two years back, when Sutter and I had arrived at 3:00 a.m. at Gable's home in the Hollywood Hills. He was tied hand and foot with leather straps, and his scrotum was bound in dental floss that had all but disappeared into swollen blue flesh.

The fact that he was high as a kite was a help. It'd kept him calm — jolly even — while I set him free, restored his circulation, and tended to his lacerations. He was downright courtly to the frightened young dominatrix whose knots and inexperience had led to his predicament, and whose panicked call to Gable's manager had brought Sutter and me out. Despite his careful manners, she'd run off just after dawn.

The drugs had mostly worn off by then, but not Gable's charm. He was affable, unpretentious, scrupulously polite, and entirely unembarrassed, and he insisted that we stay for coffee and then for a full breakfast. His appetite for sexual adventure, coupled with some awesomely bad luck at it, had brought Sutter and me around three more times to tend to Gable and his pretty pals — the only repeat business we'd ever had. A Viagra overdose, a violent allergic re-action to skintight vinyl, and a muscle spasm around a mercifully empty split of Veuve Clicquot were all near-disasters for Will Gable, but quite lucrative for us. Sutter took Ocean north, and then got on the PCH.

The gray stone manse on Corona del Mar, in Pacific Palisades, was a recent addition to Will Gable's real estate portfolio. It had high hedges, iron gates, and sweeping ocean views, and there were two cars in the cob-bled court. I knew Gable's R8, but not the candy-apple Tesla. The double front doors were unlocked, and we heard a woman's voice as we came through. At first we thought she was crying, but as we sprinted through the house it became something else.

Laughter. They were weeping with it as they rolled, naked, across Gable's vast bed. Their legs were intertwined, and they gripped each other's asses with both hands. They stopped rolling with Gable on top and the girl's face buried in his shoulder.

"Dr. X!" Gable called, craning his neck to look at me. His smile was wide and cheer-ful, and his dark hair was damp with sweat. "Long time, doctor, and thanks so much for coming." He looked at Sutter. "And hello to you too, Mr. X! Always a pleasure."

Gable looked at the girl. "See, I told you they'd come. The X's are totally reliable and totally discreet. Say hello to them." The girl giggled and said something that might've been "Hi."

I recognized the red hair that fell across the sheet like an autumn cape, the long creamy legs, and the cool green eyes that peeked over Gable's shoulder — they were on the cover of the latest *Vogue,* and on the billboards over Sunset that advertised her latest album, which had been locked at the top of the charts for weeks. Tawny Mack. She giggled some more, whispered something, and Gable giggled too.

"You got this, brother," Sutter said, laughing. "I'm going to find the bar. Shout if you need me."

I nodded and looked around at the wreckage of the room: the strewn clothing, bedsheets, and pillows, the overturned ashtrays, wine bottles, and crumpled tubes of lube. There was music playing — Tawny Mack covering Carole King — and a muted TV on the wall tuned to CNBC. The air was scented with booze and weed and sex and something else — something chemical, familiar, but elusive.

"What can I do for you, Will?"

This brought on more laughing. Gable

174

struggled to keep it together enough for speech. "Tee has a gig later tonight, doc — a surprise thing on the roof of the Roosevelt." He looked at me over his shoulder, waiting.

"And . . . ?"

"And she needs to get up and get ready. Plus, we need to pee."

"And . . . ?"

There was more laughter from both of them, and Gable looked at Tawny's graceful white hands on his ass. She wiggled her arms, but her palms and fingers didn't budge. "We went overboard with the Super Glue," Gable said, giggling.

Indeed they had. Besides gluing hands to asses, they'd managed to weld parts of their thighs and bellies to each other too, though fortunately their genitals were joined in only the usual way. Between blushing and giggling, Tawny said it was like they were engaged.

"Let me know where you're registered," I said, and Will Gable blanched. "Do you have nail polish remover?" I asked. Gable didn't think so, but Tawny had some, at the bottom of a turquoise Hermès bag large enough to hold a pony. It didn't take long to free them, after which they raced each other to the bathroom.

Traffic was slow as we headed back toward Venice, but the wind off the ocean was soft. Sutter handed me an envelope.

"I took mine out already," he said.

I opened it and looked at the bills. "This puts me over a hundred. Finally."

Sutter nodded and glanced over at me. "That's good, right?"

"Not good enough for a down payment. Not yet."

"And you're still fixated on staying put?" he asked. I nodded. "You'll get there," he said. "One step at a time."

"Feels like I'm walking to Europe."

Sutter smiled. "You know, Gable wants to hire you. Seriously — he asked me just now, when he paid. The guy doesn't even know your name, or that your degree isn't from a cereal box, but he wants you to be his regular doctor."

I laughed. "I like the kid, but he's nuts."

"Totally. Still, the guy loves you."

"All my best references are from crazy people."

"Story of my life," Sutter said.

CHAPTER 16

The Brinkley's interpretation of a California clambake entailed no bare feet, no bonfires, no sand, and no visible clams. It did feature trays of raw oysters on crushed ice, lobster empanadas, grilled scallops, Kobe beef on skewers, puff pastries that smelled of jasmine, a full sushi bar, and a very full bar bar. It took place in something called the Regal Room, and spilled onto a large adjacent terrace with views of the dark Pacific, which was the closest it came to a beach. The music was live, vaguely Brazilian, and with a heavy elevator inflection. The waiters and waitresses were all actors — lovely, bored, tired, and bitter.

Sutter had been right about the evening's timing: the fund-raisers and donors were still in the midst of hors d'oeuvres when I arrived, and were convivial without yet being comatose. They ranged in age from early-middle to early-old, and I was relieved to find that they were not in black tie. My blue blazer and tan were adequate camouflage, as long as no one looked too closely at my shoes or my watch, which — once I'd lifted an unclaimed nametag from the unattended reception table — no one did.

No one paid much attention to my nametag either, which was a good thing, because I'm sure I didn't look much like Suresh Mittal. I helped myself to a flute of California not-champagne and wandered through the crowd, scanning for anyone who resembled the pictures I'd seen online of Hoover Mays: blond, blocky, square-faced, early fifties. I saw many people who met the criteria, but none who had Hoover's expression, of a mildly surprised pig, and none with the right nametag. I was leaning against the terrace rail, the Pacific and the Ocean Avenue traffic moving restlessly at my back, when a woman took my hand.

She had a nametag, but in place of her name she'd substituted a smiley face with X's for eyes and a shaky, anxious line for a mouth. Her Capri pants were white, her sleeveless silk blouse was turquoise, and the square-cut diamond on her finger was yellow and a little smaller than a golf ball. She was tall, fortyish, and expensively blond — just the kind of toned and bored housewife

I'd be cruising for if I was the dissipated tennis pro Sutter said I resembled.

"Dr. Mittal is in the gastroenterology department at USC," she whispered. "He fixed my husband's duodenal ulcer six months ago, and you are not him." Her voice was years younger than she was, and her tone was light and conspiratorial. Her diction was very careful. Drunk, but pleasantly so.

"I'm not even in the gastro department," I said. "Suresh gave me his ticket."

"Not a gastro — then what the hell are you?"

"ED."

She squinted, then smiled slyly. "Erectile dysfunction?"

"Emergency department."

"So, if I want you, all I have to do is call 911?"

"Only if it's a real emergency."

She slid her hand over mine, and up to my biceps. "Oh, trust me, it is."

I laughed. "Suresh told me to look out for Hoover while I was here. Hoover Mays. Have you seen him around?"

She put on a melodramatic frown. "What do you want him for?"

"Suresh told me —"

She waved away my explanation. "Excuses, excuses," she said, and pointed at the ceiling.

I looked up. "He has a room upstairs?"

She shook her head gravely and kept pointing.

"He's in heaven?"

She barked a laugh. "Not hardly. There's a bar on the roof. Last time I saw Hoover, that's where he was headed." She tilted her head sideways and flicked my nametag with her finger. "He might not be glad to see you, Suresh."

The penthouse of the Brinkley had a big round bar for posing and smiling, curtained nooks for intimate dining, a fireplace and soft leathery furniture for lounging, innocuous electronic music for ignoring, and windows and postcard views all around. But Hoover Mays wasn't there for the views or airy music; he was there to drink and brood. He sat in a wing chair not far from the fire, hunched forward and staring at the dregs of something in the rocks glass he held in his pudgy hands. A waiter hovered near, and I heard Mays order a gimlet as I took a seat nearby. His voice was low and tired, and I didn't think it was his second drink, or even his third.

He wore a navy linen jacket, a pale-pink

shirt, white linen pants, and supple-looking loafers without socks. The clothes were well tailored but — like his expensive haircut — could only hide so much. Neither clothes nor coif could disguise the scratches on his face and neck, the split lip, or the ugly contusion — a fading eggplant color — on his right temple. None of the injuries was fresh, and my guess was that they were a week to ten days old, roughly the vintage of Elena's injuries. The waiter offered me a drinks menu. I declined.

"A gimlet sounds good," I said, nodding at Mays. "I'll have one of those."

The waiter vanished. Mays glanced my way but said nothing. My drink arrived with his, and I took a sip and sighed. "That was good advice," I said. "Thanks." Mays grunted softly. "You escape the clambake too?" I asked.

Mays looked up and squinted. His little blue eyes were unfocused. They took in my nametag, but it looked like work. He nodded at me. "It was crowded," he said.

"Crowded and boring," I said. "But they need the money."

"They seem to need it all the time."

"You don't think it's a good cause?"

He shrugged. "I go where she points me. She tells me to sign a check, I sign a check."

I chuckled. "Who is *she*?"

He swallowed some of his gimlet. "The wife," he said. He absently touched a finger to his bruised temple and winced.

I pointed to my own face and then to his. "That looks painful. What happened?"

He looked at me again, and for a moment I thought I'd lost him. "Car accident."

"You have it looked at?"

"It's fine. Nothing broken."

"Where'd it happen?"

His eyes darted around and he took another drink. "What — the accident?"

"Yeah. Where were you?"

"The 405. Coming off the 405. Onto Sunset." He squinted at me and looked for my nametag, but I'd taken it off and put it in my pocket. "Do I know you?"

I shook my head. "Lot of broken glass in your accident?"

"What?"

"Was there a lot of broken glass? I ask because those lacerations on your neck might be from broken glass."

Mays nodded. "Yeah. Plenty of broken glass."

I swirled my glass and watched the ice cubes bump around. "But they could also be scratch marks. They look more like scratch marks."

Mays was wide awake now. He put his glass down carefully, and sat up straight. "What the . . . Who the hell are you?"

"To me it looks like Elena gave as good as she got. A few inches and she would've caught you in the eye instead of the temple, and then we could be talking detached retina or —"

The porcine face went ashen. Mays looked around the room and back at me. He leaned toward me and his voice fell to a whisper. "For chrissakes, keep quiet. Who . . . who's Elena?"

"That might be more convincing if you hadn't turned gray first, Hoover."

"Who *are* you?"

"Siggy didn't tell me you'd screw around like this."

"Siggy sent you?"

"Why else would I be here?" I said, nodding. "You're supposed to go over it with me."

"Go over what?"

"What happened with Elena." I put up my fists in a boxing pantomime.

Mays looked me over again. "I told him all this. And how do I know he sent you? You don't look like —"

"Siggy doesn't hand out ID cards. You want to call him, go right ahead. I'm sure he'll be happy to hear from you. Maybe he'll send over those guys that don't look like me. They'll fit in well around here. Your friends will like meeting them."

He went even paler. "Jesus — no."

"Okay, then. Tell me about Elena."

Mays gave another furtive glance around. The room was filling up and he didn't like it. He cocked his head at a corner alcove, and we carried our drinks there. Up close, his bruises were uglier and angrier, and one scratch — a long one down his neck — looked infected. He stared at the tabletop and kept his voice low. As he spoke, his cheeks reddened, and his face took on a stricken look, as if he were listening to the story rather than telling it, and didn't like what he was hearing.

"There isn't much to say. Last time I saw her was a week ago last Thursday, in the afternoon, at three. My usual day, at my usual time, and everything was . . . as usual. Everything was normal. She was the way she always was — a little shy at first, and then . . . Everything we did was . . . It was just like every other time."

"I get it. Go on."

"And, just like always, I took a bath afterward. Usually, I take a long one — there's a big soaking tub in the apartment, and sometimes Elena gets in, and we go again. Sometimes I fall asleep in there. The only thing different that day was that I couldn't stick around long. I had a thing in Malibu and I needed to get going, so, even though she had the bath waiting, I had to make it a short one.

"I was in the tub for a little while; then I put on a robe and went out to the living room, and there was Elena with my wallet and my car keys, headed for the door. I grabbed her arm, but before I could ask what the hell she was doing, she was all over me, punching, kicking, scratching — biting, for chrissakes. She was out of her skull. I seriously thought she was going to kill me." Mays looked up at me, embarrassed. He was more than a foot taller than Elena, and outweighed her by at least a hundred pounds.

"So you hit back," I said.

"I defended myself. I . . . I slapped her a couple of times and we wrestled, and then we were down on the floor. And then I saw stars. She clocked me with something — a lamp — and by the time I got myself together, she was gone — along with my car keys, my wallet, my phone, and all my goddamn clothes. She even took the fucking bathrobe."

"You called Siggy then?"

Mays shook his head. "With what? There's no phone in the apartment, and I wasn't going to look for one wearing nothing but a napkin. I . . . I didn't know what to do, so I waited. Finally — a few hours later — one of you people came around.

"Siggy told me to say I got mugged if anyone asked, and to report the car stolen. I didn't want to at first, because I didn't want anything to do with the police, but Siggy said that wouldn't be a problem."

"So you reported it?" Mays nodded. "You hear anything back?"

He squinted again. "A few days ago, the cops called. They said they found the car someplace east of downtown. A really crappy neighborhood."

"The car, but not Elena?"

"Not that anyone's told me." Mays squinted at me again, and I could see gears turning through the gimlet sludge in his head. "Don't you know all this already?"

"Just connecting the dots," I said, and wondered how long it would be before Mays did the same. "Did she know anybody in town?" I asked.

"*Know anybody?* She was fresh off the boat when I started seeing her — just like every other girl Siggy's set me up with. She

186

was straight from who knows where — some Romanian pig farm or something. She didn't know anybody when she got here, and she still doesn't; Siggy doesn't let these girls out. Well, you'd know more than I would about that." But from the sidelong glance Mays shot me, it was clear he had his doubts. The gimlets were losing their efficacy.

"What did you say your name was?" he asked.

"Sergei."

"Bullshit — you're not Russian."

I shrugged. "And the apartment where you saw her — where was that?"

Mays squinted. "How can you not know that?"

"How many girls do you think Siggy has? How many apartments? You think I keep track of them all?"

"I . . . I think I should call him."

I shrugged. "You do that. In the meantime, I'm going to the bar. I don't know where the hell that waiter disappeared to. You want anything?"

Mays was pulling out his cell as I rose. He rose too, as if he wanted to stop me, or follow, but then he thought about it and sank down again. He shook his head. I grinned

at him and walked to the bar and past it,
out the door.

CHAPTER 17

Sutter was at the Arsenal, on Pico, and it took me half an hour to get there from the Brinkley. There were a lot of old weapons on the wood-paneled walls — rifles and swords, daggers and flintlock pistols — and shiny red leatherette on the banquettes and booths. There were candles on the tables, in red glasses that threw a dim, diabolical light. The crowd was dense and noisy for a weeknight, and I had to edge and elbow my way through.

On the phone Sutter had said he was wrapping up a meeting, and there were two guys with him at a booth in back. They were doughy bookends: balding and pale, with stylish scruff on their chins, artfully frayed jeans, tee shirts with the names of bands I hadn't heard of, and watches that cost more than my car. Sutter glanced my way and nodded toward the bar. I drank cranberry juice and club soda there while he finished, and carried my glass over when the book-ends left.

"Hard to believe those guys have jobs," he said as he folded a check and tucked it into his pocket. "They're like little babies."

"Jobs doing what?"

"Television. They sold a cable series and they're looking for a combat consultant — that's what they called it. Somebody to teach their underfed leads a little pretend Krav Maga."

"And that's you?"

"For five episodes, guaranteed, if the check clears."

The waitress came and smiled at Sutter and put a hand on his shoulder. He ordered a bourbon, and when she went to get it I told him about my conversation with Hoover Mays.

When I finished, Sutter was quiet. "No applause?" I said after a while. "I thought I did pretty well."

"Yeah, just great. So great that you pretty much guaranteed another visit from Siggy's boys, just as soon as Mays sobers up and finds the balls to tell Siggy about you. It won't take him long to do the math and send some Ivans back to the clinic. And this time there won't be any foreplay."

It was my turn to be quiet. "Shit," I said

eventually.

"Shit for sure, but that's not even the bad news."

"I don't follow."

"Turns out Siggy's not your worst problem. I ran the tag you gave me, brother, and the company it belongs to makes Siggy's crew look like Jehovahs going door to door. They call themselves Petro Risk Partners, which makes them sound like they're in insurance or heating oil, but they're not."

"What are they?"

"Their Web site says *security consultants to the energy industry,* but that's sort of bullshit too. They actually have just one client, and they're not so much consultants as they are a private army."

"Whose army?" I asked. "Who's their client?"

Sutter grinned. "Bray Consolidated."

It took a moment for the penny to drop. When it did, I found it hard to swallow my drink. "As in Harris Bray?" I said.

Sutter nodded and looked at his phone, scrolling. "Yep. As in Bray Oil and Gas, Bray Chemicals, Bray Agriculture, Bray Logistics, and Bray Media, not to mention the Bray wing at the art museum, the Bray Pavilion at Palms-Pacific Hospital, and that new opera house downtown. I was surprised at the list when I Googled." He slid the phone over to me.

"Shit," I said, reading.

"Oh yeah. And, see, he also bankrolls that stupid whatever the hell it's called — Fundamentalist Fuckheads Forum. You know, the assholes who want to rewind the country back to 1951."

"Fundamental Families something?"

Sutter nodded. "That's them. And he funds that other thing too — the American Penises Institute."

"American Pinnacle Institute? That's a think tank."

"My version's better. Anyway, this is the guy that employs Petro Risk — exclusively. So, if PRP's looking for the kid, it means Bray wants him."

I shook my head and looked at the other booths, and the red candle flames flickering beneath laughing faces.

"Why?"

"You're asking the wrong guy."

"And these Petro guys are badasses?"

"I wouldn't say *badass* so much as bad, and I don't think it, brother, I *know* it. I *know* these douche bags."

"From where?"

Sutter frowned. "Nigeria. A few years back — after I left the C.A.R. but before I quit private security altogether. I was babysitting these Brit engineers who were surveying pipeline routes. We were out of Warri, but we were always inland or upriver, which is where I ran across PRP. Bray Oil and Gas had a big thing going with Nigerian National Petroleum, developing new fields, and for about ten days me and the Brits were set up in a village where Bray was just finishing construction on a new facility. Their place had everything: barracks for the oil crews, an infirmary, mess hall, water treatment, movie theatre, even a brig and a helipad. It was twice the size of the village and ten times as nice.

"PRP had a big footprint there — there were as many of them as there were construction guys — and they were a mixed bunch. Americans, Brits, Irish, Aussies, Kiwis, some Ivans, some Germans, even a few Albanians and Boers — all ex-military, and all white. I noticed that right away.

"Still, they were friendly enough, and we were fresh blood for their card game. Pretty much every night, there was poker and the usual bullshit session — crappy ports I have known, most fucked-up ops, you think your army's screwed, let me tell you 'bout mine — that kind of thing. After about a week, over a late-night hand, I mentioned that things seemed pretty calm in the neighborhood, security-wise. I brought it up because, until then, me and the Brits had had to look out for insurgent crews that were still kicking around the river delta, despite the amnesty deal the government signed. They liked to tap the pipelines and siphon off crude they could sell for guns, and they weren't above snatching the odd Westerner for ransom, or just shooting some for laughs.

"I asked the PRP guys what their secret was, and what I got back was weird silence — just snorts and glances, and finally somebody said something about *day care,* followed immediately by somebody else yelling, *Shut the fuck up.* I felt like there was a joke somewhere but I wasn't in on it.

"Couple days later, I brought it up again, with a kid from Abilene I'd gotten to know a little. He was a driver, not a shooter, and not one of the poker players. He had some drinks in him, but my questions sobered him up fast. He definitely didn't like the subject, and he hemmed and hawed and kicked the dirt a lot. Then I mentioned *day care,* and he turned white and looked liked his grandma had just caught him tugging one off.

"I pressed some more, and finally he grabs my arm and whispers: *You want to know how we do it? You want to know about day care?* Then he leads me to the far corner of the compound, to a Quonset hut I'd thought was just another barracks. There was a padlock on the door, but he points to a little window, and I look inside."

Sutter paused and looked at his bourbon. He shook his head. "The hut was filled with women and kids, probably twenty souls in all, ages forty down to four years."

A shiver went through me and I squinted at Sutter. "What the hell?"

"That's what I said. The guy told me that PRP had had big insurgent problems when they first came into the area — firefights every few days, sabotage, even IEDs. Lots of injuries, even more equipment damage, and no work getting done. The guerrillas wanted protection money to go away, but PRP didn't want to pay. So instead they spent a few weeks gathering intel on them, and especially on the bosses — who they were, where they came from, where exactly they lived, that kind of thing. Then they took hostages."

"Hostages?"

"The insurgents' wives and kids — they went out and grabbed them up. They'd been holding them for the better part of a year. As long as the security situation stayed calm, the hostages would be taken care of; otherwise . . ."

"Fuck," I whispered.

"For sure," Sutter said. He ran his palm over his nearly shaven head, and looked at the ceiling.

"What did you do?" I asked.

He sighed. "About the kids? Probably not enough. Two nights after I cleared my Brits out of the village, I went back to the Bray compound, quietly. I clipped the lock on the Quonset hut and opened a hole in the fence behind it. I told the women and kids who could speak English or French or Swahili to wait fifteen minutes and then take off. Then I crossed the compound and started a fire in a Dumpster — big and bright and smoky. Don't know how many of 'em made it out, or if any did. The next day, I called a *Times* stringer I knew, but I never saw any news stories about it."

I nodded. "Hard to corroborate, I guess."

"And the Brays have a long reach."

"You come across PRP again?"

"Anyplace there's oil — in the Gulf, Africa, Lat Am. And they always operate on the bleeding edge. Torture, extortion, kidnap, bribery — they do it all. One of their guys in Nigeria — one of my poker pals — joked that their company motto should be

196

The Balls to Cross the Line. It's a point of pride with them."

I took a deep breath. I put my glass aside and signaled the waitress. When she came, I ordered a bourbon of my own. "So what the hell do these people want with Alex?" I asked again. "What is he to them — another hostage?"

Sutter shook his head. "Between PRP looking for him, and Siggy after his mom, the kid's in a world of shit."

My bourbon came, and the sip I took was a flame licking down my throat. I looked at Sutter. "We can't let them have him."

He nodded, and bumped his glass against mine.

CHAPTER 18

Tuesday was hot and airless downtown, and the clinic was a blur of faces and symptoms, questions and equivocal answers, and diagnoses and treatments of varying degrees of certainty. In the pauses between patients I tried to think only of the next cup of coffee, the next appointment, of putting one foot in front of the other. And I emphatically did not think about Siggy Rostov, Harris Bray, or all that I hadn't told Lydia and Lucho.

I spoke to them only on medical matters that day, and was silent on the topic of Monday's visitors, but the air was thick with the unsaid. The closest I came to any of it was to ask Lucho how Alex was doing. He looked at me for a long moment, and so did Lydia, and then he told me that Arthur had spoken to his sister late last night and that everything was fine.

"He's eating," Lucho said. "He's watching TV; he likes her dog."

I nodded, and they looked at me some more; I went back into the exam room.

When we ran out of patients, I ran out too — upstairs, into the shower, and then into my car and west, to meet Nora Roby. She had plans to order in, and I was invited. The menus were fanned on her coffee table like a poker hand when I arrived.

"I'm okay with any of those," she said. "You pick, you order, you open the wine. I'm taking a shower."

I chose Chinese, from the Palace, and ordered dumplings, cold noodles, scallion pancakes, duck, and salt-and-pepper shrimp. Then I opened the bottle of Merlot Nora had left out, and poured two glasses. I was thinking about drinking one when she emerged from the bedroom in yoga pants and a loose-fitting tank top, and with her hair in a towel. Her skin was pink and she smelled of pears, but there were shadows beneath her eyes, and lines around her mouth.

"Long day?" I said.

She picked up a glass, took a sip, and nodded. "One of my first-years — probably the smartest one — told me she doesn't think she wants to do it anymore. One year out of med school and she's fried — exhausted, disillusioned, depressed, anxious all the time. I didn't know what to tell her."

"Tell her that in another fifteen or twenty years she won't notice anymore."

Nora smiled thinly and shook her head. "And I had two referrals for oncology today — a boy and a girl, seven and ten. The parents were devastated, terrified. . . . I don't know — those words don't begin to cover it."

"Is the outlook —"

"Bad, for both of them."

"Fuck," I said.

"There was a really crappy moment talking to the boy's parents when I found myself going through the motions of empathy — making the right faces and noises — and wondering if I had any actual empathy left, or if it was all just . . . performance."

"That's a defense mechanism."

"Could be, or maybe my resident has a point."

She took another sip and paced the tile floor, to the desk, to stack some papers; to the French doors, to stare at the dark patio; and back to the sofa, where she sat, sighed, stretched her long legs, and put her feet in my lap.

She squinted at me. "And you? You look worse than the last time I saw you, and you had a hangover then. You're not hungover now, are you?"

"Just a lot of mileage since the weekend," I said. Then I gathered my breath and told her about my search for Elena, and about all my uninvited guests. I told it carefully, and paused only to refill our glasses, to pay the delivery guy, and to eat dumplings and scallion pancakes. When I finished, Nora was quiet and busied herself mixing the cold noodles. Then she looked at me and shook her head.

"What are you into? Hookers, Russian pimps, thugs in back alleys and in your waiting room — with your patients, for chrissakes. And Harris Bray! You know how many things around town are named after him?"

"Sutter read me the list."

"It's a long one. One of these days they'll add the whole Republican Party to it — *brought to you by Harris Bray.* The Russians sound bad enough, but Bray — he's a different league of badness."

"I know."

"You know, and yet . . ." Nora sighed, and shook her head.

"What?"

"You're not stupid, Adam. The risks you're taking are more than plain. Why invite this kind of trouble?"

I drank some wine. "I'm not inviting any-thing."

"Of course not. Why would you? It's not as if running that clinic isn't trouble enough. Who in their right mind would go looking for more with the authorities, or criminals, or a fucking oligarch?"

I reached for a dumpling with my chop-sticks. "I'm not."

"What you're *not* doing is explaining."

I ate the dumpling and looked at her. "I'm not sure how to, not without sounding like a self-dramatizing ass."

Nora smiled and poked at the shrimp. "Take a chance."

"Okay. I guess it has to do with favoring the weak over the strong, kindness over cruelty, victims over bullies, the Golden Rule over zero-sum games. Whatever risk I'm taking, it's because I think the boy and his mom need help that they won't get from DCFS, and because I think it's the right thing to do. How's that?"

"Heroic," she said quietly.

"Then I told it wrong, 'cause that's not me."

"That's a relief."

"What — you don't believe in heroics?"

"I think few things are more reductive than rescue fantasies — or more dangerous.

Not much in the real world boils down to black-hat versus white-hat. Actual people are complicated, and their motives and intentions are almost always tangled and obscure, even to themselves. Especially to themselves. I'm sure there are people — a few — whose noble impulses are just what they appear to be. For most people, though, it's more . . . complex."

"Complex, as in *crazy?"*

She shrugged. "You see it in our field: dysfunction channeled into heroic behavior. What looks like heroic behavior, anyway."

"You have someone in particular in mind?"

She smiled and picked up a shrimp and licked the salt and pepper from it. "It must've been scary when those people came to the clinic."

I nodded. "The Russians were bad, but that happened fast. The corporate thugs — the guys from PRP — were worse, more threatening. That's what they were trying for, and they succeeded."

"Lucho and Lydia must've been upset."

"The PRP guys didn't tell me anything I didn't already know about them, but, yeah, they were upset. They still are, and I haven't even told them about the Russians yet, or about the Harris Bray connection."

She raised a dark eyebrow. "Shouldn't you?"

"I'm waiting for the right time."

"Which you'll know how — by the pigs flying past your window?"

"Funny."

Nora put down her chopsticks and picked up her wine. "The stuff they said about you, in Africa . . . I've seen the scars on your side and your leg, but you never say much about it. Who was the nurse they were talking about?"

I sighed and filled my glass. "Merry. Her name was Marie-Josée, but she spoke so fast it sounded like *Merry*-Josée when she said it, so . . . Merry. She wasn't much more than a kid when she came to the field station, and she had a little boy, Mathieu, who was maybe four. His father died before the kid was born, killed with most of Merry's people in a militia attack on their village.

"Her education was minimal, but she was a great nurse — tireless and careful, and she had that innate clinical radar some people just have. You know — someone who can tell at a glance who's turning the corner, and who's not going to make it till morning." Nora nodded.

"On top of which, patients loved her. She calmed them down, made them laugh, made even the ones who were circling the drain feel like it was all going to be okay. Especially them." I took a deep and shaky breath. It'd been a long time since I'd talked about this, and it was no easier.

"Our field station was small, and the village wasn't much bigger — a crossroads, really — which was good and bad. It was accessible for patients, but also for assholes with guns, and there were a lot of those. *A fluid security situation* is how they put it in the head office. We'd get alerts all the time, and the security contractors DTR employed would sweep in and sweep us out for a while. Most of the time nothing came of it — an excess of caution. Until it wasn't.

"It was after the rainy season and the floods, and we were seeing all the things you'd see then, an uptick of vector-borne stuff: yellow fever, dengue, chikungunya, and malaria, of course. We were full up, but DTR had made allowances for that — they'd arranged to relocate the patients too. The problem was, about two hours after the trucks left with the last patients aboard, five more people came in — four women and a teenage boy, all with high fevers, diarrhea, dehydrated, two of them hemorrhaging, one of them pregnant. It was amazing they'd made it to us, but there was no way they'd survive a four-hour ride in the back of a truck. And anyway, DTR was fresh out of trucks. So when our ride showed up — the transport for the rest of the staff and me — I made the call that I would stay behind with them. I put the pregnant woman in my seat.

"It was against DTR protocol, I knew, but it seemed like the only thing to do — a risk, but a low one, given all the false alarms we'd had. And given the condition of the patients, I just didn't see . . ." I swallowed hard and fought to get some air in my lungs.

"In fact, it seemed like such a good idea that Merry insisted on staying too. I told her no way, and we argued and argued until the transport had to leave. She put Matty on board, with one of the other nurses, but said she wasn't going anywhere until I did. So off they went, and there we were."

Nora's dark eyes were huge and gleaming and fixed on me. I fought for breath. "Of course it went south," I said finally, "about an hour after dark. They came in numbers, and they were fucking crazy. Kids, most of them — teenagers, armed to the teeth. I don't know what they wanted; I'm not sure they knew either. They took what little we had in the way of meds, and they started fucking with the patients — wanted to know where they'd come from, who their people were, their religion — the kinds of questions that never lead to anything good over there, or anywhere else. DTR protocols talk about *minimal engagement,* and *no resistance,* but I guess I didn't do it right. I wasn't . . . deferential enough. I don't know. I thought we were home free when they got in their trucks and drove off, but I was wrong. They came back about an hour later and unloaded right into the field station. They must've emptied every magazine they had, and when that wasn't enough they pulled out the RPGs."

Nora shook her head and sighed. "Jesus," she whispered.

"I woke up in a hospital in Bangui, but I didn't stay there long. They shipped me to Lagos to remove the bullets and the shrapnel."

"And Merry? Did she —"

I shook my head. "Besides me, only one of the patients made it. She had burns, but she survived.

"When I was well enough, DTR flew me to the head office in Brussels and read me their report — the long and short of which was that it was on me, all of it. The breaches of protocol and misjudgments, the deaths — Merry, the patients — all on me."

"There's no way you could've known."

"They disagreed."

Her cheeks colored and she shook her head. "And after Brussels?"

"I came here. I was in the Brussels Airport with a ticket to New York, an empty head, and mostly empty pockets, and Sutter called me. He'd heard what had happened from friends of his over there, and he'd been trying to track me down. Said if I wanted to give L.A. a try he had a sofa I could crash on. It was the best offer I had. Also the only one."

"A friend in need."

I nodded. "He has ideas about balanced ledgers."

Nora drank some wine and looked at me. "What happened to Merry's son?"

I took another deep breath and shook my head. "I tried finding out, but things deteriorated badly over there. It was hard to get information without contacts in-country, and none of mine wanted to know me. Merry had no people left, but I guess one of the other nurses might've taken Matty on, or . . . I don't know."

Nora put her hand against the side of my face. Her palm was cool and soft and smelled of soap.

CHAPTER 19

For a man who made his living from en-
gorged appetites, Siggy Rostov's own hun-
gers were strictly managed things, at least at
breakfast. He had a plate of egg whites
before him, a pitcher of ice water with
lemon slices in it, black coffee, toast that
looked like baked gravel, and half a grape-
fruit. This lavish spread was served up on
bone china, laid out on white linen, and set
on a table in a stone courtyard, beneath the
shade of a coral tree whose flowers were
colorless and shriveled.

By early afternoon every table in the
courtyard — in the whole restaurant —
would be full, and by evening the line of
cars for valet parking would jam traffic on
Sunset. But just then, at seven on Wednesday morning, La Bouche d'Or was empty
save for Siggy, his kitchen staff, his soldiers
and lieutenants, and a queue of petitioners
waiting at the edge of the courtyard. Sutter

and I were at the end of the line.

According to Sutter, Siggy held court like this every Wednesday and Friday, at one of the several trendy eateries he owned on the Westside. Sutter thought it better that I go to Siggy than wait for his goons to come to me, and more prudent if he came along, and we'd been waiting for nearly an hour. The men ahead of us were a motley bunch, of various ages, colors, nationalities, and styles of dress, but they had in common a grim, resigned expression, as if they were waiting for lab results and bracing for bad news. They approached Siggy tentatively, and made their pitches in low, stumbling tones.

Siggy seemed to pay them no attention, but his number one, a dark man who sat beside him and had a face like a toad and a body like a sprung sofa, would nod and consult a laptop. On rare occasions the dark toad would glance at Siggy, who would look up momentarily from his iPad, though no words passed between them. Then the toad would speak, sometimes in Russian, sometimes in English, always softly, and the petitioner would move off. Some men looked more frightened as they departed, others just looked numb. I had yet to see anyone who looked pleased.

Siggy himself looked rather like his breakfast — pale, lean, and flinty. He was in his fifties, with close-cropped white hair, a gaunt, gray face, and eyes the color of overcast. He had an angular frame, and strong, bony hands like white machines. His shirt was white with gray stripes, and expensive-looking, and his wristwatch was a weighty chunk of steel that looked like a spare part from the Large Hadron Collider. Besides the watch, there was a bandage on the back of one of his hands, and a whiter patch on the white skin of the other. There were more white patches on his face — on his chin and on his right cheek. Sutter saw me looking at them.

"Looks like tattoo removal," I said.

Sutter nodded. "Siggy's campaign to get respectable. The restaurants are another part of it."

One of Siggy's guys — the same one who'd frisked us at the door — shot us a dirty look and grunted some Russian.

"No talking in line," Sutter said, chuckling. "It's like seeing the pope, only it's not his ring we're supposed to kiss."

Siggy's guy was about to say something else but stopped. The toad was standing, beckoning. The other petitioners had gone; it was our turn. Sutter crossed the courtyard and I followed, my heart pounding.

Siggy Rostov set aside his iPad, sipped his coffee, and said something softly to the toad, who shook his head and moved off. Siggy looked at Sutter.

"The very careful soldier," Siggy said. "So very picky about the work he takes. I still regret not hiring you sometimes. Also I regret leaving you aboveground." His voice was deep, and his speech was deliberate but without accent.

Sutter laughed. "You do fine without me, Siggy, better than fine. You're aces."

"I lost men I shouldn't have — men I wouldn't have lost if you'd been there."

Sutter shrugged. "Should've, could've, might've — you never know how things work out. I would've held you back."

Siggy looked at me. "But you're not so very picky now, eh? This who you're working for?"

"This is Dr. Knox —"

Siggy cut him off. "I know who he is."

"He's a buddy of mine. From Africa."

Siggy pursed his lips and nodded. "He doesn't look African." He turned to me. "And you, Dr. Knox, what makes you fuck with my livelihood?"

"I wasn't trying to do anything to your —"

"You weren't *trying* — like that means something. You go around asking about my lost property — threatening my associates, scaring my fucking customers, giving my men a hard time. You —"

"To be fair, Siggy," Sutter cut in, "it was me who gave your boys a hard time."

"So they tell me," Siggy said, and he looked behind us.

There were voices, and the two men from the clinic alley stepped into the courtyard. Cornrows wore a blue French soccer jersey today. Tats wore the same ill-fitting pin-striped pants and pink shirt as he had in the alley. He gave Sutter a mad-dog stare, said something in Russian, and spit at Sutter's feet. Some of Siggy's men laughed.

Sutter smiled. "Speak of the devil."

Siggy smiled too. "These two would've been to see you the next day if I let them, but I told them to wait. They don't like it on the leash."

"Maybe they'd like muzzles better," Sutter said.

Tats spit again and growled something and grabbed his own crotch.

Sutter replied in rapid Russian, and the only words I caught were *tvoyu mat.* Whatever it meant, it was more than enough for Tats, who turned a volcanic shade, lowered

213

his head, and charged.

It happened quickly, in a fluid, twisting instant — like a pennant snapping, or a wave breaking — and it was oddly muffled, so that the only sounds were fast, shuffling steps, an explosive breath, a grunt, a gasp of pain, and then a meaty thud. And then Tats was on his back on the other side of the courtyard, his nose pulped, his right wrist, elbow, and shoulder all grossly dislocated. And Sutter somehow had a gun in his hand, a shiny automatic that he pointed at Siggy.

A smile flickered on Siggy's lips, and he shook his head. He looked over at his number one. "We stopped patting people down? Too much work, *mudak*?"

Sutter put the gun up and let the clip drop from the grip to the courtyard stones. Then he worked the slide and ejected a shell. "Not his fault. I took it off your boy as he went past."

"Asshole," Siggy said, though I wasn't sure to whom. He looked at me. "Enough with this fucking dinner theatre. You understand that if I want to hurt you I can. And I will — even if your friend here pushes my overhead up. He knows I'll pay the price, yes? So you tell me why I don't want to hurt you."

"I'm not interested in interfering with

your business. I'm just looking for the girl — Elena."

Siggy's eyes grew colder. "The girl *is* my business, doctor."

"I didn't know that when I started looking for her."

"Finding out didn't stop you."

I took a deep breath. "She has a child — a little boy. He —"

"Maybe she has five kids. Maybe she has an old babushka too, and ten cats and a blind goat — I don't give a shit. She owes me and she's got to work it off."

"How much does she owe you?" I asked, and I heard Sutter sigh wearily.

"She comes off the boat owing me forty grand for travel expenses."

I nodded. "Forty thousand," I said. "Forty thousand is —"

"Forty is *not* the number," Siggy said. "Forty is what she owed me off the boat. There's interest on that, which for the three months she's here comes to another five, and room and board on top of that, which is another fifteen — which, let me tell you, is a fucking bargain for West Hollywood."

"Sixty thousand, then."

"Which might've been the number, if she hadn't beat the shit out of one of my best customers, who — by the way — is close personal friends with half the fucking city council."

Sutter cleared his throat. "So what is the number, Siggy?"

"The fact that there's a number at all — the fact I'm willing to *think* about not putting her down, and this doctor too, is because I know you, Sutter. Because we've got some history, and you've got a little credit with me."

"And I appreciate it, I really do. What's the number?"

"Seventy-five."

Sutter laughed. "Seventy-five thousand? You're —"

"It's seventy-five *now.* How long it stays that way — does it go up tomorrow, does it go away altogether — nobody knows."

Sutter tossed the empty automatic on the table. "A number like that — it takes time," he said.

"Take all the time you want. My guys won't stop looking, and if they find her first, then I guess they save you some cash."

CHAPTER 20

"Seventy-five," I said, and then I said it again.

Sutter laughed. "You think, if you keep saying it, it's going to appear in a puff of smoke?" We were in his BMW, headed east on surface streets, and the morning rush was starting to thicken around us. "Anyway, you've got it — you've got more than enough. If you want to spend it."

"That's down-payment money."

"Like I said — *if you want to spend it.*"

"And if I do, what about Siggy?"

"I think he meant what he said: we come up with the scratch before they come up with her, he'll take our money."

"And forget about the girl?"

He shrugged. "He won't forget anything, but he'll move on. So you've got some deciding to do."

Sutter worked his way east and south, and I thought about the clinic, and about where else to look for Elena, and where else Siggy's men might be looking. I didn't get very far, and Siggy's white, automaton hands kept intruding on my efforts.

We came to City Hall Park and took a right off First onto Spring Street. There was a kid — a teenager — on the sidewalk, weaving lazily on a skateboard. He was skinny and his hair was dyed bright blue.

"Shelly," I said aloud.

Sutter looked at me. "Who's Shelly?"

"She's a streetwalker — a patient. She was at the Harney the first time I went over there. I thought she had something to say to me, but she took off when she saw Troop watching."

"She work out of there?" Sutter asked, and I nodded. "So she might've met Elena, or at least seen her around." I nodded again. "You know where to find her?"

"Might have a number on file. Other than that, the Harney is my only guess. But the Harney makes me nervous — Siggy's guys could be hanging around, or maybe those assholes from PRP."

Sutter said nothing, but turned the car onto my street. We were still a block from the clinic when he pulled to the curb. "I wouldn't worry about PRP's stakeouts," he said. "I think they've moved on to other things."

Sutter pointed toward the clinic. There were three cars parked out front — a sedan and two SUVs. The sedan was beige with a whip antenna, and looked government-issued; the SUVs definitely were. One was gray and had a city emblem on the door; the other belonged to the LAFD. The door to the clinic was propped open, and patients were streaming out, looking bewildered, irritated, and skittish. I climbed from the BMW and headed down the block at a run. Lydia and Lucho met me in front of the clinic.

"What the fuck?" I said. Lucho caught my elbow as I made for the door.

"They showed up twenty minutes ago," he said. "A guy from the fire marshal, and some guys from Buildings and Safety. They say somebody called about code violations. They say we have to stay out for now."

"What kind of bullshit is that? What code violations?"

"They didn't explain," Lydia said. "They said they didn't have to."

"That's crap. Did you call Anne Crane?" Anne was the clinic's pro bono lawyer.

Lydia nodded. "Her assistant said she's in court all day."

I shook my head. "Is somebody in charge here?"

Lucho pointed to a paunchy guy leaning on the beige sedan. "Maybe him."

I turned toward the sedan, and Lydia called behind me, "Don't make things worse."

Close up, the paunchy guy looked like he had a hangover, and a massive weight riding his stooped shoulders. His thinning hair, short-sleeved poly shirt, rumpled pants, and the heavy folds of skin on his face and neck all matched the color of his car. He had a large paper coffee cup in one hand and a cigarette in the other.

"You want to tell me what's happening here?" I asked.

He swallowed hard and put his cup on the roof of his car. He plugged the cigarette into the corner of his mouth and pulled a square of paper from his pocket. He unfolded the paper and smoothed it on the car hood. His bloodshot eyes ran up and down the page. "You Dr. Knox? Adam Knox?" His voice had the faint twang of a Texas childhood.

"That's me."

"You run this clinic?" I nodded. "We spoke to your landlord — Kashmarian — and he said you were the guy to talk to."

"Sure. Let's start by you telling me why you've fucked with my practice, and put my staff and my patients on the street."

The man coughed, and put his hands up. "Take it easy, doc, we're all on the same side here — public safety, and all that." He reached into his pocket and offered me a business card. It was wrinkled and damp. "I'm Stengal, from Buildings and Safety. We got a report of violations, and we have to —"

"What violations? Report from who?"

The man drew on his cigarette and took a step back. "Report's confidential, doc — you can understand that. People call, they want to do their civic duty. They don't want trouble."

"What about my trouble? Doesn't that count?"

"We get a report of fire hazards, wiring problems — at a clinic, no less — we have to investigate. Kashmarian said you could let us into the apartment upstairs."

"You need to search my apartment?"

Stengal put his hands up again. "I wouldn't say *search,* but we got to check the whole place out — gas lines, wiring, that kind of thing."

"And you go through all this for every anonymous call you get?"

He shook his head. "Seriously, doc, I'm not tryin' to bust your stones, but I'm on the downhill side of things, you know what I mean? As in the direction shit flows. People talk to people somewhere over my head, and finally my phone rings. I'm just doin' a job here."

I counted to ten while he puffed nervously. His face was darkening and there was a vein throbbing in his neck. I sighed. "How long is this going to take?"

Stengal looked relieved. "A place this size won't take but a couple or three hours, and we won't leave too much mess."

"Mess?"

"It happens when they have to go into walls — but, hey, maybe it won't come to that."

Of course it came to that — gouges and channels in wallboard and plaster, vinyl flooring pulled back in spots, ceiling tiles askew or broken. Stengal's people, having found nothing to cite us for, made a show of sweeping up, but Lucho, Lydia, and I still spent an hour scrambling around the place with dustpans after they left. By one o'clock, the waiting room was full again, and we were jumping until six.

There was little time that afternoon for

talk about much besides cases, and in those brief periods, Lydia was ominously mono-syllabic. Lucho and I gave her a wide berth, and when the last patient was gone and the door was locked, we waited for the explosion. There was none, which was worse.

She sat heavily in a swivel chair at the reception desk. She pushed a hand through her thick, dark hair and sighed. She looked up at us. I could smell disinfecting soap, her flowery perfume, her sweat.

"Is this the way it's gonna be now, doctor — this kind of thing every day? People come in, they threaten, they send firemen, inspectors — who next? The sheriff? Drug cops? La Migra? You saw the way people ran out of here this morning. You think they all came back? I got news for you, doctor: they did not. And it won't take many more days like today before they stop coming at all — and not because they're all of a sudden healthy." Lydia shook her head and sighed again, more deeply this time.

"But maybe that's for the best, yeah? Maybe we should stop kidding ourselves we're doing any good here — stop running around like one-armed jugglers and just shut this thing down."

Lucho shook his head. "Jesus, *tía,* what the hell —"

She pointed at him. "Watch your language, *mijo.*"

"I'm serious," he said. "What's with this talk?"

Lydia's voice was soft and frayed. "I'm tired, *mijo,* that's what's with it. I been doing this forever, and it's hard enough work when nobody's trying to stop you from doing it right."

"And even harder," I said, "when your boss gets you caught in a shit storm."

"Shit storm?" Lydia said. "You don't even know *what* this is, or how to get out of it. How long do you think this can go on? How do you think it's gonna end?"

"I don't know how it's going to end, Lyd, but I hope it won't take much longer. I found out a little about his mom, and maybe that'll help us find her."

"*Us* — you and that pirate."

"Sutter's all right, *tía,*" Lucho said.

She snorted at him. " 'Cause your time running with the Avenue Kings makes you such a great judge of character. Every time he goes off with that one . . ." She threw up her hands and hoisted herself from the chair.

"We'll sort this out, Lyd," I said. "I promise."

"Don't throw that word around, doctor.

And even if we do get through this, what about next time? And the time after that? What about the rent, and the next paycheck? Is another magic cash deposit gonna take care of that? And when the lease is up — then what? We're living on borrowed time here."

I didn't have answers to her questions, and Lydia didn't wait for any. She grabbed a stack of patient folders from the in-basket and carried them to the file room. In a moment I heard angry tapping at a keyboard. Lucho looked at me and shook his head. He took another stack of folders from the basket and rolled a chair over to the computer.

"I don't like this domestic shit," he muttered, and started updating records.

I took the remaining folders to my office and banged away for I don't know how long. I typed and clicked and tried not to think about Siggy Rostov or the bull-necked PRP men, or Lydia's accusing looks, or Alex, or Elena. Still, they swam up at me from the depths of the monitor.

My cell phone rumbled in my pocket, and brought me back. It was Sutter, with traffic sounds behind him.

"Go out to your car," he said.

"What?"

"Your crappy Honda — go out to the alley and open it and check the glove box."

"What the hell are — ?"

"Humor me. I'll hang on."

I rubbed my eyes and pushed back from the desk and headed down the hall. A blast of hot air shoved me as I opened the back door. The alley was dim and smelled like a burnt skillet. I opened the Honda's passenger door and flipped the latch on the glove box. On top of the owner's manual and the gas receipts were two identical plastic boxes, shiny black and slightly larger than my iPhone. They were featureless but for a large adhesive square in the center, and a tiny column of Korean characters along one edge.

"You still there?" I asked Sutter.

"Yep."

"What are these things?"

"I took one off Lucho's car and one off Lydia's while you guys were working. There was one on your car too."

"What the hell are they?"

"Trackers. South Korean models. Kinda crappy, really. The GPS units are okay, but the power units are unreliable."

A cold knot tightened in my stomach. "GPS trackers? On our cars? Where the fuck did they come from? And how long have they been there?"

"They're courtesy of PRP, and they've only been there a few hours. I watched one of those bristle-heads plant them this morning, while you were dicking around with the inspectors."

"You hung around?"

"I figured firemen were just the opening act."

I shook my head. "You said there was a tracker on my car too."

Sutter laughed. "Yeah — I put that one under the bumper of a tourist bus — you know, one of those double-decker nightmares — *See All of L.A. in a Day.* Right now I'm at the Farmers Market, watching some confused-looking PRP grunts follow it around in a Suburban."

"Jesus. They haven't figured out you messed with their stuff?"

"Not so far. I guess they're too lazy to run a proper tail — they're just relying on what the GPS says instead of using their eyes. I tell you, this has really lowered my opinion of these guys. Substandard equipment, sloppy tails — this is definitely not the A-team."

"You think trackers are all they did? Could they have put something inside the clinic?"

"You mean mikes and cameras? No —

they wouldn't have sicced the building inspectors on you if they'd done that. You might want to stay away from the landlines for a while, though."

"Shit. And out front — what am I going to find there? More Suburbans? Maybe they'll just pull an RV up and move in."

"You should be okay. The only PRP clowns I saw in your neighborhood were the ones I'm watching now, and they were parked three blocks away."

I looked at the trackers and sighed. "Small favors," I said. And then I heard myself speaking Lydia's words. "How long can this go on?"

Sutter made a clicking noise. "Until they find the kid, or Bray calls off the dogs."

"Well, let's hope the former doesn't come to pass — but God only knows how we get the latter to happen."

"Figuring out why they want him would be a good start," he said.

"Any bright ideas about how?"

Sutter was quiet for a moment, and the traffic sounds grew louder in the phone. "You gotta wonder why they haven't called the cops," he said finally. "I mean, they've shown you how well connected they are — why haven't they called their pal the police chief, have him send a few tactical units down to your place? Why wasn't that the first call they made?"

"Yet another in a long list of questions I can't answer."

"Ask the PRP guys," he said. "It won't be long before they come around for another talk."

"Fuck."

Sutter laughed loudly.

"What's funny about that?" I said.

"I'm not laughing at you. My tour bus is circling the block again, and I'm watching these dumbasses follow it. It never gets old."

CHAPTER 21

Arthur's sister, Danni Silva, lived in Echo Park, at the top of a small hill, on a dead-end street off Lemoyne. I could see a dome of white light off to the east — a night game at Dodger Stadium — as I pulled to the curb, and I could smell a charcoal fire somewhere, and grilling meat. I checked my rearview yet again. It was dark and empty, as it had been for many blocks.

Danni's house was a green clapboard shotgun-style, with white trim, a gray Prius in the carport, and a camellia climbing along the chain-link fence. The front door was open, and I heard a woman's voice from inside. A chocolate Lab barked once and blocked my way as I came to the threshold, and I stopped. Danni was in the middle of the long, open space. She had a phone to her ear, but she smiled widely and waved me inside.

She was thirty, dark and compact, with

big brown eyes, quick, vivid features, glossy black hair razored short, and four silver rings in her left earlobe. She wore black shorts and a plaid shirt with the sleeves cut off, and she had ink on her right forearm — a mermaid with a cigarette and a naughty smirk — that was new since the last time I'd seen her. She winked at me, put up fingers in a *two minutes* sign, and walked to the back of the house trailing rapid, irritated Portuguese.

Even at night, her little house was bright. The walls and floors were white, and the sofas and chairs were rumpled and comfortable-looking. She was a graphic artist, and most of the place was her studio. There were long drawing tables along the walls, easels, white metal files and supply carts, and a pair of Macs with giant screens.

Alex was on a stool before one of these, his small hands poised over the keyboard. He wore a red Azul tee shirt, black track pants with a white stripe, and white socks. His dark eyes were fixed on me, and I waved. He smiled minutely.

I closed the door, and the Lab circled me and sniffed at my jeans. I knelt and put out a hand and he backed up, barked at it, then gave it a sniff and a lick. I scratched him behind his ears, and his tail gyrated wildly.

"What's his name?" I asked Alex.

He looked at me for a while before he answered. "Joe," he said finally. "It's her boyfriend's name."

"Ex," Danni said, returning from the other end of the house and pocketing her phone. "And he was *way* more of a dog than this cutie." She slipped into flip-flops and dug through her purse.

"Thanks for coming, doc — there was just no way I could get out of this thing tonight. The network's been my bread and butter for a while, and when they say show up at our party, then show I must."

"Can't afford to piss off the paycheck. I really appreciate you letting Alex hang out."

"This dude?" Danni said, grinning at him, "He's the best, but I think I talk too much for him — no, *gato*?"

Alex smiled and made a low whistle. Joe trotted over to him and dropped a big paw on his leg. Alex turned back to the monitor, which was filled with video zombies in a vegetable garden. Danni caught my eye and flicked her head at the door.

"See you in a few, *gato*," she called, and headed out. I followed.

Danni looked up at me when we were outside. "I don't know shit about kids," she whispered, "but I'm worried about that guy."

I nodded. "He's been through a lot," I said.

"Artie told me. You know, he was crying last night — in his sleep. He stopped when I woke him. He's really quiet too — most of the talking he's done is to Joe. Plus, he's a nervous little dude. I see him tense up every time I move quick."

"Is he eating?"

"When I put food in front of him. Otherwise, he doesn't ask. He hasn't had dinner yet."

"Does he ask for anything?"

"Not a thing," she said, and she vanished into her Prius.

Inside, Alex was throwing video vegetables at the zombies, Joe the dog at his side. They both eyed me suspiciously as I shot the deadbolt and crossed the room, but neither spoke.

Danni's kitchen was an alcove off the hallway. She had a lot of coffee and yogurt, some skim milk, and some oddly furred mangoes, but nothing in plain sight that might be dinner. With more rooting I discovered pasta, sauce in a jar, and a bag of frozen vegetables. I read the labels carefully for any mention of nuts, and finding none, I heated things. Along the way I tried to talk to Alex. It was slow going.

"You like spaghetti?"

"You like broccoli?"

"You like video games?"

"You like dogs?"

Most of these elicited no more than a shrug, though the last one earned a tiny, considered nod and the whisper of a smile.

I put pasta in a bowl, topped it with sauce and broccoli, and placed the bowl, along with a glass of milk, on one of the long tables in Danni's studio. I pulled up a stool for Alex.

"TV?" I asked, as he climbed up. Alex tilted his head, which I took as a yes, and I rummaged on the coffee table for Danni's remote.

It had been a long while since I'd watched any television, and things had only gotten weirder. Beauty pageants for infants; ruddy men in trucker caps fighting over abandoned storage lockers; public shamings of compulsive hoarders and pre-diabetics; affluent suburban women made up like transvestite hookers, competing with each other in feats of coarseness and cruelty; barely literate pregnant teens with tattoos, unfocused eyes, and futures like wrecked cars; apoplectic crypto-fascists spitting bile and paranoia; a carnival midway of weight loss devices, hair growth creams, erectile dysfunction potions, and pottery from which herbs grew like green hair. It was like the day room of a surrealist mental hospital, or any big city ER on a summer Saturday night. Alex and Joe squinted at me as I surfed.

Deep into the triple-digit channels I came upon some cartoons, but Alex seemed uninterested. I pressed on until I found a nature show — three polar bear cubs with their mom. Alex's eyes locked on the screen and he nodded slightly. I put down the remote.

I fixed a bowl of spaghetti for myself and leaned on the kitchen counter, watching Alex as he ate. His gaze flicked between the polar bears and Joe, and only occasionally went to the pasta, a significant percentage of which might've ended up on Danni's floor if not for the dog. Alex smiled at the antics of the bear cubs and at Joe's midair catches. It was the happiest and most relaxed I'd seen him.

I wound spaghetti around my fork and thought about Lucho and Lydia. They were volunteering at a quarterly blood pressure screening clinic that Lydia had organized two years back. It always drew a crowd, possibly because of the snacks, and if tonight's event was like the last one, they'd be there past midnight.

I hadn't told Lucho or Lydia about the tracking devices on their cars. I'd thought hard about it, but ultimately couldn't see the point. They already knew the crew-cut guys were watching us, and they were already looking out for them. I didn't see anything to be gained by inflaming their paranoia, or making their skin crawl with the idea of someone creeping around underneath their cars and tracking their moves on a laptop. It was bad enough that I was trying to wrestle down those images.

I washed my bowl and put it in the dish rack. The polar bears were gone from the TV, replaced now by a family of prairie dogs. Alex and Joe were rapt. Their eyes, identically large and chocolate-colored, followed the darting images across the screen. I heard Ben Sutter's voice in my head: *Figuring out why they want him would be a good start.* I sighed, and rolled a chair over to one of Danni's big screens and put a keyboard in my lap. I typed *Bray Consolidated* into Google, and hit return. Many pages came back.

The first dozen or so covered the same ground Sutter had when he told me about PRP and its only client, though in much greater detail. There was a long list of companies under the Bray Consolidated umbrella, many more than the ones Sutter had recited, and most in energy and energy-related businesses. There were Bray's numerous charitable contributions, mainly to high-profile cultural and medical institutions. And there were Bray's many political investments — truckloads of cash to feed a lunatic menagerie of right- and ultra-right-wing causes, from expelling immigrants, combating mythical voting fraud, and denying global warming, to privatizing Social Security, Medicare, and public schools, dismantling every regulatory agency of the federal government, dissolving the Federal Reserve, and pulling out of the UN.

Commentary on Harris Bray and his politics was also plentiful, with much more of it coming from his detractors than from his supporters. To the left, it seemed, Bray was more or less the unclean offspring of a demonic three-way between Ayn Rand, Robert Welch, and Dick Nixon; and he and his political foundations were the bogeymen under every progressive bed — the dark engines driving every imaginable conspiracy, from Ford's Theatre to the grassy knoll to hanging chads in Florida. It was fascinating stuff — for the plausibility of some of it and the paranoia of the rest — but there was nothing that shed a photon on why Harris Bray might be interested in Alex.

I scrolled to the biographical stuff, and learned that Bray's father, Garth, an oilman from Pennsylvania and before that Connecticut, was at least as politically zealous as his son. Garth was a Roosevelt-hating isolationist, who in his later years was a generous donor to any number of groups that touted white Christian supremacy, before finally coming out as a full-throttle neo-Nazi. He died in his late nineties at his home in Greenwich, wearing an authentic SS uniform, with an authentic Luger in his mouth.

Harris himself was, ostensibly, less exotic. He went to boarding schools in Connecticut, to Harvard afterward, and to the engineering and business schools of Stanford after that, and he was — according to several magazine profiles — utterly single-minded in transforming Garth's medium-sized pipeline company into a vast, privately held empire. There was nothing flashy in his business strategy — he bought often, and always on the cheap, and he rarely sold. His personal life was similarly staid: a marriage after B-school to the youngest daughter of a Kentucky horse breeder, the birth of a son,

Kyle, a few years later. Relocation of his company and his family to SoCal followed not long after. As far as I could tell, Harris was still married, and Kyle Bray — by now in his early thirties — worked at Bray Consolidated.

There were pictures too, from corporate reports, press profiles, and benefit red carpets, and they were mostly unremarkable. Despite his opponents' vivid imagery, Harris Bray sported neither horns nor fangs nor cloven hooves. He was in fact a tall, stoop-shouldered man, with a square face, a fringe of gray hair around a great bald dome, and watery blue eyes behind rimless rectangular glasses. Maybe his teeth were overlarge, and his mouth was too wide and thin-lipped; maybe his eyes had a slight hyperthyroid bulge; still, the overall effect was of beige blandness, and if someone told you he was a senior partner at an accounting firm, you'd believe it. Mrs. Bray — Audrey — looked like an aging Barbie doll, though thicker and with a less natural smile. Kyle's was the only vaguely interesting face in the bunch.

He had his mother's blond hair, narrow head, and precise, molded features, though his mouth was too wide, like his father's. His orthodonture had been better, though, so he wore his smile more handsomely, and his blue eyes were more sleepy than watery. In a few of the photos — the ones from the charity fests — he looked drunk, and maybe a little bored. Or was that anger?

I glanced up at Alex. He and Joe had moved to one of the slouchy sofas, and had moved on from prairie dogs to tiger cubs. Their attention was total. Alex's bowl was empty and so was his glass, and I put them in the sink. I dug around in Danni's freezer again and found a bag of frozen strawberries and another of frozen blueberries. I pulled these out, along with a tray of ice cubes and a tub of vanilla yogurt from the fridge. There was a blender on the countertop, and I was thinking about smoothies.

I looked over at Alex and cleared my throat. He looked up and so did Joe. I was about to ask about dessert when Joe's ears lifted. A low growl came from deep in his chest, and he looked down the length of the house to the glass doors at the rear. Then he bared his fangs, leapt off the sofa, and ran barking toward the back door. He was just about there when a metallic clang came from the backyard, then a thud and the sound of breaking pottery. Joe's paws skittered on the hardwood and he slid to a halt at the door. He growled and whined and glared at the door. His tail was down and the fur along his spine was stiff.

My heart rate spiked and I climbed off the stool and peered through a side window. I saw nothing but my own reflection, hanging in darkness. Joe kept growling, and I walked down the hall, casting about for a flashlight. There was a tug on my shirt, and Alex was behind me. His face was white and his eyes were wide and terrified.

I squatted down and put my hands on his shoulders. "It's okay, buddy," I said quietly. "You hang here while I check out back." I led him into the kitchen alcove, then went to the hallway again. On my way, I slid a boning knife from the block on Danni's counter into my side pocket.

Joe was at the back door, growling and barking and scratching at the doorjamb. I passed Danni's bedroom and glanced in. There was a king-sized bed and a nightstand beside it. I stepped to the nightstand and opened the top drawer. There was a flashlight inside, a heavy black aluminum model that cops favored. I switched it on. The beam was a dim yellow, but the weight was comforting. I went back into the hall, switched off the lights, and managed not to jump out of my shoes when Alex grabbed my wrist. His fingers were cold and damp.

I knelt down in the dark and put a hand to his neck. His pulse was racing. "Deep breath, buddy — nice and slow," I said, and tried to take my own advice. "We're fine here." Joe came over and whimpered, and pushed his snout in Alex's ear. "You and Joe wait in here," I said, and I ushered them into the bedroom. "I'll be right back."

I shut the bedroom door and moved down the hall, trying to regulate my breathing. Adrenaline grabbed at my throat and arced through my limbs. I came to the rear door, looked through the glass, saw nothing. I listened but, besides Joe's snuffling, heard nothing. Dire scenarios — PRP thugs bursting through the back door while Siggy's boys battered down the front — raced through my mind, and I pushed them out before they gained a beachhead. I adjusted my grip on the flashlight and unlocked the back door.

Outside, the sky was the color of tea. The air was soft and smelled of blossoms, earth, damp fur, smoke, and something else. Wood smoke? Cigarettes? Both. My pupils dilated, and the darker masses resolved into a small deck, a low rail, bucket-sized terra-cotta pots, a charcoal grill, shrubs, a short gnarled tree, a high wooden fence, a gate to the alley. A small breeze threw whispers into all of it. I drew a shaky breath, slid the knife from my pocket, and switched on the flashlight.

I ran the dim beam around the deck and then beyond, around a small patch of grass and dirt. And then there was thrashing in the bushes along the fence, hissing, and a scrabbling in the dirt. A dark shape broke cover, and scuttled low to the ground along the back fence. I caught it for an instant in a yellow cone of light, and saw a burglar's mask above bared fangs, a fat gray body, and a thick gray tail with black rings.

"Fuck," I whispered, and the raccoon hissed at me and disappeared under a gap in the back gate. "Fuck," I said again, and laughed with relief.

I locked the back door behind me and turned on the light to find Alex and Joe side by side in the hallway.

"So much for waiting in the bedroom," I said. They looked at me. "It was nothing," I said, "just a raccoon looking for food. Everything's fine." They kept looking at me. "You okay?" I asked. Joe wagged his tail and let his tongue loll. Alex was less expressive, though I thought he nodded. Then he took my hand and the three of us headed toward the front of the house. I was about to ask Alex about dessert when he stopped in his tracks. His hand gripped mine and his nails dug into my palm. He was white and shaking, and his eyes were wide.

"Alex, it's okay," I said. "There's no one outside." But he wasn't listening, and his eyes were locked on something over my shoulder. I turned to follow his gaze, to the Mac I had been using, and the image I'd left on the screen: a gala at the Museum of Modern Art in New York, and Mr. and Mrs. Harris Bray and their son in evening wear.

CHAPTER 22

"I don't know why he was scared of them, Lyd — I just know he was. The kid was freaked out."

Lydia leaned in the doorway of my little office, Lucho looming behind her. It was just 7:00 a.m. on Thursday, and we were about to open the doors. The blood pressure clinic had gone late the night before, and they were bleary-eyed. I was worse. Danni hadn't gotten home until nearly two, and found Alex, Joe, and me on the sofa. Alex and Joe were sleeping, and I was awake, and more or less a pillow. Joe had his snout on my thigh, while Alex was curled next to me, his hand in mine and his head against my arm. It had taken nearly an hour for him to stop shaking, and afterward he'd fallen fast asleep. Danni made up a chaise with pillows and blankets for him, and I carried him over and tucked him in. Joe had followed, and settled himself on the floor alongside.

"You didn't ask how he knew them?" Lucho said.

"I asked if he knew who they were. He didn't answer — I'm not even sure he heard me — and I didn't press. The guy's been traumatized enough."

Lydia shook her head slowly. "And these people he was scared of — they're the ones who sent the *soldados* to threaten us, and those fire inspectors." She made a face as if she wanted to spit.

"Christ knows what they'll do next," Lucho added. I thought about the trackers in my glove box, but said nothing.

In truth, I'd been up most of the night wondering the same sorts of things about the Brays. I switched on my computer when I returned from Danni's house, and Googled Bray Consolidated again, and scanned page after page of articles about Bray — the company and the family — and looked at countless pictures of them, but found nothing that suggested a connection with Alex or his missing mother. I did find several references to a Bray subsidiary in Romania, but there seemed nothing remarkable about it — Bray Consolidated had subs in many countries, nearly every country that had any sort of oil industry. There'd been a pale ribbon of light in the east when I stretched out on my bed, and my alarm went off about a minute after my head hit the pillow. It was like being a resident again. Coffee was keeping me going — though just barely — and I was hoping that the only visitors we had that day were patients.

As it happened, they were, and in large numbers. There was a norovirus going around, so in addition to the usual complaints — injuries of various sorts, and the collateral effects of substance abuse, mental illness, poverty, or a questionable immigration status — we had a half-dozen people with some combination of diarrhea, vomiting, muscle aches, and low-grade fever. All were miserable, though only one — a badly dehydrated man who dragged himself in at the end of the day — needed hospitalization.

Lucho was lining up a ride for him to County-USC, and I was trying to figure out if I had enough juice to make it upstairs or if I should just lie down in one of the exam rooms, when Lydia appeared at my office door.

"Can you do a house call?" she asked.

I lifted my head from the desk. "You're kidding, right?"

She shook her head. "I'd do it, but it's

Maria Ruiz, and she says she only wants you."

"Which Maria Ruiz?"

"The older one, with COPD and the bad hip."

"I remember. What's her problem?"

"Sounds like another norovirus, but she says she can't make it over here."

I sighed. "You got another iced coffee for me?"

Lydia smiled. "It's on my desk."

"Where does she live?"

Maria Ruiz was on Crocker, just off Fifth, in a walk-up that looked like a sagging bale of hay: faded yellow, raggedy, a gust or two from breaking up and blowing away. There was no buzzer on the front door — perhaps because the door had no lock — and there were no names on the mailboxes. A step across the thresh-old took me from baking sun to catacomb darkness. The urine stench didn't fade as I climbed the pitted stairs, and I hitched my backpack higher on my shoulder and breathed through my mouth.

The Ruiz apartment was on the second floor, in front, and a girl in cutoffs and a wifebeater answered my knock. She was young — maybe fifteen — with dark skin, peroxided hair, a blue glass stud in her nose, and sloppy tattoos on her neck and hands. Her arms and legs were without fat or muscle, and her knees and elbows were chapped and swollen. I could see her nipples and ribs through the faded fabric of her tee shirt. Her face was bony, and her teeth were gray and soft-looking — the beginnings of meth mouth.

She turned a feral eye on me, and then past me, into the hall and down the stairs. "Where the fuck is Toodie?" she said.

I clenched my jaw. "No clue," I said. "Where's Maria?" I didn't wait for an answer, but stepped around her into the apartment. It was a dim room with a pocket kitchen along one wall. The furniture was old, mismatched, dying or dead, and the place smelled of cigarettes, old food, and vomit. There were bedsheets hanging from clotheslines in two corners — the walls of makeshift bedrooms.

The girl looked into the hall again, then closed the door. "Who the fuck are you?"

"Maria's doctor. Where is she?"

A thin voice called from behind one of the bedsheet walls. "Here, doctor."

I crossed the room and pulled aside a sheet, and the vomit smell hit harder. Maria Ruiz was in a camp bed, beneath layers of dirty blankets. Only her face was visible —

flushed, drawn, and full of pain. She was in her middle sixties, but that evening she looked about a hundred. There was a cardboard box beside her, doing duty as a table, and a plastic bucket beside that, overflowing with vomit.

"¿Qué tal, Maria?"

She shook her head. "Not good, doctor. My stomach — nothing stays down. And my arms and legs — it feels like somebody's been kicking me."

I knelt beside her and found gloves in my backpack. "There's a lot of that going around." I put fingers to her neck. Her skin was dry, and her pulse was racing. I found a strip thermometer in my pack and pressed it to her forehead; 101, high for a sixty-seven-year-old. Her lips were cracked, and crusted with dried vomit. I tore open a packet of wipes and cleaned them off. There was a shadow behind me. The girl was there, her thin arms crossed, her eyes on my backpack.

"When'd she call you?" she said. I ignored her. "You really a doctor?"

"How about you get her some water?"

The girl snorted. "How about you kiss my ass?"

I stood, and she took a step back. "Either be useful or go away."

She put up her hands. "Who the fuck are you, coming into my place, acting all fucking bossy?"

"The water," I said, "in a clean glass."

The girl snorted again, and went away, muttering.

"I'm sorry about her, doctor," Maria Ruiz said in a whisper.

I shook my head. "Who is she, anyway?"

"Mona. She's my niece — my grand-niece — my sister's granddaughter. She's up from Chula Vista. She was supposed to stay a week, but that was a month ago."

I took a blood pressure cuff from my pack and folded back the blankets. A humid wave rose up — sweat, body odor, vomit, urine. Maria Ruiz shivered when the cooler air hit her skin. I found her arm — a reed, a feather — and her hand, a stubborn knot wrapped around a cell phone.

"If I let go of the phone, I won't get it back," Maria whispered. "But I didn't want to call the police, and your number was the only one I could remember."

"No problem." I slipped the cuff on. She winced, and I saw the bruise on her forearm. "She giving you a hard time, Maria?" I asked.

Maria managed a tiny shrug. "She's a greedy girl — she always was — and kinda stupid. She has people in here all hours."

Her BP was low. I took the cuff off, carefully, and covered her again. I flicked on a penlight and checked her eyes and her throat. There was a bruise on her neck. I turned around. Mona was there again, with a glass.

"It's clean," she said. I took it from her. She pointed at my backpack and made a sly smile. "You got anything good in there?"

I shook my head. "When's the last time you emptied that bucket?" I said.

The girl scowled. "Echh — that thing? Never."

"Well, give it a try now."

"Fuck you," she said, and went away.

I knelt by Maria Ruiz again and held the glass to her lips. "Just a sip," I said. "Not too much."

"I can't keep it down."

"Just a little — you need fluids."

I heard the door open, and voices — Mona's and a new one, a man's. The bedsheet wall was pushed aside.

"You really a doc — like the kind can write me a 'scrip?"

The man was about thirty, large, and without a neck. He was white, with close-cropped bleached hair, close-set blue eyes, a three-day beard, and a stray-dog meanness.

He wore baggy shorts that came halfway down his calves, and a baggy Lakers jersey with brown stains in front. Mona was behind him, smiling nastily.

"Now *you* can empty the fucking bucket," she said triumphantly.

"I guess this is Toodie," I said.

The man squinted at Mona, his mean look somehow meaner. "You give him my name, bitch?"

Mona shrank back, scared. I put my hand up. "Don't get hung up on that, Toodie — she didn't mean anything by it. What you two want to focus on now is that Mrs. Ruiz needs to get to a hospital. She's got a viral infection, she's badly dehydrated, and somehow she's sustained suspicious injuries — contusions, cuts — the kind we associate with domestic violence."

Mona made a squeaking noise. "Domestic what? I barely touched that old cow."

"Shut up, girl," Toodie said. "What the fuck you get me in the middle of?"

"The desire not to be in the middle of things," I said, "now, *that* I understand."

"What the hell are you talking about?" Toodie said.

"I'm talking about the fact that I'm going to call 911 and get an ambulance over here for Maria, and that means cops and questions and a bunch of shit I'm sure you guys don't want any part of."

"Fuck," Mona shouted, and she wrapped her thin arms across her thin chest.

Toodie was less intimidated. "So maybe you don't make that fucking call — and then I'm not into anything. Maybe instead you give me your phone, and your doctor bag there, and your car keys and wallet, and you write me up a few 'scrips for the road." His smile was ugly as he took a step toward me. He stopped when I held up the scalpel.

I shook my head. "I guess that's one way it could go. The other is that I could call for two ambulances."

He squinted. "You — that's bullshit. Doctors don't do shit like that."

"They don't make house calls either, but here I am."

Toodie got red and his nostrils flared, and he looked like he might paw the ground. Then he lifted the hem of his dirty Lakers jersey until it came to the waistband of his shorts and I could see the little automatic there. "Maybe it goes another way," he said softly.

My joints locked up, and my chest got tight, and it was with much effort that I managed a shrug. I kept my voice soft and steady. "It's not the first gun I've seen,

Toodie."

"Yeah? Maybe it's the last."

"Was that what you had planned for today — to lay out three people?"

"I only see one of you."

"You're not worried about loose ends, then? Mona seems like a solid bet to you? Personally, I'm not so sure, and between her and me and Mrs. Ruiz, I count three. That's all of a sudden a busy day for you. Maybe busier than you had in mind when you got up this morning. Maybe it turns out you've better things to do."

I tried to keep my breathing under control and my heart rate down below 180. Maria Ruiz coughed weakly, and I nearly jumped. Mona made a whimpering sound, and Toodie gnashed his teeth while steam rose from his head. He rocked on the balls of his feet and flicked his hand, as if he was shooing a fly.

"Fuck it," he said finally, then looked at Mona. "We gotta be in the Valley anyway." He turned and walked from the apartment. Mona grabbed a pair of flip-flops and a fraying cloth bag and hurried after him.

I let out a long breath, and knelt again by the camp bed. Maria Ruiz's dry cheeks were streaked with tears. "It's all right, Maria," I said softly, and pulled out my phone.

■ ■ ■ ■

The sky was a dusty plum by the time the ambulance took her. On the sidewalk, the air was heavy with exhaust, but it was spring water after that apartment. My car was across the street, and I got in but didn't turn the key. Adrenaline was still bumping and burning in my veins, and the thought of going back to the clinic, empty and dark now, didn't appeal. I thought about calling Nora, but knew she had meetings with her residents on Thursday evenings. I checked my watch and looked up at the street signs. I was just a couple of blocks from the Harney, and it would be another hour or so before Nora was free. I got out of my car, locked it, and went in search of Shelly.

It was busy in front of the Harney in the dusk — girls strolling, waving at the slow-rolling cars that flashed their high-beams, climbing in, climbing out, sometimes alone, sometimes with men, whom they led into the hotel. I scanned the block, but saw no sign of Shelly's bleached and blue-streaked hair. A couple of the girls approached me — a tall Hispanic girl in track shorts and a halter top, and a taller black girl in red plastic sandals and with an appealing gap-toothed grin. She hit me with it full-force, and bumped me with her hip.

"Dr. Knox, what you doin' out here? If you're lookin' for company, I got you covered."

"How're you feeling, Franny? No more dizzy spells?"

"Nah, I'm good, doc — I can even wear my boots again. But what the hell you up to here?" Franny took my arm, and walked me down the block, out of earshot of the Hispanic girl. Her voice got low and urgent. "Seriously, doc, this is not a place you want to be."

"I'm looking for somebody, Franny — a white girl named Shelly. She's got a bleach job with a bright-blue streak in it."

Franny nodded. "Yeah, I know her. Try around the corner, on Sixth, but you want to stay the hell away from here."

I wanted to ask her why, but Franny was in no mood to talk more, or even to stand next to me, and in an instant she was halfway down the block. I walked in the other direction and around the corner.

Shelly was hard to miss, even in the failing light. Her white hair shone against a scarlet macramé vest, her green vinyl skirt glittered in the passing headlights, and she looked like an ornament off Charles Bukowksi's Christmas tree. She glanced up as I headed toward her. I waved, but she spun around and jogged across the street against an oncoming phalanx of cars. She kept jogging down the opposite sidewalk and into an alley.

When the cars passed, I sprinted after her. I was ten yards into the alley when a black SUV blocked my way, and three large, crewcut men in black suits emerged and beckoned to me with guns.

CHAPTER 23

They were mostly quiet, and when they weren't they were clipped but polite. They took my backpack and cell, but weren't overly rough about it. They didn't hide their faces or cover my eyes, though I wasn't sure if these were good or bad things. We took surface streets, and it was seven-thirty when we turned off Santa Monica onto Century Park East, then down a ramp into the maze of parking beneath Century City.

We pulled in amid a herd of identical SUVs, and the crew-cut men walked me to an elevator. Our footsteps echoed, and the air smelled of exhaust and motor oil. I heard other cars but saw none, nor other people. We rode to the fourteenth floor.

The doors opened on a darkened reception area with no company logos or names, but with low, sleek furniture and views to the ocean. I paused, and one of the crew cuts took my elbow.

He led me down a hall to a conference room that had glass walls and a view of office towers studded with lights. There was a glass-topped table in the center of the room, and swivel chairs around it. I recognized the man sitting in one of them. It was the soldier from the clinic's waiting room, the fifty-something shark with the white crew cut, the Naugahyde skin, and the burn scar on his neck. He wore the uniform of the day today — a black suit and tie, a crisp white shirt, and spit-shined brogues. He glanced at my escorts, who nodded in unison, pivoted, and left. The shark gestured toward a seat with a ham hock hand.

"You want coffee or a soda? How about something stronger?" I shook my head. "Chow, maybe? We got decent mess."

I rolled a chair out and sat. "No, thanks. Who are you?"

The shark smiled. His teeth were massive. "Conti, doc. Jimmy Conti. The boys call me Tig — for Tiger."

"And you are what at PRP — the scout leader?"

Conti grinned wider. "So you know us now. I guess that's no surprise, given the game with the tour bus you ran on my boys. I thought it was cute, but I'll tell you, I got a couple fellas did *not.* They knew you were up here now, they'd want to have a talk, if you know what I mean."

"That doesn't answer my question about what you do here."

He shrugged. "This and that. But getting back to your little trick — you think that one up by yourself? Or maybe that gang-banger candy striper of yours helped out? Though I'd have put that out of his league."

I shrugged back at him. "*This and that* is kind of vague, Mr. Conti."

Conti smiled some more. "You sure you don't want something?" He heaved his massive frame from the chair and crossed to a credenza against the wall. There was a small fridge inside, from which he produced a little bottle of tonic water. Conti twisted off the top and emptied it in one swallow.

"You could tell me what you want with me."

He took his seat and sighed. "*I* don't want anything, doc — this ain't my party. I'm just the travel agent."

"Whose party is it?"

Conti looked over my shoulder. "And the devil appears," he said quietly, and rose again. Kyle Bray walked through the door.

He was handsomer in person than in the online photos — bigger, broader through the shoulders, his features finer and haughtier, his eyes more vividly blue. But he was also more smudged. Not his clothes — the close-cut pinstriped suit, pale-purple shirt, and eggplant tie were impeccable — but everything else about him: his sallow, grainy skin, chapped lips, bloodshot eyes, and greasy hair. He was like the floor model of an expensive shoe — well crafted but too much handled, scuffed, and permanently finger-stained. And pictures couldn't hint at the nervous energy that coursed through him and made him shift and twitch like a skittish hound. His blue eyes bounced around the room, lit on me, bounced away again. When he spoke it was to Conti.

"You offer him a drink, Tig? Maybe a sandwich? He looks hungry to me."

Conti's mouth tightened. "He passed."

Kyle Bray smiled. He went to the little fridge in the credenza and found a tall brown bottle with a Japanese label. He pried off the cap, drank, and sighed.

"Can't interest you in a beer? This is the good stuff." I shook my head. Bray looked at Conti. "I don't know, Tig — he looks underfed. But maybe that's just the way he looks. Is that just the way you look, Dr. Knox?"

I didn't respond, and Kyle smoothed the lapels of his suit. He sat down at the end of the table, opposite Conti, and took another long pull on his beer. "Underfed, under-slept — you pick up those habits in med school, or was it later on?"

Before I could answer, Conti cleared his throat. "You need me for this, Kyle?" he said.

Kyle shot him an irritated look. "I don't think I need you for anything, Tig," he said, and flicked a dismissive hand. Conti ambled out the door, and left me with what might've been a sympathetic glance.

"So what about it — hungry and tired something you learned in med school?" Kyle's smile flickered like a flame in a breeze.

I stretched my legs out and crossed my ankles. "What am I doing here, Mr. Bray?"

"I knew a bunch of premeds at Santa Barbara, and some med students at SC, and they were always grinding it out. Work, work, work — and for what? The pay was never very good, and now that we've got socialist medicine it's only going to get worse. Seems like there ought to be a better ROI — am I right?"

"I doubt many doctors in this neighborhood complain much."

He drank some more beer, wiped his mouth with the back of his hand, and put the bottle on the table. He ran a finger along the collar of his shirt and touched the large knot of his tie. "Don't kid yourself — doctors complain about everything, especially the old ones. But maybe geography *is* the main issue. The doctors I know *do* look better fed than you, and they're all driving Beemers and Benzes. But all of them are on the Westside. Do all the docs in your neighborhood look like sorry sacks of shit?"

There was movement in the hallway, beyond the glass wall — a cleaning woman pushing a cart. Kyle watched her, then pointed at my scrub shirt and jeans and laughed. "I mean, seriously, the washwoman's better dressed than you."

I sighed. "Am I here to talk wardrobe?"

He stood, and struck a pose by the window — legs apart, hands clasped behind his back, the captain on the bridge. "You know why you're here, Dr. Knox. My men told you what they wanted the day they walked into your shack, and they've sent you messages a few times since then."

"They were interested in a little boy. I gather they still are."

"You *gather*? You fucking *gather* right."

"And now you're going to threaten me some more? Maybe read from my high school transcript?"

264

Bray shook his head. "I looked at your file, and I didn't think there was much in there, except maybe the part about you getting kicked out of Doctors Transglobal. I figure an outfit like that would be desperate for cheap labor, so you'd have to fuck up big-time to get fired. Tig's theory is that it was black market stuff — that maybe you were raiding the drug supply to make something extra on the side. Me — I'm simpler. I figure you got a thing for dark meat, and they caught you fucking patients. That's a thing doctors do, right? One of the perquisites?"

I sighed. "I thought I made it clear to your people — I don't talk about my patients."

"Which isn't the same as you not knowing where he is."

"I *don't* know where he is."

"And I say you're a little bit full of shit."

"Then I guess we're at an impasse."

"Except you're not going anywhere until I say so."

"Why do you want this kid, anyway? What is he to you?"

Kyle smoothed his tie and put on a brittle smile. "You're here to answer questions, not ask them."

I shook my head. "If you're not going to explain what you —"

He puffed his chest and jabbed a finger at me. "*I* don't explain, fucker!" he shouted. "*You* explain!"

I got the impression he'd practiced the line often, and probably in a mirror, but his voice broke when he said it, and he looked and sounded like a schoolyard ayatollah — the opposite of intimidating. I laughed. Which was probably not the wisest choice.

There was a heavy silence afterward, and Bray stared at me and colored deeply. He looked at the Japanese beer bottle on the table, whispered "Motherfucker," and grabbed it. I rolled back in my chair as he came around the table, and I kicked one of the empty chairs into his path. He stumbled, but kept coming. I stood, and grabbed his right wrist with my left hand.

I didn't get into many fights as a kid — some sloppy punches and grappling on the soccer field after one too many fouls, a more concerted effort with two douche bags in boarding school who had a penchant for racist jokes, and again in college with two other douche bags who were giving a waitress a hard time. Always the results were equivocal. I was strong enough, and quick, but I was untrained. Then I met Libby. She was an EMT in San Francisco, on the crew I joined for med school ride-alongs. She was five four and 120 pounds with change in her pockets, but she routinely brought down and restrained rampaging drunks and dopers twice her size with a mix of Brazilian jujitsu, aikido, and pressure-point control techniques. She took pity on me after I'd gotten bounced around a few times, and shared her secrets; over the years, in ERs, in Africa, and in my own clinic, I'd had plenty of opportunities to practice.

I pulled Kyle into his stumble, and let momentum carry him past me and into the table. I tangled his ankles so that he sprawled on the tabletop, and as he went over I dug my fingers into his wrist, into the median nerve. He yelped, and the beer bottle fell to the floor. I stepped behind him, twisted his arm back, and pressed my right thumb into the mastoid process behind and beneath his right ear. He screamed and stopped struggling, and then there were dark-suited men in the room.

Two of them pulled me off, and back into my seat. Then they stood on either side of me as Conti picked up the beer bottle and helped Kyle to his feet. Which just made Kyle angrier.

"Fuck off, Tiger," he snarled, and rubbed his wrist and his neck. He looked at the other PRP soldiers. "And you guys can fuck off too. Just leave me alone with this ass-hole."

The soldiers looked at Conti, who shook his head. "I leave you with him, someone's gonna get hurt."

Kyle smoothed his tie. "That's the point, dick."

"You sure you want to take things in that direction just now?" Conti said carefully.

Kyle glared. "Are *you* sure you want to keep patronizing me?"

The men beside me stiffened, and Conti's tanned face grew darker. His hands clenched and a tremor went through his shoulders, but otherwise he didn't respond. For a moment all I heard was Kyle's excited breathing, and then a cell phone pinged.

Conti fished it from a jacket pocket, scanned the screen, and looked relieved. "You're wanted on the phone, Kyle."

Kyle's face tightened. "Give it here."

"The call's waiting out at reception," Conti said.

Kyle looked like he might spit. He stared at Conti for a moment, then brushed his lapels and left. Conti looked at the two soldiers. "Give it five and take him to the elevator," he said. Then he raised an eyebrow at me and followed Kyle from the room.

268

The soldiers were silent while we waited; then one of them led me to the reception area. There was a woman there, in the shadows by the elevators, listening to the rumbling whispers of a tall, stoop-shouldered man, and nodding as the man spoke, in agreement or obedience. The man glanced at me before he stalked off, and I glimpsed a square face, a massive bald head, and a look of icy contempt.

CHAPTER 24

I thought she was a girl at first. She was small, with dark-blond hair in a pixie cut, brown button eyes, and a pink, eager face, like a pretty child's. My second look took in the trim curves, the diamond stud earrings, diamond tennis bracelet, weighty square-cut engagement ring, immaculately tailored black suit, and black suede pumps — definitely not a school uniform. She smiled at me, and her teeth were even and very white.

"I came over as soon as I heard they'd brought you in, doctor," she said. Her voice was also young, and there was a twang to it — not quite Southern or Southwestern. "Those are yours." She pointed to my phone and backpack atop the empty reception desk. I picked them up and looked at the phone. It was still locked.

"There wasn't enough time to break into it," she said, still smiling. "Not that they didn't try."

I slipped the phone into my pocket and nodded. "I appreciate the honesty."

"It's one of my many virtues. Kyle give you a hard time?"

I shrugged. "You know he's squirrelly, right?"

"Is that a professional opinion?"

"I see a lot of it in the course of a day."

"No doubt," she said, laughing.

"You work for PRP?"

"Actually, they work for me."

"You're with Bray?"

"I *am* a Bray. Well, sort of."

"I didn't think Kyle had siblings."

"Cousin. Amanda Danzig — Mandy." She put out her hand. Her grip was strong and warm.

"Adam Knox," I said, cautiously.

She giggled. "I know who you are. After all, you've been my prisoner for the past two hours, including travel time." Mandy's smile was intimate and conspiratorial, as if we were sharing a naughty joke. It was an effort not to smile back.

I held up my phone. "Which is why I'm calling the cops."

Mandy laughed again and crossed the reception area to the windows, and a pair of low-slung leather sofas. There was a silver coffee service laid out, with china cups and

271

lacy cookies. She sat, filled two cups, and patted the seat next to her. "C'mon — I promise I'm not Kyle. And anyway, we both know you're not going to call the police."

I went to the windows but didn't sit. "No?"

The smile turned coquettish. "Nope."

"Because . . . ?"

"Because if you were you would already have done it. Days ago. Look, you said that you appreciated my honesty — let me give you some more. We know Alex went into your clinic last Friday evening, and we know he didn't come out. So it's a pretty sure bet that you have him, or that you know where he is."

"I told Kyle — I've told all your people — I don't talk about my patients. And I don't —"

Mandy shook her head. "Just for argument's sake, let's pretend I'm right. Then the question is: why haven't you given him to us? Maybe it's because that girl told you some story. Maybe you think you're playing hero for her, or for the boy. But I'm going to say that it was our bad, doctor: I think we got off on the wrong foot with you."

"You're definitely right about that."

She dropped a sugar cube into her cup, stirred, took a sip. "To the extent Kyle thinks — and it's really very little — he thinks there's only one way to sort out a problem." She put her cup down, made a fist, and drove it into her open palm. The sound was like snapping wood. "And while he's not as rash as Kyle, Tiger has a preference for those methods too — it's what he's used to. So Kyle got panicky, and got Tiger wound up, and sent him half cocked right into your clinic — big boots, big noise, big mess. But, lucky for you, I'm here to make things right."

I looked down at Mandy. Her face was bright in the colored light that came through the windows, and her smile was wide. "Lucky for me. How do you propose doing this?"

"It's simple: I'm going to ask you what you want, doctor — what it is that we can do for you."

"I don't —"

She held up her hand. "Maybe you're not sure what you want — in which case, take a little time to think it over. Or maybe you know, but you're too shy to ask — in which case, don't be; I don't judge. Or maybe it's what in B-school we called a *pricing uncertainty problem* — you've got something in mind, but you don't know what the market will bear, and you don't want to undercut yourself, or maybe price yourself out. Well, I'm here to tell you, the market will bear *a lot.* Seriously. A lot."

I shook my head slowly, but Mandy pressed on.

"Don't overthink this, doctor. I promise you — I'm not being cagey or cute; I'm not playing you with some nefarious strategy. I'm offering you a lot of money, or a lot of whatever it is you want, for help getting Alex back. That's it, full-stop."

I smiled, despite myself. I sat down opposite her, picked up my coffee cup, and took a sip. It was excellent. "*I promise you* — is that something else they taught you in business school?"

"I learned that in Brownies, actually."

I laughed. "What are you at Bray Consolidated, Mandy?"

"My job title? It's senior vice-president of development. Fancy, right?"

"You don't seem old enough to be *senior* anything, except maybe senior class president."

She laughed. "You wound me, Dr. Knox. Plus, that's a deeply ageist crack — and probably sexist too. And besides, I'm a few months from thirty — which isn't so young."

"It's practically diapers. What's your fancy

title mean?"

"That I follow my uncle around. I'm in training — learning how the company operates, how each part works, how the parts fit together. How to run the thing. He's a great believer in apprenticeship."

"Like Donald Trump. You're taking over for him one day?"

The pretty white smile flickered for an instant, then came back full-strength. "My uncle has plenty of years left."

"That was him, wasn't it — by the elevators? He keeping an eye on you? Giving you your brief?"

Mandy colored. "He's very hands-on. But if you're wondering whether I'm empowered to make a deal, the answer is yes."

"Let's not get ahead of ourselves. I've got questions."

She nodded encouragingly. "Fire away."

"Why do you want Alex? What's he to you?"

"He's my cousin."

"Your cousin? So he's . . . Kyle's son?"

"Maybe now you can excuse the rashness. I mean, what wouldn't a parent do for a child?"

"Kyle's more than just rash."

"You'll get no argument from me. Next question?"

"That *girl* you mentioned . . ."

"Elena."

"Who is she?"

Mandy's smile vanished, and her eyes fixed on something in the darkness. "An opportunist. Someone who thinks she sees a big payday. She may also be . . . disturbed."

"She's not Alex's mother?"

She shook her head. "Sometimes she claims she is; she may have even told Alex some story to that effect; maybe she told you the same thing. Who knows, she might even believe it herself."

"Wouldn't Alex know the truth?"

Mandy's voice softened. "He was young when his mother died — too young to remember."

I caught a scrap of Mandy's perfume. Magnolia and something else. "So Elena's not related to him?"

"An aunt. But she doesn't know anything about him, except she may've seen him once when he was an infant."

"Back in Romania?"

Mandy gave me a sharp look. "You *do* know her."

"I heard her speak."

She nodded. "Yes, she's from Romania."

"So what's going on here? A custody dispute? Some kind of shakedown? A kidnapping?"

"All of the above, maybe; we're not sure. And, honestly, we don't even care that much. We just want Alex back, safe and sound."

"Then why haven't you called the police, or the FBI, or someone? You've made it pretty clear that you're seriously connected."

Mandy leaned forward and rested her elbows on her knees. She pressed her fingertips to her eyes. "It's not that simple. Alex has been through a lot in his life. Nobody wants to make him the center of protracted legal warfare or — God forbid — a media circus. And we certainly don't want to make him a target for more . . ." She ran a hand through her cropped hair and sighed. "Look, I'm authorized to make a deal with you, not to air my family's laundry. The bottom line is, we want to get him home — quickly, quietly, and safely."

"You think he's in danger?"

She looked at me. "You probably know more than I do about that."

I shook my head. "You think he's in danger with Elena?"

"He's a little boy, doctor. If he's not with his family, he's at risk. Does that take care of your questions?"

"For the moment."

"Great. Then, getting back to mine . . ."

"I don't know if I can help you, Mandy."

She drank some of her coffee and smiled knowingly. She put her hand on mine. Her nails were smooth and glossy; her fingers were hot. "Don't say anything, then. Take some time and figure out what you might want. Something for the clinic, maybe, or for yourself — it doesn't matter to us."

Mandy finished her coffee, squeezed my hand, and rose. She placed a cream-colored business card with her name on it next to the coffee carafe. "Our only concern is time, doctor — we want Alex home ASAP. You've seen how impatient Kyle can be, and who knows what harebrained ideas he might come up with. Calling people we know at Immigration, maybe, or at the state medical board, or having your malpractice insurance yanked — and let's not even contemplate his felonious notions. Tiger tries to rein him in, and so do I, but we can only do so much. I can keep him quiet for a few days, maybe. After that . . ."

She brushed off her pants, adjusted the lines of her jacket, and walked to the elevators. A door slid open as soon as she touched the button, and she stepped inside. She mimed a telephone with her thumb and pinkie and put it to her ear. "Call me," she mouthed as the door slid shut.

CHAPTER 25

"I wondered why your car was parked in the same spot for so long," Ben Sutter said, and he blew a long plume of cigar smoke into the night sky. We were drinking beer on the roof of my building, and I'd just finished telling him about the earlier part of my evening. Sutter was sprawled on a mesh-and-metal lounge chair, and I was perched on the coping of the low wall that ran around the rooftop. Two bottles of Populist IPA had begun to leach some of the fear and adrenaline from me. The night was warm, and there was a breeze that carried off Sutter's smoke.

I squinted at him. "How'd you know how long my car was parked?"

"The tracker I put on," he said.

I thought for a moment about being angry with this, but decided I was touched instead. I nodded at Sutter and drank some beer. "Were you ever going to check out why?"

"I was curious, but then you called. Speaking of which, let me see your phone."

I dug my phone out of my pocket and tossed it to Sutter. "Why?"

Sutter took the cover off my phone and examined the edges. Then he took out his key ring, and selected a slim tool from it. He slipped it into the phone casing, twisted, and lifted the back off. Then he pulled a penlight from his cargo shorts.

"I'm checking for spare parts," he said. "Like trackers."

"Shit."

"No worries there," he said as he slid the phone case back on and tossed the phone back to me. "How about your backpack?"

"Under your chair."

After ten minutes searching through the pack, Sutter held up what looked like a gray pen cap. He looked at it for a moment, then crushed it under his heel. "Tracker," he said.

"Shit," I repeated, and let out a long, shaky breath.

Sutter smiled ruefully. "That Kyle guy sounds like a dick."

I nodded. "Without a doubt. Too much money, everybody around him saying yes all the time . . ."

"Always a healthy mix. The cousin seems like fun, though. She cute?"

"If you like naughty elves."

"My favorite kind. She smarter than Kyle?"

"Smarter; more manipulative. She had a nice way of offering the carrot, but she never let me forget about the stick."

"You buy her story?"

I shrugged. "It explains why the Brays are after Alex."

"And that business about why they haven't called the cops or the feds, or the National Guard?"

"That makes less sense. I know the Brays are private people — that's what everything I've read about them says, anyway. And, given what they've got with PRP — their own little army — they clearly have no problem cutting the authorities out of things when it suits them. But bypassing the cops seems like a damn big risk to take when your son or your grandson is missing. And then there's Elena."

Sutter shifted in his lounge chair and tilted the back down farther. "Is she or isn't she the kid's mom?"

"That's the question. When Alex's airway was closing up, Elena was freaked in the way that only parents get. But Lydia's had her doubts from the start — how she left her kid with total strangers, et cetera. I

chalked that up to fear and desperation —
being chased, wanting to protect Alex —
but now I'm wondering."

"You're not going to have an answer until
you find her."

"No shit. But I'm still waiting for a brilliant idea of how to do that. Mandy said
she'd give me a little time to think things
over, but that's measured in days. Or less."

Sutter smiled. "*Mandy* — that's nice. She
have a pet name for you?"

"Not that she mentioned."

"Probably waiting for the second date."

"Which I'd prefer to pass on. She may be
cute, but she's also scary, and I take her
threats seriously."

Sutter nodded slowly. "Yep. These folks
haven't been the slickest operators so far,
but it's not for lack of trying. Eventually,
they'll get lucky."

CHAPTER 26

By Friday morning, no ideas — brilliant or otherwise — of how to find Elena had announced themselves, though a headache, as gray and dispiriting as the marine layer that squatted over the city, had. Advil did a little something to cut the pain, and coffee did a little more. I poured a third cup and drank it, and thought about Amanda Danzig and Kyle Bray and carrots and sticks. Then Lucho called from downstairs to tell me the waiting room was filling up, and I turned on the shower.

It was another busy day, with more norovirus cases in the morning, and in the afternoon the principals in a pickup-versus-SUV collision a block away, who very nearly came to blows at the reception desk. Lucho was threatening violence to the pickup driver, and I was ushering an SUV passenger into the exam room, when Mia came in. She was wearing jeans and a halter top, and she crossed the waiting room to catch my sleeve.

"I need to see you, doc," she whispered.

I looked her over quickly, and saw nothing beyond pallor and nervousness.

"Check in with Lucho, Mia — it's crazy today."

She was pacing by the front door next time I passed through the waiting room, looking paler and jumpier.

"What's Mia in for?" I asked Lydia.

She shrugged. "She wants to talk to you."

"About what? The cut on her leg bothering her?"

"She just said she needed to talk."

I looked across the waiting room. Mia was buried in her cell, worrying her lower lip. "Okay," I said. "After the UTI in Exam Two."

The urinary tract infection was barely out of the door when Mia swept into the exam room, her usual flirty cool nowhere in sight. I motioned her to the exam table, but she didn't sit. Her sandaled foot tapped nervously.

"What's up, Mia? The leg okay?"

"It's fine, doc. You need to come with me."

"What?"

"You need to come with me, like on a

285

house call. Like now."

"A house call? I've got patients out there." She pressed fingers to her temples and sighed. "What's the matter?" I asked.

"It's . . . it's Jerome, doc — he's not doing good."

"What's wrong with him?"

"I . . . I'm not sure. That's why you need to look at him."

"He can't find another doctor?"

"He needs to see somebody *now.*"

"If it's an emergency, he should call 911."

"He . . . he can't, doc. He just needs . . ."

She rubbed her temples again. She was paler and more frightened than I'd ever seen her. I checked my watch. "Let me see if I can get away." Relief crossed Mia's face like the sun coming out.

Lydia said she could cover the rest of the day's patients, and I grabbed my backpack. "Let's go," I said to Mia.

She smiled and nodded. "Let's use the back door. I got my car in the alley." I nodded and led her down the hall.

Mia's car was a Golf that was once red, with a soft top that was once not mostly duct tape. Inside, the Golf was surprisingly tidy, and Mia played electronic dance music at a deafening volume as she angled expertly west and then north. We were nearly in

Little Tokyo when she pulled into a spot in front of a shuttered store that used to sell soccer equipment.

"This is where Jerome lives?"

Mia locked the car. "On the second floor."

We went through a metal door and up a dim staircase. There was a short hallway at the top, with flimsy-looking doors at either end. Mia paused.

"Which way?" I asked.

She shrugged her broad shoulders and looked down at the mildewed carpet. When she looked up, her face was red. "I . . . I'm really sorry."

My pulse spiked, and sweat prickled across my forehead. "Sorry for what?"

"I owed, doc, and I had to pay off."

"You . . . Mia, what did you do?"

She shook her head and turned and ran down the stairs. I started to follow but froze when the door to my left opened. "Don't blame her," a voice said from the darkened doorway. "She didn't want to lie to you. I made her do it."

It was a small, tired voice, and it came from a small figure with bleached-blond hair streaked blue in front. Her left arm was folded across her chest, and her left hand pressed to her right shoulder, where her shirt was crusted with dry blood.

She stepped into the hall and I caught her as she sagged against the wall. "Jesus, Shelly, what happened to you?"

"It hurts like a bastard," she said, "but she's in deeper shit." She pointed into the apartment, and I looked past her, to a spavined daybed and Elena upon it, beneath a thin and bloody blanket.

CHAPTER 27

Shelly had a contusion, purple and swollen, under her left eye, and a flap of skin like the sole of a shoe hanging from her right deltoid — painful, ugly, and possibly infected, but, with cleaning, stitching, and meds, not life-threatening. She was conscious, coherent, and ambulatory. She was the lucky one.

"Call 911," I said, and left her in the hall. I crossed the room, knelt at the daybed, and pulled back the blanket. Elena lay on her left side, hunched around her pain. She was white — almost gray — and her breathing was fast, shallow, and desperate. I snapped on my gloves.

Elena's eyelids fluttered when I touched her neck, and she shrank from my hand. She tried to roll away, but pain or weakness stopped her. I found her carotid and felt her pulse careening beneath my fingers — 120 at least.

"It's all right, Elena," I said softly, "I'm

going to help you. Remember me from the clinic — Dr. Knox? I took care of Alex." Her eyes opened wide at the mention of his name, and darted about. She tried to speak but had no breath.

"I need to check you out," I said, and turned her onto her back. Her jeans were dark and damp with blood at the beltline, and so was her Little Mermaid tee shirt — darkest and dampest around the long slash on its left side. I tore the shirt open from hem to collar.

Elena's breasts were small and blue-veined, her nipples like dark-red beans. The skin of her torso was paper white, and painted all over with tea-colored daubs — blood from a laceration across the lower left quadrant of her abdomen, from above her hip to her navel, and from a smaller wound — a puncture — on her right flank, just below the sixth rib. I slipped on my stethoscope, and placed the chest piece above Elena's left breast. I heard breath sounds — fast and labored. I moved it to the right side and heard . . . nothing.

Shit.

I pulled the stethoscope off, splayed my left hand on Elena's chest, just above her left breast, and rapped my middle finger with the middle finger of my right hand.

There was a dull *thock*. I moved to her right side and percussed her chest again. It sounded like a hollow gourd.

Shit.

Elena had a tension pneumothorax — an air bubble in her chest cavity, between the chest wall and the lung, that was pushing against her right lung, squeezing it and starving her of oxygen. Killing her, if I didn't pop her chest. I rummaged in my pack. In another world, I felt Shelly behind me.

"Last ten minutes, she's been panting like a dog," Shelly said. "She gonna be . . . okay?"

I found Betadine, tape, and packs of sterile gauze. Where was the needle? "What happened to her?"

"Motherfucking Russians happened. One of them had a knife like you clean fish with, and went at her like she was a tuna, the fucking prick."

"When was this?" Where was the needle?

"This morning, around seven, maybe. Is . . . is she gonna be okay?"

Seven a.m. — more than enough time for pressure to build, and for a simple pneumo to become a tension pneumo. *Shit.*

"The knife probably nicked her lung, and now it's collapsed," I said. Shelly gasped. I

291

dug deeper into my pack and found it — a syringe with a fourteen-gauge needle.

I looked at Elena's chest. Her ribs were plain beneath her white skin. I touched her clavicle on the right side, slid my finger to the midline, and counted down to the second intercostal space. I squirted Betadine over her second and third ribs, and wiped the area with a gauze pad. Then I sprayed lidocaine on the same spot. I tore open the syringe and tossed the plunger away.

Elena stared at the needle. "Close your eyes," I told her. She nodded and closed them.

"You want to take a step back," I said to Shelly. "There may be spray." Then I pushed the needle slowly into Elena's chest, at a ninety-degree angle, in the space just above her third rib.

Push, push, push, and there it was: a pink mist in the barrel of the syringe, and a hiss, strong and steady. Almost immediately, Elena's breathing deepened and slowed. I slipped on the stethoscope and heard breath sounds from both sides of her chest now. Her color began to return. I checked her pulse again: ninety-five and slowing. I released a long-held breath of my own, and taped the needle in place.

"Better?" I asked, and she nodded, panic fading from her eyes.

"Alex," she said in a hoarse whisper.

"He's fine," I said. "Let me look at those cuts."

I took a squeeze bottle from my pack, ran sterile saline over her wounds, and wiped away dried blood. The puncture wound had closed. The belly cut was thin and clean-edged — almost surgical — a single curving stroke made with a very sharp blade. A film of clotting blood had begun to form over the seam. I had no idea how deep the cut went, or if there were bleeders inside, or if — worse still — her abdominal cavity had been punctured and her gut was leaking. I pressed my fingertips into her belly to check for rebound tenderness. There was none, and that was a good sign, though the folks in the ER could tell for sure. They could also see to the fresh cut on her lip, and the new bruises on her head, her arms, and God only knew where else. A shiver ran through Elena's pale body. I pulled the thin blanket over her, careful not to cover the syringe. She sighed deeply and closed her eyes again. I sighed too, and looked at Shelly.

She'd retreated to a corner — to one of the folding chairs set around a card table. Her gaze flicked between the dusty screen of a television perched on a plastic crate, and a bar of greenish light that came through a window. I carried my pack to the table and knelt at her side.

"Is she okay now?" Shelly asked.

"She can breathe again," I said softly. "The rest of her problems will keep till she gets to the ER." Shelly stared at the floor. "Let me see the shoulder."

I pulled on fresh gloves, and Shelly turned in her seat. She slowly took her hand from her shoulder. Unlike the surgical wound on Elena's belly, this was a butcher's cut, through layers of skin and muscle, nearly to bone — a hack with a thick blade and a heavy hand.

"Can you move your arm?" I asked, and Shelly showed me that she could, though with pain. "How about your hand and fingers?" She demonstrated those too. "Lucky," I said, and squeezed some normal saline over the wound. Shelly winced, and cursed when I started cleaning. "Tell me what happened," I said.

"I told you already. *Fuck* — that hurts!"

"Tell me more. It'll take your mind off the pain."

"We were on San Pedro, by Fourth Street, headed over here, and those Russian pricks showed up from nowhere. One grabbed me by the throat, started shaking me, and — boom — my girl Ellie goes up on his head with a tire iron. Don't know where she was keeping that. Then this other asshole gets on her. She fought — whacked him good a couple of times — but then he pulls a knife and I hear her yell. I'm not too sure what happened after that, 'cause the first guy got up, screamin' bloody murder and wavin' a goddamn meat cleaver around. Caught me in the arm with it, and then I was runnin', draggin' Ellie down the street, and a cop car came up San Pedro, and the Russians took off the other way. *Ow!*"

"How do you know they were Russians?"

Shelly grimaced at me. "C'mon, doc, I'm not stupid. Those assholes work for Siggy Rostov. They're at the Horney twice a week, when they come around to collect. And lately I see 'em every day — following you all over the place, and asking anybody who can breathe if they've seen Ellie."

"Elena's been with you the past week?" Shelly nodded. "I've been looking for her too, you know."

"I know — and you're like the one person she hasn't been hiding from. She wanted to get in touch; she's worried sick about the kid. But between the Russians and the other guys looking for her — those big-neck creeps you drove off with last night — she was, like, crazy paranoid. She didn't want to be on the street; she didn't even want to call you. She thinks your phones are bugged or something. I tried to get word to you for her, but every time I saw you or went by your place you had company."

I finished cleaning the wound, and taped a loose dressing over it. I pulled off my gloves and checked my watch. "There are pieces of your shirt in there that need to come out, and you need a tetanus shot, but that should hold you till the ambulance gets here. Which should've been twenty minutes ago."

Shelly looked down at her sandals. "About that," she said. Her voice was small and choked.

"About what?"

"About the ambulance. I . . . I didn't exactly call for one."

"*What?*" I stood, dug in my pocket, and found my cell. "What the hell's the matter with you, Shelly? Elena's been knifed, you've almost had your arm hacked off — it's only sheer luck you're both still breathing. Why're you fucking around?"

Shelly's small, blood-blotched hand closed around my wrist. Her eyes were wide and pleading. "You can't, doc! She made me promise — no cops, no 911. She made me swear to it!"

"You're not calling them — I am."

"Please! She said the hospital meant cops, and cops meant the end for her. She said if they got her then Siggy would get her, and if not Siggy, then Immigration, and either way she'd never see the kid again."

I pulled free of her grip. "She's in a bad way, and you are too. I can't —"

"You fixed her up — she can breathe now — and you patched my shoulder too. Just give me some pain meds and I'm good to go."

"Neither of you is good to go anywhere except a hospital. All I did was stabilize you; you need more than that."

"Can't you do it here?"

"You've barely got running water here, Shelly."

"Then how about at your place?" she said, and took hold of my wrist again. "Please, doc. Ellie's serious. She said if they take the kid then she hopes Siggy gets her, 'cause she'd rather be dead." Shelly's face was pale and glazed with sweat, and I could feel the fever in her hand.

I shook my head. "You're killing me, Shelly," I whispered, and touched a number from my phone book. I put the cell to my ear. "Lucho, it's me," I said. "Did you drive your van to work today?"

CHAPTER 28

It was dusk when Lucho pulled his van into the alley behind the soccer equipment store, and dark by the time we got Shelly and Elena into it. Lydia met us at the clinic's back door, with solicitous efficiency for the two injured women, and opaque silence for me. She and Lucho settled the women in exam rooms while I washed, changed my shirt, and called Ben Sutter. Then I went into Exam One.

Elena was stretched out on the table, her breathing steady and careful, her dark eyes wary. Lydia had already swapped what was left of her bloody clothing for a gown, given her a tetanus shot, and started her on IV fluids. She was cleaning Elena's cuts and scrapes, and examining the knife wounds suspiciously.

"I checked her belly," Lydia said. "No peritoneal signs. Yet."

I nodded, and put on my stethoscope. I

checked her chest again. "Her breath sounds are better, but I'm hearing a pneumohemo."

Lydia nodded. "She needs drainage," she said quietly. "Of course, she could use imaging too, and a few other things you'd find in a hospital."

"Let's start with drainage."

"I'll set it up," Lydia said, shaking her head. She went down the hall to the supply closet, and I took over the cuts and scrapes.

Elena fixed her eyes on mine and touched my arm. Her hand was cold. "Alex," she said in a slow whisper.

"He's fine. You'll see him soon."

Elena's eyes widened and tears welled in them. She took a deep, shaky breath. "Men . . . look for me. Also Alex."

"I know about them."

Her grip tightened on my forearm. "Please, you must not —"

"No one's going to bother you here, Elena. Not you or Alex."

Lydia cleared her throat. She was standing in the doorway, holding the Pleur-evac drainage unit and a surgical kit. Her look was accusing. She shook her head some more and moved to the sink, where she washed and put on a mask and gloves. Then she started laying out the drainage gear. Despite her years away from the OR, Lydia was still the precise scrub nurse. She spread a sterile pad over a tray and carefully laid each instrument on it, in the order in which it would be needed.

"You want to give her Ativan?" she whispered. "Or are you worried about the belly wound?"

I nodded. "We'll stick with the local."

Lydia nodded and prepared a syringe and laid it on the sheet. Her voice dropped even lower. "You know, you shouldn't promise things you can't deliver," she said.

"I'm not," I said.

Lydia rolled her eyes. "Sure. Between six and seven?" she asked.

"Six and seven," I said, and she painted the white skin over Elena's sixth and seventh ribs brown with Betadine.

The drain went in easily, and Elena uttered not a word of complaint while we worked. The only sign she gave of pain was a stiffening of her features now and then, and a narrowing of her eyes, which were locked on me. Lydia stayed with her afterward, to monitor her vitals and periodically check her belly for indications that the cut had done more than superficial damage. I went down the hall to look in on Shelly.

Who was also wearing a gown, sitting cross-legged on the exam table, and giving

301

Lucho a hard time.

"I'm like a fucking prisoner, doc. He won't give me my clothes, won't let me out of this room, won't give me any good drugs — he just sits there looking like a scary totem pole."

Lucho smiled and shook his head. "She's not that scared."

"I agree. You want to keep an eye out back, for Sutter?" Lucho nodded, and closed the door behind him.

"How's the shoulder?" I asked.

"It fucking hurts."

"Is it still mobile?" Shelly demonstrated, and cringed only a little doing it. I nodded. "If you'd let me send you to an ER, they would've cleaned that wound some more, given you a tetanus shot, started you on IV antibiotics, and stitched you up, so that's what I'm going to do."

"And pain meds?"

"If you behave."

"I mean good shit, not that Tylenol-with-codeine crap."

"We'll see. So how about, while I'm cleaning you up, you tell me what the fuck is going on."

"I told you about the Russians already."

I picked up a squeeze bottle of normal saline and a forceps. "Then tell me some-

302

thing new. For starters, tell me how you know Elena."

"From the horrible Horney, of course. That's where I met her — her and the kid. The first couple days, they had a pretty rough time there. Every time they set foot out of their room, some asshole would fuck with them — sayin' shit to Ellie, even with the kid standin' right there. And Troop was always sniffin' around her. She had to go out and get stuff — food and shit — but she didn't want to take the kid, and she sure as shit didn't want to leave him alone. Finally, she comes up to me and asks would I go to the bodega for her."

"She must've thought you looked trustworthy."

Shelly laughed and nodded vigorously. "That's what she said. Actually, the first thing she said was she liked my hair. What I think really is, she heard me cursing out some paint drinker in the lobby for messing with a new girl, and she figured that made me okay."

"Did she tell you she was on the run from Siggy?"

"After a while," she said, and shivered as I tugged a scrap of tee shirt from the cleft in her shoulder. "It took me by surprise."

"I bet. Didn't she know that a lot of the

girls at the Harney work for him?"

"She had no clue," Shelly said. "Her bad luck."

"What did she tell you about the kid?"

"Only that people were looking for him too. She didn't tell me who or why."

"I didn't think her English was that good, but I guess you were able to communicate."

"Ellie understands everything, and she talks fine if she's not rushed. Or scared."

"And you two are like BFFs now?"

Shelly looked down. "I like her. She's a tough bitch, and there's nothing she wouldn't do for the kid. Who's awesome, by the way."

"Yeah?"

"Yeah — he's funny, and sweet as hell."

"I think he's a good guy too," I said, nodding. "And you did a lot for them — took some big risks, probably got on Siggy's bad side."

"Bunch of pricks — him and all his guys. I been flippin' 'em off forever."

"Could be Siggy's finally taken notice." Shelly shrugged and her face screwed up in pain. "Anyway," I continued, "you risked a lot for people you've only known for a couple of weeks."

She looked at the floor again and took a deep breath. "It wasn't much. And anyway,

I . . . I owe them."

"Owe them for what?"

"For . . . for the kid. For what happened to him when he came to you. I . . . He got that candy bar from me."

"The one with the peanuts?"

Shelly's face got red, and there were tears in her eyes. "It was a Snickers. They're my favorite, and I thought he would like it. I almost killed the fucking guy."

"You couldn't know. Elena didn't know."

Shelly swallowed hard and shook her head. "You done yet?" she whispered.

I squeezed her good shoulder. "Almost," I said.

I gave Shelly something for the pain, and left her dozing in the exam room. When I stepped into the hall, Sutter was there.

"Another busy night?" he said, smiling.

"We're putting up a velvet rope soon. You see anybody lurking?"

"Everybody around here lurks. But, no, I didn't — which doesn't mean nobody's watching. The street out front looked clear, and you couldn't hang in the alley without being seen, but there're a couple of rooftops nearby that would give you decent sight-lines. If I were the PRP guys, that's where I'd set up."

"So those assholes may have seen us come in with Elena and Shelly?"

"Always best to assume the worst. Besides which, Siggy must've heard about the dustup his boys had this morning, and that they cut up these girls a little. It won't take him long to figure out where they might've gone for help."

"Excellent," I sighed. "So everybody knows where they are."

Sutter grinned wider. "Only for a little while."

CHAPTER 29

I rode shotgun in the black Escalade that Sutter had conjured from somewhere, but I still had a hard time following the twists and turns and loop-backs he drove from the clinic to the house in El Segundo. Elena and Shelly were quiet in the back seats, as they had been since Lucho had doused the alley lights and we'd taken them out the back door. Their faces were pale against the black leather upholstery, and they both grimaced when we went over bumps.

The house was a tidy stucco ranch, sherbet pink in the Escalade's headlights, with white trim and a lawn like a swatch of green suede. The furnishings were simple and bright — fresh from the IKEA box — and the floors were shiny oak. The smells of paint and varnish still lingered. Sutter moved from window to window, lowering shades.

"New tenants come in a couple of weeks,"

he said, "so you're good till then."

Shelly eased herself carefully into an armchair. "Nice," she said, looking around. "Clean. What do you get for a place like this?"

"Thirty-seven hundred a month. Why — you in the market?"

"Sure," Shelly said, smiling. "Siggy's monkeys have probably moved into my old place by now, so I can't go back there. This is a little out of my way, though. Got anything downtown?" Sutter smiled back and shook his head.

I helped Elena to the sofa, got her feet onto the coffee table, and put the Pleurevac on the floor by her side. Her eyes roamed around the room, settled on Sutter, and narrowed. "We are close to the airport?" she said.

Sutter nodded. "South runways at LAX are two blocks away."

"First week in Los Angeles, I was close to the airport," she said. "An apartment. They move me after that."

"To another apartment?" I asked. Elena nodded. "In West Hollywood? The one where you met Hoover Mays?"

Her mouth turned sour. "You know Hoover?"

"I spoke to him," I said.

"I thought maybe he's killed," Elena said, sighing. "I hit him hard." I wasn't sure if she was relieved or disappointed. Sutter snorted.

"It looked to me like he hit you hard too," I said.

She nodded minutely. "Where is Alex?"

"He's fine. He'll be here in the morning."

"Not now?" Her voice trembled.

"It's too late. I didn't want to wake him in the middle of the night. I didn't want to scare him." She looked into my eyes for a while and then nodded. "Let me listen to your lungs again," I said.

I put my stethoscope on. Both lungs sounded good, and no fluid had drained into the Pleur-evac for over an hour.

I smiled. "You're doing well."

Elena looked down and touched a finger to the drainage tube where it snaked from beneath the gown she still wore. "You can take it out?"

"Yep — it's pretty much done its job."

"Before Alex comes?" I nodded. Elena studied the edge of her gown. "Is there something else for me?" she asked. "Other clothes?"

I nodded. "My nurse found some clean sweats and a tee shirt for you. Tomorrow morning you can wash up and change. Let me take the tube out, and then we can talk."

"Talk about what?"

"About what's going on, Elena — about why people are chasing you and Alex. About the trouble you're in."

She sighed. "You helped already, doctor — Alex and me. You do not need to do more. To be more . . . involved."

"Unfortunately, that's out of my hands." Elena squinted at me, puzzled. "I'm involved whether I want to be or not. People know I've helped you. Siggy knows; so do the Brays."

At the mention of these names, Elena's face froze. Then she sighed again, deeply. "Can be later we talk, doctor? I am so tired."

I nodded again. "I'll take the tube out."

"You need an extra pair of hands for that?" Sutter asked. I shook my head. "Then I'm going to walk around the block," he said.

Elena watched him go and then looked at me. "That one — he is your friend?" she asked. Her voice was a whisper.

I nodded. "He's helped you out a few times too."

"So you trust?" I nodded again. "He is what — a soldier?"

"Used to be. Now he does a lot of things. Like real estate."

She squinted at me. "But you trust?"

"With my life," I said. "Now, the tube." I dug in my backpack for gauze, and Elena sighed and closed her eyes. I pulled on yet another pair of gloves, and folded back her gown. Shelly fidgeted in her armchair.

"You just yank that thing out of her?" she said. "Right now? Right here?"

"I'm going to try not to yank."

"There gonna be blood?"

"Shouldn't be."

Shelly shivered and shook her head. "And I thought my job was gross."

The tube came out the way it went in — without a hitch and without a sound from Elena — and by the time I finished taping gauze over her ribs, her eyes were closed and her breathing was deep and regular. I was covering her with a blanket when Sutter returned. His walk around the block had included a trip to Vons, and he was carrying three plastic sacks.

"Sandwiches, fruit, cheese, crackers, a loaf of sourdough, and seltzer," he said.

"No doughnuts?" Shelly said. "No chicken wings? You a fuckin' health freak?"

"Have an apple," Sutter said, and tossed her a Granny Smith. "You'll live longer."

Shelly caught it with her good arm, and

winked at him. "That all it takes?"

Sutter and I went into the little kitchen. He unwrapped a chicken salad sandwich, and I peeled a banana. I twisted the top from a liter of water, drank from the bottle, and passed it to Sutter.

"Called a buddy to hang outside for a while," he said. "Remember Tommy?"

"Tall guy, weird hair, bullet holes in his left leg?"

"That's Mosul Tommy; this is Kabul Tommy I'm talking about. Anyway, he'll be around if you want to head home."

"I should keep an eye on them — especially Elena. Make sure her gut's okay."

Sutter smiled. "She seems to have no problem in that department."

"Neither one of them."

"You bringing the kid over?"

"Arthur's sister is, tomorrow morning."

"And then what?"

I shrugged. "A mother-and-child reunion."

"It'll be beautiful, I'm sure. You going to send photos to Siggy and the Brays? You think that'll make them go away?"

I drank some more water. "I'm not counting on it."

Sutter took the bottle from me. "You got that right."

CHAPTER 30

Danni brought Alex over at nine the next morning, and when he walked through the door, Elena sobbed and opened her arms. She was sitting on the sofa, in clean sweats and a tee shirt, and her hair was damp. She was still pale and exhausted, but color spread across her neck and cheeks when she saw the boy, and her smile was wide. Alex was across the room before Elena could rise, and he buried his face in her neck. The coiled watchfulness in their dark eyes vanished, and tension slid from their shoulders like an overcoat falling. They quivered as they held each other, and Elena stroked his hair and cooed to him in words I didn't understand.

I offered Danni breakfast but she begged off. When I'd seen her to her car, I walked around to the backyard. Sutter and Shelly were drinking coffee at a redwood picnic table and watching planes cross the sky. Sutter raised the coffee carafe and pointed at an empty mug. I nodded.

"How's the little dude?" Sutter asked, pouring.

"Happy," I said. "Crying. Elena too."

Shelly nodded sagely, her blue forelock sweeping across her pale face. "Shit, yeah. They're tight."

I drank some coffee. It was thick and biting. "She never said anything about who was looking for him?"

Shelly shook her head. "I told you — she didn't say much about anything. She talked about Siggy — about clocking some Westside john and taking off from one of his apartments, and that Siggy was going to skin her alive. She said nothing about the kid's problems."

Sutter chuckled to himself. "Need-to-know, huh?"

"Fuckin'-A," Shelly agreed. "Ellie doesn't give away shit. Getting her to tell about Siggy was like pulling teeth, and even then it was only 'cause she had to — I had to know who we were running from if I was going to help her run."

I drank more coffee, leaned back against the picnic table, and stretched my legs. I'd gotten maybe two hours sleep the night before, and my head was flopping like a sawdust doll's. The sky was milky, and there was a tang of kerosene that waxed and waned with the passing planes. But the air was soft, and the small breeze carried the smell of bread baking not far away. My stomach grumbled. Sutter laughed.

"Got a couple of popovers here," he said, and slid a pink bakery box across the table. "Fresh this morning."

I took one from the box and pulled it apart. The warm yeasty smell made me dizzy. I ate it and drank more coffee, but when Sutter offered another I shook my head. I rose. "No," I said, stretching. "I've got to pull some teeth."

"Didn't know you were a dentist too," Shelly said, and laughed.

Elena had made toast for Alex, and sliced an apple and some cheese for him. They were sitting at the little kitchen table, and she held his arm and watched him as he ate, as if a wind might carry him off if her grip or her vigilance faltered. Alex looked up as I came in. He smiled.

"How goes it, bud?" I said.

"Good," he said behind a mouthful of apple.

"He is hungry," Elena said.

I nodded. "Alex, you okay taking your

breakfast out back? You remember Shelly?" Alex smiled and nodded. "She's out back with my friend Ben. They're watching the planes come and go. They fly low, and it's kind of cool."

Alex looked at Elena, uncertain, and she looked at me.

"We need to talk," I said.

Elena's face sagged. She squeezed his arm and nodded. "Go, *pui,*" she told the boy. "But finish the food."

I held the kitchen door for Alex, and he carried his plate from the table. I ruffled his hair as he passed, and then I took his seat.

Elena stared at me, her oval face still and utterly opaque. She picked up the paring knife.

"You want toast? Apple?" she asked. I shook my head. She smiled thinly. "You just want a story, huh?"

"I need to know what's going on, Elena. If you want help, you —"

Her face tightened. "I don't want help."

"Then you're stupid."

Elena straightened and almost smiled. "Thank you, doctor. Very kind."

"Stupid — because you obviously need help, you and Alex both. And I'll give it to you, but you need to tell me what I'm in the middle of."

"You are going to help me? How? You go-
ing to scare that Russian prick away? Or the
Brays? You got more money than them?
More soldiers?"

I sighed. "I can't know what to do until I
know what's going on."

Her fist tightened around the paring knife.
"What's to know? I sold myself to Siggy to
get here, I run from him, I take back my
kid, and here we are. Good enough story?"

"I already knew most of that."

"Then why you asking?"

I sat back, crossed my legs, folded my
hands in my lap, and said nothing.

Elena muttered something and ran a hand
through her hair. "I don't know where is
the start. I don't know where it begins."

"How long have you been here?" I asked.

"In Los Angeles? Three months and
twenty-two days. For nineteen days before,
I was traveling here."

"Traveling from Romania?"

She nodded. "From Lanurile. A little town
— village — not so far from Constanţa."

"On the Black Sea?"

"Lanurile is inland. A guy Kurt — friend
of my stupid brother Nico — from him I
meet another guy there — Vladi." Her
mouth twisted like there was something
spoiled in it. "Kurt tells me Vladi can get

317

me to Los Angeles, no passport, no questions. Vladi works for Siggy, getting girls. Recruiting. I take a car with him from Lanurile to Constanţa, and then to Varna, in Bulgaria. Then no more Vladi, but more people who work for Siggy. I take a truck to Burgas, and then into Greece — Xanthi, Kavala, some other place on the coast, I don't know where. Then a little boat across to Athens. From there, a plane to Canada — Montreal — then a plane to Vancouver. Last part was a boat down here. San Pedro."

"That's a long road."

She nodded. "You don't know," she said softly.

"Alex was with you?"

Elena shook her head. "He has been here more than a year."

"You traveled by yourself?"

"There were other girls — getting into truck, getting off if they cry or complain too much. Disappearing. I don't know who they were or where they go. And there were men — the ones who drove, the ones who watched us. The ones who . . . They all work for Siggy."

Elena's voice choked and her face hardened. "There was a doctor too — in Constanţa — to make sure I was healthy enough, no AIDS or anything else. That I was worth to send all the way to Los Angeles. I don't know if he was any good — he smelled of cherry brandy and he didn't even know I had a baby. Maybe I could've told him I was virgin and he'd believe it. Anyway, he says I'm healthy — good to send — so they should take care with me. So that was something."

"Did they take care with you?"

Her laugh was short, metallic, and full of hate. "Sure. When they raped me in Varna, and again in Burgas, and in Xanthi, and in Athens, it was only one guy at a time, and they used condoms, and didn't cut me. So, sure, better than some girls."

For a moment I couldn't get enough air into my lungs, and then I couldn't get it out again. "I'm sorry," I said finally. "I'm sorry that that happened to you."

Elena shook her head. Her hand was tight around the paring knife. "It's not like I didn't know, doctor. They tell the girls some story about how jobs are waiting for them — nanny, maid, whatever. It's bullshit, but some girls believe, or pretend to. Me — I knew."

"Then why did you do it?"

She squinted at me, as if I'd asked why the sun rose. "You don't have kid," she said finally. "Otherwise, you know — there's *nothing* you wouldn't do. *Nothing.* There's nothing I wouldn't do to get here — to get him back."

"There wasn't another way for you to come over?"

"What other way? Those bastards left me empty pockets. No money, no family, no passport or visa, and they owned the fucking cops there — they buy anyone they need in the fucking government. I had nothing."

"Which bastards are you —"

"Brays, Brays — who else I am talking about? They buy what they want, and they take everything else. Like they take my *bunica* — my grandma — who raise me. Like they take Nico, my stupid brother. Just like they take my boy."

"Kyle is his father?"

Elena flicked her hand as if she were shooing a bee, and she looked as if she might spit. "They say Alex is theirs — like they own him, like he's a car or house, or one of their companies. He is not owned." She took a deep breath, and a vein in her neck pulsed rapidly, as if she were sprinting.

"How did you get tangled up with the Brays?"

"Tangled?"

"Involved. How did you meet them?"

"Through Nico. My brother worked with many foreign companies in Bucharest. He help them do business — show them how things are done there, introduce them to people in ministries, in unions, in the prefectures. Nico knows everybody, some big people, yes, and all of the people in the middle — the ones who really do things. So he helps these foreign companies get permits for things — buildings, whatever, helps them with licenses, documents for import, export, this kind of thing."

"He was a fixer."

She didn't know the expression, and furrowed her brow until she decided it worked. "Fixer — yes. He fixed things for these foreign companies, so everything worked for them. For the foreign people too. He take them around Bucharest, the places to eat, the places to party. The places to meet people. To meet girls."

"He did that for Kyle Bray?"

Elena looked at the tabletop, her hands, the knife. She tightened her grip on the handle. "Yes," she said softly. "Nico worked for a company the Brays bought — Petroplan Ploieşti — and Kyle came to Bucharest to run it. To play at running it. Nico was fixing things for them, and he liked Kyle — liked his cars and suits and his big watches.

Liked how Kyle spent his money — how much he didn't care about it. Of course, this is what they care about most, the Brays.

"So Nico fixed a job for me with Petroplan. The company was trying to win a contract with the Ministry of Industry, and they are hiring people. I was in school for geology until our *bunica* got sick and I had to go back to Lanurile, and my English was good enough, and I knew the technical words for things. Nico got me a job as a translator."

"You met Kyle there?"

Elena nodded. "He saw me in the office and said he needed an interpreter. My speaking English wasn't good enough, I told him. He didn't care." Elena shifted her grip on the paring knife, holding it like a pencil, and she poked delicately — poke, poke, poke — again and again, at the wedge of Swiss on the table.

"You worked for him?"

She nodded. "Work, and more than work." Poke, poke, poke. "I . . . I don't know why."

"You must've liked him."

She looked up at me and nodded. "Maybe for the same reasons Nico liked him. The car, the clothing, the big suite at the Carol Parc. The dinners and the drink. He didn't know anything about Romania, but he seemed to know everything else. It was like a movie . . . like he came from another planet, where they know so much more than us it's like . . . magic." Poke, poke, poke. "Yes, I liked that."

"So what happened?"

"Happened? We run around Bucharest for six months. I'm basically living at the Carol Parc with him. We're out every night, drinking, dancing, big parties, whatever. We go away on weekends, to Constanţa, to Istanbul, even to Dubai and Paris. I don't go to the office anymore, and he barely does. The business — Petroplan — I guess is going to shit, but he doesn't care too much. Then the father comes to town."

She pronounced the word *father* with a strangled snarl, and buried the knife hilt deep in the cheese. She looked at me and worked the blade free. "The father comes, and that is the end of things."

"His father wasn't happy."

Elena smiled grimly, and rose from the table. She walked around the kitchen, the knife still in her hand. Her movements were slow and cautious, guarded, but she showed no signs of pain.

"Not happy. Not with anything. Not with Petroplan, not with Kyle. Not with me. He comes to Bucharest on a Monday morning

— walks right into the suite at the Carol Parc. The hotel manager is cringing like a dog behind him. He stands at the end of our bed with his . . . his soldiers. He's looking at us, not speaking, just shaking his big head. Then he says something to his guards, and they open the curtains and turn on the shower and pull Kyle from bed and carry him to the bathroom. Kyle doesn't even fight. The father takes a suit from the closet, and a shirt, and goes into the bathroom after him and closes the door. I hear voices, but I can't understand anything — I'm just trying to cover myself, and the guards are staring. Finally, the door opens and Kyle and the father come out. Kyle is looking at the ground, walking between his father and a guard. He doesn't say anything to me, or even look. He walks out, and the rest of them walk out, and I'm alone. Alone until the maid comes and tells me I have hour to leave or they call the police."

I watched her as she moved carefully about — watched her face, which remained shuttered, watched her breathing, which had settled down, watched her hand around the knife. She was silent for a long while, and then she sighed.

"I went back to Lanurile that night. I had nothing in Bucharest, nowhere to go. My flatmates had rented out my room. Nico didn't want to see me. He was mad when I called, said I'd screwed up a good thing and cost him a customer. I had my clothes and whatever money I could find around the hotel room, so I got on a train. My *bunica* was happy to see me."

Elena returned to the table and sat. She sighed again and looked at nothing.

"You were pregnant then?"

Her eyes flashed and she looked at me hard. "I didn't know then; I didn't know for six weeks. After, there was no mistake. So tired, throwing up like crazy . . ." Her voice grew soft and there was a wistfulness to it. Then she shivered. "My *bunica* knew. She took care of me. Of us. She was the only one."

"Your brother didn't help?"

Her mouth turned bitter. "Nico? No. I didn't hear from him at all. He was traveling then, taking Germans and Russians all over the country. He didn't call us or visit, not for years."

"And no help from Kyle?"

Elena shook her head. "What help did we need? When I stopped throwing up, I got a job. Nothing much — there was a factory not far, and it had an office. I worked there awhile, and they let me come back after

Alex was born.

"And then, for short time, everything was okay. Fine. I went to work. My *bunica* took care of the boy, and she worked too, like she always did — washing clothes, ironing, mending. She even made dresses. They all looked like the curtains in her kitchen, made everybody look like potatoes in a flowered sack, but the old ladies liked them." Elena smiled and chuckled softly. "We were okay. Fine. Until Nico decides after a few years it's time to visit." Elena rose again, and this time she froze in the middle, and put a hand to her belly. Her face was gray.

"You all right?" I said, and put a hand out.

She brushed it away and shook her head. "First time I see Nico since Bucharest. Last time too."

"Was he still angry at you?"

"No, no — he was . . . he was friendly. He had a new car, money in his pocket, and he wanted to be friends. He brought flowers and chocolates and a bolt of fancy fabric for our *bunica*, and he had Italian wine and a bottle of vodka, and . . . then he saw Alex. He saw his nephew for the first time."

"He didn't know you'd had a baby?"

"He didn't know anything," Elena said. She walked to the sink, touched the taps, but didn't run the water. "Nico just stared at Alex, watched him chase a little football — soccer ball — around the sitting room. Finally, he asks how old, and I tell him almost four years, and I see him doing sums. Then he asks if that bastard sends us money, and I say he should leave it alone. I tell him the Brays know nothing about Alex, and that he's not their business, and he should leave it alone. But I can tell by his voice and his crazy eyes and how red his face is getting that he won't. I beg and plead with him, and so does our *bunica.* We cry, we get angry, but it doesn't matter to Nico. He's drinking the vodka from the bottle, the wheels are turning in his head, and he doesn't listen. He drives to Bucharest that night.

"Two days after, the police call. Nico's car went off a road somewhere, and into a ditch, and there was a fire, and maybe bears or an earthquake too. I didn't know what the hell they were saying, but I knew it didn't matter. I knew they were full of shit. I knew what happened to him." She touched the taps again, and this time she turned them on and watched the water.

"What did you think happened?"

"Not *think,* doctor — I *know.* I *know* what happened. Nico went to Kyle and wanted money and God knows what else. He got paid another way."

"Kyle was still in Romania?"

"Oh yes. Petroplan was running fine again — better than ever. They bought other companies, they get bigger, important contracts with the government, and Kyle was the big fish in the little sea."

"And you knew that Nico went to see him?"

She nodded over the sink, and took the steel plug from the drain. She turned the taps some more, and the water flowed faster. "I knew Nico, and I knew what he did. I just never knew they would . . . I never thought of it." And then Elena vomited into the sink.

I was at her side fast, and caught her around the shoulders. She shrugged my arm off and pushed me away. She rinsed her mouth and spit, then wiped her lips on the back of her hand. She ran water in the sink until the vomit was gone.

"Are you —"

"I'm fine. It comes whenever I . . . It comes every time."

I nodded. "What happened next?" I asked.

"What happened? I went to work the next day, and the days after that. I had to go — I needed that job. But the policeman who called me, to tell about Nico, I called him up to tell him what really happened. He didn't want to hear from me — not at all. He was angry and said he was busy, and that I could get in trouble with that kind of talk. He said I should never call back. I didn't care. On the weekend, I went to Bucharest, to talk to police face-to-face. That was worse. These two guys, they put me in a room for hours, with no water or food, no one else, no bathroom. Then they questioned me about Nico — did we get along, where was I that night, that kind of thing. They yelled and slammed the table and grabbed my arms, and it was midnight when they finally threw me out and told me never to come back. Fucking bastards."

She wiped her mouth again and looked at her hands. "Then, the next week, I start seeing a car, a big black SUV with black windows, like we don't see in Lanurile, parked down the street, parked outside my work, near the market, parked everywhere I go. I look at it or walk toward it, it drives away. I go a different way to work or the market, it's behind me anyway. This goes on for two weeks. I talk to the police — not the pricks in Bucharest, the local pricks — and they do nothing. But nothing. They laugh."

Elena turned quickly and bent over the sink, and I thought she might vomit again, but she didn't. "Then, one day — a Tuesday — I go to work and, finally, I don't see the car. Nowhere. And when I get home, my *bunica*'s apartment is like . . . It looks like thieves were there, or animals — everything smashed, broken, torn apart. And blood." Elena's voice tightened and stopped. She was breathing hard.

"Your grandmother?" I said after a while.

"Dead. Beaten. Arm broke, ribs broke, neck broke. She is seventy-one. Did she even weigh fifty kilos?"

"And Alex?"

"Gone," she whispered, and her shoulders shook and fat tears fell down her cheeks. She covered her face with her hands, and the tears seeped between her fingers.

I put my hand on her back, and she shuddered but didn't shake it off. Her skin was burning through the thin fabric of her shirt. "Sit down," I said. "Let me get you some water."

"I don't want water, and I don't want to sit. You wanted your story, and you're going to have it." Her voice was low and choked. "I called the police, and they came and looked around and talked to some neighbors. And finally they say it is robbery. Thieves. Thieves steal my child, and steal my grandmother's life."

I shook my head. "What about the kidnapping? Didn't they do something about that?"

"It's like they were sleeping, those bastards. They did nothing. They take a picture of him from me — that's it. They say they talk to neighbors, put out bulletins, but find nothing. They *do* nothing."

"You told them about the SUV, about Kyle?"

"It's the first thing I say. I say I know who did this! I say where to look for my boy — who to talk to! They look like I'm telling them to clean the toilets. They tell me they talk to Kyle, or to *his people. His people* say he went back to America weeks before, and *his people* don't know nothing about my boy. But they know enough to tell the police that I'm some kind of crazy woman, some crazy ex-girlfriend."

"Did you try the U.S. Embassy? If they took him out of the country, they would've had to get him a passport."

She laughed bitterly. "You think Kyle travels on a regular plane? You think any of them do? They have their own planes. And you think they couldn't get a little boy" — she lost her voice again, and for a while gasped for breath — "my good little boy — you think they couldn't get him on their plane without anyone seeing? You think they couldn't pay people not to see, the way they paid the bastard police in my country, and anybody else they wanted?"

"You think that's what happened?"

"I thought you had to be smart to be a doctor. Of course that's what happened. And I said so to police, people at the embassy, everybody I meet. And you know what happened? They throw me out of the embassy, out of the police station, out of my job, and out of my grandmother's apartment — right onto the street. So I take my suitcase and I go to a girl I work with — worked with — and she lets me stay with her, until, one day, a man visits. A big man, old, with big arms and short white hair, and skin like leather, and burn marks along here." Elena ran a hand along the side of her neck.

"Conti," I said.

"I don't know his name, but I see him right before I come into your clinic with Alex. He is one of the bastards chasing us. I see him again, I'm going to stab his eyes."

"What did he do to you back in Romania?"

"What he did? He grabs me like this" — she wrapped a hand around her own neck — "and holds me up against a wall and says if I don't shut my fucking mouth he's going to cut my tongue out. Then he throws me in a corner, goes through my things — all of my things — until he finds the little bit of money I have and my passport, my driving license, my identity cards, and these he burns right in front of me. He holds them under my nose and waves them around — I can still smell the burning — and he says, *Now you stay close to home, keep your head down, don't bother people, and maybe you get to live.* I can hear him say it."

"Christ," I whispered.

"My friend throws me out after that — she's scared — and I go to police again. This time they lock me up a few days and hit me a little. After that, I go for new passport. The ministry won't give it me, though — I got no permanent address, they say, no identification papers. Without those, it's like I'm not even a person. They throw me out, and I sleep on the street a few nights, and spend my days in the library.

"Finally, one of the ladies there, behind the counter, she takes pity on me. She lets me stay all day in the library if I do some cleaning, and she lets me sleep in back at night, on a mattress in an empty room. There's a dead rat in there, and spiders, but they got Internet, and I do a lot of reading. All about the Brays, the things they own, about Los Angeles, and about how people — girls, young ones — can travel to the States, even with no money and no documents. I knew about girls who did this, and it didn't take much to find Kurt, and then that shit Vladi." I thought for a moment she might spit on the floor, but she shook her head and wiped a hand across her mouth. She looked at me.

"When I get here, Siggy puts me in apartments, first near airport, then in West Hollywood. I knew before I left Romania where Brays live — I found it on the Internet, like I found the school they sent Alex to, the same school Kyle went to, with Bray library and Bray gymnasium. I knew where to find Alex, and when it was time, I . . . I took Hoover's car and his money and his clothes. I drive over to Alex's school. I park, I wait, and when he is on playground, and people are not watching, he comes with me. We run."

Elena sighed deeply, and ran a hand through her hair. "So now you got my story, doctor. You happy now?"

I was exhausted, shocked, deeply sad, and more than a little nauseated, but not remotely happy. I sat at the table again and rubbed my eyes. "And now what?" I asked. "Now that you have Alex, what're you going to do?"

Elena ran cold water, drank from the faucet, and splashed some on her face. "Do? I want to go home, doctor — I want to take my little boy home. But it turns out I got no passport, no money, no home to go to. And the only people I know with these things is the fucking Brays. They got to pay, doctor. They got to pay for me and Alex."

CHAPTER 31

I never saw Kabul Tommy, but when he left he was replaced by Yossi, a tall guy with a three-day beard, a deep tan, and a line of Chinese characters tattooed down the side of his neck. He wore wraparound shades and an automatic on his hip, and Sutter said he would stay with Elena and Alex and Shelly for a while. When we left, Elena and Alex were in the kitchen, holding hands and whispering, and Shelly was staring into space. Yossi was at the front window, scanning the street.

Sutter swung the Escalade onto Acacia and then Loma Vista, and drove widening circles around the house, looking for a long time at cars parked on the street. Finally, he turned onto Sepulveda, headed north. He looked at me.

"What's the deal with your girl?" he asked.

I told him what Elena had told me, and Sutter listened and nodded occasionally.

When I was done, he let out a long breath.

"She's badass," he said. "Like a fox that chews its leg off to get out of a trap."

"If it's true."

"You have doubts?"

"First thing we learned in med school: patients lie."

"And not just them," Sutter said, laughing. "But this particular patient . . . ?" He raised his eyebrows quizzically.

I watched the traffic stop and go in Culver City, and squinted into the hard glare off windshields and car hoods and white pavement. We drove beneath the 405, and the darkness of the underpass was a relief.

"I don't know," I said. "Her story explains why the Brays haven't gone to the cops; I'm just not sure it's the whole story. She's not the most forthcoming person I've met."

Sutter smiled. "Whole truth or not, it doesn't solve today's problems. Like getting Siggy off her back, or the Brays off of the kid's."

"Siggy wants money. As for the Brays — the only thing they want is the kid, and I don't know how to change their minds about that."

"Sounds like Elena has the start of a plan: she needs cash, and the Brays have plenty of it."

"So — what — we get the Brays to pay off Siggy? How the hell do we manage that? I expect they'd be pretty damned happy if Siggy just swallowed her whole."

"It's not about making them happy — it's about motivating them."

"Motivating them with what?"

"With what scares them."

"Murder and kidnap allegations."

Sutter nodded. "It's why they haven't called the cops, right? If you buy Elena's story."

"But we have nothing to make those allegations stick — nothing besides Elena's say-so. And that didn't work out too well for her back in Romania."

"Maybe they don't need to stick. Assholes like the Brays might be bothered by the charges alone — especially if they were made in public and very loud."

"So that's the plan — threaten to say bad things about the Brays on Facebook unless they pony up some cash?"

"I wouldn't say it was exactly a plan yet," Sutter said as we turned onto Culver Boulevard. "You have something better?"

I thought about it for a while, as I watched shopping strips and gas stations and crappy little apartment buildings slide by. Finally, I shook my head.

"Not a damn thing," I said.

It was past noon when he dropped me at the clinic. There were no afternoon hours that Saturday, and Lydia and Lucho had seen the morning's patients and already locked up. The clinic was cool and quiet inside, the street noise muted and far off. There were messages on my desk, three of them from my landlord, Tony Kashmarian, and one from our lawyer, Anne Crane. I looked at the pink slips and thought about what they might want, and then I heard a tired sigh and the sound of papers from down the hall.

Lydia was at the desk in the records room. She had a stack of charts before her, and a chipped coffee mug that said *Big Nurse* on it. She'd taken her scrub top off, and the blue tee shirt underneath had a faded marlin on it. She looked up at me; in the cone of dusty light from the gooseneck lamp, she looked a couple of decades older than her fifty-five years.

She sighed again, more deeply this time. "I didn't think you were gonna show," she said. Her voice was low and scratchy.

"Not too bad this morning, I hope."

"Pretty slow, for us. Two more cases of the runs. A guy from the flower market who had too many Red Bulls and vodka and thought he was having a coronary. An eight-year-old girl with a fractured arm."

I leaned in the doorway. "Shit," I said. "We know her?"

"Never seen her, or the woman who brought her in."

"She wasn't the mother?"

Lydia shrugged. "She said she was."

"You think she was beating on the girl?"

Lydia turned her palms up like a scale. "Not sure."

"You call Family Services?"

She shook her head. "No clear indicators. I put the girl in an air cast and sent them to County. Told an ER nurse over there to keep an eye out, but who knows if they'll show up."

It was my turn to sigh. I took a folding metal chair from the corner, opened it, and sat across the desk from her. "There any more of that?" I asked, pointing to her mug.

"Help yourself." She slid the mug across to me.

I drank and made a face. "That sucks."

"Bottom of the pot. How's Shelly doing?" I told her, and she nodded. "And Elena?" I told her that too, and that Danni had brought Alex to his mom that morning.

"That's good," she said. "That's nice. For

him. For her too. And now that they're back together, what next?" she asked. "They going on their way?"

I looked into Lydia's coffee mug, at the muddy dregs. "It's not a simple situation," I said.

Lydia took a file off the stack in front of her, swiveled in her chair, and started typing. "Of course not," she said softly.

Her back was solid, and there was a faint line of sweat on her blue tee shirt, along her spine. I watched her for a while, and then I took a deep breath and told her Elena's story. At some point she stopped typing, but she didn't turn around. The quiet was thick in the little room when I'd finished, and then Lydia began to type again.

"There's nothing you can do for them," she said after a while.

"I'm not sure."

"That wasn't a question, doctor. I'm saying: there's nothing you can do for them. Their trouble is big and complicated; you can't solve it."

I sighed and rubbed my eyes. "Half the people who come here have big, complicated problems. We help them."

"We *patch* them. We get them well, some of them, or well enough so they maybe can get back on their feet. So they can go on a

341

while longer. That's all we do — that's all we *can* do, and it's more than most. But sometimes — like with this girl and her little boy — you get an idea that you can . . . I don't know what. Fix them? Fix their lives?"

"Don't you ever want that, Lyd — something more than a temporary patch? Don't you want an outright win sometimes?"

Lydia wiped a hand across her forehead and looked at me with a mix of disbelief and pity. "You know better, doctor — you know, unless you got a magic wand, that's not gonna happen. And while you try, you're risking this place."

"I'm not risking —"

"Sure you are. Those people she's involved with — they have a lot of juice. More than enough to shut us down. And those Russian pigs — I'm surprised they haven't torched this place already. They still might."

Lydia turned in her chair. Her face was lined and sagging. "I know you worry about the people who come in here, doctor, even the ones you don't see. I tell you about some girl with a fracture and you're worried she's in trouble, and you don't even know her. You care about them. So don't you want to keep doing what you can for them? Why put that at risk?"

"I'm . . . I'm not."

She pursed her lips and looked at me for a long time. Then she shook her head. "I'm going out to the desert this weekend, with Junie. We're going to work on that cabin of his. No Russians, no skinheads in polo shirts, just sandpaper and paint — nice and quiet. Nice when we have some of that around here."

My face burned. "Lydia, I —"

She reached across the desk and put her heavy hand against my neck. "I'm not looking for promises, *chico* — I know what happens with those." Then she patted my cheek and picked up her coffee mug. "Now, go away. I got all this shit to update."

"You want some help?"

Lydia laughed and shook her head. "That's almost funny, doctor."

CHAPTER 32

My apartment smelled of old coffee and dust and weed. I slung my backpack on a chair, emptied my pockets on the table, kicked off my shoes, and stretched out on the bed. I thought that the night on the sofa in El Segundo would catch up with me and that sleep would come fast, but I was wrong. Elena's voice whirled in my head, not her words but the sound of it: its hard, dispassionate shell, the way it broke in places, the pain and molten rage that surged in the cracks. I looked at the ceiling — white and shot with fault lines — and after a while Lydia's voice mixed with Elena's. Fear, fatigue, and a hefty slug of fatalism sifted with anger, like flour in a bowl. I touched my cheek where Lydia had patted it. She'd never done that before.

But sometimes — like with this girl and her little boy — you get an idea that you can . . . I don't know what. Fix them? Fix their lives?

Dangerous fantasy, I knew — paving stones on the road to hell. I wished I could say that Lydia had it all wrong.

I awoke from a dream about Africa: the forested hills around my last field station, the dense, corrugated green, the screaming and thrashing in the branches sometimes, at dawn and dusk, the silence that descended before a storm, Mathieu standing on a trail that led into the woods. . . . I tried to find the narrative, but the dream broke and faded as I chased it.

I sat up and ran my hands through my hair. I was looking at my dresser and wondering which drawer might have some weed in it when the phone rang. It was Anne Crane.

"I left you messages," she said. Her voice was scratchy and tired, and there were traffic sounds and wind behind it. I pictured her in front of her firm's Century City office building, her cropped gray hair tousled by the breeze, a cigarette dangling from her lip. Anne and her pro bono efforts had come with the clinic — along with the crumbling infrastructure and the negative cash flow. I didn't know what debt she owed my predecessor, Dr. Carmody, only that it was something big. I was just grateful she didn't yet feel it paid in full.

"I got them. You still smoking?"

"Bad enough I'm in the office on a Saturday — I don't need guilt. Did you get Kashmarian's messages too?"

"Yep. I haven't called him either."

"Well, I can save you the minutes. He wants to tell you he has an offer on your building."

I stood. "An offer? I thought I had months before it was even on the market."

"You do, technically."

"Technically?"

"Kashmarian can't offer it for sale for another three months, and you have right of first refusal, but, assuming you don't make a matching offer, he's saying he's already got a willing buyer lined up. Someone who reached out to him."

"For this place? Who?"

"He didn't volunteer that."

"How would anybody even know it's for sale?"

"Beats me. How does anybody know anything in this town?"

"Did he say what the offer was?"

There was silence on the line, and then Anne cleared her throat. "He said they came in at full ask."

"For *this* place? Full fucking ask?"

"Calm down. That's just what his message said. I haven't actually spoken to him yet, so who knows if it's true."

"Shit." I sighed. "I can't match full ask."

"We don't even know if it's for real yet," Anne Crane said again. "But in the event . . . do you have a Plan B?" I said nothing, and Anne sighed. "I'll take that as a no, despite the fact that I've been telling you to make one for the past six months."

"My plan is to put together a down payment."

"Fantastic. How much do you have?"

"A hundred grand."

Anne made a noise that might have been a laugh being stifled. "That's it — a hundred? A hundred thousand? That's a down payment on, like, a toolshed. And not in a good neighborhood."

"That's what I've got so far. I'm still working on it."

"You better work faster," she said.

It was after eight by the time I found parking off Los Feliz Boulevard. The air was cool on my face as I walked toward Hillhurst. I'd managed no more sleep that afternoon, just fitful turning in my bed for a while, and then much coffee and a scan through that week's medical journals — all the while trying not to think about the Brays or Siggy circling the clinic like sharks. My eyes were still gritty and hot.

I was meeting Nora at Airstream. Like the trailer, it was low-slung and industrial, shiny and metallic. Everything there looked new, including the customers, who seemed fresh out of school — possibly middle school.

Bright faces were gathered at the bar, which was shaped like an airplane wing, and I scanned its length for Nora, pausing at each dark ponytail. I found her at the far end, leaning away from an eager hipster with white arms, a belly like a soft volleyball, a smudge of beard on his chin, and a turquoise bowling shirt with an old Northrop logo on the pocket. He scowled when I walked up. Nora smiled, drained her wineglass, dropped off her stool, and smoothed her flowered skirt. "Good luck with that pilot," she said to the hipster, and hooked her arm in mine.

Our table was outside, where it was cooler and the sky was purple. We were near a gas fire, burning in a wide copper brazier, and the heat rolled across me in waves. Its flickering light made Nora's face quick, sinister, and sexy.

The waitress came and Nora asked for another glass of wine. I had coffee. Nora squinted at me. "Planning a wild night?"

I shook my head. "Anything stronger and I'll be having a pillow and blanket for dinner." She raised an eyebrow and tilted her head, and I took a deep breath and once again told Elena's story. It was the third time that day, and that just made it worse.

Nora was still and silent when I finished. A chopped salad had been delivered at some point, but she hadn't touched it. "Jesus, Adam," she said finally. Her voice was soft. "This woman, her son — they need help."

"I know," I said, and pushed away my salmon.

She leaned toward me. "I mean, *serious* help."

"I know that. That's why —"

"Help you can't give them. If her story is true, this woman has been the victim of several violent crimes, including multiple rapes. She's lost her close family to murder, lost her son to abduction, and been forced into sex slavery. She's massively traumatized — almost certainly suffering from PTSD — and her little boy . . . God only knows what he's been through, what he's seen. You've done what you can for them — you saved both of their lives and brought them together — but you're not equipped for what they need now."

"I know I'm not, but what am I supposed to do?"

"Call DCFS, or the police, or both."

"And then what happens? Elena's an illegal, a sex worker, a witness to who knows how many crimes that Siggy Rostov and his boys have committed — not to mention the miscellaneous felonies she's committed herself. Do you honestly think the authorities are going to let Alex stay with her? And that's without Harris Bray putting his thumb on the scale. How long do you think it'll take him to get ahold of Alex again, once cops get involved?"

"None of that is certain. And are you sure that it wouldn't be in Alex's best interests to be back with his father and grandparents?"

I sat up. "Back with the people who arranged for his abduction, and caused most of the shit that's happened to his mother? You can't believe that."

Nora shook her head. "Everything I know is secondhand, so I don't know what to believe. Which is okay, since I'm not setting myself up to make custody decisions for Alex."

"If you saw him with Elena, how they are together, you'd know they belong together."

Nora nodded slowly and swept a wing of

black hair behind her ear. She picked up her wineglass, swirled it, and took a sip. "The bond between them isn't the only consideration. With what Elena's been through, she may not be the best person to look after Alex — not right now, at least. Her behavior might be erratic. Her judgment might be impaired."

"I've seen traumatized mothers and children before — whole villages of them, half a country, it seemed like — and I don't know that separating kids from their moms improved anybody's health."

"These circumstances are different from what you saw in Africa, and you know it." I shrugged, and Nora's mouth became a hard line. "Anyway, DCFS actually specializes in making those kinds of calls."

The look on my face made Nora pause, sit back, and change tacks. "Do you believe everything that Elena's told you?" she asked.

"I'm not sure she's told me everything, but I think the part she's told me is true."

"Doesn't it bother you that she might be holding back?"

"What she's been through doesn't make people trusting. I'm more bothered by the fact that the Brays still haven't called the cops. Like that's not too suspicious — people with that kind of sway, reluctant to use it. Or how about their approach to this whole thing — strong-arm tactics, and offers of a bribe? Do they sound like people with nothing to hide?"

"Which is a great reason not to get involved with them."

"And also a great reason not to hand them that little boy."

"Point taken," she said. "And very heroic." She wasn't smiling.

We prodded and picked at our food after that, but ate little and spoke less. I had another coffee and Nora had another glass of wine.

A thaw set in when we left Airstream and walked along Hillhurst, and when we turned onto Franklin, Nora leaned close and took my hand. We were on Vermont, headed for Skylight Books, when a silver Mercedes pulled up ahead of us and rocked to a halt with its front tire over the curb. The driver's door swung wide and scraped against asphalt. Climbing from the car, Kyle Bray seemed not to notice.

He wore a dark-blue shirt with the sleeves pushed up, gray trousers, black loafers with no socks, and black aviators. When he pulled them off, his eyes were red and unfocused, his pupils pinpricks. He smiled and pointed at us, and I moved in front of

Nora. My pulse revved.

"You took your time over dinner, doc," Kyle said. He had a drunk's overcareful pronunciation. "You order everything on the menu?"

"You're following me now, Kyle?"

He leaned back against the Mercedes. "I have people who do that. They called when it looked like you were staying put for a while."

"What do you want? Mandy said —"

"I don't fucking answer to my bitch cousin, doc."

"Do you answer to your father? Because I caught sight of him at PRP, giving Mandy what looked a lot like marching orders."

Kyle's face tightened and his voice was brittle. "When it comes to my kid, *no one* tells me what to do."

"That's nice, Kyle — touching — but I don't want to get caught in the middle of a family feud. Maybe you, your dad, and Mandy should sit down and make sure you're all on the same page with the threats and everything, just so I don't get confused. And maybe then I could say it just once, to all of you: that I really can't help you out."

Kyle snorted. "Too late for that, doc — you're already in the middle. But something you might think about is how many other people you want to drag in with you. Like, for example, your girlfriend here. That's who she is, right — your girlfriend?" I said nothing, and Kyle smiled. "Though she's no girl, is she? She's got a nice MILF-y thing going on." Behind me, Nora snorted.

I sighed. "What do you want?" I asked again.

"You know the answer to that, asshole — I want my kid."

"And you know what I've said every other time you people have asked. Did I not say it loud enough, or do you have some kind of aphasia? Or are you just fucking stupid? Maybe that's why Daddy put you on the bench and put Mandy in the game instead."

Kyle colored, and balled his fists. Then he took a deep breath. He looked past me, at Nora. "All the tough talk for her benefit? You like an audience?"

I shrugged. "Maybe you want to step away, and we can finish what we started back in that conference room."

Kyle laughed. "That's tempting, doc — believe me. But I've got plans with two blondes and a suite in Vegas tonight, and I'm not gonna fuck those up, even to kick the teeth out of your head."

A Volvo cruised by and slowed as it passed Kyle's Mercedes, angled into the curb. The driver honked and stared and shook her head.

"What the fuck are you looking at, bitch?" Kyle yelled, and grabbed his crotch. "You see something you like?" The woman blanched and sped off, and Kyle laughed.

I cleared my throat. "Then I remain confused, Kyle. I don't get why your men are following me around, or why you're here. You have nothing new to say to me, and I have shit to say to you, so —"

"That's where you're wrong, doc — I do have something new. I'm here to introduce you to your new landlord." Then he put out his hand and laughed.

CHAPTER 33

Monday was like any other day at the clinic, which itself seemed odd. After a Saturday evening of incipient argument with Nora, and stalking and threat from Kyle, and a Sunday of sleep — interrupted only by making rounds in El Segundo — a typical workday, full only of the sick and their treatment, was disorienting and strange. Like the calm after a storm. Or before one.

Though probably not what most people would consider a calm. The norovirus continued its march through our corner of the city, and we saw three more miserable and messy cases, along with an unmanaged hypertensive, an unmanaged diabetic, a badly infected spider bite, two STDs, miscellaneous lacerations, sprains, and fractures, and a pale and wiry young woman in the waiting room who wore sweatpants, an overlarge pink tee shirt, and a layer of grime, and who started screaming when

Lucho asked her name. Somewhere in the midst of it all, Mrs. Guzman delivered a cake.

We had vaccinated her three granddaughters several weeks back and treated the youngest for ringworm on her scalp, and because she hadn't been able to pay us for any of it, she'd made a *tres leches* cake and brought it in a foil pan. The custard smell filled the office, and my stomach crooned to it all afternoon. It was five-thirty before I made my way to the file room for a slice and a coffee, and when I did, the baking pan was empty and the coffee pot was dry. I stared at them, feeling forlorn.

"Fucking Lucho," I muttered.

"Don't worry," Lydia said, "I'm looking out for you." She was in the doorway, holding a steaming mug of coffee and a big square of cake on a paper plate. "My boy's got a sweet tooth, so I knew to put some aside for you." Lydia smiled at me, and her stern features softened. I felt a rush of affection for her, followed immediately by a rush of guilt. I hadn't told Lydia about the bid on our building — hadn't told her about a lot of things lately — and I didn't have the energy or courage to start just then.

"You're the best, Lyd."

"You bet your ass," she said, and handed

me the coffee and the cake.

I was about to have a bite when my cell burred. It said *unknown caller* on the screen, and I thought for a moment about not answering, but then I did.

Mandy's voice was arch and teasing. "It's been *days,* doctor — *days.* I'm not used to waiting so long for a guy to call. But I guess being the savior of the dispossessed is a full-time gig. Or are there other things that have kept you hopping?"

I looked at the cake. "I have patients, Mandy."

She giggled. "I'm sure you do. And I have *patience,* doctor, but it's not infinite."

"I don't know what to tell you."

"Tell me that you've decided what you want. Tell me what I can do for you."

I laughed. "What is this — good cop, bad cop with you and Kyle?"

There was silence for a moment, and then a deep breath. "What are you talking about?"

"I'm talking about Kyle, two nights ago — following me, accosting me on the street, threatening me. Are you going to pretend that's news?"

Mandy sighed. "I had no idea, doctor — really. Kyle gets out of hand sometimes."

"You'll forgive my skepticism. And you'll

forgive me if I get back to work." I put my phone down and picked up the paper plate and put it down again, because my appetite was gone.

I got out of the clinic just after dark, and drove west until I got to The Grove. I pulled into the big white parking structure, up the ramps to the fourth level, and into a space not far from a stairwell. I got out and locked my car, and Sutter appeared from the shadows.

"Shopping at Crate and Barrel today?" I asked. Sutter smiled minutely, glanced behind him, and said nothing. I followed him to the stairs. "Was that your Escalade I passed on three?" He nodded.

We walked up to the fifth level and found a gray Mazda there, parked facing out. Sutter opened it and we got in and drove. We took Fairfax out of The Grove, and went south and west, toward El Segundo.

I looked over at him. "If not Crate and Barrel, then what's with The Grove? And what's with the car swap?"

Sutter chuckled this time and checked the mirrors. "Siggy's boys have been like lint on me today. He's using lots of bodies and not trying to hide any of 'em. It's not subtle, but it gets the job done. Hence The Grove and the car swap."

"He doesn't care that you see his people?"

"He wants me to see — wants to make sure I haven't forgotten about him. And let me tell you — it's a real pain in the ass. I've got people to see and business to do, and none of it happens with these poodles around."

His mouth settled into a tight line and we drove in silence for a while. I watched the mirrors until everything seemed suspicious. Then I sighed.

"I had a poodle of my own on Saturday," I said, and told Sutter about my run-in with Kyle Bray. He listened and nodded imperceptibly a few times, and when I was done he looked sideways at me and laughed.

"The new landlord, huh? Maybe he'll spring for clean carpet in your waiting room."

"I'm thinking not."

"Probably right. Guy's a head case."

"I don't know if it's drugs or daddy issues or both, but his wiring is fried."

"Maybe it always was. But I bet he's extra pissed at getting sent to the kiddie table. And I'm guessing Papa Bray and the cousin won't be too happy with him wandering off the rez."

"Mandy didn't seem pleased. I just hope

they get his leash back on."

Sutter nodded and checked his mirrors again. He was mostly taking La Cienega, turning off sometimes and looping back to check for tails. The strip malls were unending and monotonous — like piles of lost luggage at the roadsides. My temples were throbbing.

Sutter pulled into a side street, into a space by a fire hydrant. He switched off the lights and the engine and watched the mirrors. They were black. He turned and looked at me.

"You're juggling chain saws, brother, and you got me juggling 'em too. It can only go on so long."

I sighed. "I know, I know, and I'm sorry. I —"

"I'm not looking for apologies, but we need to get out of this holding pattern. No more waiting around for shit to happen."

"So we do what instead?"

"We had a plan, the start of one, anyway — about squeezing the Brays, so that they lay off the kid and cough up some cash. About telling Elena's story out loud otherwise."

I looked at Sutter and said nothing.

He sighed. "We gotta do something, brother. You got crazy Kyle stalking you and buying your building out from under you; you got his daddy and the little piranha cousin threatening you; and let's not forget about Siggy."

"I haven't forgotten him."

"Neither have I, as I sit here in not-my-car. I'm thinking we get Elena on video, telling her story. Arrange it like a deposition — have her under oath, with a lawyer asking the questions — then we make a highlight reel for Bray. We threaten to put the director's cut on YouTube, or send it to MSNBC."

I thought about it and shook my head. "I just don't see how this scares someone like Harris Bray. He'll have an army of lawyers and press flacks on deck, just waiting to rack up billable hours for him. Not to mention those bullet heads from PRP."

"He's got all that firepower on tap 'cause he's a big name, brother, and that's what we've got going for us: he wants to protect himself. You know firsthand the hoops even little tiny names jump through to guard their precious reputations. Harris Bray's got a whole lot more to lose. He's got bankers and business partners to worry about, not to mention all those high-profile boards and good works he's involved with. He doesn't want all that splashed with shit. And he's

362

got political enemies too. I gotta think there're a few senators or congressmen or ambitious prosecutors who'd love to make their bones looking into these kinds of allegations."

"We go public with Elena's story, we go public with her being an illegal," I said. "Then ICE gets involved, and after that, who the hell knows what happens — to her or to Alex. Who knows where he might end up?"

"It won't come to that."

"You're sure about that?"

"Nothing's for sure, but Harris Bray — hell, all his companies and his whole damn family — have a long way to fall. I just don't think they're gonna go that route."

I sighed again, and we were quiet for a while on the dark street. "We'll need DNA tests to go along with Elena's deposition — in case the Brays try to sell their story of her not being his mom."

Sutter slapped the steering wheel and smiled. "Now you're talking."

"And we've got to get Elena's buy-in," I said. "If she says no —"

"She won't," Sutter said. "Girl wants her pound of flesh, and this is the closest she's gonna come to it." Then he started the car and pulled from the curb.

CHAPTER 34

Yossi answered the door in El Segundo with a big automatic held down along his thigh. He scanned the street as we stepped inside.

"Everything copacetic?" Sutter asked.

Yossi nodded. "Five by," he said softly.

Shelly was sprawled on the sofa, in cutoff sweats and an oversized Dodgers jersey. Her legs were thin and white, and there were old scrapes on her knees, and yellowed bruises. Her hair was tied back, all but a faded blue forelock that fell across her cheek. She looked at Sutter.

"Dude, you got something against entertainment? No Internet here, no TV — you trying to turn us into Mormons or something?"

Sutter smiled. "Mormons watch TV, little sister. You're thinking of the Amish."

"So you say. How about a cell phone?"

He shook his head. "You shouldn't be texting anybody yet, or e-mailing."

Shelly scowled. "There're gonna be people wondering about me."

"Yeah — people like Siggy," Sutter said. "I'll hook you up with some cable, and if you're really nice, maybe a book."

Shelly raised her right arm, to flip Sutter the bird, and winced. I took a knee by the sofa. "How's the shoulder?" I asked.

"Crappy," she said.

"Let's have a look," I said, pulling on a glove.

Shelly gingerly snaked her arm out from under her jersey, and looked away as I touched her.

In fact, Shelly's shoulder wasn't crappy at all. Her wounds looked okay — no signs of infection, and the sutures still nice and neat — and Shelly herself had no fever and said her appetite was good.

"Let me see you move it," I said. "Nothing too aggressive: just roll your shoulder a few times, and stretch your arm out. Stop if you feel anything pop, or tear, or if it hurts too much."

She looked skeptical. "What's too much?" she said, but went through the motions with only a wince or two. I helped her back into her shirt.

"Try doing that every couple of hours," I said.

"Sure — it's more fun than I'm having now."

"I get that you're going stir-crazy, Shelly, but —"

"Hey, I'm all good here, doc — I know what the other option is, and I don't mind the rest. But how long can we do this? A few days? A week? And then what happens? Siggy won't forget about us too fast, and who the fuck knows about those douche bags after the kid? I got family up in Portland I guess I could see, but Ellie and the kid — where're they supposed to —"

"Nobody has to go anywhere yet. We're going to figure this out."

"Yeah, definitely *figure it,* doc," Shelly said. "I just hope what you come up with involves greasing Siggy and as many of his shitbags as you can. And in the meantime" — she looked at Sutter — "some cable would be good."

Elena and Alex were in the back bedroom, cross-legged on the double bed. A copy of the *Times* was open before them, and their heads were together as they read it, as if they were trading secrets. They looked up at me. Alex smiled. Elena's face stiffened, and she nodded.

"How're you two doing?" I asked.

Elena and Alex looked at each other. She put her hand on the back of his neck. "Yes, okay. I think maybe he is hungry."

"I'm pretty sure we can do something about that," I said, and smiled back at Alex. "Come out here and we'll get you fed, and in the meantime I'll see how your mom is doing."

Alex exchanged another look with Elena and rolled off the bed. He followed me into the hall and stopped when he saw Sutter.

"You need some mess?" Sutter asked him. Alex grinned.

"Nothing with —"

"No nuts — I know, doc. C'mon, little brother."

Alex followed him, and I returned to Elena, who was folding the newspaper. Her movements were deliberate. "How about you?" I asked. "How's your appetite?"

Elena shrugged, and put the paper on the floor. "I should lie on bed?"

I nodded, and pulled on a clean pair of gloves.

Elena was unmoving as I examined her, and terse and without affect when she answered my questions. Pain is less, breathing okay; no fever; yes, eating and drinking; yes, passing water; no bowel movement yet. Her small white body still read like an atlas of violence, but, like Shelly, she seemed to be healing nicely. Her several wounds showed no signs of infection, and though her newer bruises were yet ripening, the older ones continued their yellow fade. She rose when I was done, tugged her sweatpants over her narrow hips, and tied the drawstring carefully below the dressing on her belly.

"So far, so good," I said. "You're doing okay."

Elena looked at me as if I was selling magic beans. She nodded vaguely and sat on the edge of the bed, her feet together, her white hands in her lap. "Okay to travel, then? To go on plane?"

"We have to be careful about the lung, but, yes, health-wise it should be okay for you to travel pretty soon."

"So we go home pretty soon, Alex and me."

"We need to talk about that," I said, "about how we get that to happen." And I told her about Sutter's idea: money and passage home from the Brays in exchange for silence; criminal prosecution and devastating embarrassment otherwise. When I finished, Elena frowned.

"I used to think about something like this," she said, "but then I learn a few things. About money the Brays have, and what they do with it.

"Why they gonna care what I say, or who I say it to? Why they give a shit what people think? They don't — it doesn't matter to them. They have money, so it doesn't matter. Brays want people to think something, Brays tell them what to think. They don't want you to hear something, forget it — you won't hear about it. Like it was never there, like nobody ever said anything. Things they want, happen; things they don't want, don't." She shook her head some more, and color rose in her cheeks. "Your friend's idea is no good."

"No one's saying it's certain, but they do have a lot to lose. They're a very high-profile family, with —"

"I know them, doctor," she said coolly. "I know them better than you."

"Then you know how much people like them value control. What we'd be doing by making your story public is taking some of their control away. Once your story is out there, they can't control it, can't know what the consequences might be. It makes their money and power maybe not irrelevant, but at least less of a guarantee."

Again there was the magic-bean look. "You don't know what they did to me in my own country — in the town where my grandmother lived most of her life. Every door was closed to me — everybody deaf and blind all of a sudden. People get some money in their pockets, it's like I'm a stranger. You think this place is different? Maybe it's worse here. Here I know nobody — I am nobody — but this is where they live. Yeah, here is worse."

"You know a few people here."

Elena smiled bitterly. "Yeah, I meet nice guys here. Real great."

"I wasn't talking about Siggy and his customers."

Her gaze softened minutely. "Okay, you been good to me and Alex, doctor — you and your friends. But you're not Brays. You don't have their money, or their . . . *influenţă*?"

"Influence."

"Yeah — influence. Sorry, doctor, but you're almost nobody too."

"The Brays can't control everything. They have enemies here, and if your story gets out it will give their enemies power. The Brays won't want that."

Elena rose from the bed and paced — from the door to the windows that looked out on the backyard, from the closet to the small white desk, around the perimeter of the bed. She moved carefully but was steady enough on her feet, and I could almost see gears turning furiously in her head.

"You have a better idea?" I asked.

She looked at me and shook her head. "How we would do this?"

"It's not like I've got a blueprint," I said, but I laid it out for her as well as I could. I explained about having an attorney take down her story in an affidavit, and about getting it on video. When I got to the part about a DNA test to prove that she and Alex were in fact mother and child, she went stiff and her voice quivered with anger.

"What — you don't think I'm his mother?"

"I didn't say that. But the Brays might try to tell that story. They tried to tell it to me."

"And you believed?"

I shook my head. "But I've seen you with him — how you are with him, the two of you together. Other people won't have seen that, and it's better if we don't give the Brays even a chance to try that bullshit."

Elena's mouth was like a seam in a stone. "*Other people* — what *other people*? Who else I need to worry about?"

"If the Brays aren't scared, or scared enough, about you going public with your story, then we need to be prepared to follow through. That means, at a minimum, the cops, child services, Immigration, the FBI, maybe even the press. You'll be talking to a lot of people."

"And they're gonna believe me?"

"You tell it to them the way you told me and they will. The DNA will make it easier."

Elena nodded slowly. "You take it from me and him both?" I nodded back. "It hurt?"

I shook my head. "Just a cheek swab. I can do it right now if you want."

She crossed the room. "So once we have all this — this video and this test — then what do we do? What happens?"

"We meet with the Brays, show them a sample, and make our pitch."

"Pitch," Elena repeated. She looked through the window into the yard and spoke the word softly, over and over. Then she turned to me. "Who you make the pitch to? Who you will talk to?"

"I don't know yet."

"To Kyle?"

"Probably not."

Another bitter smile. "No, not Kyle. The father wouldn't let him. Wouldn't trust him."

"Kyle has a cousin. Maybe her."

Elena's brow went up. "A girl? No. No,

the father would not trust a girl."

"Maybe somebody else — I'm not sure. Why?"

Elena returned to the bed and sat at the edge. She tucked one bare foot beneath her and dangled the other. She reached down and scratched the top of her foot, her ankle, and then she pulled the leg of her sweatpants up to her knee. She touched her calf and studied her white leg for a while, and then she looked up at me. And suddenly, as if a switch was thrown, there it was again — the crackling, electric charge of her sexuality. I'd felt an attenuated version when she'd first appeared in the clinic, but this was something else. Bruised and battered as she was, with chunks beaten and carved from her, still it was an insistent, relentless thing, like a riptide. Like gravity. She pursed her bow lips and lay back on the bed until she was propped on her elbows. I took a slow breath and a step backward.

"I got something else I want from them — besides their money and a ride home. I want something else." Her voice was soft. Intimate.

"What else?" It was an effort to get words out.

"I want to see the old man — face-to-face. I want that bastard to apologize for everything they did to us. To my face, I want him to beg forgiveness."

"I don't think that's a good idea, Elena, and I doubt they'd agree to it, anyway."

Elena smiled. "This is not bargaining, doctor. I am not asking — I am telling."

CHAPTER 35

Yossi was relieved by a cheerful Brazilian kid named Franco, who wore his blond hair in a ponytail and had the stars and shield of the São Paulo Football Club tattooed on his forearm. He looked more like a rock climber than a soldier, or maybe like a bike messenger, but beneath the chuckles and easy smile he was as watchful as Yossi, and at least as well armed. He unloaded two black semiautomatics from his backpack, along with spare clips, a pair of throwing knives, a six-pack of Red Bull, and a bag from a dim sum place out in Rosemead. He and Sutter spoke in low tones, in a mix of English and Portuguese, and then Franco put his food in the fridge and took up station in the living room. Shelly winked at him and he winked back. It was ten when Sutter and I left.

As he drove, I told Sutter about my conversation with Elena. When I got to the part about Elena's demand of a personal apology from Bray senior, he laughed.

"Style points, definitely," he said. "It'll never happen, but you gotta like her balls." Things loosened in Sutter's voice and shoulders, and I felt the relief too. I still had no great confidence in this plan, but I was glad Elena was willing to try it. Direction — any direction — was better than drift.

"You want to get a drink?" he asked. It was nearly eleven, and I had that jumpy, gritty-eyed post-call feeling.

"Maybe more than one," I said.

He punched up some music — Laura Mvula singing "Green Garden" — and we drove to Venice Beach. Sutter said nothing to me as we went, but sang along and drummed lightly on the steering wheel. I put my head against the window and closed my eyes, and when I opened them we were turning into the alley behind his house.

The passage was a gray tunnel, and the streetlights and security spots only made the shadows deeper. The alleyway looked empty to me, but Sutter must've seen something, because he stopped fifty yards from his place, killed the music, the engine, and the lights, and pulled a black semi-automatic from somewhere.

"Hang for a second," he said softly, and

slipped from the car into the dark.

I was wide awake now, the post-call raggedness banished by the hammering of my heart on my ribs. I gripped the door handle and stared into the night for some sign of Sutter, or of anything at all. I saw nothing. After five minutes — or maybe it was an hour or two — I took a deep breath, opened my door, and stepped into the alley. Adrenaline was coursing through me, making my knees quiver. I heard nothing but my own breath, the pulse that rushed like a tide in my ears, and my suddenly loud sneakers. I moved slowly toward the back of Sutter's house, still peering ahead. I was at his back fence, at the gate that opened to his carport, when the lights came on around his patio.

"I thought you were waiting in the car," Sutter said. He was in the threshold of a sliding glass door. The gun was in his belt, and his voice was flat and exhausted.

"I got bored. Everything okay?"

Sutter sighed and shook his head. "Not so much," he said, and walked back into the house. I followed. He went into the kitchen and opened the fridge. I stopped in the living room.

"She tells me her name is Ingrid," Sutter said.

She was crouched on one end of the sofa,

a frightened girl of maybe nineteen, slender and pale, with long black hair and darting blue eyes. Her dress was little more than a silk slip that fell off one shoulder and didn't reach her knees. Her legs were white and flawless but for the purple scars of what looked like cigarette burns on her calves, and a handcuff locked around her slender ankle. There was a yard of shiny chain running from the cuff to a steel ring that had been sunk into the stone of Sutter's floor. The girl shrank back when I looked at her, as if she wanted to bury herself in the sofa cushions. The chain was loud across the stone.

I nodded at her. "You okay?"

She nodded back. "I . . . I guess I am." Her voice was wispy and sweet, like cotton candy.

I looked at Sutter. "What's she doing here?"

He came out of the kitchen carrying three bottles of Lagunitas IPA. He handed one to me and one to the girl. "Tell him, Ingrid."

Her eyes bounced from Sutter to me to the beer to the floor and back to me again. Finally, she took a sip. "Vicky brought me — Vicky O — him and two guys that work for him. I don't know their names. They brought me over and . . . left me here."

"Vicky O is Viktor Ostrow," Sutter said from behind his beer. "Runs girls in Sherman Oaks. Middle management for Siggy."

"Why?" I asked Ingrid. "Why'd they leave you?" She looked confused.

Sutter drank more, and knelt by Ingrid's ankle. "Tell him about the message," he said, holding her foot and inspecting the handcuff.

She nodded. "Right, right — I gave him the message," she said, pointing down at Sutter. "About lunch."

"Lunch?"

"Yeah. Siggy wants him to come to lunch. He wants his friend to come too. Some doctor."

"Knox?"

"Yeah — Dr. Knox. Is that you?"

I nodded and looked at Sutter. "This is all to invite us to lunch? Couldn't he have just picked up the phone?"

Sutter drained his beer and got up. He crossed to the kitchen, rummaged in a drawer, and returned with a flat leather pouch. "Lunch isn't the message," he said, kneeling again. He unzipped the pouch. "The message is: *Look how easy it is. Look how I come into your house and do what I want. This time I left one of my girls in there; I could just have easily left a body — this girl's;*

yours, maybe. That's the message."

My stomach clenched. "Where's the cat?" I said.

"She's okay," Sutter said, and pointed behind me. "Plenty freaked out, though." I turned and saw Eartha beneath a wrought-iron chair on the patio, her green eyes glowing. She looked at me, licked a paw, and retreated into shadow. Sutter selected a pick and worked it in the handcuff lock. Two turns and it opened.

Ingrid drew her legs up and rubbed her ankle. "You're . . . you're supposed to say about lunch — if you'll have lunch with Siggy."

Sutter rubbed the back of his neck. "We'll do it."

"Tomorrow? 'Cause that's what Siggy said."

Sutter stretched his legs out and sat on the floor, his back against the sofa. He sighed. "Tomorrow," he said.

"What if we said no?" I asked.

The girl's already pale face went paper white, and her lower lip began to tremble. "But you said . . . Siggy told me you *had* to come, that if you didn't . . . If you don't come he'll —"

"We'll be there," Sutter said.

Ingrid took a deep breath and let it out

very slowly. "Okay," she said. "Okay. I . . . I'm supposed to text when I'm done here. Am I done, or am I . . . are we gonna do something?"

"You're done," Sutter said.

Ingrid nodded and produced a phone, possibly from her underwear. She tapped away, waited, and tapped again. "My ride's down the block," she said.

"Don't let us keep you," Sutter said.

Ingrid nodded, looked at me, and smiled tentatively. I smiled back. She placed the beer bottle carefully on the floor, headed for the front door, stopped halfway there, and spoke in her spun-sugar voice. "Sorry for the . . . Sorry." And then she was gone.

The door closed and it was quiet in the house, just dry leaves scudding on the bricks of Sutter's patio, the low grind of distant traffic, and the muted, steady push and pull of the Pacific, like an endless freight train, endlessly passing. Sutter was motionless on the floor, looking down at the lock picks and Ingrid's handcuff. A wave of exhaustion swept over me and I swayed. I wanted to sit, but wasn't sure my legs would cooperate. Eartha broke the stillness with a leap from somewhere onto an arm of the sofa. She padded across the cushions and paused by Sutter's head and pushed at him with her nose. Then she leapt to the floor and followed the chain to the steel ring and the shattered slate.

Sutter shook his head. "Can you believe what they did to my floor?" he said. "I spent a shitload of time laying that."

"What was the point of the chain?"

"Besides showing me he can fuck up my house? I guess it's another part of his message — something about property. That Elena is his property, just like Ingrid, that he keeps his property on a short leash. Who knows what goes on in his crazy Russian melon?"

"Is that all? Something about it seems a little more . . ."

"Personal?" I nodded and Sutter sighed deeply. "That's 'cause he means it to be. Back when, when he wanted me to soldier for him, he wasn't too happy when I said thanks but no thanks. If he hadn't had his hands full already, he might've pressed the point."

"And now?"

"Now maybe he wants to press it, or at least remind me how much he's come up in the world." Sutter shook his head. Eartha padded across the floor and onto Sutter's outstretched legs. She walked up them and stopped when she got to his lap. She looked at him, kneaded his crotch with her fore-paws, and sat.

"You think he's done with his point?"

Sutter offered his beer bottle to the cat. She sniffed it and touched the rim with her small pink tongue. "I guess we'll see," he said.

"Sorry," I said. "About your floor. About Siggy."

"You should be, brother," Sutter said, looking up. "Knowing you is not an easy thing."

CHAPTER 36

I called Anne Crane early Tuesday morning and asked her if she could take a statement from someone, and if she knew a videographer who could get it all on tape.

Her voice was tired and furry. "Get what on tape? Statement from who?"

"Her name's Elena."

"Just Elena, no last name?"

I realized that I didn't know it. "Ask her when you take her statement."

"Statement about what? I need a little background if I'm going to ask her questions."

"She . . . she's in the country illegally. I want you to ask her about how she came here, and why."

"That's not nearly enough information."

"I'll fax you some notes."

"What the hell is going on, doctor?"

"I'll bring her by your office tomorrow, after hours. Does that work?"

"I have to check with the video guy. And you haven't answered my question."

"My notes should explain it."

"Somehow I doubt it."

Lydia gave me a suspicious look when I told her I needed to be out of the clinic by one that afternoon, but she didn't ask why and I didn't tell. She was watching from the front window when Sutter and I drove off in his bullet-holed BMW.

Sutter was wearing jeans and a white shirt with a buttoned-down collar. His clothes were fresh and pressed, but his eyes were bleary. "Lunch is at Siggy's house," he said.

"Is that a good thing?"

Sutter shrugged. "The food should be decent, so that's something. On the other hand, it'll be easier for him to shoot us."

I looked over. "You think that's what he has in mind?"

Sutter smiled thinly.

Siggy lived up in La Cañada Flintridge, north and east of Glendale. Sutter got on the 5 and then the 2, and despite his skill the drive took an hour. It was shimmering hot when we turned onto Foothill Boulevard, and the San Gabriels were close, black, and serrated, like the fossilized plates of an ancient, armored thing.

Siggy's place was south of Foothill, on a quiet lane off Berkshire Avenue. Dense hedges hid the wire-topped wall that circled his property, and an elaborate gate guarded the cobbled drive. Three of Siggy's steers guarded the gates. They patted us down and pointed us to a golf cart that one of them then drove up to the main house. The cart had a red-and-gold striped canopy that matched the awnings over the terraces and piazzas of Château Siggy — a freakish Valley Versailles, with more than a little Vegas in its bloodlines.

The golf cart parked at a fountain that featured many frolicking, gilded sylphs, and we followed the driver's bulk down well-groomed paths to a sunny plaza behind the house. A lawn in Technicolor green unspooled to a glass-walled pavilion beside a long white pool. The golf cart driver pointed, another large man beckoned from the pavilion, and Sutter and I set off across the lawn.

"Lots of water to keep this green," I said as we walked. "Hasn't he heard about the drought?"

Sutter nodded. "When I first knew him, Siggy operated out of a warehouse in San Pedro. Had a cot and a hot plate, a little fridge, and a view of the cargo cranes."

"Now he's living the dream."

"Somebody's dream."

Siggy's toadlike lieutenant waited outside the pavilion. His blue linen suit fit like a sack, and emphasized the lumpiness of his frame and the gun under his arm. He had a soldier with him, who frisked us again and pointed us inside.

Siggy was at a black refectory table large enough for a couple of dozen diners and a few roasted boars, but holding just then only an iPad, three iPhones, a copy of the *Financial Times,* a coffee carafe, and a china coffee cup. Siggy held a glossy brochure on Gulfstream jets in his white machine hands, and he didn't look up when we came in, or offer us seats, perhaps because his was the only one in sight. The lieutenant and the soldier took flanking positions behind him.

"We late for lunch?" Sutter asked.

"You're right on time," Siggy said, still looking at the jets. "But I was hungry an hour ago, so . . ."

The soldier snickered. Siggy brushed something imaginary from the sleeve of his pale-blue shirt and turned the glossy pages of his brochure. I looked around, at the glass walls and the long green views. There were two women on the far side of the swimming pool, one tall and slender, one short and thick, walking three borzois with delicate legs and long curved tails. A little blond girl, maybe four, ran ahead of the group in an aimless zigzag through the grass. The dogs tracked her as if she were a rabbit. I looked at Sutter, who was staring at Siggy.

Siggy glanced up, his colorless face impassive. There was a fresh bandage on the side of his neck — another tattoo erased. "There's pizza at the shopping center on Foothill," Siggy said. "You probably passed it on the way. I hear it's good."

Sutter nodded slowly. "Yeah, maybe we'll grab a slice on the way back. So, if that's all you wanted to say, we'll find our way out." He pivoted for the door and Siggy chuckled.

"Not yet, soldier."

"Well, can we get the hell to it? 'Cause I have things to do, Siggy — crap to clean up around the house, that sort of thing."

The lieutenant didn't like that and neither did the soldier, and they both straightened up and leaned toward us. Siggy waved them off. "I'm still missing property, and I still want it back. You forget about that?"

I glanced at Sutter, who was looking out at the lawn. He ran his fingers along his chin. "I didn't forget."

"And?"

"And I might have a line on her."

Siggy closed his brochure and sent it skidding across the tabletop. "*A line?* That's it?"

"You think I have her in my car?"

"My guys say you have her somewhere."

Sutter shrugged. "What can I tell you, Siggy? Your guys can't hold a tail, so they think the worst — *if* they think at all."

"You're funny today, soldier. You have her or not?"

"Like I said, I might have a line. I have to see how it plays out."

"And were you gonna call and tell me about this? Or did you forget that too?"

"I didn't forget anything."

"So what — you think you don't *need* to call me? You *wanted* to piss me off. You *wanted* to say *Fuck you, Siggy*?"

"You know I'm not rude like that. I just didn't see the point in wasting your time if things didn't pan out."

"You don't decide that — *I* decide. Just like I set the price on that bitch. Or is that another thing you forgot?"

"I didn't forget about the seventy-five either."

"No? Well, it's a hundred now. Cash. Or you bring her back. Your choice."

"Still that simple?"

"I like simple. You remember that much, don't you, even with your leaky fucking memory? Maybe your pal should check you out. Maybe you got Alzheimer's. Maybe I should write things down for you, tattoo them on your head: *$100,000, one day.*"

Sutter smiled thinly. "One day? That's not enough time to locate her or get any cash together."

"That's not my problem, is it? You don't have the money, give me back my property. It's one or the other; otherwise, you're a thief. You're stealing from me."

Sutter sighed again. "You like simple? A week and no trouble is simpler than a day and trouble, isn't it?"

Siggy sat up, and his men shifted behind him. "You threatening me, soldier?"

"I'm making an observation."

"How about I observe Josef putting you down right now, you and your friend both? How about if that's the simplest thing?"

Sutter shrugged. "If Josef can manage it. And even if he can, it leaves you without the girl or the cash."

The men behind Siggy suddenly had guns in their hands. I felt my throat close and my shoulders tighten. Siggy smiled. "But it'd leave me with one less pain in my ass, soldier. And maybe it'd just make me happy."

"You used to have more self-control than

that, Siggy, more discipline. Don't tell me this large life has made you soft."

The gaunt face froze. "I can afford to be impulsive now, soldier, or any other damn thing I like."

"So you can afford a little time to —"

"Don't tell me what I can afford. Don't tell me anything. You just do what I fucking say."

Sutter smiled and shook his head. "You make it sound like I work for you, Siggy."

Color bloomed on Siggy's ropy neck — an angry red that rose to his ears. "You think that you don't?"

"Didn't I take a pass on that, once upon a time?"

"Maybe you get another chance now. One more chance."

"You don't need me."

Siggy's hands were like bone on the black table. He pushed his chair back. "You think you're above things, don't you? You think you're fucking special, that the rules don't apply. Like you're exempt. Let me tell you — you're not."

Sutter sighed deeply. "Are we really going to do this — a pissing contest? Here and now? Who benefits from that? You want me to say that you're the man? Fine — you're the man, Sig, biggest guy in the city, in the

391

Valley, in all the Southland. I bow down to you — whatever you want. But I'm still gonna need a week."

"A week." Siggy spit the words. He shook his head and looked at me. "You hear this, doctor? All his shit? You get that he's dragging you into this, right?"

"I get it."

Siggy pointed a white finger at me. "So you're on the fucking hook too," he said. "Three days. I give you three days — the money or the whore."

Sutter nodded. "Three days, then," he said. "And thanks again for lunch." He touched my arm and we turned to the door, but Siggy raised a hand.

"Three days, plus I want the other bitch."

Sutter turned. "What're you talking about?"

"The other whore — what's her name, Josef?"

"She goes by 'Stella' sometimes, sometimes 'Shelly,' " the lumpy lieutenant said, never taking his eyes from Sutter.

"Who is that?" Sutter said.

"Tell him, Josef."

"She's a nothing street whore, works downtown and east, on San Pablo sometimes, not far from his shithole clinic. Our guys say she helped Elena run away. They saw the two of them together. Almost got 'em both a couple of days back."

Sutter looked at Siggy. "I don't know anything about this, and if you're trying to squeeze more cash —"

"I don't want money for her," Siggy said. "Her you deliver."

"I'm not fucking FedEx. I don't know this girl and I don't know where to find her."

Siggy looked at me. "And you don't know her either?"

"Doesn't ring any bells."

"Well, I want this fucking girl. She talks shit about me, she gets in the way —"

I cleared my throat. "You don't think that looks bad?" I said. "I mean, if she's such a nothing, why bother with her? It makes you look small."

Siggy froze, his colorless eyes locked on me. His face was like a flint hatchet and his voice was low. His gaze shifted to Sutter. "Your friend's a pretty stupid guy, for a doctor," he said.

"He doesn't have your range of experience," Sutter said.

"Stupid," Siggy said. "Explain it to him."

Sutter nodded. "People get ideas," he said. "Siggy doesn't want people getting any ideas."

"Damn right," Siggy said. "Now get him the fuck out of my sight."

CHAPTER 37

We were hungry after our nonlunch with Siggy, and we stopped for pizza at the joint he mentioned, in a shopping center on Foothill. We ate Sicilian and drank beer, and Sutter sighed when he finished the last slice, breaking the silence that had enveloped us since we left the pavilion.

"He wasn't lying about the pizza," he said.

"Yeah — he's better than Yelp," I said. "But how about the rest of his speech? How much of that was bullshit?"

Sutter drank some beer. Food and drink had revived him somewhat, but he still looked weary. "Bluster, maybe, but not bullshit. He's serious about wanting the girl or the money, and serious about coming after our hides otherwise."

"I guess that's not all he's serious about."

Sutter squinted at me. "You think?" he said. His voice was bitter. He shook his head. "Sorry. Yeah, Siggy's got a hair up his ass about me. And if he starts thinking I've made him look bad in front of his guys — made him look weak — it's only going to get worse." He finished his beer and set the bottle carefully on the table. "Got a cure for that? A hair extraction procedure?"

I shook my head. "Cash might work. Lots of people swear by its soothing relief."

He smiled. "We can hope."

"The problem is, we're not going to get anything out of the Brays in three days' time — if we get anything from them at all."

Sutter shook his head. "How're you fixed for cash?"

I watched the traffic on Foothill, which passed in an endless, hypnotic stream and fluttered in waves of heat from the pavement. I sighed. "I've got what I put aside for a down payment on the building. It's a little over a hundred grand."

Sutter nodded slowly. "If things work out, you can take it out of what we get from the Brays."

"And if they don't work out?"

He shrugged. *"Mi sofá es tu sofá."*

The clinic was closed when I returned, buttoned up and dark. I felt guilty about running out at midday, but grateful that I had to face neither patients nor Lydia. I climbed the stairs, kicked off my shoes, and lay on the bed; I was drifting into sleep when my phone chirped.

"Tomorrow night's good," Anne Crane said. Her voice was clipped and tired, and there were other voices in the background. "My video guy will be here, and I have a conference room booked for eight o'clock, and a stenographer."

"Thanks, Anne. I appreciate it."

"Just be here at eight with . . . whoever," she said, "and don't forget — you're supposed to send me notes." And then she was gone.

Along with any chance of sleep. I sighed and cranked up my Mac, and spent forty-five minutes drinking coffee and typing three pages of bullet points that I e-mailed to Anne. Then I grabbed my car keys.

Jiffy-Lab was a twenty-four-hour drug, STD, and DNA testing lab in a Koreatown strip mall, wedged between a martial arts studio and a UPS store. And Nate Rash, who worked there, owed me for restarting his sister's heart when she stopped it with heroin. It was past eight on Tuesday night when I parked my Honda out front. The UPS was dark, and the sensei was locking his dojo, but the gruesome fluorescents were still lit at Jiffy-Lab. I killed my engine, and Nate climbed into the passenger seat.

He was red-haired and gangly, with a patchy beard and piercings in his nose and both ears. His purple scrubs were wrinkled and dotted with what I hoped were food stains.

Nate eyed the plastic zip bags in my hand. His voice was soft and reedy. "Those for me?"

I nodded. "Two buccal samples. A is a woman, B is a male child."

He took the bags. "Mother and son?"

"That's what you're going to tell me."

"I guess you're not worried about chain of custody."

"We'll get to that later, depending on what you say. How long?"

He shrugged. "A couple days."

"Sooner would be better."

"Getting paid wouldn't suck either," he said, and climbed from the car.

The parking lot was quiet, and I sat there for a while, my hands at twelve o'clock on the steering wheel, my forehead on my hands. The air in the Honda was stale, and smelled of exhaustion and fear — chronic conditions of late. I'd been driving with one eye on my rearview mirror for days now, jumping at shadows, and searching passing faces for ones I'd seen too many times before. Worse still, I was getting tired of looking over my shoulder — too tired to take care. That, I knew, was when bad things — lethal things — could happen. I thought about turning the key in the ignition, but my hands were suddenly like someone else's hands, and my arms felt like lead. The smart move was to head home, bar the doors, raise the drawbridge, and pull the covers over my head, but the thought of the empty apartment in the empty building — the dark clinic like a cave below, the echo of my footsteps on the stairs, and the silence afterward — turned my chest icy.

There was a rap on the car window and I bolted up. It was a woman, worried-looking, with one earbud plugged in and the other dangling near her clavicle. I ran the window down.

"You okay?" she asked. "You looked like you passed out or something. Or like you were crying."

"I'm all right," I said, and the woman nodded. I watched her climb into an ancient Volvo, and watched the car dissolve into the blur of headlights on Third Street. Passed out or crying — that seemed to cover the range of my options just then.

CHAPTER 38

They were fond of gray at Burnham Fiedler. Smoke, dove, steel, pearl, and charcoal
colored the walls, floors, and furniture,
along with most of the lawyers I'd met
there, and I found it hard to spend time in
their offices without feeling that my head
was wrapped in fog. But there were no gray
lawyers around at 8:00 p.m. on Wednesday,
when Sutter stepped off the elevator with
Elena — no one but me and a cleaning
woman, who was wrestling with an asthmatic vacuum.

Elena took careful steps, and her dark eyes
darted left and right as she came into the
reception area. Sutter had conjured a dress
and accessories for her from someplace, a
simple blue shift that she wore with a gray
belt, flat gray shoes, and a kerchief with pale
flowers on it around her neck. A blue ribbon held her ponytail in place, and she
looked like a Mormon girl setting out on

her mission.

The cleaning woman cursed softly in Spanish, and Elena froze. Sutter put a hand on her arm.

"Right on time," I said. "Any problems?"

Sutter shook his head. "Didn't see anything. Yossi was watching our backs, and he says we're cool. I just wish we weren't quite so close to those PRP dicks."

I followed Sutter's gaze to the windowed wall and the neighboring office tower that looked close enough to touch. How long since I'd been over there with Amanda Danzig and Kyle Bray? A few days? A year?

"I think their windows face the other way," I said. "Who's with Alex?"

"Evie, Franco, and three other guys."

"Have I met Evie?"

"You'd remember if you had."

"We're down here," I said.

Anne Crane was at the end of a dark hallway, in a conference room that had a long glossy table, chairs that looked like parts of a spaceship, a legal stenographer in a short green skirt, and a man with tattoos and many black nylon gear bags. The man fixed a camera atop a tripod, and pointed it at the head of the table, at a pair of chairs and a pair of microphones there. He checked the viewfinder, then crossed the room to adjust another camera aimed at the same spot.

Anne was sitting, looking at the pages of a fax, and adding to a long list of notes on a yellow legal pad. She wore tailored navy pants and a pale-pink blouse that was untucked in the back. She looked up at me when I stepped in, and then beyond me, into the hallway.

"That's Elena?" she said quietly. I nodded. Anne lifted the fax pages. "And the notes you sent? This stuff is really . . . for real?"

"I'm pretty sure."

"Christ," Anne said, shaking her head. "Is the little boy with her?"

"He's with babysitters tonight."

Anne peered into the hallway again, at Sutter this time. "Babysitters like him? He looks like a ninja."

I nodded. "He's a friend of mine. He does security work, among other things."

Anne's eyes narrowed. "Is security going to be a problem tonight? Because, besides the building guys, we don't have —"

"It's covered."

"By your ninja pal, all by himself?"

"He's got a friend downstairs."

"Interesting social network you've got. How's the little boy doing?"

"He's okay, I think. I hope. He seems to be a pretty tough little guy."

"He'd better be. You might want to think about DNA testing for —"

"The samples are in the lab."

Anne nodded. "Should we get started, then?"

Anne made brief introductions, and Elena said a quiet hello and took a seat in front of the microphones. Anne invited Sutter and me to leave.

"The fewer distractions, the better," she said, and she closed the conference room door.

We went back to the reception area, and then Sutter disappeared down another corridor. He returned a few minutes later, laughing and speaking amiably in Spanish to one of the cleaning guys.

"Later, *hombre,*" he said to the cleaner, who pushed his cart down another hall. Sutter took a seat next to mine, stretched out his legs, and sighed. "We should be good up here. Only access besides the elevator are fire stairs on either end of the floor, and they don't open from the stairwell side."

I nodded, and looked at our reflections in the big windows. I was pale in the glass, and rumpled, and Sutter looked like weather-beaten totem. In the years I'd known him, I'd seen him look this tired only a few times, and all of them after firefights. He pulled a black semiautomatic from behind his back, checked the magazine, and yawned. He put the gun in his lap and closed his eyes.

"Should I wake you if Siggy's guys come off the elevator?" I said.

"I'm not sleeping — just resting my retinas."

"When's the last time you actually slept?"

"Not sure. How about you?"

"I think I did last night, but it didn't do much good."

Sutter smiled. "You got the itch. I got it too."

"What itch?"

"Between your shoulder blades — from being in somebody's crosshairs. It makes you a little crazy. Used to drive me nuts back in the sand pile. It was between the shoulder blades for me; other guys got it other places. I knew one dude got a purple rash the size of a quarter on his forehead, right between the eyes."

"So what's the treatment, Dr. Sutter?"

Sutter slouched lower in his chair and smiled. "Me — I find whoever's on the other end of the scope and . . ." He made a gun with thumb and forefinger of his left hand.

"That doesn't work for me."

"Trust me, brother, it works — but it's the side effects you got to worry about. They build up over time."

"I imagine."

"That's why I try not to. . . ." Sutter paused and sighed deeply. "But I tell you, Siggy doesn't make it easy."

"You think that's what it's going to come to with him?"

"It will if he doesn't get his money. Which is why we're seeing him tomorrow night. With the cash."

I nodded. "I'll go to the safe-deposit box in the morning."

Sutter sighed and closed his eyes again. "It sucks, right — paying off a guy like that?"

"A little bit."

"Think *bridge loan* — you and your girl in there are going to shake some cash from the Brays."

"I wish I was that confident."

Sutter opened one eye and looked at me, but said nothing.

Cleaners went to and fro through the darkened reception area, and finally decamped altogether, but still we waited.

405

Lights winked out in the nearby buildings, and jets crossed the sky, and my reflection floated in the black window glass like a rumpled ghost. Sutter was silent and still. It seemed that days passed, but it was two and a half hours. Sutter stood suddenly and the gun disappeared, and a moment later Anne was there, with Elena two steps behind. Anne was bleary-eyed and white, and she caught my elbow and led me to a corner.

"This is the audio," she said, handing me a flash drive. "I can give you video and a transcript tomorrow."

"How'd she do?"

"She's . . . she's a good witness. She keeps things simple and lets the facts do the work. And her English got better as we went along. What you laid out in your notes was bad enough, but when she tells it it's much worse — maybe because she's so matter-of-fact about everything. That makes it more horrible. If I was in a courtroom and she was a witness for the other side, I'd be thinking hard about settlement."

I nodded. "I hope that comes across."

"It will. She couldn't care less about the cameras, or who else was in the room, and that makes for a good video." Anne paused and glanced across the room, at Sutter and Elena, who were standing near the elevators. "Something else comes across too, though," she said softly. "Something you want to be careful about."

"What something?"

"She never lost her shit when she was making her statement — nothing even close — but, still, I got the feeling that Elena is a seriously angry girl."

"How can she not be — given everything she's been through?"

"I'm talking *Carrie* kind of angry, if you know what I mean. Like rage. You want to take care around somebody like that."

"Thanks, Anne."

She nodded and disappeared down the hallway, and I joined Sutter and Elena at the elevators. "How're you feeling?" I asked her.

Her voice was empty and exhausted. "I want to go to Alex now."

CHAPTER 39

In a bathroom that was spartan at best — cracked tile, rust-stained porcelain, and failing grout — my showerhead was the single luxury. The owner of a plumbing supply around the corner had sent it over last year by way of thanks after I'd patched up his son, who'd driven a forklift off a loading dock, and who'd already had one DUI arrest that week. It was a brushed steel bell, and on the right setting it could scour the hide off a rhino at fifty paces. I had it dialed to something more gentle on Thursday evening — no more than a mild sandstorm — and I'd been under for twenty minutes, washing away a long day of people with lice in their hair, voices in their heads, a host of untreated chronic diseases, and a miscellany of maimings and acute infections. I'd been riding a wave of adrenaline and caffeine since early morning, and if I could muster enough energy to turn off the water,

408

I wanted nothing more afterward than to crawl into my bed. But that, I knew, wasn't going to happen. Sutter would be by any minute.

Through a supreme act of will, I spun the handles and climbed out of the shower. I toweled off and pulled on a clean shirt and pair of jeans, and while I was buttoning these I once again looked over the package Anne Crane had sent.

It had arrived this afternoon, with a bound transcript of Elena's statement inside, along with a DVD of her making the statement, a sheet of paper with a URL and password to the online version of the video, a flash drive with excerpts, and a handwritten note from Anne in her neat, Catholic-school script. *Check out the highlight reel. Four stars — impossible not to take her seriously.*

I'd watched a few minutes of excerpts between patients, and I watched a few minutes more as I slipped into loafers and buckled my belt. Elena looked young and vulnerable on the laptop monitor. Her skin was pale against the blue of her dress, and faint blue veins were visible in her neck. Her eyes were guileless and shy, and her voice was flat. Her speech was clear, even with her accent, and the accent was endearing, and somehow lent credibility to what she said. I agreed with Anne Crane's review, and hoped the Brays would too. My phone chirped with a text message from Sutter; he was in the alley. I took a bulky yellow legal-sized envelope from the table, and walked downstairs.

Sutter was waiting in another new car — a Lexus RX, in steel gray with smoked glass.

"Where do you get these cars?" I said as he drove down the alley.

"This came from the guy who bought my Simi Valley house. He didn't have all the cash, so he threw in the car. I'm gonna give it to my mom, I think — her Audi's getting raggedy, and she'll like the color."

"Plus, there are no bullet holes in it. Yet."

"Let's hope we don't pick up any where we're headed tonight."

"And where's that?"

"Not far. Siggy just bought himself a lounge downtown — one of those speakeasy theme parks, with artisanal cocktails and ice made from unicorn piss and middle-aged dudes from the Westside playing Humphrey Bogart."

"That doesn't narrow it much."

Sutter laughed. "I guess not. It's called Lacquer." He glanced at the envelope in my lap. "That the cash?" he asked.

I nodded. "A hundred thousand doesn't

take up much space."

Lacquer was on Sixth Street, near Main, and as Sutter drove past he tilted his head at a silver Bentley moored in a no-parking zone at the mouth of an alley. There was a big guy in a dark suit leaning on the driver's door, smoking.

"You like Siggy's ride? His wife's got a matching one in gold."

"Classy."

"Nothing but," Sutter said. He parked on the street, a few doors away. He pulled a backpack from behind the driver's seat and held it open.

"Drop the cash in there," he said. I did, and we climbed from the Lexus. Sutter locked the car with a remote and spun the key ring on his finger.

The entrance to Lacquer was down an alley, through a metal door beneath a caged lightbulb. Inside was a velvet-lined hallway with a hostess at the end — a sullen redhead in a green silk slip dress, who had a rascally cat tattooed a few inches north of her left nipple. Sutter grinned and coaxed a flickering smile in return. Before she could say good evening, or anything else, two large shapes stepped in front of her podium.

There was a blond guy with cauliflower ears, and a blonder guy with a neck like a

411

fireplug. They knew Sutter, and moved cautiously around him.

"You here to drink, or what?" fireplug asked. His accent was more Oxnard than Moscow.

Sutter laughed. "Are you taking cocktail orders now, Stevie? That's a step up."

Stevie ignored the remark. He pointed at the backpack. "What's in the bag?"

"It's for Siggy," Sutter said.

Cauliflower shook his massive head. "We gotta check."

Sutter lifted the pack from his shoulder and tossed it to Cauliflower. "Sure. But you open it, you guarantee the count to Siggy."

"The fuck does that mean?" Cauliflower said.

"It means if all of Siggy's money isn't there it's on you."

Fear and confusion chased each other across the man's thick features until Stevie spoke. "He's messing with you, dickhead. Just check the fucking bag."

Cauliflower's puzzlement turned into anger, and he snorted. He opened the backpack and rooted inside, then threw it back to Sutter. "Cunt," he muttered.

"I need to pat you down," Stevie said. "Both of you."

Sutter spun his key ring some more.

"Knock yourself out," he said, chuckling, and he winked at the redhead, who winked back.

After the frisk, Stevie led us through the club, which was as Sutter had described. The light was sepia-toned, the walls were bare brick, and the booths were dark leather and wood. The customers were silhouettes, leaning together or posing for each other, or for the lovely bartenders and waitresses, who came from the same casting agency that supplied the dour hostess. The cash register was a chrome beast crouched behind the bar, flanked by battalions of bottles and shining glassware. The music was Edith Piaf, but no one cared. We came to a padded leather door, guarded by Cauliflower's uglier brother. Stevie whispered something and he moved aside, and we stepped from speakeasy fantasy into disco nightmare.

It was a long room, with silver wallpaper and a mirrored ceiling. The carpet was white shag, the furniture Lucite, white leather, and tubular chrome. The music was Donna Summer, and the scent in the air was of cigars, powerful cologne, and sweat. Siggy's lieutenant, Josef, was sprawled on a white love seat near the door, leafing through a catalogue from an auction house, and two more of his soldiers were on an adjacent sofa, watching a soccer game on a flat-screen. Siggy himself was on the far side of the room, at a desk like a wide white mushroom, in pursuit of his own interests.

Fairly conventional interests, as it happened. There was a bottle of Belvedere vodka in a Lucite ice bucket on top of the desk, and some shot glasses, and next to them a half-dozen brightly colored vials of amyl nitrate that looked like prizes from a gumball machine. Next to these was a small berm of cocaine. Beneath the desk was a blond woman in a sports bra and yoga pants, bending her head to Siggy's lap. She was energetic and noisy, if not entirely sincere, but Siggy was responding as he might have to dental work — with a look of impatience and mild discomfort. Our arrival didn't change his expression, but his men looked up, grunted some Russian at each other, and laughed brutally.

Sutter chuckled. "Didn't know it was date night, Siggy."

Siggy glanced up and murmured to the woman, who ceased her labors, wiped a forearm across a bruised-looking mouth, and rose. She said something in Russian to Siggy, scooped a few milligrams of coke onto a long fingernail and into her nose, straightened her bra, and left.

Siggy looked us over as he did up his fly. His gaze fixed on the backpack and he smiled. It was a nasty thing, with many large teeth. "It's too small for her, unless you made pieces — and I know that's not your thing. So I guess that's my money."

Sutter nodded and held out the backpack. Siggy pointed to Josef. Sutter swung the pack in a neat arc, and it landed at the lieutenant's feet. Josef unzipped it, tore open the envelope, and dumped the money on the love seat — ten packs of ten thousand. He picked up each one in turn, ran a thumb across the top and made two stacks while Sutter twirled his keys. Josef nodded at Siggy.

The cash — or maybe the vodka, or coke, or the blow job — made Siggy more affable. "You start to listen to reason," he said to Sutter. "That's good." He picked up the bottle of Belvedere. "Come on, soldier, sit down and have a drink."

Sutter and I traded looks. He shrugged, and I followed him to Siggy's desk. We sat on Lucite chairs, and Siggy filled shot glasses. He pushed two toward us and raised his own.

"So — what do we toast?" Siggy asked. "Old days? New opportunities? Endless demand for pussy?"

"Still the poet," Sutter said. "How about we drink to done deals?"

Siggy tossed back his drink, and Sutter and I did the same. The vodka was a cold wire down my throat, and then a flame.

Siggy made a contented sigh and refilled our glasses. "Except this one's not quite done, is it, soldier?"

Sutter didn't freeze beside me; he played with his keys some more, then reached for his glass. But there was a change in the room, as if the atmospheric pressure had suddenly fallen and a storm was going to break. Siggy's men felt it, and looked over and shifted in their seats.

Sutter sipped his vodka and smiled. He cocked his head toward the sofa and the money. "That was the only thing on my to-do list, Siggy."

"Then I guess you weren't paying close attention."

"No?"

"Or else you forgot about me wanting the other whore" — he looked at Josef — "what's her name?"

"Shelly," Josef called.

"Her. You forget I want her too? 'Cause I don't see her in that backpack."

Sutter sighed deeply, and sat back in his chair. "Did *you* forget that I said she wasn't

416

on my radar? I'm not looking for her; I have no business with her. I'm —"

"You got business with *me,* and I got business with *her* — the math isn't hard, and you're a bright guy."

"My business with you is done."

Siggy pushed the Belvedere bottle around in the ice bucket. "You keep saying that."

"But somehow I'm not getting through."

It was Siggy's turn to sigh. "You didn't want to work for me back then; all right, that's something I guess I understand. I was a risky proposition then: it was hard to say how things would break, or if I could make payroll week to week. But now it's not hard. Now everything breaks my way, soldier — everything. So you've got nothing to worry about. A solid payday, and zero risk for you — not to mention for your friend here." Siggy looked at me as if I was a fish of dubious freshness.

Sutter shook his head. "He's not in this." His voice was low, and I felt my heart rate spike.

"But here he is anyway," Siggy said, and turned to me again. "You have an opinion on this, doc — anything you want to add? Some particular way you'd like things to work out, maybe?"

I swallowed some vodka, and the flame in

my stomach burned hotter. "Peacefully?" I ventured. "That's better for business, isn't it?"

Siggy pointed at me and bared his big teeth. He made a barking noise that I eventually realized was laughter. "*Peacefully* — that's not bad. Yeah, peace is good for business. Unless you're in the business of war. Right, soldier?"

"But that's not your line of work, Siggy — not anymore. It's not mine either."

"No?"

"From what I see, you won all the wars. And now you're enjoying the spoils."

"That's the way it looks to you? Then you don't look hard enough. There's always shit that needs doing. That's how you keep the peace."

"But it's low-level stuff, right? And you've got Josef and all the Mouseketeers for that. They're more than enough."

Siggy filled his own glass and offered the bottle to Sutter, who declined. "I decide what's enough," Siggy said, and then he sipped some vodka.

Sutter sighed. "You're still carrying a torch? Is that what this is about?"

Siggy barked again. "Yeah, soldier, I got a broken heart right here," he said, and grabbed his crotch.

Sutter laughed too, then leaned forward and rested his arms on the desk. He spoke softly, nearly in a whisper. "Seriously, I'm not worth the heartache."

Siggy leaned in. "No?" he whispered back.

"Not at all."

"Because . . . ?"

"You said it yourself — I'm a pain in the ass. My boss from when I was private sector would tell you, so would my old CO, if he was still walking the earth. And, really, nobody needs another pain in the ass."

"So maybe I just take you off the board."

Sutter's voice got lower. "We keep coming back to that, and I gotta tell you, Sig, the cost to do it might be steep. Might make it not worthwhile."

Siggy leaned in closer. "Yeah? See those guys there? I snap my fingers, they'll empty their clips in you and your pal, right here, right now. Wouldn't cost me a thing."

Sutter looked over at Josef and the soldiers, still lounging on the sofas, absorbed in the soccer game, laughing, pointing, and cursing. He looked back at Siggy and held up his Lexus remote key. "See this button over here — this red one?"

Siggy laughed. "What're you going to do — flash your lights at me?"

Sutter smiled and his voice dropped to a

whisper. "Sort of, but instead of the car alarm it sets off a frag charge I tucked in the shoulder straps of that backpack on the sofa. It's small enough that we'll be fine over here — nothing worse than blown eardrums — but those guys will be seriously fucked, and of course your cash will be confetti."

Siggy cocked his head. "What the fu—"

"And before the smoke clears, I'll be on your side of the desk. And I bet I can find a piece back there, and if not, I'll have plenty of time to break your neck."

Siggy squinted. He was quiet for a while, and then he shook his head. "Do you have any fucking idea what you're starting?"

Sutter smiled, and winked at him.

Siggy shook his head some more, and smiled nervously. "You're full of shit," he said slowly.

Sutter grinned wider, and leaned in again. "Sure I am," he whispered. "Or maybe not. Who the fuck knows? Should we find out?" He glanced over at Josef, who was gesticulating at the television and saying something to the soldiers, who laughed. The backpack was beside him on the sofa. Sutter put his keys on the desk. "Or maybe it's not worth it," he continued, "having to explain to your missus how her big brother's head got turned into so much borscht."

Red patches bloomed on Siggy's face, and his lips disappeared. His eyes flicked to me, to his desk, to his men across the room. My pulse spiked again, and adrenaline sizzled through every vein. "You fuck," he said, his voice a low rumble. He took a deep breath and reached for his glass.

Siggy drank, hand shaking, and worked a hideous smile onto his mottled face. "You are so full of shit, Sutter — it's fucking funny. You're unbelievable."

Sutter sat back, nodding. "Like I said, I'm a pain in the ass."

Siggy smiled at Sutter for an endless minute. When he spoke, his voice was loud, and full of manufactured good humor. "Now get the fuck out, you and your pal both. I got more important things to do than screw around with you two."

Sutter smiled back. "So we're done now, yes? I mean *done* done, Siggy."

Siggy went back to a whisper. "I said *get out* — so go, before I change my mind."

"Dr. Knox first," Sutter said, and looked at me. He flicked his head toward the door. When I stood, one of the soldiers did too. He looked at Siggy, who nodded. I crossed the room on legs that were suddenly rubber, and opened the door, and stepped back into the sepia-toned saloon.

I made my way to the bar and found a stool and looked at the office door. One of the slinky bartenders came over and spoke to me, but I couldn't make sense of what she said. I must've looked as shaky as I felt, because she brought over a glass of ice water. I drained it in one swallow, and as I put the glass down, the office door opened and Sutter strolled out, the backpack on his shoulder. He walked over to the bar.

"I wasn't sure you were coming out," I said. "And I wasn't sure what to do if you didn't."

"Have a little faith, brother. But now we roll — unless you want another drink."

I shook my head and climbed off my stool. "Was that for real — that business with the backpack?" Sutter smiled but said nothing. We crossed the room and made for the door, pausing only once, so that Sutter could exchange numbers with the hostess, who seemed surprised to see us again.

CHAPTER 40

My pulse was thrumming all the way back to the clinic, and my left knee was bouncing. Sutter pulled his car into the alley.

"So that's it with Siggy, then?" I asked as he rolled up to my Dumpster. "He's going to leave Elena alone?"

"Us too, I hope."

"*Hope?* I'd think a hundred grand would buy something more definite."

Sutter shrugged. "Siggy's a dick, and his ego is bruised, but he's a businessman. He understands costs and benefits." I nodded. Sutter watched me and chuckled. "You look disappointed," he said.

"Me?"

"You. But not to worry, brother — the Brays have plenty of guns too. More than enough to keep you entertained."

I flipped Sutter the bird and climbed out of his car. He laughed some more and drove away.

Lydia or Lucho had slipped my personal mail under the door, and it slid across the bare floor as I entered my apartment. There wasn't a lot — a couple of medical journals, a *donation, please,* letter from my college, catalogues of things I had no interest in and anyway couldn't afford, a postcard meant for someone else. I gathered it up and stood in my gloomy living room for a while before I switched on the lights and the television. I drank a beer and flicked through the channels.

It was the same old shit — a lot of noisy nothing. I stopped on a nature channel and sat, but couldn't sit still. Monkeys chattered and screamed at each other, and it felt like they were in my clothes. I got up and checked the answering machine. There was nothing.

The package Anne Crane had sent — the video and transcript of Elena's statement — was on the kitchen counter. I stood there and leafed through the transcript again. I paused at the section about her journey to the States — the truck ride into Greece, the repeated rapes. Then I skimmed backward, to the part about her grandmother's apartment — the smashed furniture, the blood. Then forward again, to the apartment in West Hollywood, where she met men. I took a deep breath. The transcript was the size of a small phone book, but you couldn't turn three pages in a row without a new horror. I went to the fridge for another beer.

I should have felt some comfort now that we'd dealt with Siggy — relieved that there was one less danger to worry about. But somehow I didn't. Somehow it made the Brays loom even larger in the landscape of threat.

It was time to call Amanda Danzig, I knew — time to meet with her and make my pitch for Elena's and Alex's freedom — but something stopped me. It wasn't Elena's story, which was awful and compelling, powerful and powerfully told. If that didn't convince the Brays to make a deal, it wouldn't be because it lacked in dreadfulness. And though I hadn't yet heard from Nate Rash at Jiffy-Lab, I was certain that the DNA results would bolster her tale. No, it wasn't what I knew of Elena's story that worried me, it was what I didn't know — the nagging sense that there was a chapter that I hadn't read yet, but which the Brays perhaps had.

I drank more beer and went back to the television. The monkeys were gone, and in their place was a sea turtle, dragging through the sand of an empty beach to lay her eggs in the moonlight. The ocean was flat and black behind her, and she herself was inky and gnarled against the pristine sand — scarred, barnacled, and exhausted, but still grinding through the ancient dictates of her genes. Her eyes were black and shining, at once dogged and resigned, and I walked closer to the screen to look at them. There was something familiar there, I thought. I knew that look somehow, but from where? The bottom of a beer bottle, I thought, and my laugh echoed stupidly off the bare walls. Then, suddenly, Mandy's voice was in my head: *What wouldn't a parent do for a child?* What indeed.

I paced some more, trying and failing to slow the racing engine of speculation and suspicion in my head, and soon it felt as if the monkeys were going through my pockets again. My watch said almost eleven, and I knew Nora would be home from an evening clinic at UCLA but not yet asleep. I reached for my car keys.

Nora's Lexus was in the driveway, so I parked farther down the hill, on Berendo Street. There were deep shadows on the sidewalks as I walked back to Nora's house. Porch lights were on outside many of the bungalows, and windows were dark or glowing blue with television. A little wind blew in the trees, no more than a sigh, and then I heard the faint throb of an engine behind me. I turned and saw headlights rounding a far corner.

I turned left on Cromwell Avenue, walked past three dark houses, and stopped at Nora's brick path. There were ground lights along its edge, and big cactus plants in terra-cotta pots, and it curved up to three brick steps and the front door of her Mission-style cottage. Her lights were on, and an angular shadow moved across the big window. I texted her — *Out front* — and sent a smiling frog too. In a minute, the door opened and Nora was there. She was barefoot, in black yoga pants and a black tank top, and she was holding her phone.

"You don't call first?" she said, as I came up the path. "And, seriously, an emoji? What are you — in middle school?"

I stood at the bottom of the steps. "Middle school kids are too cool for that. Besides, I wasn't sure you'd take my call."

"I'm not sure either," she said, smiling ruefully. "It wasn't exactly the perfect date."

"No, it wasn't."

Nora's smile broadened. "Come on — I've got Chinese."

I smiled back. "Cold noodles?"

"Yes, cold —" Then there was sound behind me — footsteps on brick — and movement, and Nora Roby's eyes went wide. I crouched reflexively and spun, and something like a bowling ball glanced off my right shoulder. My arm went numb and then burned, and my feet went out from under me. I was on my ass on the bricks, looking up at a broad-shouldered silhouette.

"You fuckin' pussy — you had to go cryin' to him! I talk to you on the street, and you get scared and cry like a fuckin' baby to him." Kyle Bray's voice was shrill and drunken, and his face was a mask of rage. His arm swung down and there was a whipping sound, like a golf club cutting air. I scuttled backward, and stumbled on the steps.

"You want more, you fuck — or you want to tell me where the kid is?" There was a metallic scrape, a line of sparks on the bricks, and then something lashed at my calf and left it first numb and then burning. Kyle held what looked in the dark like a stubby golf club — a putter, maybe. He raised it above his head again, and I saw that it was a telescoping metal baton.

"Tell me where he is or I'll split your fucking head," Bray said, slashing the air, and then I threw one potted cactus at him, and then another. The first, a quilled soft-ball, caught him in the center of his tee shirt, and stuck there. He yelped and stepped back. The second cactus was like a spiked baguette, and it caught him full in the face. Bray yelled and dropped the baton, and I kicked out and swept his ankles. He fell backward, screaming, into another cactus pot, and then screamed louder.

"Stay still or it's going to hurt worse," I told Kyle Bray, and I pulled his hand away from his face.

"Get 'em out! Just get them the fuck out of me!"

He was squirming on the tiled floor of Nora Roby's entrance foyer. His shirt was spattered red, front and back, and still bristling with brown needles, but the real problem — and the real pain — was in his face. The cactus had caught him on the right side, on the eyebrow, eyelid, nose, cheek, and upper lip. The barbs had gone deep, and his clawing had made things worse. The side of his face was like a road stripped for paving.

Nora had an orange backpack with all the essentials in it, and she dropped it, along with a white trash bag, at my feet. Then she walked into the living room, sat on the sofa, and glared. I opened the pack, found forceps, alcohol, sterile gauze, tape, and gloves.

"Keep still," I told Bray again, and batted his hand away. I took the forceps and pulled a spine from his right nostril and dropped it in the trash.

"Fuck!" he yelled.

"Fuck yourself," Nora muttered from the sofa.

Bray tried to focus with his one good eye. The smell of liquor mixed with sour milk came off him in waves, and I was pretty sure he didn't understand much of what anyone was saying. Sweat soaked his tee shirt and beaded on his face. I pulled two spines from his cheek, and he cried out twice more.

"You followed me from the clinic?" I asked.

"The PRP boys did."

"And they called, and you came over?" I pulled a spine from the bridge of his nose.

"Ow! Yeah, they called."

Nora snorted. "And you came to do what — kill us?"

Kyle Bray squinted at her and shook his head and winced. "Should I just call 911, and get you to an ER?" I said. "Then you can explain all this to the cops."

"No," Bray moaned. I pulled out another spike, sunk deep in his eyebrow. He screamed.

"What *did* you think you'd do — besides bash my head in?"

Bray sighed a boozy cloud at me. "I wanted to get the kid back. You know where he is, and I couldn't stand listening to that shit anymore."

"Listening to what shit?"

"All his shit. About *half-measures,* and *half-right is all wrong.* About how I can't even hang on to my own kid, much less raise him. All his usual shit."

"Who says all this?" I asked.

Kyle Bray furrowed his brow, which must've hurt. Still, it stayed puckered as he spoke. "Cap — who else but Cappy? Who else can go on forever about what a fuckup I am?"

Bray made a swipe at his face again, and I caught his wrist and pushed it down. "Who is Cap?"

"Cappy? That's *Captain* Bray."

"He was in the military?"

Bray snorted. "Connecticut Air National Guard. He spent the end of Vietnam on his ass in fucking Windsor Locks. I'm not sure where that is, but I bet there weren't a lot of VC around. He likes for everybody to call him Cap, though. Like he's fucking Captain America."

"And Captain Bray would be your father?" Nora asked.

"Of course my fucking father. Who else?"

Nora looked at me. "He's crazy drunk."

I stood, and my knees creaked. "That's part of it," I said softly. I pointed at his neck and face and mouth. "See the acne there, and what's going on with his teeth and gums? And you catch that smell coming off him?"

She stood, walked over, and squinted. Then she nodded. "You think — what — methamphetamine?" I nodded.

Nora looked at me. "And you bring him into my house. Great. Thanks for that, Adam." She shook her head and turned on her heel and went into the kitchen.

I sighed and crouched by Bray, who was pawing at his face again. I pushed his hands down. "Open your mouth for me, Kyle. I want to make sure none of these punctures went all the way through." He nodded vaguely and opened up, and I swabbed the insides of his cheeks.

It took me another twenty minutes to finish cleaning Kyle's wounds and dress the worst of them with gauze. Bray's fidgeting lost steam, and his yips of pain were fewer and softer by the time I taped the last dressing to his forehead. I was just standing when

Nora's doorbell rang. Nora came in from the kitchen and looked at me. Kyle made a moaning sound that turned into a snore.

Nora's voice was a tense whisper. "Who the hell is that?"

I shook my head. "You expecting anyone?"

"I wasn't expecting *you,* for chrissakes!"

The bell rang again, and I stepped across Kyle and picked up his metal baton.

"Jesus," Nora whispered.

There was a speakeasy panel set into the front door, and I opened it and peered through the wrought-iron grill. I saw a blond pixie cut and button-bright eyes, diamond stud earrings, and a very white smile. Amanda Danzig looked up at me and waved.

"Hey, doc! Sorry if I'm interrupting your fun, but I need to collect my cousin. I understand you've got him in there." As she spoke, two large men appeared behind her. Mandy watched me watch them and smiled. "Don't worry — they're just here to lift, if Kyle needs lifting. Which I suspect he does."

"Last we spoke, you said you'd give me some time to think things over. What happened to that?"

Mandy smiled. "You're right. I made you a promise, and Kyle and his antics tonight were strictly out of bounds."

"I guess that happens a lot with him."

Mandy shrugged. "Do we have to talk through this door, or is it okay with your girlfriend if I come in?"

I closed the speakeasy panel, and opened the front door. Mandy stepped in. She barely glanced at Kyle, but scanned Nora's house — and Nora — with interest. Then she looked at me.

"So this is your thing? The yoga MILF? You don't think she's a little old?"

I laughed. "She's my age, Mandy. And she's a doctor."

Nora snorted. "Who *is* this, Adam?"

"Her name is Amanda," I said, "and she's just here for a second, to pick up her . . . lost property."

"You know this isn't the lost property I'm interested in, Dr. Knox," Mandy said, and kicked Kyle's leg lightly with the toe of her black pump. "Still, he's what I'm here for." She glanced behind her at the two men on the porch, and pointed down at Kyle. They lumbered in and hoisted, supporting him between them, his arms across their shoulders, his head lolling. They paused in the doorway, and Mandy inspected Kyle's face.

"What'd you do to him?" she asked.

"He fell on a cactus."

Mandy smirked. "*Fell* — I bet. Nice patch

434

job, though — makes him look like a Picasso."

"He could probably use a tetanus booster. He should also think about rehab."

Mandy nodded, and the big men carried Kyle out. She looked at me and shrugged. "Yeah — rehab — that might be a good idea. But you know how it is. You can lead a horse to water. . . . It's hard to get Kyle to listen, which is why you shouldn't let this linger much longer, doc."

"Is that a threat?" Nora said.

Mandy looked at her and shook her head and laughed. "Nice meeting you, doctor," she said, and left.

There was long silence when she'd gone. Nora looked at me, and at the trash bag at my feet. Her voice was low and tight with anger. "Take that crap with you when you leave," she said, and went into her bedroom, and shut the door.

My feet were loud on the pavement as I walked back to my car, and the night was darker. The porch lights and televisions were out, and the little wind was gone. I tossed the trash bag into my back seat and shut the car door; it sounded like a thunderclap. I put my hands on the wheel, and the cold went up my arms. I closed my eyes.

"Shit," I said to no one. Then I took some deep breaths and pulled out my phone. It rang just once before Mandy answered.

CHAPTER 41

Amanda Danzig's waiting room was nicer than mine, which was very short on polished stone floors, Barcelona chairs, Japanese ink-wash paintings, glossy trade magazines that made oil pipeline valves look glamorous, and a robotically genial young woman named Jenny who produced superb espresso, seemingly from thin air. I was working on my second hour of pacing in Bray Consolidated's black glass tower in Westwood, and on my fourth coffee, and I had memorized the twentieth-floor views of the UCLA campus, the Federal Building, and a traffic-clogged stretch of the 405. Through the tinted windows, the cloudless sky was mauve.

I sighed and ran my thumb along the Bray coat of arms, emblazoned on my demitasse cup — a black shield with two red maces crossed in the center, and underneath, also in red, *Sine missione.* I emptied the cup and sat, which was Jenny's cue.

"Another coffee, sir?" she asked, smiling.

I wondered if she'd been given instructions to induce tachycardia, or maybe kidney failure. I smiled back but declined cup five.

I thought again about calling Nate Rash at Jiffy-Lab for the results of the DNA tests I'd requested, but he hadn't answered his cell a half-hour before, and the woman I spoke with at the lab wouldn't say when he'd be in.

I also thought about calling Nora Roby. She hadn't answered my calls last night, after she'd kicked me out, or this morning, and the messages I'd left had yielded only dead air. What could I say that I hadn't said already? *I'm sorry that a lunatic has been following me around, and that he bled all over your foyer? I'm sorry that his slightly less crazy cousin brought her thugs into your home, and insulted you?* I took a deep breath and untied the cord that bound the red file folder in my lap.

The contents hadn't changed since the last time I'd checked: the printed transcript of Elena's statement and a disc with the highlights. It would've been nice to have the DNA test results too, but I hoped Elena's statement would be enough, and that its threat to Bray-world would be clear. Still, my stomach turned over. A pair of doors opened, and I looked up to see Amanda Danzig beckoning.

"Dr. Knox!" she said, surprised and delighted, as if we'd bumped into each other at the polo matches. She wore black pumps, a snug gray skirt, a fitted white blouse, and a Bluetooth earpiece in her right ear. Her cropped blond hair was slicked, and her teeth were very white. There was a thick platinum chain around her neck, and an emerald pendant on it the size of a table grape.

"Look at you," she said, smiling, "All dressed up in khakis and a nice blue blazer — it's like Parents' Day at Choate."

I stood, and looked down into her button-bright eyes. "Even so, the guys in the lobby almost made me use the service entrance."

"They're paid to be superficial. But, fortunately for you, I see beyond the cosmetic." Her eyes went to the file folder under my arm. "I have to tell you, I was surprised to hear from you last night, doctor. I thought after Kyle and I screwed up your date with Dr. MILF —"

"Don't call her that."

Mandy chuckled and raised her hands. "Sorry, sorry. Anyway, I'm glad you phoned.

Surprised, but glad. Now, have you been thinking about what you want? Is that a Christmas list you have there?" She didn't wait for an answer, but took my elbow and led me into her office.

It was even nicer than her waiting room — larger, brighter, and with more view. Her desk was a sweep of steel and glass that ran along some of the windows. Along some others was a seating area — more Barcelona chairs and sofas, and a glass coffee table holding a bowl of cut flowers, bottles of water, and yet more coffee. "So tell me what I can do for you, and tell me where I can find my cousin."

I followed her to the seating area, where she perched on a sofa, kicked off her shoes, hitched up her skirt, and tucked her neat legs beneath her. I took one of the chairs, but before I could speak, Danzig held up one finger and touched another to her ear-piece.

"I'm still here," she said to someone else. Then she frowned, shook her head, and spoke in Russian. She spoke for a while, looking down at her knees as she did. She finished in English. "No. And don't waste my time with those assholes again. Call me when we actually have something to talk about, or don't call at all."

Danzig pulled out the earpiece, tossed it on the table, and smirked. "Moscow office. Bunch of crazy bastards, if you ask me — half drunk all the time. You want coffee? Water?"

I shook my head. "Speaking of crazy, how's Kyle?"

Danzig laughed. She reached for a bottle of water, twisted the top, and took a sip. "He's gone — what — eighteen hours without a brawl. That could be a record for him. I'm pretty sure he still hates you, though."

"You might be feeling the same way soon."

She put on a theatrical pout. "About you, doctor? I couldn't. Or are you telling me that's not a wish list you've got there?"

I took a deep breath. "What I have is Elena's story," I said. "I found it convincing, and I think anyone else hearing would agree." Then I handed her the folder.

Amanda Danzig scowled as she opened the folder. She took out the thick sheaf of the transcript, and then the disc. She shook her head. "What am I supposed to do with this, besides marvel at the waste of paper?"

"You should read it, when you've got some time. For now, you should put the disc in your Mac and watch."

"You disappoint me," she said, shaking

her head, but she slipped into her shoes and carried the DVD to her desk.

I watched her as she watched Elena and listened to Elena's flat, accented words, but Danzig's face remained perfectly blank. When the highlight reel ended, she picked up a thick silver fountain pen and tapped it lightly on her desk for what seemed a long time. Then she looked at me.

"So — that was it? That was your shot? And — what — am I supposed to curl into a ball now? Am I supposed to weep? Anyone can tell a story, doctor — and with a little imagination, they can make it a real tear-jerker too — a lurid, harrowing, heartrending tale of woe. But the fact that you've made a nice video of it, dressed up with a lawyer, doesn't make it true."

"She's not his aunt, Mandy, she's his mother. If you saw them together, you'd —"

"That's what you're banking on — how they look to you, side by side? You have any facts behind that?"

"DNA doesn't lie."

"DNA may not lie, but sample collection, testing facilities, procedures, all those things do. That's why they ask about that shit in court. And is that really where you want to go with us, doctor, into a courtroom? 'Cause I guarantee you, we're going to have a lot of company in there, and you're going to feel pretty lonely. Maybe more lonely than you feel already. Think hard on this, doc, because if we head down that road we won't turn back. Not ever.

"You want to have a court swab Elena and Alex, or you want your lawyers to do it — that's fine. They can swab Kyle too, while they're at it. I'm confident of the results, so long as everyone involved keeps an eye on the samples.

"And then what — the case becomes a custody battle? Is that really appealing? On one side you'll have what, with all modesty, is a fairly prominent family: philanthropists, generous donors to noble causes, employers of many thousands of worker bees around the world. And on the other you'll have a twenty-something prostitute from East Mudhump, Romania, an illegal alien to boot, with God knows what kinds of vices a motivated investigator might find. And I assure you, doctor, our investigators are highly motivated. Which one do you think would provide a better environment for raising that boy? What do you think a judge would think?

"But when it comes to it, you won't have time to worry much about it. You'll be too busy trying to find a new home for your little health-care bodega, and a new place to live besides. And that's before we get to kidnap charges, attempted extortion, defamation, and those are just the appetizers. But, sure, if that's the way you want to go . . ." Mandy twisted a finger in her necklace, and her pendant flashed green as it caught the sun. Her cheeks were pink with excitement.

I shrugged. "You seem to want to go that way — you've got it all planned out. In which case, I guess I should stop ducking the reporter who's been calling me. I don't know how he got my name, but it sounds like he's got a corner of something, and a whole bunch of questions, and if we're headed to court I should probably get my story out there."

Danzig squinted at me, took a breath, and opened her mouth, but whatever she might've said was lost when her office doors swung wide. The lovely Jenny was there, but decidedly less genial. She was trying — without success — to impede the progress of a large man with a white crew cut and Naugahyde skin.

"I'm sorry, Ms. Danzig," Jenny said, "but he wouldn't wait. He wouldn't listen to anything —"

Danzig's face darkened. "It's all right, Jen.

Tiger, what the *fuck* do you think you're doing?"

Conti stepped around the assistant and smoothed the lapels on his black suit. "Sorry, Mandy —"

"You can call me Ms. Danzig."

"Yeah, sure. Anyway, Cap wants to see him." Conti flicked a thumb in my direction.

Danzig stood, and her chair rolled away behind her and rebounded off the window glass. Her hands were balled into white fists. "He wants *what*? I'm in the middle of something, for chrissakes."

Conti walked slowly to the desk and dropped a meatloaf hand on my shoulder. He shrugged at Mandy. "Guess you have to take that up with the Captain. Ms. Danzig."

CHAPTER 42

Conti didn't take me to a conference room or to another office suite. Instead, he led me into an elevator, out again, up a short flight of metal stairs, through a metal door, and onto Bray Consolidated's rooftop helipad. There was a chopper waiting there, a sleek white machine with the Bray coat of arms on its side. Its engines were idling and its rotors spinning slowly. The pilot donned his headphones and adjusted his mike when he saw us coming. Fuel vapors pricked my eyes.

Leather seats faced each other across a leather-lined passenger cabin. Conti waited until I climbed into a window spot and then took a seat opposite. He pulled the hatch shut and pointed at my seatbelts while he fastened his. When I'd buckled up, he tossed me a set of headphones.

"The jack's in the armrest," he said, positioning his own headphones over his ears. He swung his mike down and spoke to the pilot. "We're all good back here, Jerry."

Jerry's twang came through my headphones. "Roger that, Tiger. We are wheels up." The engines revved, the cabin vibrated and swayed, and then the rooftop slanted away.

I looked out the porthole at the world rotating below — the 405, the cemetery, Brentwood, and, to the north and west, the brown, shadowed folds of the Santa Monica Mountains and a bright haze off the Pacific.

Conti's voice was in my ear again. "You're not gonna puke, are you?" His shark grin was wide. I shook my head. "Then you want a drink?" He pressed on the divider between his seat and the next, and a panel slid away to reveal a bar. I shook my head again and he shrugged. He reached in and pulled out a small bottle of tonic water. He opened it and drank.

"I thought you'd put up more of a fight," he said. "Or at least ask questions."

I pulled my own mike down. "What's the point? I want to talk to the guy who can make things happen. Apparently, that's not Amanda." Conti snorted. "I guess now we're going to see that guy."

"Got that right," Conti said.

I looked through the porthole again. The

ridges and ravines of the Santa Monicas were closer now, and away to my left I could see a white strip of beach and the PCH running alongside. "I thought Bray lived in Bel Air," I said.

"That's one place. Malibu's another."

The chopper dipped lower over a canyon — Topanga I thought, from the tortuous road that wound down to the ocean, and from the size of the homes on its slopes. Pools and tennis courts and vast decks were like shining tiles on the parched hillsides, a mosaic that spelled out *money* in the Ur-language of real estate.

"Keep an eye out — you almost always see tits around here, a couple pairs at least, lying out in the sun. Nice ones too. Don't know if they're real or not, but from up here they look good. Sometimes the chicks wave." I looked at Conti and shook my head.

He squinted at me. "You don't like tits? Or you see so many in your line of work, the magic is gone?"

I ignored his questions. "Bray senior keeps an eye on Mandy's appointments?"

Conti barely shrugged. "It's his company and his building. Everything goes on there is his business."

"And he pays you to watch over it?"

"That's as good a job description as any."

448

"That include babysitting?"

"Ask him yourself. We're almost there."

The engine sounds changed, and so did the vibrations through the cabin, and we slid to the right. The sea rotated in the cabin window — slate blue, with breaking waves like lace. There was a stretch of sand like a tawny thigh, then the green of an irrigated hillside, and then a slab of white cement as we hovered above a helipad. And then we were down.

The pad was on a terraced slope far above the ocean and the PCH, but below the hilltop. I followed Conti up a stone path through manzanita and yarrow and salt air, and another man followed behind us. He had a crew cut and made no effort to hide the gun beneath his suit jacket. The ocean swayed and sighed behind us, and gulls hung overhead.

Near the crest of the hill we came to a line of wind-twisted scrub oak. Beyond were a meadow, a horse paddock, stables in whitewashed stucco, and then the main event — a Spanish Renaissance palace in white stone, with a green tiled roof and leaded glass windows. It looked like the Beverly Hills City Hall, only larger and without the tower.

Conti led me past a fountain full of

mottled koi, and up steps to a wide patio. The highway was invisible from this vantage, and so was the beach — the view was all ocean and sky — two things Harris Bray could yet aspire to own. Unless they were his already.

There was furniture on the patio — wrought-iron chairs and glass-topped tables — and signs of recent entertainment, but no guests. The only other people were four waiters in white shirts and black vests, moving silently among the tables, clearing empty highball glasses, hors d'oeuvre plates, and crumpled cloth napkins. Conti stopped and put out his hand.

"Cell phone," he said. I dug my phone out and gave it to him. He powered it down and gave it to the crew-cut man. "You'll get it back when you leave. Arms out to the side." Conti demonstrated, and the crew-cut man ran a wand up and down my body, pausing at my belt and wristwatch.

"He's good," Crew Cut said. He hung back while Conti and I crossed the patio to a set of French doors on the far side. The doors were open, but Conti stopped at the threshold.

"A minute," he said softly. He slipped a cigarette from his breast pocket and dangled it, unlit, from his lower lip. He turned to watch the ocean, and I looked inside.

The room was a rosewood chapel, with paneling and bookshelves that ascended to a coffered ceiling, and a red-tiled floor covered in Persian rugs. The books were leather-bound, and so was much of the furniture. The green silk drapes were pulled back, and sunlight fell on an ebony standing desk. There was a phone on it, a keyboard, a thin monitor, a highball glass with something amber at the bottom, and a stack of papers. A leather chair crouched before it — a place for supplicants to sit and stare upward and await the word of God.

Harris Bray stood behind the desk, nearly motionless. He was dressed not for an afternoon in Malibu, but for a board meeting in New York, or maybe a centerfold in *Forbes.* He wore a snow-white shirt, gray tie, navy trousers, navy suspenders, and gleaming wingtips. His navy suit jacket hung from an ebony peg on the side of his desk.

Bray wasn't handing down law just then, but listening to a man's voice from a phone speaker. I couldn't make out the words, but the voice was pleading and desperate, which seemed to make Bray angry. His jaw was rigid, and his large mottled hands clutched at each other. His own replies were curt and chilly — ice on a windowpane. His words too were lost to me, but his scorn hung like a fog in the air.

My glimpse of Bray, in the PRP corridor, was of little more than a looming shadow, and the photos I'd seen were of a beige Rotarian — an auditor or a pasty tax attorney — if not genial, then at least reassuringly bland. In person, up close, he was not. Cameras hadn't captured his crowding, aggressive presence, his heavy, sloping shoulders, long arms, and thick, hard torso. And they'd softened and civilized a face that in reality was brutal and crudely made — hacked from ice, and animated by contempt.

Bray wore rimless glasses, and behind them his eyes were flint splinters, and as jangly as Kyle's. His nose was a hatchet, and his mouth a bitter seam, too long and nearly lipless. His skin was pale even against the collar of his white shirt, but pink patches bloomed on his cheeks whenever the man on the phone spoke. Flushing isn't necessarily a symptom of hypertension, but I wondered if something wasn't ready to rupture beneath that ridged white scalp. He leaned forward as he listened, and his hands strangled one another.

Bray's frozen whisper rose to a growl, and he stabbed a thick finger at his phone. The pleading voice cut out, and Bray smoothed his tie. He read something on his computer screen and tapped at his keyboard.

"He's here?" he said without looking up.

Conti nudged past me and through the French doors. "Right here, Cap."

Eyes still on his screen, Bray pointed at the chair in front of his desk.

I shook my head. "I've been sitting all day."

Bray sighed and looked at Conti, who took my elbow. "That wasn't an invite," Conti said, ushering me to the chair.

I sat, and Conti retreated to the patio. I watched Bray scan his monitor for a few minutes, and type in rapid bursts. The color was gone from his face, and so was any expression. When he looked at me again it was disconcerting, like locking eyes with a statue.

"Do you know why you're here?" he asked. His voice was low and rumbling now, and like an inquisitor's — uncomfortably close, but without a trace of warmth.

"I assume you were listening to my conversation with Mandy." Bray shot a glance at the patio and Conti. "He didn't say anything," I continued, "I'm a good guesser. So my guess is that you didn't like how Mandy

453

was handling things, and decided to take over."

Bray pursed his lips minutely. "My niece has strengths, but she doesn't always recognize when the time for conversation has passed. It's a limitation of her sex, I find."

"Does that mean you didn't bring me here to talk? Because I thought that was the purpose of meetings — to converse."

Bray lifted the highball glass from his desk, turned it in his hand, and extended it toward me. He tapped on the black shield, red maces, and Latin script printed underneath. "You know what this is?" he asked.

"Your company logo?"

He made a disdainful noise. "It's our family crest, and our motto — *sine missione.* I don't expect you know what the Latin means. It translates as —"

" 'Without quarter,' if I remember from high school. *Sine missione* — without quarter."

Bray lifted an eyebrow. "My niece forgets that these aren't simply words. They are a fundamental principle of operation. A code of behavior. A way of being. *Without quarter.*"

"Did you bring me out here to threaten me, then? Because if that's the purpose —"

"My niece is the one who threatens, doctor, and promises. She's the one who pretends to listen to what people say, and pretends to care. She can even charm at times. In your case, she's threatened to bring pressures to bear on you if the child is not returned to our family immediately. And she's made promises as well — implied that certain benefits might accrue if you bring him home. I don't operate on those terms.

"Instead, I *act*. I don't *say* that harm may come — I *do* harm. And not only to you, doctor. So the *purpose* of this meeting is not to converse. It's for me to describe the mace that's poised above your head, and above the heads of those you care for."

He checked his watch again, and took a sheet of paper from the small pile on his desk. He cleared his throat. "And so, as of nine-fifteen this morning, Southland Liberty Development Corporation became the sole owner of Kashmarian Properties, assuming its various assets and obligations, including and particularly the property which currently houses your clinic and is your residence. Southland Liberty, by the way, is a division of Eureka Pacific Real Property, which is a wholly owned subsidiary of Bray Real Estate Development. I —"

"You can't do that. My lease gives me the right of first refusal on any sale of the building. I'm supposed to receive notice of a proposed sale."

"You have a lease with a corporation, doctor, and that hasn't changed. I simply bought that corporation. But by all means, consult your attorneys; take the matter up in court. My lawyers assured me this wasn't an issue, and I'm told Mr. Kashmarian made no mention of it at the closing — though the price he was paid may have left him speechless."

"I —"

Bray held up his white palm. "It's in your interest to keep still, doctor. Now, in a separate transaction that took place late this morning, Southland Liberty also assumed ownership of a second property, a six-unit rental building on Roderick Road, in Glassell Park, the current residence of Mr. Luis Enrique Torres, who is your employee, and Mr. Arthur Silva, who is an information technology consultant. Your consultant."

Bray rubbed his fingers across his marble chin and held up more papers. "We will return to Mr. Silva in a moment, but before we do, I direct your attention to these. These are two complaints, one against yourself that will be filed shortly with the Medical Board of California, and another against Lydia Torres, your nurse, that will be filed with the state Board of Registered Nursing. The complaint against you is made by a Flora Brickel, and alleges that you sexually assaulted her during a medical examination. The complaint against your nurse is made by a Patrick Goins, who alleges that Ms. Torres offered to sell him a dozen oxycodone tablets, though no doctor had prescribed the medication for him, and that she also offered to sell him a forged oxycodone prescription."

I wasn't aware of standing, but suddenly I was up and halfway around the desk. Bray took a step back and Conti was on me, with an arm across my throat and a gun in my kidney.

"You don't want to go that way, doc," he whispered in my ear.

I didn't fight, but I didn't move either. I stared at Bray. "That's bullshit! Flora's a mean drunk, who'll say anything for the price of a box of wine, and Goins is a pimp and a junkie. I haven't seen either one of them in over a year, and those complaints are nonsense."

Bray smiled, small and nasty. "I'm sure. And the licensing boards may reach the same conclusion — eventually. But Tiger's people assure me that Ms. Brickel and Mr. Goins will remain committed to their stories. And who knows how many corroborating witnesses or other complainants may come forward in the meantime." Bray looked at Conti. "Sit him down."

Conti led me to my seat and stood behind me. "And now back to Mr. Silva," Bray said, and the smile broadened across his brutal face. "He has many other clients besides yourself, all over the city — a thriving little business. But I doubt it will survive after his clients are made aware of certain files hidden on their servers, certain photos and videos that only someone with Mr. Silva's access could have placed there. I'm referring to quite disturbing images, doctor — altogether sickening, I'm told, and entirely illegal. People in this city may tell themselves they don't mind living alongside of homosexuals, but I doubt their liberal attitudes extend to pederasts."

I tried to stand, but Conti dropped a hand on my shoulder. Bray looked at his watch and sighed. "As I said, the mace is raised, and not just above your head. And it will come down, I assure you. The only person who can stop it is you, Dr. Knox. You have twenty-four hours to decide if you and your nurse will spend the next eight or ten months defending yourselves before licensing boards, if your clinic will be evicted from

458

its current space, if you and some of your employees will be evicted from your respective residences, and if your consultant will lose his business and be brought up on child pornography charges."

His words barely sounded through the rushing in my head. My pulse was bounding, and I could feel it in my carotid. My face was hot. I took a deep breath, and let it out slowly. I smelled eucalyptus and sage and sea air, leather and liquor and old paper. Harris Bray propped his forearms on his desk and stared down at me, as if I was an ant beneath a lens and he was waiting for the first wisp of smoke. I took another deep breath.

"If you were listening to me and your niece, then you heard Elena's story. You know —"

"Let me stop you there, doctor, because you're already spouting irrelevancies. It doesn't matter one iota what I heard or what that woman has to say — you might as well be reciting last month's weather reports. The only thing that matters to your situation — and the situation of your makeshift family — is what you decide to do about the child. Everything else is noise." Bray's eyes were somehow darker and shining, and they bored into mine.

"If you were listening," I continued, "then you know Elena insists that Alex is her son. DNA testing will confirm —"

Bray made an irritated wave. "I heard all that. I also heard Amanda ask you if you wanted this to devolve into a custody battle. She didn't think it was to your advantage, and I couldn't agree more."

"DNA —"

"Assuming the results are what you think they will be, do you really think we can't produce adoption documents, doctor?"

"Valid ones?"

He smiled. "I imagine only Elena would say otherwise, but she wouldn't be able to prove it. And then will follow much legal posturing about the best interests of the child, who is the more fit parent, and so forth. It will be lengthy and expensive and tedious, but the results are a foregone conclusion."

"And you're not worried about Elena's story getting out? You must see it's beyond damning — to your company, your family — to your son especially. If the press got ahold of —"

Bray laughed, a rough barking noise. "Is that a *threat,* doctor? Are you threatening me with the press? Do you really think any news outlet would run that story? What editor or news director would do something so foolish? Assuming you could find a reporter stupid enough to write it."

"A story like that would sell a lot of advertising."

Another bark, and his nasty smile got wider. "Are you really so naïve? The people who make these decisions answer to management — chief operating officers, presidents, CEOs — who themselves answer to boards of directors. I happen to sit on several boards, doctor, including the boards of media companies, and I assure you that, while they might find an incremental bump in ad revenues appealing, they would find my lawsuits completely terrifying. The huge legal fees, the years of distraction, the potential for crippling judgments against them, not to mention the reputational wounds — they would simply have no appetite for it; the cost-benefit equation would never make sense. Though, really, I doubt my lawyers would ever have to take things that far."

"No?"

He shook his head. "Because the editors and news directors — even the reporters — who might bring this woman's nonsense to public attention are all human beings, Dr. Knox. And as such they operate according to their own self-interests. They have assets they wish to protect, secrets they wish kept, loved ones they wish to safeguard, and when they understand what they must do to achieve those ends, they will act accordingly. I promise you, faced with a situation like the one you are in, none of them would take as long to make the only rational decision."

"There are other ways her story could get out — social media, blogs. . . ."

Bray shook his head. "*Publicly held* social media companies, doctor, blogs hosted by *publicly held* firms and written by human beings. I'm afraid it all comes back to risk, reward, and self-interest."

"*Risk, reward, and self-interest* — is that how you dress it up?"

Bray took up his highball glass again, tapped a finger on his family crest, and drained it. He sighed and looked at me. "Dress what? It's all about self-interested actors competing in a free marketplace, nothing more. It's the way of the world."

"This is theatre, right — for my benefit? You can't really believe that crap."

Bray barked out another laugh. "Your immaturity is amazing. What I *do* find hard to believe is that you spent time in Africa, yet apparently find these concepts so alien. The continent provides so many splendid models of the power of unfettered markets."

"If by that you mean the power of warlords and child soldiers over unarmed men, women, and children, then, yes, I'm well acquainted. Except that what you call pursuit of *self-interest* I call intimidation, coercion, extortion, rape, and murder."

"A distinction without a difference."

I let out a long breath and shook my head. "You set a new benchmark for arrogance, Mr. Bray."

He straightened up. "And you, doctor, are smug and superior even by the standards of your profession. So certain you know what's best for the world — precisely how to improve it. Honestly, do you think you're the first scruffy man to stumble out of the jungle with fantasies about changing the world? Your story is unoriginal, doctor — old, boring, and fundamentally wrong-headed. The world is what it is — what it's always been. It doesn't want changing; it doesn't accept it. And it's the height of hubris to think you're at all qualified to try.

"In any event, I've indulged this pointless rambling for too long. You have twenty-four hours. Tiger will give you your phone back and give you a number you can call. Or don't call. You know the outcome. *Sine missione,* doctor." Then Bray took his suit jacket from the peg, crossed the room, and disappeared through a paneled door.

Conti tapped my shoulder. "Ride's waitin', doc," he said. He went to the patio and I followed. Outside, the sun was lower over the ocean and the air was cooler. The gulls were closer and more angry.

CHAPTER 43

The noodle shop was on Sawtelle, not far from Bray Consolidated. It was a new place — sharp-edged and colorful, like something made from Legos — and I'd pulled in when I noticed that my hands were shaking and I had no idea at all where I was driving. I took a table near the open kitchen and called Sutter. Then I spent the next half-hour drinking iced matcha and watching steam rise from the shiny ranges. A narcotic flow of electronic music seeped from speakers in the ceiling, and the comforting aromas of soy and ginger and simmering broth washed over me, and by the time Sutter sat down across from me, I'd managed to purge a few of the visions of Lydia and Arthur getting hauled off to jail from my head.

Sutter squinted at me and looked as if he might ask something, but then the waitress came. Sutter ordered a Kirin and I finished my matcha and ordered the same. Then I told him about my day. The story carried us through one round of beers and part of the next.

"The evil emperor himself," Sutter said when I finished, "and he brings you to the Death Star. Awesome." He made room on the table for the steaming bowls of ramen that were approaching.

"It was more San Simeon Lite than Death Star," I said, "though I saw a few storm troopers."

"Probably more you didn't see." Sutter picked up chopsticks and turned the ramen in his bowl. A thicker cloud of steam rose up. He looked at me through it. "You read him as serious?"

"As cancer."

"So you've got a decision to make."

"I'm not giving him the kid."

"Which means?"

"I don't know what the fuck it means," I said. It was louder than I meant it to be, and the other customers turned to look. Sutter smiled and lifted some noodles from his bowl. We ate and drank in silence for a while, and then Sutter drained his second beer and sighed.

"You don't give him the kid, you're going to war with him, and he's got the tactical advantage. He rolled out the shock and awe today to tell you that — to tell you that your choices are surrender or suicide."

"I got that. I just can't believe those are my only options. Maybe I don't want to believe it."

"Maybe they're not."

I looked up. "Then what?"

Sutter caught the waitress's eye and held up his empty glass. "I'm not saying you've got *good* options. But maybe you can run the clock a little, distract Bray, give him some other things to worry about for a while."

"Like what?"

He shrugged. "In another part of the world, or another part of town, you could blow up some of his shit. But here — maybe the niece."

I sat up. "Mandy? You're not thinking of — ?"

Sutter laughed. "Wrapping her in duct tape and throwing her in the trunk of my car? No, but I'm thinking maybe we wire you up and send you back to talk to her some more. You whisper some bullshit in her ear, whatever, and get her to threaten you — get it on tape. Then we turn the recording over to some wannabe Glenn Greenwald, and turn him loose on Mandy."

"Which accomplishes what?"

"Throws her off balance, scares her, makes her go running to Uncle. Best case, the recording makes Bray reassess, or at least pause. It buys you some time."

"Time for what? Nothing I heard today leads me to believe he isn't going to make good on his threats."

"Time to prepare, time to mitigate, time to think of something else. A holding action's the best you can do, brother. Of course, you want to go another way — I always have a few spare rolls of duct tape around. But I don't think you want to go that way."

"Give me a minute."

Sutter frowned. "Seriously, that's what this boils down to. The old man is going to war. Unless you are too, a little extra time's all you're going to manage."

I finished my beer and took a deep breath. "I've got to tell them. Lydia and Lucho and Arthur — I've got to tell them what's happening. What could happen to them."

He pushed his chair back from the table and shook his head. "That won't be pretty."

"No. They didn't sign up for any of this, didn't want any of it. Lydia has thought that we should stay the hell away from this since the day Elena and Alex turned up, and she's made no secret of it. Lucho has mostly kept his own counsel, but I know he thinks our day jobs are hard enough without the extracurricular shit. And Arthur — half of what he does for me is on a pro bono basis, and now . . . Shit."

"Noncombatant casualties. Collateral damage. It sucks."

I looked at my empty beer glass and thought about having another one, maybe ten more, but didn't. "I don't even know how to tell them," I said.

Sutter nodded. "While you're figuring that, work out what you're going to tell Elena too."

"Shit," I said again. "Shit."

CHAPTER 44

Sutter drove to El Segundo, and neither of us said a word the whole way. It was nearly dark when we got there, and another one of Sutter's mercs, a sinewy black woman with scarred forearms and a Glock on her hip, spoke to him in French.

Shelly was at the kitchen table, working on a burrito the size of a cat, and Alex was just finishing a plate of enchiladas verdes. Alex smiled and waved and Shelly said "Yo" through a mouthful of rice. Elena was curled on the sofa, eating yogurt from a cup, and she rose when she saw me, as if she knew I had news.

"Let's talk in back," I said to her. She shuttered her face, put her yogurt cup on the kitchen counter, and walked down the narrow hall to the rear bedroom. She sat on the edge of the bed. Her feet were flat on the floor, and her mouth was a straight line.

"So?" she said.

I nodded and told her about my meeting with Mandy, its interruption, and my visit to Malibu. I didn't go into the details of Bray's threats, but I did say that I thought he was serious.

"He wants Alex returned, and he wants it on his terms," I said, limping to conclusion. "He left no room for negotiation."

Elena's silence was long and heavy, and neither Shelly's pitchy laughter from the other room, nor Alex's giggles made a dent in it. Her gaze was fixed on the window behind me, and the darkness beyond.

"So you meet the old man, face-to-face," she said finally. "What you think?"

"Scary guy," I said. "Maybe a little crazy."

"No maybe. And not a little," she said. "How he scare you?" Elena's eyes were locked on mine now. I swallowed hard.

"He threatened to shut down my clinic, and to hurt some people I care about."

She nodded. "But if you give him Alex, then everything's fine. For you."

"I'm not going to do that, Elena."

She nodded again, slowly. Her gaze went back to the black glass. "So — what are you going to do?"

I took a deep breath. "I'm still working on that. Sutter had an idea about trying to get Mandy on tape, making the same threats her uncle did. That might give us some leverage."

A smile flitted across Elena's small mouth so quickly I wasn't sure I'd seen it. She shrugged. "Sure, that could work, or maybe something else. You keep thinking."

"I will. And you just sit tight. You and Alex are safe here."

Elena's eyes didn't stray from the window, but the little smile came and went again. "*Sit tight.* Sure — what else I'm doing? Nothing but sitting."

Sutter brought me back to my car. I drove home slowly and reluctantly, trying as I did to come up with a way of telling Lydia and Lucho and Arthur what Harris Bray had said that made his plans for them seem less disastrous than Godzilla's for Tokyo. Trying and failing.

The clinic was dark when I got there, but I could feel Lydia's irritation and exhaustion in every room, like background radiation, even before I found the note taped to my desk chair: *Sent 7 to ER @ County this afternoon. Assume they went. Hope so. Assume you remember we're open both days this weekend. Hope so.* Her handwriting was firm, precise, and angry.

I dropped into my chair, and dust rose in

472

the darkness. It settled around me as I debated not calling Lydia and Lucho and Arthur just then, and instead waiting until morning to tell them. Or perhaps crawling upstairs, into my bed, and not coming out again. Or perhaps never moving from this chair. What difference would a few hours make, with a giant radioactive dinosaur bearing down? Better to let the good citizens of Tokyo have a few hours more of sleep and blissful ignorance. Somebody should dream — why not them? Then I thought about the files Bray said were squirreled away on the servers of Arthur's clients. God only knew what kind of sewage they contained, and a few hours might make the difference between finding and not finding them, between defusing the situation and having it detonate in Arthur's face. I sighed heavily and reached for the phone.

Of course they knew it was bad news. Why else would I call Lydia and Lucho back in at nine in the evening? Why else would I ask Lucho to bring Arthur along? They looked vulnerable in the waiting room's plastic chairs, in their after-hours clothes — tee shirts and sagging jeans, Lydia in a faded tracksuit — like our patients, pale, small, disheveled, and bewildered. Lucho brought coffee for me. I took it from him but couldn't bear to drink it.

"It's Kashmarian, right?" he asked. "He's selling the place on us? We gonna shut down?"

I shook my head and told them, without preamble or pause, and without looking any of them in the eye.

The silence afterward was leaden and sickening, and went on for a long time. Then Arthur muttered "Motherfucker" and sprang up and disappeared down the hall. In a moment I heard the sound of rapid fingers on a keyboard. Lydia made a shuddering sigh, put her head in her hands, and murmured *"Dios."* Lucho squinted at me and shook his head.

"What the fuck, doc? This asshole is the kid's grandfather? And he bought my fucking apartment building — and this place too — just so he could kick us to the curb? Who does that? And what the fuck does he want from Artie? Artie never did anything to him, or to anybody — he doesn't even work here, for chrissakes. What the *fuck*?"

Lydia looked up. "It's got nothing to do with Arturo or you or me," she said, her voice low and tight. "It's got to do with *him.*" She pointed a blunt finger, and I thought she was about to stand, to come at me from across the room. But then the breath and everything else left her, and tears ran down her face. When she looked at me again she was a decade older. Her voice was quiet and beaten.

"I'm not even going to ask what you'll do — I don't want to hear it. Anyway, it's always the same: you do what *you* want to do, like always, and the hell with what anybody else wants, or what it costs them."

"Lyd —"

She held up a hand, as if she were warding off the evil eye. "Don't. Just don't fucking bother."

CHAPTER 45

It was quiet on the roof. The wind was small and soft in the rust-colored sky, the traffic was distant, and the usual nighttime soundtrack, of shattering bottles, shouted curses, sirens, was muted. Still, my head was full of a chanting chorus: Arthur and Lucho and Lydia, their anger, fear, and disappointment. Not that they'd said much more to me after I'd given them my news. Lucho had joined Arthur in the file room, and the two of them had spoken in low, tense tones while Arthur typed madly. Lydia hadn't moved from the waiting room chair — had barely moved at all except to stiffen when I'd tried to talk to her again. When her shoulders began to shake I'd retreated to my office, and reemerged only when I'd heard them heading for the door.

"I thought you guys should know about Bray," I said. "But I don't want you guys to —"

"You don't want us to what, doctor?" Lydia said, turning. Her eyes were red and wet. "To worry?"

"Bray's not . . . That stuff he talked about is not going to happen, Lydia. I'm going to make this right."

Her mouth puckered, as if she'd tasted something spoiled, and then she left. Lucho and Arthur followed, and after I heard their cars pull away, and listened to the A/C push stale air through the vents for a while, I'd gone to the roof.

The little wind flicked at the lapels of my jacket, and I was surprised to find I was still wearing it. *Like Parents' Day at Choate,* Mandy had said. I took it off and folded it over the low coping and rolled up my sleeves. I sat on the lawn chair, and its metal joints creaked. So did mine. I sighed, and life seeped from my bones.

The shaky, leaden, post-call feeling swept over me, and I closed my eyes. The night-time city vanished and was replaced by jagged pieces of the very long day: the fish like ancient coins in Bray's fountain; the thrum of chopper rotors running in my chest; the cut flowers in Amanda Danzig's office, the sunlight on her desk and on her glossy blond head; Elena with her hands in her lap, staring out the bedroom window; Bray's somber library; the shield and maces of the Bray sigil, the Latin motto; the look in Lydia's eyes.

I rubbed a hand over my face, thought about Sutter's words: *The old man is going to war. He rolled out the shock and awe today to tell you that — to tell you that your choices are surrender or suicide.* No matter how long I stared at it, I still couldn't see a third option — a way to make it right for Lydia and Lucho and Arthur that wasn't paid for by Elena and Alex.

I reached into my jacket and pulled out my phone and the card Conti had given me. I looked at the number and wondered who would answer if I called, and what I could possibly say.

The old man is going to war.

Sutter's words were loud in my ears, and as I listened I wondered: *Why now?* What had made Harris Bray decide on war today? Why not tomorrow? Why not yesterday, or last week? What had happened?

I sighed and called Nora again. And once again listened to the rings, and then her message. "You have reached . . ." It was the same message as always, but somehow her voice was unfamiliar to me, and impossibly remote. I hung up before the tone.

I looked at Conti's card, and put my finger

on the number. *Why today?* My phone chirped suddenly, and I nearly dropped it. I caught it and thought it must be Nora. I checked the screen, but didn't recognize the number. I didn't recognize the woman's voice either, not at first.

"Doctor — you're still alive!" she said. "That's a nice surprise."

"Mandy?"

Her laugh was bright and brittle, her speech overly precise. "One and the same, doctor. And so very glad to hear that Tiger didn't misplace you out the chopper door."

"Are you drunk, Mandy?"

"Not nearly enough. How about you?"

"Not at all, sad to say."

"No? That is plain unacceptable, my good doctor — we'll have to fix that. What do you like to drink? Do you favor rye whiskey? Do you perhaps like a good Sazerac? Because I mix a very fine one, and I've had lots of practice tonight."

"I don't know that I've had a Sazerac."

"Well, that's a real void in your education, doctor — one I'd be more than happy to fill, if you'd like to meet for a lecture and demonstration."

"It's late, Mandy. I think I'm fine where I am."

"Oh, you *are* fine, doctor," she said, and

479

giggled. "And pray tell: where exactly have I reached you?"

"At my place, on the roof."

"As it happens, I'm not far from you."

"What the hell are you doing in this neighborhood?"

"Well, not exactly your neighborhood, doc — I'm outside a club on Figueroa — a place some new Chinese partners wanted to see. They're still seeing it, but I got bored. I'm ten minutes by car from you. Maybe fifteen."

"Tell me you're not driving, Mandy."

She laughed. "I'm in back, all by my lonesome, doctor. It's a silver Mercedes — keep an eye out. I don't make house calls very often." And before I could argue, she was gone.

It was ten minutes exactly, and the silver Mercedes was an SUV, with smoked windows, black leather, a fully stocked bar, and a raised partition between the driver and passengers. Mandy's spicy perfume wafted out when the rear door opened, along with the smell of whiskey.

"Look at you," Mandy trilled. "You've still got your little outfit on."

"It's been a busy day; no time to slip into something more comfortable." I squinted into the shadows of the back seat. "I see you had no time either." Mandy wore the same gray skirt and fitted blouse I'd seen her in in what seemed like a hundred years ago. Her hair was still slicked, but her blouse was untucked and unfastened by a button or two. Her eyes were shining and unfocused.

She grinned. "I did take off my panty hose, doctor. Now climb in here, before the wolves start circling. I've got a Sazerac with your name on it."

I got in and shut the door, and Mandy's driver pulled away fast. I wasn't quite seated and lost my balance. I landed on my knees, with my cheek pressed against Mandy's thigh. It was firm and warm and fragrant.

"Talk about a cheap date," Mandy laughed. "Not a taste of your cocktail and you're good to go! I *do* like your style." I found my seat and Mandy handed me a glass. "Check that out."

I took a sip, and heat and then a cool, evaporating sweetness spread through my chest. I nodded. "I could get used to these."

Mandy had a glass of her own, and she took a drink and sighed. "That's life-changing, right there." The Mercedes turned onto San Pablo, and she looked out the window at the line of tents and even more provisional shelters, the campfires made of garbage, and the figures hunched around them. She shook her head. "Speaking of which — yours could use some changing. Your ZIP code, anyway. It's like the fucking Dark Ages out there. Or a Bosch painting."

I shrugged. "Poverty's not pretty; neither is mental illness. And by the way, this is your ZIP code too now — or your uncle's."

She chuckled. "What the hell are you talking about?"

"He didn't tell you? Your uncle bought out my landlord this morning — all of his real estate holdings, including my building. That was one of several things he wanted to discuss."

There was silence for a moment, and then a stream of profanities I didn't entirely catch, but in which "fucker," "fucking," and "high-handed motherfucker" featured prominently.

"Guess he forgot to mention it," I said.

"Yeah," she said, drinking. "But I shouldn't be surprised. Information only flows one way with him. You know that son of a bitch had my office bugged?"

"I connected those dots."

Her button eyes narrowed. "So, once again, I'm the last to know," she said, and laughed ruefully. "Once again, I fetch and carry and do the trench work, so he can swan in and . . . You know, *I* was supposed to take care of this shit with Alex — I *was* taking care of it — and then . . . Can you believe he *bugged my fucking office*? That's trust for you, huh? That says, *I trust you with the future of this business,* right?"

It was my turn to laugh. "Let me get this straight, Mandy — am I supposed to feel sorry for you because your uncle robbed you of the chance to intimidate and coerce me, and to take Alex from his mother? Because if that's what you're —"

She wasn't listening. "This isn't the first time with him — it's not even the tenth time. I've had deals teed up in Alberta, in the North Sea, Nigeria, partnerships negotiated with the Indonesians and Australians, acquisitions agreed to, restructurings arranged, and in every case he comes in, in the eleventh *fucking* hour, and invites me to step away from the big table. To be a good girl and take a seat along the wall, so the grown-ups can do business. And by grown-ups he means the ones with dicks.

"I guess I should count myself lucky he didn't invite my moron cousin in this time. He does that, you know. I think he thinks that Kyle might learn something — by osmosis, maybe. As if — with all the brain cells Kyle has scorched. The only things that get through his thick skull lately are meth and vodka." Another swallow and another bitter laugh. "Not that I'm judging."

I shook my head. "You're seriously complaining to me about the glass ceiling at Bray Consolidated?"

She made her small, manicured hand into a fist. "He bugged my fucking office!"

"You sound shocked. Is it such a surprise that a guy with his own private army might take his management style from Dick Cheney? I thought you were smarter than that."

"I'm plenty smart, doctor — believe me. I'm the only one fucking smart enough to run that company for him. The only one with any kind of vision. The only one with balls."

"And yet he doesn't trust you. So sad."

She crossed her bare legs, laughed bitterly, and took another drink. "I sense a certain lack of sympathy on your part, doctor, to say nothing of empathy. They didn't cover this in med school — under the heading of bedside manner?"

"I'm weeping for you on the inside."

Mandy took another drink and flipped me the bird. "Once upon a time he used to say I was the son he never had. What a bunch of bullshit."

"He said that in front of Kyle? Because, if

he did, it explains a lot."

"He used to say it when Kyle was in the hinterlands — over in Europe, trying to play good soldier. Cap was definitely *not* impressed with his efforts. He stopped saying it when Kyle came back, though."

I shook my head and swallowed some of my drink. "*The son I never had* — very nice. So what happened to make him pull the plug on us this afternoon? Did your uncle just suddenly recall that you don't have a penis, or was it something else?"

"Who knows? He probably thought I'd waited too long to start the waterboarding."

"I gather he's not much for conversation. Personally, I thought we were doing okay, you and I."

She looked at me, patted my leg, and sighed. "We were doing just fine, doctor. We were having a pleasant chat about custody hearings, and you were threatening me with reporters, and then — boom — we were done. Maybe your reporter talk pissed him off. Maybe he thought I should've just clubbed you when you mentioned it — like a baby seal."

Strobing lights flashed past us — a prowl car running silent in a red-and-blue blur. I slid the window down, and warm air rushed in. I took a deep breath. "Maybe," I said.

Mandy yawned. "Put that up — it's too windy."

I looked out at the streets. We were on Olympic, just east of the 110. "Where are we going, Mandy?"

"West. The general direction of my place."

I laughed and took another drink. "I don't think so."

Mandy laughed. "Because of Dr. Yoga MILF? Are you guys, like, going steady? 'Cause I'll tell you, I sensed some tension last night. I think she was sort of pissed at you. Or maybe she's always that way."

"A: don't call her that. B: I really don't know what she and I are doing, since she's not taking my calls. And C: yes, she was definitely pissed, thanks to your cousin and you."

Mandy reached over and ran a fingertip around my earlobe. "So let me make it up to you," she said softly. "I'm not as old as you apparently like, but I'm limber."

I batted her hand away. "Don't you have a boyfriend or something?"

She laughed and stretched her legs into my lap. Her bare soles were hot on my thigh. She held up her hand and made a show of inspecting her engagement boulder. "I have a fiancé, which I guess is close enough, but he's in Shanghai right now.

Anyway, he has nothing to do with us."

I smiled. "It'll be an amazing marriage, I'm sure. But sleep would be the best thing for you right now, Mandy —"

"We can sleep. Eventually."

"Sleep and lots of water. I don't think you're going to feel that great tomorrow."

Mandy sat up, slid across the leather, and ended up mostly in my lap. Her lips were soft on mine, and her tongue insistent. She tasted of Sazerac, and when she pulled away she left the same heat and vanishing coolness on my lips.

She kissed my ear, and whispered: "There's the blah, blah, blah coming out of your mouth, and there's all the stuff going on inside. You've got to get your stories straight, doctor."

"Mandy —"

"Too much talk," she said, and she hitched up her skirt, swung a leg across me, and straddled my lap. Her mouth was hot pressing down, and her body was strong and lithe and burning. Her breathing was quick, her hips were achingly slow, and her spicy, whiskey scent was everywhere. I don't know how long our fevered grapple lasted, but we were on Melrose, in West Hollywood, when I came up for air. My shirt was open and so was hers. Her bra was a pale web of lavender lace, half falling off.

Mandy's face was above me — pink and shining and swollen-mouthed. "Jesus," she whispered, and bit my lower lip.

"Indeed," I said, and I hoisted her off my lap and back onto her own seat.

"What the fuck?" she said, scowling.

"I need to catch my breath, Mandy."

She laughed. "What — you want candy and flowers, or something? 'Cause, from what I could tell, you were DTF."

"I don't even know what that means."

"*Down to fuck,* Gramps, and don't tell me that you weren't — that you aren't."

I fumbled with my shirt buttons. "Maybe it's a generational thing, but I'd like to know who exactly you'd be fucking — me or your uncle?"

Mandy straightened her skirt and looked down at her blouse, but didn't bother to close it. "I could ask you the same, Dr. Freud, except that I couldn't care less."

"Like I said, maybe it's a generational thing."

Mandy sighed, found her glass, and took another drink. "I think you just like saying no to me, doctor. I think it turns you on a little bit."

"It's possible you have that backward, Mandy. It's called projecting, if I remember from my psych rotation."

She raised an eyebrow and smirked at me over her glass. "You may be on to something, Sigmund." Then she flicked a switch on her armrest and spoke to the driver. "You can stop over by the Urth, Gus. The doctor will get out here."

The Mercedes pulled to the curb near the corner of Melrose and Westmount. "You're dumping me here?"

"No one rides for free, doc," she said, chuckling, and pushed open the door with her foot. She was still laughing when the Mercedes rolled away.

I took an Uber home, and along the way didn't think of the heat of Mandy's body, her lips, the dizzying scent of her, but wondered instead about her family — her uncle and her cousins.

Mandy was wrong, I thought, about what had pissed her uncle off enough to send Conti barging into her office to collect me. It wasn't my threat about reporters — we were right in the middle of that discussion when Conti appeared. And I doubted it was our back-and-forth about custody fights — that had taken place only a minute or two earlier. No, what had upset Harris Bray — and maybe what had driven him to war — was something Mandy and I had talked about before that. The more I thought about it, the more certain I was.

When the car dropped me at the clinic, I didn't go in, but went around back to the Dumpster, where my Honda was parked. I looked through the filthy window at the white garbage bag, still slumped on the rear seat. Then I got behind the wheel and started the engine. I dug out my phone before I shifted into drive, and put in a call to Jiffy-Lab.

CHAPTER 46

It was dawn when I said goodbye to Nate Rash and got in my car and pulled onto Third Street. I hadn't slept in twenty-four hours, but my mind was oddly clear as I headed east, as if a stiff ocean breeze had swept away my shaky fatigue, thoughts of impending doom, and any other anxious cobwebs. The sky was pale and brightening ahead of me, and the streets as close to empty as they got. I stopped for an egg sandwich and a bucket of coffee at Bottega Louie, and rolled up to the clinic as Lucho was opening the doors.

I ran my window down, and he walked to the curb. His green scrubs were pressed, but he was not. His skin was sallow, his broad face lined, and there were gray pouches beneath his eyes.

"You're early," I said.

"Not a lot of sleep goin' on at our place. Artie was at the keyboard all night."

"He get anywhere?"

Lucho shook his head. "He found foot-prints or something — I'm not sure what that is — but he said the fuckers who did this were good at it. They didn't make it look like this porn crap was just being stored on his clients' servers; they made it look like the servers were being used to exchange this shit. He still hasn't found the actual files they put out there — he said that'll take more time — and he's still try-ing to put together some proof that he had nothing to do with any of this."

"Is he going to reach out to his clients — to explain things, and get ahead of this?"

"We talked about it, but it's not so easy to explain, right? Not without sounding like you're a little crazy yourself. That's why he wants evidence before he gets into it with them — something that'll calm 'em down when they freak. He's afraid some of 'em will call the cops no matter what."

"Artie could call the cops."

Lucho squinted at me for a while. "So could you," he said finally.

I nodded. "Has he thought about a law-yer?"

Lucho rolled his eyes. "We talked about it, but . . ." Lucho rubbed his thumb over his first two fingers. "We were thinking about Anne Crane. Maybe she'd throw some pro bono our way."

I nodded, and cursed to myself for not having thought to call her. "I bet she would. I'll phone her."

Patients started showing up around six-thirty, by which time I'd left a message for Anne, showered and changed, and started coffee brewing in the file room. We were working on the second pot when Lydia appeared. She'd never been so late before, or looked so rumpled or distracted. She offered no explanation of her late arrival, or any word at all beyond asking me about the patients in the waiting room, and the ones I'd seen already. She didn't look at me when she asked, or when I answered.

I filled my coffee mug and took cover in an exam room, hiding behind a line of patients from thoughts of Lydia's anger, Harris Bray's promises, and other shoes dropping. The motley parade marched all day, and the caffeine flowed, and my sense of clarity somehow persisted. Until it shattered into a thousand pieces at around four-thirty that afternoon, when a messenger walked in. He had a clipboard, and sweat stains under the arms of his polyester shirt, and he brought me an eviction notice, which he made me sign for.

CHAPTER 47

"You should've called me, for chrissakes." Anne Crane let the letter from my new landlord fall to her desk. "Right away — as soon as Bray turned you loose." We were at Burnham Fiedler's offices — mostly empty on a Saturday — in Anne's gray, glass-walled box. Fading daylight came through the window and fell on a desk cluttered with dog-eared documents, cups from the Coffee Bean, an empty yogurt cup, and a half-eaten salad in a plastic container. Anne wore jeans and a rumpled pink blouse with an umlaut of raspberry jam on it. Her gray hair was pulled into a short, ineffective ponytail.

"What would you have told me?" I asked.

"I don't know — but I would've had twenty-four more hours to think about it, maybe to figure out some things. If nothing else, we'd have had an extra day to find these people — Brickel and Goins — and remind them of the downside of making false accusations."

"Good luck with that. They don't have addresses, or much of anything else besides the clothes on their backs. They're litigation-proof, Anne, just like Bray."

"Harris Bray's got plenty of assets."

"So? Bray's insulated — even I know that. The real estate transactions are separated from him by who knows how many layers of companies, and I'm sure we could look for a long time without finding a link from Bray to what's happened to Arthur and his clients, or to the charges against me and Lydia. His private army is good at that stuff. All these are going to look like discrete events, and I'm the only one to say differently. It'll be my word against his that this is — what — a conspiracy? Coercion? Is there something you would have said to make that argument sound more plausible?"

She picked up the eviction notice again and shook her head. "This is shit, you know. Your lease doesn't permit —"

"This is just a shot across the bow, Anne — the first one. And while you're filing whatever you can file about this, Lucho and Artie are going to get their own eviction notice, and Lydia and I are going to hear from the licensing boards. Not to mention Artie's clients. Speaking of which . . ."

"I'm not sure what I can do for him. I — Burnham Fiedler — represent the clinic and maybe you personally, if we stretch things. We don't represent your employees or your contractors."

"But you could, couldn't you?"

"And do what — assuming my masters let me do anything at all?"

"I don't know, help him calm his clients down, maybe. Help him if the cops come around."

"For that he'll need a criminal lawyer. I don't do —"

"He's a bystander, Anne — they all are. You guys must be able to do something."

Anne winced. "I'll talk to my bosses. But the bigger question is: what are *you* going to do about all this? This is a world of shit, doctor. Have you thought about —"

"He's not getting the kid — that much I know. Beyond that, I have an idea about getting Mandy to say incriminating things on tape."

"Why would she do that?"

I shrugged. "She's . . . weird. And she kind of likes me." Anne squinted. "She called me last night. She was pretty drunk, and pissed off at Bray, and —"

Anne's squint became a smirk. "She drunk-dialed you? What — she got bored

497

with Tinder?"

I felt my face redden. "The point is: she's not overly fond of her uncle. It turns out, on top of everything else, he's a sexist — big surprise — and Mandy's a disgruntled employee."

"Poor baby. But is she disgruntled enough to bite the hand?"

"I guess we'll find out, unless you have a better idea."

Anne picked up one of the cardboard coffee cups on her desk. She looked inside and swirled it around and shook her head slowly. "I got nothing," she said.

I left Anne wilting in her office with her salad and her documents, and rode the elevator to the garage. She had promised to call after she spoke to her bosses, though she couldn't say how long that would take on a weekend. Still, I was hopeful when my phone chimed as I was unlocking the Honda. I shouldn't have been.

Sutter's voice was low and tense. "I'm in El Segundo," he said. "You need to get over here."

"What's happened? Is Elena okay? Alex?"

"Don't know if they're okay, but they are definitely gone."

I pulled into the driveway behind an SUV

and sprinted up the path. The front door was open, and Sutter was in the living room with Yossi, the tall, dark man with Chinese characters on his neck, who looked more sheepish than dangerous now.

Sutter put up his hand like a traffic cop, and I stopped at the doorway while he spoke quietly to Yossi. I couldn't hear what he said, but I saw Yossi go from sheepish to pale and nervous. Yossi nodded as he listened, and when Sutter was done he started to answer. Sutter raised a finger and stopped him. Sutter spoke some more and put a hand on Yossi's shoulder. Yossi nodded again, visibly relieved, then slid past me, out the door.

"You want coffee?" Sutter asked, and walked into the kitchen. I followed.

"Coffee, some clue as to what's going on — either of those would work."

"They bolted, all three of them," Sutter said as he scooped coffee into the machine. "Out the bedroom window, over the back-yard fence, and — poof. About two hours ago. Yossi thought Elena and the boy were asleep, and that Shelly was taking a bath, and he was mostly watching the street. He's embarrassed as hell, if that makes you feel any better. And he's worried that he won't get any work out of me again. He's got that right, the sloppy fuck."

"Two hours ago? How far could they get in that time?"

"On foot, figure three miles an hour times two, but we'll find out. I've got Franco and Evie looking."

I was adding milk to my coffee when the front door opened and Franco walked in, followed by Evie — the sinewy black woman with scars on her forearms. They paused when they saw me, and Sutter waved them on.

"We spiraled out," Evie said in a heavy French accent, "on foot and in the car. Seven-mile radius, and we got nothing."

"Maybe not total nothing," Franco said, and pointed toward the rear of the house. "You know the place behind this one, with the carport? When I'm here before, I always see a pickup in it."

"Blue Ford," Sutter said. "Kind of beat up."

Franco nodded. "That's it. Evie says she thinks the guy lives there works a late shift, comes back late morning, leaves the truck in the carport, sleeps all day, takes off again around nine at night. Truck's not there now, but it's not nine yet. We go up close and find the kitchen door jimmied. I look in — very quiet — I see a wallet on the kitchen floor, looks empty."

Sutter looked at me and smiled ruefully. "You think they jacked the truck?" I asked.

Franco nodded. "Me and Evie make a bet. I say the blonde did it; she thinks no. But that blonde is tough."

Evie shook her head. "You know shit about women, *cher.* It was the little dark one, the mother. She watches everything — everybody — all the time. And she plans — you see it in her eyes. Out there in the yard or from the bedroom, I know she sees that house and that truck, that guy on the night shift — same as me."

"I'm with you," Sutter said. "I don't guess either of you caught the tags on that Ford." Franco and Evie shook their heads. "Me neither, but if it was boosted, the guy next door will be calling it in soon. When he does, I can get 'em from a guy I know with the Sheriff's."

"Which will tell us what?" I asked.

"Tag numbers make finding the truck easier."

"Isn't that a needle in a haystack in this town?"

"Yeah, but I think we can rule out Holmby Hills and Brentwood. I assume Shelly's driving, and she's gonna go where she knows. What do you know about where Shelly hangs out, or who she hangs with?"

I shrugged. "I've see her on the streets, near the Harney, but I don't think she's going back there anytime soon. As far as friends, Mia's the only one who comes to mind, and, given what Shelly brought to her door last time . . ."

"Burnt bridges — I get it," Sutter said. "Still, Mia might be a place to start. You know how to find her?"

"I'll see what contact info we have at the clinic," I said. "If we have anything."

Franco and Evie left, and the little house was quiet but for a drip of water from the tap into the kitchen sink — as flat and insistent as a bill collector's knock.

Sutter stared at the sink. "I got to fix that," he said eventually.

"If Elena's a planner," I said, "what's her plan?"

He shrugged. "You tell me."

"She wanted money from the Brays, and passage home for her and the boy. And she wanted an apology."

"She doesn't strike me as someone who changes her mind easy."

"But I have no clue how she'd go about pursuing any of that — not on her own, anyway. What's she going to do, go to the press herself? Stake out all the places the Brays live?"

Sutter shook his head. "Who the fuck knows? But I'd focus less on her plans if I were you, and worry more about your own."

I squinted at him. "What am I missing?"

"Your girl has left you deeper in the shit, brother, if you can believe your shit can get deeper. Even if you wanted to do a deal with Bray, you can't now. And how do you think the old man will react when you tell him you have no idea where his grandkid is? Or when you tell him, *Now that Alex and Elena are in the wind, I got no dog in this fight?* You think he'll say, *Solid, my brother; no harm, no foul, nice doing business with you?*"

"Fuck," I whispered.

Sutter's smile was tight and grim. He drank his coffee, and the dripping tap held sway again.

CHAPTER 48

There were two guys at the end of the alley when I parked behind the clinic, dividing the contents of a suitcase that looked mostly made of duct tape. Caught in my headlights, their smudged faces were furtive and hungry and mad. One elbowed the other, and together they dragged their treasure into deeper shadow. I dragged myself upstairs.

I found a yogurt that was only slightly out of date in the fridge, and a brown banana, and I stood by the kitchen window while I ate them. I looked again at the eviction papers that had come that afternoon, and thought about what Sutter had said — *Your girl has left you deeper in the shit* — and found nothing I could argue with.

What little leverage I might've had with Bray, any marginal sway over this slow-motion train wreck, had bolted out the back window of the house in El Segundo, and driven off in a stolen truck. Harris Bray hadn't believed me before, when I said I couldn't produce Alex. What reason would he have to believe me now, or even to listen? A helicopter flitted in the western sky, above Pershing Square and the towers along Grand Avenue, and I thought about my recent chopper ride — the sky sliding across the cabin window, and Conti's suntanned bulk. Perhaps the question of Bray's believing me was beside the point. Perhaps, having raised up his mace, he just wanted to bring it down.

I dropped the eviction notice on the counter, and wondered what messengers might arrive at my door — or Lydia's, or Lucho's — tomorrow, and with what ugly news. Then I dug in my pocket for my cell. Talking to Harris Bray was a nonstarter, but maybe someone else would take my call, and maybe she'd be drunk again.

Amanda Danzig answered on the fourth ring but, unfortunately, was sober. There were people talking in the background, and music playing. "Kicking yourself over missed opportunities, doctor? Wondering if that ship has sailed for good?"

I laughed. "That wasn't the main purpose of my call, but we can talk about that if you want."

Mandy laughed too. "I haven't had nearly

enough wine for that. What do you want?"

"I don't know where Alex is, and I don't know where or how to find him. I want you to get your uncle to believe that and to lay off me and mine, before this gets out of hand."

Another, chillier laugh. "Out of hand for who? As far as I can tell, my uncle has the reins firmly in his grasp."

"Did he share the particulars of his plans with you?"

There was quiet on the line for a while, just dinner party sounds from wherever Mandy was. Then she sighed. "He did not, doctor, which is not atypical."

"So you said, last night."

"Christ — I really *was* in the bag."

"There's nothing wrong with venting."

Mandy laughed again. "The two of you must really have hit it off. I'd have paid to be a fly on the wall."

"If you had been, you'd know the overkill that he's got in mind — and not just to punish me. There are innocent people —"

"None of this is remotely surprising, or remotely my business. Not anymore."

"No? I thought you were concerned about the big picture at Bray Consolidated."

She sighed. "Doctor, as appealing as you may be in certain ways, let me assure you that you and your friends and this whole messy business with my baby cousin constitute not the smallest pimple on the ass of the big picture of Bray Consolidated."

"Maybe not, but what your uncle's planning — coercion, conspiracy, inducing perjury — that kind of stuff is messy. It shows up on the radar, and in the press."

"Again with the power of the press! That must be a generational thing, doctor, this overestimation of the power and incorruptibility of the Fourth Estate. It's sweetly retro, and much less annoying than porkpie hats."

"I'm serious, Mandy. If you're concerned with your company —"

"It's *not* my company, as my uncle has made abundantly clear to me. And my role is to stay the hell out of this and say: *Good night, doctor.* So: good night, doctor."

My phone went quiet, and I put it on the counter and took a long, slow breath. Then I opened a bottle of Carta Blanca and went downstairs to pull Mia's records.

CHAPTER 49

We held a podiatry clinic that Sunday — soaking, debriding, clipping, scraping, lancing, salving, and bandaging feet that looked like they'd marched the long way from Bataan. Lydia usually ran these things, with help from some of our part-timers and from Bruce Welker, a mostly retired podiatrist from the Valley who volunteered. But Lydia was a no-show when the first patients tottered in, so management fell to Dr. Welker, who seized command like a gnomish Mac-Arthur. I was glad of it, because I had an overfull dance card of my own.

Injuries and STDs, mostly. Syphilis, chlamydia, ankle sprain, fractured ulna, scalp laceration, genital herpes, syphilis, syphilis, fractured ribs, second-degree burn, chlamydia. In between, I tried and failed to reach Mia on the several phone numbers we had on file for her. It wasn't until two that afternoon that I took a break. I was eating an apple at my desk, listening to another of Mia's phones ring, when Lucho stuck his head around the corner.

"You hear from Lyd, doc?"

I shook my head. "You?"

"Not yet."

"Not even a voice mail?"

"Nope. I'm gonna give her a call."

"She didn't have much to say yesterday — not to me, anyway. Maybe five words altogether."

"She's pretty worried, doc. We all are."

I nodded. "How's Artie doing?"

Lucho shrugged. "Not sure. He's been at his office since . . . I don't know when. He's gonna start calling his clients today." He paused and looked down at his big, scarred hands. "I'm gonna call Lyd," he said, and headed for the file room.

"Let me know when you talk to her," I called.

By five he hadn't, nor by six, nor by seven o'clock, when we were turning out the lights.

"I tried her house and her cell a couple times," Lucho said. "I'm gonna go over."

"I'll do it," I said. "You go home to Artie."

"He's not home yet."

"Then go to his office. I'll see Lyd."

Lucho frowned and looked at his feet.

"Maybe she won't be glad to see you."

"There's no maybe about it," I said.

The sky was a muddy violet when I got to Highland Park. There were lights on in most of the little houses that I passed, and cars in the driveways. I turned onto Repton Street and slowed when I saw a woman who at a glance looked like Lydia. On closer inspection, she was smaller and younger, and I drove on.

There were kids on Lydia's block, a pair of ten-year-old boys, shoving each other, laughing, sprinting past her house. Lydia's windows were dark and empty, as was her driveway. The gate on her chain-link fence was unlatched, and swung slowly in the evening breeze. I parked in her drive and walked up the path to the porch; I stopped halfway there, when I saw that her front door frame was splintered, and that there was a large black boot print on the door itself, just under the knob.

I waited on the porch for a moment, until my heart climbed back behind my sternum, then pushed open the door and called Lydia's name. I called three times and got no answer, and prayed it was because the house was empty. I found my cell phone, and the flashlight app, and threw a small white circle into the foyer. There were black scuffs on the floor, and broken crockery, and a small upended table with a broken leg.

"Fuck," I whispered, and found the light switch. Then I searched the house.

I went through it twice, my breath fraying in my lungs, and found more broken things, but no blood and no body. Lydia's sofa had been pushed up against the wall, and I slid it back to where it usually was and sat down heavily. I pulled out my phone again, but I didn't know whom to call. Lucho? Sutter? The police? My phone made the decision for me. It glowed and burred, and Lydia's name came up. A shuddering sigh went through me as I pressed the phone to my ear.

"Jesus, Lyd, where the hell are you?"

The voice that answered was heavy, dark, and Russian. "The bitch is here, doctor," the man said, "but she can't talk right now."

CHAPTER 50

Sutter looked down at his living room floor and touched the toe of his sneaker to a stone that was newer-looking than the others around it, but webbed with cracks. He shook his head and sighed. "I just fucking replaced this," he said softly. "Now look at it." He looked up at me. "Tell it again — everything the guy said."

The glass doors to the patio were open, and the ticking of insects came in with traffic noise and a tired breeze. I was on the sofa, and Eartha stepped from the cushions onto my shoulder. Sutter was pacing too, slowly, from the kitchen to the edge of the patio and back. He held a beer bottle in his hand, but hadn't yet had a sip.

I nodded. "It wasn't much. He said: *It's not complicated — we have your nurse and we want the boy. A simple swap.* He said to tell you to call about the details. I tried telling him I didn't know where Alex was, but

512

he ignored me. He kept saying I should talk to you, and that you should call. Then I pointed out that you and Siggy had a deal, and he laughed at that. He said: *They still do. The deal was, he pays and we forget about the girl. This has nothing to do with the girl; we forgot about the girl. This is a new deal.*" I sighed. "Do I call Lucho?"

Sutter shrugged. "What's he gonna do?"

"If Lyd doesn't turn up tomorrow morning, he'll want to know why — assuming he doesn't call before then."

He looked at his watch. "You open at, what, seven a.m.; that's eleven hours from now. She'll be back by then."

"How's that going to happen?"

" 'Cause I'm going to get her now."

Sutter said that I didn't have to come, that I shouldn't come, but I didn't answer him, and he didn't press. I waited in the living room while he went upstairs. He was back in ten minutes, having swapped sneakers for black boots, and wearing black Kevlar over his black tee shirt. He carried a gray duffel that looked heavy, and that made clanking sounds when he slung it on his shoulder.

"Might as well be useful," he said, and tossed me car keys. We got into the GMC in his carport, and headed for the Valley.

There was traffic on the freeway, but it was fast. The only sounds in the car were of tires hissing on pavement, Coltrane playing softly, and the metallic snap, latch, and rack of magazines and weapons as Sutter checked them.

"Siggy has her at his house?" I asked, as we turned onto Foothill.

"I don't know where he has her. I know where he'll bring her."

Sutter had me pull off Berkshire Avenue onto a narrow street that bordered the back of Siggy's property. It was hung in drooping pines and shadows, and the only streetlight was fifty yards from where I stopped.

"Lights," Sutter whispered, and I killed the headlamps. Sutter got out, carrying the duffel, and disappeared into shadow. When my eyes adjusted I could just make him out, crouched beneath a pine at the foot of Siggy's wall, a cell phone to his ear. In a moment he rose and fastened a belt around his waist. He Velcroed the holster around his thigh, and slung another gun on his shoulder. He slid the duffel into the back seat and came around to my window.

"Your phone on?" he asked. I nodded. "Good signal?" Another nod. "Put it on mute, put it on the dash, and hang here until I call. When I do, don't answer, just

514

drive around to the main gate, and drive quick. Shouldn't be longer than fifteen minutes, give or take. You might hear noise while you're waiting. If you do, don't worry about it. If you don't hear from me in twenty, take off. Go to that shopping center on Foothill — the one with the pizza joint — and wait there. Park out front; wait in the car. Somebody will come."

"Somebody who?"

"Somebody. Did you get all that?"

"I got it. What if cops come?"

Sutter's grin was bright in the shadows. "Not to worry, brother — the neighbors are far away, and nobody in there is calling 911." Then he tightened his Kevlar vest and vanished.

I put the phone on the dash, and waited and watched as the numbers changed. The night air was soft and full of pine resin and chirping and the quiet creak of branches, but all I could hear was the hammering of my heart, and all I could taste was metal on my tongue. In about an hour, ten minutes passed and I heard — thought I heard — distant shouts and flat popping sounds. An hour or a minute later, I saw a flash of red at the top of the wall. After an eternity — at the fourteen-minute mark — my phone glowed with Sutter's number. I started the engine and pulled out.

The GMC slid around the first corner on a patch of pine needles, and slid again on the next one, and I tapped the gas coming out of it. It was dark on Siggy's block but for the lights at his gates, which winked out just as I got there. I hit the brakes, and the GMC skidded and swayed and threw up a heavy cloud of dust. The gates swung open and Sutter was there — a silhouette walking backward from the haze, dragging Siggy by the back of his pants. Siggy was barefoot and stumbling, and his wrists were bound in back with zip ties. There was a strip of duct tape over his mouth.

Three of Siggy's men followed them down the drive, ranged in an arc, about twenty yards away. All three had guns — automatics with straps and skeleton stocks and big magazines — but only one seemed to know what to do. He was in the center, squinting down his sights at Sutter. Sutter stopped and pointed a finger at the center guy. When he did, a red line cut through the hanging dust and a red dot appeared on the man's head. The gunmen didn't notice, but then the center man's head snapped back, and I heard a sound like a cough behind me, and the man's legs collapsed beneath him. He lay motionless on the cobbles, and the other two gunmen stood frozen, staring at him and at the red dots that hovered on their own chests. I opened the driver's door, and Sutter called without turning around.

"Stay in the car. That guy's done, and these two aren't as stupid as they look. They know if they empty their hands and put their bellies on the deck they might see sunrise. Right, boys?"

The gunmen looked at each other, at Sutter, at Siggy, who shook and grunted, and at the silent red dots over their hearts. Then they did what Sutter told them.

CHAPTER 51

"Pizza," Sutter said, and he threw Siggy onto the floor in back, climbed in after, and shut the door. "And keep to the speed limit." I nodded, but I struggled all the way to the pizza place on Foothill to go light on the gas.

The storefronts in the shopping center were dark when we got there, and Sutter told me to park in back. I found a spot in the shadows, amid some Dumpsters, and killed the lights and the engine. Sutter hauled Siggy onto the back seat and grabbed a corner of the duct tape strip over his mouth.

"When I take this off, I know you're gonna want to tell me how dead I am, how dead everyone I know is — everyone I've ever known, et cetera — and in the bloodiest, most painful way possible. Believe me, I understand the urge. But how about we skip over that part? Let's take it as a given that you're pissed and want to kill me, and that I know this, and we'll go from there. What do you say?" Then Sutter peeled away the duct tape — gently, I thought — and Siggy spit in his face.

"Killing you will be the least of it," Siggy said. His voice was low and calm. "An afterthought. But we won't get to that part for a while. And when we do, you'll be begging for it. I promise you, you'll thank me — you and this prick both. It'll be a fucking mercy. That's my *given,* soldier. Besides that, we got no reason to talk."

Most of Siggy's spit had landed on Sutter's shoulder, but he wiped off the bit that hit his jaw and smiled ruefully. "I guess you had to get that out of your system. I did fuck up your landscaping, after all, not to mention your French doors, that guy in your den, the one at the gate, and your evening in general. But let's move on, and let me tell you how wrong you are. We've got at least one thing to discuss: I want the woman back. Tonight. Now."

Siggy laughed. "Or what — you're going to kill me? Then she gets aced too, asshole. Besides, I don't think you've got the taste for it anymore. Maybe it's from hanging around with this motherfucker."

"I never had a taste for it, Sig, not like

you. Doing what needs doing is a different story."

"Bullshit — you lost your nutsack, plain and simple. You forgot what war is. So now it's your turn to cut the crap. We both know you're not going to put me down, so buy yourself a day's head start and cut me loose now."

Sutter shook his head. "You're the only one talking about killing you, Sig," he said. "I've got something different in mind." Then he reached down into the duffel, pulled out a laptop, and opened it. The computer whirred awake, and a blue glow lit Sutter's face. He typed quickly. "Gotta let the broadband connect. I could've pulled this up on my phone, but I think it's better on a bigger screen. There we go. The picture's a little grainy, 'cause it's night vision, which is cool by itself — a live feed right through the scope — but, grainy or not, I think you can make out all the highlights." Then he turned the laptop so Siggy and I could see.

He was right about the image, a grainy green-and-gray tableau, the figures and the objects in it — the tall window frames, the wall cabinets, the big double-door refrigerator, massive kitchen island, and hanging lights — all blurred at the edges. But Siggy knew what he was looking at, and lunged forward and strained against his bonds.

Sutter cuffed him across the ear, and Siggy fell back, snarling. His eyes burned in the dark.

"Bliad!" Siggy growled.

Sutter laughed. "You gotta keep your shit together, Sig, or I'm gonna put the tape back on." He held up the laptop again. "But I'm glad you catch my drift here.

"What do you think they're doing there, in your kitchen? They must be pretty worried, and I guess your little girl must be scared." He pointed to the blurred figures at the kitchen island, the taller, slender one, the smaller one. "But it looks like she's eating something, so not too scared for that.

"And how about the missus, Siggy? She's nice to look at, but is she made of tough stuff? Is she a warlord's wife? I guess they must be waiting for a call from somebody. Waiting for somebody to tell them what the fuck is going on. Is she gonna hold up under all the pressure, or freak out? You think she feels safe right now, with all those guys in the kitchen with her? Too bad none of them is smart enough to keep her away from windows, huh? Not very well trained."

Siggy was silent, staring at the screen, and I wasn't sure if he'd heard much of what

521

Sutter had said or if he was transfixed, as I was, by the crosshair at the center of the image — the way it scanned lazily back and forth, from Siggy's wife to his daughter. It was hypnotic and terrifying, and the longer I watched, the harder it was to breathe.

My voice came out in a raspy whisper. "What the hell — ?"

Sutter held up a hand. "You do get where I'm going with this, right, Sig? You understand what comes next?" Siggy's eyes were wide and damp, and he answered with a stream of menacing, guttural Russian that came from deep in his chest.

Sutter shook his head. "Stay on track. You see what comes next: *da* or *nyet*?"

Siggy nodded. "But you're not going to do it," he said.

Sutter pulled out his cell. "It's a phone call away."

"Bullshit," Siggy whispered.

Sutter shrugged, and thumbed his phone. He held it to his ear and spoke into it in rapid French, then looked at Siggy. "You want to pick, Sig, or is it dealer's choice?"

I put a hand on Sutter's arm. "For chrissakes —"

He jerked his arm away and pointed at me. "You mind sitting still and shutting the fuck up, doc? You got this shit boulder roll-

522

ing; I'm just trying to stop it."

"I'm going to kill you myself," Siggy said. "With my hands. With my fucking teeth I'll tear you apart."

Sutter spoke again in French into the phone, and put it in his pocket. Then he drew closer to Siggy, and his voice was soft and intimate.

"No, you won't. Because you can't. Do you know how long it took me to set up this little op? Not even two hours, with just three guys, not counting the doc and me. Imagine what I can do to you and yours with more time to plan, more intel, more manpower? You have a lot of muscle, Siggy, and in your own AO you do fine, because you're tough and mostly you're dealing with morons. But you have no imagination or discipline or patience, and I've got all three. Plus, Uncle spent a crap ton of time and money training me how to use them, and then sent me to the ass end of the earth so I could practice on people who shoot back with a lot more firepower than you can organize.

"You think I forgot what war is? I only wish I could. If I prayed, I'd pray for that. But the sad truth is, I can't forget it — not ever. All I can do is live with it, and try to avoid it in the future. The fact is, *you're* the one who forgot, Siggy. You're a long way away from that crib in San Pete. You're living fat now, with your nice wife and kid and your nice house out here, your place up in Tahoe, the one in Hawaii, and the condo on the Wilshire strip you hope the missus doesn't know about. You got those restaurants and clubs, all your new Westside friends, and the city councilmen who take your calls." Sutter reached out and touched a leg of Siggy's trousers. "Shit, you've got Brioni suits, Siggy. That's a lot to lose. A long way to fall."

Sutter held up the laptop. The grainy scene was still there; the crosshair now fixed on Siggy's wife. "*You're* the one who forgot about the crap-your-pants fear and the scrambling panic, about the paranoia, and jumping out of your skin when a car backfires or a fish farts six miles offshore. *You're* the one who forgot about collateral damage. Because, more than anything else, that's what war is: the slaughter of innocents while they're taking their goats to market, or coming home from school, or sitting in their nice kitchens having a fucking bowl of ice cream."

He closed the laptop and sat back and sighed. "You forgot. You took things for granted. You climbed up so high you thought there was no more gravity. You thought you were immune. I get that — it's a very human thing. But tonight I'm gravity's representative, Siggy, here with a one-time-only reminder. Your nice life can go away. I can take it away. I *will* take it away, faster than you can imagine.

"Or I won't. I don't like war and I'm not looking for one. Let go of this thing you have for me — leave me alone, leave him alone, and turn over his nurse — and you'll never see me again. Anybody asks about Siggy Rostov, I say he's a badass, somebody you never want to mess with, so scary I can barely speak his name, the one man that gives me nightmares. So it's your call, Siggy. And now's the time to make it."

Sutter put the laptop back in the duffel and took out his cell phone. He looked at Siggy, whose breathing was ragged and raspy and filled the car, and whose eyes were fixed on nothing. I felt a ribbon of sweat slide over my ribs.

When Siggy finally spoke, his voice came from the bottom of a well. "All right. We're done. After this — after tonight — you don't exist for me and I don't exist for you."

I sighed, long and shuddering, and Sutter nodded. "Who do I call?" he asked.

"Josef. His number is —"

"I know his number."

Sutter left me in the GMC with Siggy while he stood by the Dumpsters and called Josef. Siggy looked at me while we waited.

"He's crazy, your friend, you know that?" I said nothing. "You knew him when he was a soldier?"

"After, when he was private. In Africa."

"He was this crazy?"

"Pretty much."

Siggy shook his head, and Sutter opened the passenger door and held up his phone. "Siggy, tell Josef you're alive and that the swap is okay."

From the speaker, Josef's voice was tight. *"Kak dela?"*

Siggy closed his eyes. "*Horosho,* Josef. We have a deal. Do what he says."

Sutter nodded and shut the door. He was back in less than a minute, and climbed into the front seat. "Josef's dropping Lydia at a shopping center down the road. My guys will meet her there. When they tell me she's safe, we'll let you out and tell Josef where to collect you."

We waited in the car. Sutter cut Siggy's hands free and put on Coltrane again. Then he read his mail and surfed the Web on his phone, and laughed occasionally at what he saw there. "Love these cats," he said to no one. In half an hour, Sutter's phone rang.

He listened for a moment and then said *"Merci."* Then he turned in his seat and opened the rear door.

"This is where you get off, Sig. I'll call Josef when we're on the road." Siggy said nothing, but climbed out of the GMC and closed the door. Sutter ran down his window and looked at him.

"In a little while, you're gonna find yourself thinking about all this — going over it in your head. A word to the wise: don't. There's nothing down that road for you, so don't go there. Don't brood. You're getting out whole. Go back to your life."

"We have a deal. I know what a deal is."

"We had one before."

"I know what this deal is."

Siggy turned and watched his bare feet on the asphalt, and walked gingerly away from the car. Sutter called to him. "One other thing — why're you interested in Elena's kid? Was he just an excuse to fuck with me some more? How did you even know Elena had a kid?"

"You think I'm an idiot? You think I don't know other people are out looking for her too, and her kid? You think I don't know it's Bray? I guess he figured out I wanted her too, so he comes to me yesterday and offers me a finder's fee — a hundred large for the kid."

Sutter looked at me and then at Siggy. "Harris Bray came to *you*?"

Siggy shook his head impatiently. "Not him. His fucking weird son."

CHAPTER 52

It was a fifteen-minute drive to Lydia, west on Foothill, and Sutter was quiet at first, scanning through tracks on the audio system and glancing over at me. Finally, he settled on Sarah Vaughan.

"It was a matter of time before Bray's trackers ran into Siggy's," he said, "but what do you make of Junior hiring him?"

I shook my head. "Strange bedfellows, for sure. I guess Siggy didn't need much excuse to yank your chain some more, but a hundred thousand is a nice bonus."

"You think Kyle's dad knows about it?"

"I'd be surprised."

Sutter nodded. "Me too. Kinda fucks up his play with you. Muddies the waters. I don't think Daddy will be happy."

We were quiet for a block or two, and then I glanced over at him. "You think Siggy will honor this — that he'll really walk away from you?"

Sutter thought about it for a while and shrugged. "I don't know. The Siggy from San Pedro wouldn't — no way. But this is a different guy. I scared him tonight. I just hope his memory outlasts his ego."

After another few blocks of silence, he cleared his throat. "I was sort of a dick before. You get that that was for Siggy's benefit, yeah? I had to sell it."

"You did a fine job. But I was fairly certain you weren't going to do anything to the kid or the wife."

"You sure about that?"

"I just wish you'd clued me in."

"Your surprise helped the sale."

I nodded. "And that part about me getting the shit boulder rolling . . . ?"

Sutter laughed. "That? That was all true, brother."

The shopping center where Lydia waited was also dark. She was in the passenger seat of a Volvo wagon, drinking from a water bottle. Sutter's mercenary pals, Evie and Franco, were there too. Franco was in the driver's seat, looking at his phone, and Evie stood by the rear bumper. She had the hatch open, and there was a long black gun-case in back. As we drove up, she was tucking an elaborate scope into its own luggage.

"Everything smooth?" Sutter asked.

"*Oui,*" Evie said. "We drove around after the pickup. There was nobody on us."

Sutter nodded. "You two take off. I want more distance before I tell 'em where to get Siggy."

Evie nodded back and closed the hatch. She went to the passenger door and held it open while Lydia got out, then got in; the Volvo drove away.

Lydia stood in the parking lot like the last coat in the lost and found. She was creased and dazed in stained jeans, a pajama top, and sneakers with the laces undone. Her thick hair was lumpy and tangled, and her face was pale, sagging, and smudged around the eyes. There were bruises on her forearms.

I jumped out of the car and ran to her and stopped when she slapped me across the face. She pointed at me, and her hand shook and tears welled in her eyes.

"You . . ." she said. Then she got into the back seat of the GMC and slammed the door.

I climbed behind the wheel, rubbed my cheek, and looked at Sutter, who pursed his lips and shook his head.

CHAPTER 53

Lydia didn't come in the next day, and neither did Lucho, who was over at her place helping her clean up. He called to explain as I was still squinting at the overcast dawn. I asked to speak with Lydia, and there was silence at the other end of the line, and then a nervous cough.

"Now's not the best time, doc," Lucho said. "Maybe later."

"Is she okay?"

"She's fine. I mean, she's not hurt or anything. You . . . you should let her call you."

So it was chaos all day. I scrambled to find help, but none of our part-timers could make it, and the best I could do was Deirdre Zalce, a heavily inked and pierced young woman who lived somewhere east of the 101, and who sometimes helped Lucho with clerical work. She manned the waiting room, taking names and complaints, pulling files where we had them, doing what she could with the phones. She was game and highly caffeinated, but she was overmatched.

As was I. Each time I came out front to triage the room and collect the next patient, the crowd was larger, more restive, and less confident. By mid-afternoon, even Deirdre was giving me a *What the fuck are you doing?* look, and the less dire cases had begun to abandon ship. By five, we were empty and Deirdre was packing up. She pressed a wrinkled stack of phone messages into my hand before she left, shaking her head.

I carried them up to my kitchen, where I picked up an apple and a beer, and then continued to the roof. The sky was a chemical yellow, and the air smelled of scorched metal. I settled in the lounge chair and drank some beer and looked at my messages. Midway through the stack I found one from Sutter. I checked my cell phone and listened to his voice mail.

"I heard from my cop pals that they found the Ford pickup Elena boosted. It got towed last night from a lot around Seventeenth and Santee. That's practically underneath the 10, not far from the Blue Line. Wondered if it meant anything to you. Give me a ring and let me know. Hope Lydia's not hitting you anymore."

I sighed, and thought about calling Lydia, or maybe Lucho, but didn't — I didn't think I could take the anger, or worse, the silence. I took a bite of my apple and thought about Sutter's message. Seventeenth and Santee. Underneath the 10. It didn't ring any bells at first, but then there was a faint tolling. I jammed the messages into my pocket, picked up my beer, and went downstairs again.

I pawed through layers of paper on my desk and found a yellow pad with the several phone numbers and addresses I'd found in our records for Mia. At the bottom of the list was an address that wasn't from her file, but from her boyfriend Jerome's. It was on the 300 block of Washington Boulevard, which, when I checked Google Maps, was maybe a quarter-mile from where the pickup had been found. I didn't bother changing out of my scrubs, but swapped my half-finished beer for car keys.

Jerome's neighborhood — if he still lived there — was just south of the 10. Most of the buildings were long and low and beaten-looking, and most of the businesses they housed looked about the same. There were dealers in office furniture, wholesalers of cheap sunglasses, vinyl purses, and medical supplies, several dubious-looking technical schools, and more than a few Korean churches. The most common storefront sign, though, seemed to be FOR RENT.

The stretch of Washington Boulevard that fronted Jerome's place was wide and busy, and divided down the middle by tracks that carried the Blue Line back and forth between Metro Center and Long Beach. The building itself was one of the few apartment houses on the block. It was a sagging stucco box in watery pink and white, like a loaf of melting sherbet, and there were people — subsiding mounds in baggy clothes — on the stoop and the small porch. They seemed to have been there for a very long time — were maybe parts of the structure itself. I found a length of curb across from the building and killed my engine, and realized I had no idea of what to do.

I had no apartment number for Jerome, so unless his name was on a mailbox — which somehow seemed unlikely — looking for him inside meant knocking on doors, and God only knew who or what might be on the other side. And if I did find his place, what then? I sat and baked and speculated for ten minutes, wishing I had another apple or the rest of my beer. I stopped wishing when Mia walked past my car.

I'd never seen her look so unglamorous. She wore flip-flops, cutoff gray sweats, and an oversized tee-shirt with a washed-out image of Kurt Cobain on the front. Her black hair was tied in a dull bun, and the bones of her face were stark beneath sallow skin. She was carrying groceries in a white plastic bag, and looked tired and distracted as she crossed Washington. She gave no backward glance as she climbed the stairs to the front door, and so did not see me sprint behind her, across the street and up into the dim lobby.

The lobby smelled of mildew, urine, and unwashed bodies. The walls were beige, and there were sticky red tiles on the floor. It was empty, but I heard Mia on the stairs, and saw her white ankles on the landing. I followed her up three flights, and called to her as she put her key in the lock. She jumped.

"*Jesus!* You scared the piss out of me, doc."

"And yet you don't seem totally shocked that I'm here."

She shrugged. "We were saying — me and Shelly — we might have to call you. It's what Elena said to do if she doesn't come back."

"Elena's gone?"

"She took off this morning, before anybody was up."

"With Alex?"

"She left him here, with me and Shelly."

My stomach clenched. "To go where? Where is she, Mia?"

"I don't know. I was just getting dinner." Mia turned the key and went inside, and I followed.

The apartment was small and dark — a living room, a kitchen like a broom closet, a narrow bathroom, and a bedroom separated from the main room by a green curtain. Shelly was sitting on a swaybacked sofa, flipping through channels on a big flat-screen TV. Alex was at a card table, leafing through a comic book. He smiled when he saw me, jumped up, and came to stand by me.

I smiled down at him. "How you doing, bud?"

He nodded. "All right. My mom isn't here."

"I heard." Alex looked okay, if a little tired and grimy. "You hungry?" Alex nodded.

"I got you chicken tenders," Mia said. "And mac and cheese, and broccoli. And I got you milk."

Alex didn't look enthusiastic. "When's my mom coming back?" he asked me. I ruffled

537

his hair but didn't answer.

"How are you, Shelly?"

She sat up. "I'm okay, doc. And you? You pissed at us?"

"I'll get over it. What happened?"

"It wasn't my call, doc — it was Ellie. She said some of the people looking for her had you jammed up pretty bad, and she wasn't sure what you might do, and she didn't want to wait around to see."

I shook my head. "A real vote of confidence. I mean, it's not like I've stuck my neck out for you guys or anything."

"That's exactly what I tried telling her, but she wouldn't listen. She's actually pretty stubborn."

"No shit. She stole the truck?"

Shelly nodded. "She had it all planned. We got lucky and scored some cash from that house, too, and a cell phone."

"And then you called Mia."

Shelly nodded. "She owes me."

"Not anymore," Mia said. "Not after this. After this, it's all the other way."

I looked around again. "Jerome's not here?" I asked, and a nervous silence descended. Even Alex looked tense. "Where's Jerome, Mia?" She looked at Shelly, who looked at the TV. Then Mia walked to the green curtain that was the bedroom door and pulled it open. And there was Jerome, on the floor beside the bed, bruised and swollen, gagged with tape and trussed with extension cords. His eyes widened when he saw me, and were pleading.

"Jesus Christ," I said, and knelt beside him. "What the hell happened?" I pulled the tape from his battered mouth, which opened up some cuts.

"Ow! Fuck!" he said. "I'll tell you what happened — that little foreign bitch is what. She comes to my place, and outta the fucking blue she cold-cocks me, and —"

"That's a load of shit," Shelly said. Alex sidled up to the sofa and stood beside her and took her hand. "This guy was fucking creepy to me and to Ellie, and he was asking a lot of questions —"

"It's *my* place — I can say what I want," Jerome sputtered.

Shelly shook her head. "She got a bad feeling about him, and then he said something about the kid. Something . . . nasty. And that was that."

"She fucking cold-cocked me — and with the one good ashtray I had. My fucking Bellagio ashtray." Jerome shook his head sorrowfully, and I looked at Mia.

She shrugged. "It's like Shelly told. And, really, he's better this way."

Jerome glared. "You *bitch*!"

"Quiet, Jerome," I said, "or I'll put the tape back."

Jerome muttered and whined while I checked his head, neck, face, and pupils. Despite his cuts and bruises, I saw no immediate signs of fracture or concussion.

"Are you going to behave if I cut you loose?" I asked him.

"It's my place. I'll do what the fuck I want."

"You'll keep still and keep quiet, or I'll leave you where you are."

"Fine. Whatever. I won't do shit."

I looked at Mia. "Are you okay with it?"

She nodded. "I'm clearing out of here soon, and Jerome will behave himself until then. Right, baby?"

"Fuck you."

I looked at Shelly and Alex. "And you two . . ."

"What about us?" Shelly said.

"I think you'd better come with me."

Shelly glanced at Alex and shrugged. "I guess we did wear out our welcome, huh?"

Jerome struggled against his bonds. "Fuck you all. I don't care what any of you do, but I expect to get paid for what that bitch broke, and what she took."

Mia sighed. "Give it a rest, Jerome."

"You give it a rest. She broke my ashtray, she took my wallet — and I had like two hundred bucks in —"

"You had maybe fifty," Mia said, laughing.

"Bullshit. And she took my car keys. That's a good fucking car."

"That car had like half a million miles on it."

"It barely had a hundred thousand. Plus, she took my piece, and that cost me over a grand."

My stomach clenched. "She took a gun?"

"Shit, yes. A nice little nine — a Taurus. I only had the fucking thing three weeks."

I looked at Shelly. "She left here with a *gun*?" She nodded. "Where did she go, Shelly?"

"I don't know, doc, I swear to you. Ellie doesn't do a lot of talking, she just *does* shit."

CHAPTER 54

I didn't know where else to take them, so I took them to my place. Alex handled more strange accommodations with equanimity. Shelly walked through the sparse white rooms with a skeptical eye.

"You live here? Really?"

"Really."

"I guess the commute's easy. But it's kinda empty. Chilly."

"I like to travel light."

"I'm down with that, but it's like the moving van's come and gone already."

"There's food in the fridge — some yogurt, a couple of apples, peaches, some salad fixings. There are probably cans of tuna in the cupboard, some cans of soup."

"Lush life, doc," Shelly said, and snickered.

I left her in the living room with Alex, streaming video on my Mac, and I went to the bedroom and called Sutter.

He sighed when I finished my story. "I guess we gotta hope Bray has called off the hounds, at least for the moment, and that no one's been following you around."

"It . . . it didn't even occur to me."

"Water down the crapper — probably they would've grabbed the kid already if they'd been following you. Elena's the new bad news — out on the town with her nine-millimeter."

"I don't know what the hell she thinks she's doing."

"Of course you do. This chick always has a plan, brother, and you know what it is."

"You think she's going after the Brays? If she doesn't kill somebody, she's going to get herself killed doing that."

"You don't think she knows it? Why else would she leave the kid behind?"

I sighed. "I don't know what the fuck to do."

"I don't know that there's a whole lot for you to do but let it play."

"I can't just —"

"What're you gonna do? Stake out Bray's house — all of their houses and offices and clubs and whatever — and try to grab her before she gets to them? You could get yourself killed doin' that."

"I can't —"

"You don't know where she is, or where she's gonna be, or when. You got no way to contact her. She's in the wind, brother. Sitting tight is your only play."

Sutter rang off, and I was listening to nothing. I sighed again and paced, and tried to fight the jangly feel of looming doom. I looked down and saw I was still in my scrubs and thought about a shower. I reached into my pockets, to empty them, and came out with a wad of message slips. I was smoothing them out when my cell burred. I looked twice to make sure it was Nora.

There was silence when I answered, with muted voices, telephones, a woman speaking on a PA system, the electric beeps and buzzes of medical monitors — hospital noises — filling it in.

"You're still at work," I said.

"One of my residents needed help," Nora said. "He's got a girl in bad shape — immuno-suppressed, and now she's got a respiratory thing. We're waiting for labs to come back, but she's going south."

"How old?"

"Nine. Almost."

I sighed, and was quiet. "I was wondering if you'd ever call back," I said after a while.

"I wondered too," Nora said. Her voice

was low and tired.

"I'm glad you did. It's good to hear your voice, and I wanted to apologize for the shit I brought to your doorstep."

"How is all that going?" she asked. "Are you done with that business?"

Before I could answer there was a whoop from the other room — high-pitched laughter from Alex and Shelly. I looked into the living room and saw them, red-faced and giggling, watching something online. Shelly looked up.

"You gotta check this out, doc — it's octopuses that knit. *Knitting,* for shit's sake."

I put a finger to my lips and closed the bedroom door.

"You sound busy," Nora said.

"It's that business. They're at my house now."

Nora sighed again. "So you're *not* done yet."

"I'm ever hopeful."

"You know, I was going to apologize too — for overreacting, or being too preachy or something."

"You don't owe me that, Nora. You don't owe me anything."

"No, I don't. And you don't owe me anything either, and I guess that's the point. The problem."

"Which is it — the point or the problem?"

"That depends on what you think we've got going here," she said. "What we are to each other."

"Friends, right? Friends or something."

She laughed ruefully. "I guess that's one way to describe it. And if we're not *friends,* then I shouldn't give too much of a damn if you're deeply nuts or not. If you might get yourself killed. But if we are *friends or something,* then I guess I *should* give a damn. I guess we *should* owe each other something, right? Apologies, explanations, excuses, histories — something, for chrissakes. But we don't do that, do we?"

"It's one of the things we have in common," I said.

"Which makes things easy," she said, "but not necessarily good."

"We have a nice time, Nora. We enjoy each other's company."

"Like a pair of drunks."

"I would've been sorry if you hadn't called."

Nora's laugh was short and bitter. "That's what over a year of being *friends* amounts to — *I would've been sorry if you hadn't called?* That's not a lot, Adam. Is it enough for you?"

"It could be a start."

546

She laughed again, a little less bitter this time. "To what, the world's slowest —" Then there was another voice at her end, a man's, talking to her. "My cultures are back," Nora said. "I've got to go."

The phone went quiet, and I stood looking at it in my hand. "Shit," I said softly, and sat on the bed.

The phone messages were beside me, in a wrinkled stack, and I smoothed them on my thigh. There were a couple from a real estate agent who'd heard from my former landlord, Kashmarian, that I might be in the market for new offices, and a couple from two of our part-timers, looking for job references. Rats from the sinking ship, but I couldn't blame them. At the bottom of the stack were two messages from Nate Rash, at Jiffy-Lab. I checked the voice mail on my cell. There were more from him there.

"Shit," I said again, and called him back.

"Took you long enough," Nate said. "I thought you were in a hurry for these."

"The day got away."

"You have time now? 'Cause I've got your analyses."

"Let's hear 'em," I said, and Nate talked about the initial tests he'd performed, the results he'd gotten, and the additional ones he'd run. When he was done, I was quiet for a while, then made him go through it again. After that I asked him to fax the report to the clinic, and to send me another copy via snail mail. I thanked Nate after that, put the phone down, and breathed slowly and deliberately until the rushing sound faded from my ears.

I rested my forearms on my knees, and my head in my hands. I needed to make some calls, and I thought about whom to call first. Sutter first. Then Mandy, probably, and then . . . I took another deep breath and ran a hand through my hair. I stood and paced, and then I opened the bedroom door. Shelly was in the kitchen, peering into the fridge, shaking her head, and Alex was still on my Mac. He was watching something and smiling at it. His face glowed in the shifting light, soft and round and unguarded.

CHAPTER 55

Sutter told me not to force things, to take it easy — not to be overeager, or certainly not to appear that way. To be late, maybe, but above all *not* to be early.

"The problem is," he'd said, shaking his head, "you don't really listen to people, and you have the worst poker face on the fucking planet."

There was a Coffee Bean catty-corner across Wilshire from Bray Consolidated's headquarters, and I'd been sitting there for two hours, drinking coffee, watching cars push through the glare, watching their reflections slip across the Bray tower's black glass skin, checking the time, forcing myself to stay put. This meeting was three days in the making, I kept telling myself; I could wait another half-hour, another fifteen minutes, another ten minutes, another five. At three minutes before three, I stopped trying to convince myself, and tossed my coffee cup in the trash. I slipped on my blue blazer, took a deep breath, and walked out into the sun.

The lobby of the Bray Consolidated building was vast, cold, and dizzying, a marble shrine to gods of wealth and crushing power. I wasn't halfway across the polished expanse when Conti took my elbow. He wore a pale-gray suit, a white shirt, and a gray tie, and he smiled his shark smile. My pulse spiked.

"Your name's on the list, doc," he said. "No need to wait behind the rope." He guided me to the last security barrier on the left, which beeped softly and raised its steel arm in a robotic *heil* as we approached. Conti led me past the elevator banks, through double doors, and into a white corridor that smelled of car exhaust. There were more doors at the end, marked PARKING LEVEL 1. On the other side was another security desk and more turnstiles.

Parked beyond them were two Mercedes SUVs, attended by their drivers. I recognized Mandy's silver ride, but not the larger, black car. The drivers stood taller when they saw Conti, and he nodded at them and at the grunts manning the security desk. We didn't go through the barriers, but walked around a corner and stopped before an elevator door. There were no markings or buttons on it, just a card reader. Conti fished a key card from his suit jacket, along with a cell phone. He held the phone to his ear and waited.

"Comin' up, Cap," he said finally. Another pause. "Nope, just the doc." Then "Yessir."

The phone disappeared, and Conti dipped the key card into the reader. The elevator door slid open, and he ushered me into a marble-and-glass crypt — a little room made of spares from the lobby, but even colder. There was one button, and when Conti pressed it we rose smoothly and without a sound.

"Cap doesn't much care for crowds," Conti said.

I nodded. "Why am I not surprised?"

Conti showed me more teeth, and whistled tunelessly until we glided to a halt. The elevator door opened on a teakwood hallway, and Persian carpets over a hardwood floor.

"Hang a right," Conti said. I did, and passed open doors to a paneled bedroom, a white marble bathroom, and a white kitchen, all empty and dim. There were old prints in the corridor — architectural, nautical, avian — and the scents of lemons and floor wax. A line of sweat snaked down my spine.

"Right again," Conti said, which brought us to a small teak door. He stepped around me, opened it, and ushered me through.

Harris Bray's office suite was many floors higher than Mandy's, and its views made the city below even more abstract — streets and freeways no more than crosshatches; parks, fairways, and hillsides just patches of green and brown; the ocean a great, gray shoulder against the bleached sky; the people nonexistent. The walls that weren't windows were mahogany panels, broken by runs of built-in bookshelves; at the far end of the room, a pair of massive doors led, I guessed, to Harris Bray's reception area and more gatekeepers.

Bray's sofas and chairs were burgundy leather, and his desk was a massive block of elaborately worked ebony, inlaid with ivory and mother-of-pearl. Bray sat behind it, in a black leather throne, beneath a broad, ancient-looking gilt-framed map of the world, all intricate coastlines and seas full of dragons. I took a slow, deep breath.

Bray was in charcoal today, with a white shirt and a crimson tie, and his brutal face was without expression as I came through the door. He took off his rimless glasses, rubbed the bridge of his nose, and nodded at Conti, who produced a scanner like a truncated cricket bat.

"I'll be gentle, doc," he said.

"It was supposed to be just the two of us," I said to Bray.

"It will be," he answered, "as soon as Tiger makes certain."

Conti swept the scanner up and down, then frisked me thoroughly. He took a phone from my back pocket and looked at Bray. "He's clean."

"No signals?"

"No, sir."

"Then, if you'll excuse us," Bray said.

Conti nodded. "Sure thing, Cap," he said, and left the way we'd come. The door disappeared into the mahogany woodwork. Bray opened a narrow drawer in his desk, examined something inside, and closed it again. Then he folded his tailored arms, stared at me, and let silence settle. Eventually, he looked at his watch.

"You said that you were ready to resolve this situation, doctor. I'd hoped that meant you would have Alex with you. It's the only reason I agreed to meet with you. But I see that my hope was misplaced. So, unless this is some needlessly theatrical prelude to telling me where I can pick him up, there's no reason why we should spend more time together."

"Then I'll see if I can give you one. I had them tested. Both of them."

Bray looked at me impassively. "By *testing* I assume you mean DNA testing. You went through this in my niece's office. I heard then what you had to say about mother and child and DNA, and told you that the issue was largely moot. It remains so, and I remain unimpressed."

"I'm not talking about Elena and Alex."

Another blank look, another elaborate glance at his watch. "Then I don't know what you're talking about. In any event, we're done here. I wish I could say that it's been useful seeing you."

"Now who's wasting time?" I said. "You know what I'm talking about, Mr. Bray. I'm pretty certain you had them tested yourself."

Bray unfolded his glasses, perched them on his nose, pursed his narrow lips, and squinted at me. "I don't know —"

"Alex and Kyle. Their DNA match is a shade under twenty-five percent. That and the Y-chromosome analysis tell the story."

Bray turned to the windows and looked out at the white sky for a while. "This means nothing to me," he said, but his voice was lower.

I shook my head. "If Kyle was Alex's father, their DNA match would be fifty percent; if they were unrelated, there'd be no match. But there is a match, of roughly twenty-five percent, and their Y-chromosomes line up. The Y-chromosome comes down the paternal line: sons get it from their fathers. Your son — both of your sons — got theirs from you. Kyle and Alex aren't father and son; they're brothers — half brothers, actually."

Bray looked at his suit jacket and swept something off his lapel. He looked at his hands as if he'd never seen them before. Then his big shoulders sagged, and he seemed suddenly to occupy less space behind his massive black desk. He said nothing.

"I assume Kyle doesn't know," I said.

Bray looked around the room, then walked to a window and leaned against the glass, looking out. He sighed heavily and turned to me. "Why should I discuss anything with you? More to the point, why should I let you discuss any of this with anyone?"

I shrugged. "I'm happy to keep the test results to myself, if I think it's in Alex's best interests. But the only one who can convince me of that is you."

"You think I'm going to justify myself —

to *you*? I don't plead, doctor. And I don't think even you believe that Alex would have a better life with *her* than he would here, with me. He'd want for nothing here."

"It's not just a matter of money."

Bray squinted. "You have no children, yes?" he asked. I shook my head. "Then you can't understand."

"Understand what?"

"What a parent would do."

For an instant I was back in the C.A.R., at the aid station, and Merry and Mathieu were there. It was a morning after yet another endless night. Merry's hand was on Mathieu's head, which rested against her hip. He was smiling.

Bray turned to gaze out the window again, or at his reflection in it. "My father was an idealistic man. But he prided himself on being a realist — on seeing the world as it was. And that clarity extended to his family. Especially to his family. He had no illusions about his children, about our strengths and weaknesses, and where we needed to be . . . built up. Where we needed callus. I learned that from him, I suppose — seeing my child as he is. So I've never had any illusions about Kyle. I know that there has always been . . . less there than meets the eye."

Bray turned toward me, but seemed to

look right through me. "He was a handsome child. Tall, athletic, aggressive. He looked like a leader, and people — other children, even adults — were drawn to him, at least at first. As they got to know him, other traits became apparent. An intellectual mediocrity. A laziness. A tendency to lie. A tendency to bully. A lack of impulse control. As he got older, that last manifested itself in his indulgence of all sorts of appetites, along with an unfortunate inclination to violence.

"I saw all that in Kyle from the start, and for a long while I tried to . . . correct him. He was tutored; he was supervised closely; he was disciplined without hesitation or equivocation. I sent him away to school — many schools — back east, abroad, aboard a sailboat, to a work camp in the Arizona desert. Eventually, they all asked him to leave."

Bray sighed again and shook his head. "As he got older, I arranged positions for him in the company. I had some of my best managers train him, or try to. It was for naught. He was unfortunately quite . . . dependable. Consistent. The more responsibility I gave him, the more negligent he would ultimately prove himself to be. Oh, he could behave for brief periods of time — he did it in Romania — but whenever circumstances required more than simply posturing, more than just looking the part of a leader, he never failed to disappoint. Often in spectacular ways." Bray straightened, but still looked slumped and shrunken. He brushed off his trousers.

Another line of sweat slid down my spine. "So Kyle is a disappointment, and that makes Alex what — a second chance? A do-over? Setting aside how incredibly wrong-headed that is, how can it possibly justify kidnapping him, and killing his uncle and his great-grandmother? How can anything justify —"

"None of *that* was my doing," Bray said, scowling. "By the time I found out about it, it was another of Kyle's messes to be cleaned up."

"A *mess*? I doubt Elena or her brother or grandmother would characterize it quite that way."

At the mention of Elena's name a look of disgust, and something else, twisted Bray's face, and a shudder passed through him. "It was *not* my doing," he said. "It was Kyle, and several PRP assets who were . . . too eager to please."

"But you helped Kyle cover it up. That makes you an accomplice to kidnap and murder — maybe a co-conspirator."

"Kyle had the boy on one of our planes, on the runway in Bucharest, when I first learned of his existence."

"And you didn't think to stop him from running off with Alex? Or maybe calling the authorities?"

Some of the hardness came back into Bray's face. "You don't have children."

I sighed. "When did you find out that Alex was your son?"

He crossed to the leather sofa, sat, rose again, and walked to a row of bookshelves. He ran his fingers along the edge of a shelf and studied the leather-bound volumes.

"When did you find out?" I asked again.

"I had him tested a month after he got here, but I suspected before then. He had . . . *something* — an intelligence, a spark. The way he watched things, the way he played, how he went from just a few words of English to fluency in no time — I knew he couldn't be Kyle's. And his age . . . The timing was consistent."

"And your relationship with Elena — when did that begin?"

Bray recoiled, as if I'd pissed on his leg. "*Relationship?* I had no . . . There was no relationship."

"You had something."

"I met her once. One time only. The day I

559

came to Bucharest to sort out all the problems Kyle had caused."

"She told me you burst in on them in Kyle's hotel suite, that they were still in bed."

Bray nodded slowly. "I'd given him a chance with that subsidiary. We had a substantial, steady revenue stream there, and the potential for much more, and all Kyle did was waste his time and our money on entertaining the locals and himself. He was picking up tabs at every nightclub and whorehouse in Bucharest, for people who had no decision-making authority — who were barely middle management. He'd become a local joke, and worse — he'd turned Bray Consolidated into a joke."

"Elena told me that you had her thrown out. I guess she left out some parts."

Bray turned back to the window. The light was getting longer on the city, and even from up here the shadows were darker and more strange. Bray sighed again. "I'm not discussing this with you. In fact, I'm not discussing anything until I know how Alex is."

"He's safe. I want to keep him that way."

"It's the one thing we agree on, doctor. Where is he?"

"I thought we understood each other, Mr.

Bray. I haven't shared what I know with anyone, but I will unless you talk to me."

"How do I know that you've kept this private?"

"Because I'm telling you."

"And I'm supposed simply to believe you? I am not a trusting person, doctor."

"I can't help you with that."

Bray nodded slowly. "So you've discussed this with no one? Not with the people at whatever lab you used? Not with anyone at your clinic, or your friends, or your lawyer?"

I shook my head. "No one. But I promise — if you push me, I will. Now talk to me about Elena."

Bray stretched and smiled minutely. "I find that I *do* believe you, doctor, but I don't think I have anything to say to you about Elena. In fact, I believe I've finished talking altogether. Now it's your turn. You are going to tell me exactly where I can find Alex. What happens to you afterward depends entirely on whether you've told me the truth."

I raised my eyebrows. "You don't think I'm serious? You don't think I'll give the DNA analysis to . . . let's say Kyle, Mandy, and your wife, for starters, not to mention the press?"

"On the contrary, I'm certain you'd put

those results on the front pages of every paper in the country if you could. If I let you."

"But you're not going to let me."

"That is correct, doctor."

"And how do you plan on doing that?"

"Do you have to ask? Mr. Conti and a half-dozen of his men are one call and perhaps fifteen seconds away."

I shook my head. "You sure about that?"

Harris Bray sighed, and took a phone from his suit jacket. He tapped the screen and held the phone to his ear, and smiled thinly at me while he waited. The smile faded as his wait grew longer, and finally morphed into a look of sour annoyance. He frowned and tried his call again. And again. He stared down at the phone, as if there was something wrong with it, and then he looked at me.

"Conti's not picking up. Neither will your other men."

"What the hell —"

I held up a hand. "Wait," I said, "that's not the worst news." I reached into my pocket and pulled out a cell phone. "Tiger took one phone, but he left me with this other one, and I've used it to record our little talk."

Bray's face reddened and his thin lips

parted, but no sound came out.

"And if that's not bad enough . . ." I said. I went to the old map hung behind his desk. I pointed to a small black disc mounted above the frame. "You're on video too."

His lips moved noiselessly for a while, and then he pried some words free. "That's not . . . The video system is off. I made sure of it."

"Apparently, those controls don't work anymore. Apparently, it's always on."

"Tiger."

"Tiger got a better offer, Mr. Bray. I think he was worried about his future."

Bray was white now. "An offer — from who?"

There was a muted click, and the little door I'd come through swung open again.

"From me, Uncle Harry," Amanda Danzig said. "Tiger got a better deal from me."

Harris Bray stood silently, looked from Mandy to me, and swayed.

"Worse and worse," I said.

CHAPTER 56

Mandy wore black trousers and a black blouse, and she circled the office like a seal — sleek, eager, and sure.

She smoothed her hair. "Long time no see, Dr. Knox," she said. I nodded, and she looked at Bray.

"Let's make this quick, Uncle Harry. I've got a lot to do, and you're going to need a drink. Or several."

"What the hell —"

Mandy waved off his words. "You are going to announce your pending retirement. You're going to do it today, and you are going to name me as your successor. You're not going to leave right away — we don't want to spook our customers, or, God forbid, the bankers or the bond market — so the press release will talk about a graceful, gradual, and above all orderly transition plan. I'm thinking a twelve-month period — starting with me becoming COO, then president in four months, CEO four months after that, and chairman at the end. In reality, I'll start running things immediately."

Harris Bray took a deep breath. Red patches spread on his face and neck. "Amanda . . ." he said. He shook his head and managed a disbelieving smile. "Your arrogance and entitlement have finally cut you loose from reality. The only change I'm making with immediate effect is to fire you."

Mandy put her hands on her hips. "Really, Uncle Harry, I'd have thought you'd be able to read the tea leaves better than this. The doctor here is prepared to hand over everything he's got to the press. That's Elena's statement, plus the DNA tests, plus your little video. If you think that you, or the company, can survive all that, then you're the one who's seriously out of touch. As in: *fucking crazy.*"

Bray smiled and shook his head. "Dr. Knox isn't going to give anything to anyone. Call Tiger back in here, and I'll have his audio recording, the DNA tests, and Alex, and the doctor will have" — Bray looked at me and nodded conspiratorially — "whatever he wants."

Mandy sighed. "Jesus, could you be more heavy-handed? Not to mention tone-deaf. Don't you see that the doctor has his own agenda, and it isn't served by selling out to you? And, in case you haven't noticed, the same holds true for your Praetorian Guard. Tiger knows that if this shit hits the fan it's going to fly all over him, and he knows he can't buy the same legal talent that you can. He sees the writing on the wall, even if you don't."

Bray took a step toward Mandy and raised his hand, but Mandy didn't budge. Her eyes were hard and defiant; her voice was goading. "Go ahead, take a swing," she said quietly, "but don't forget to smile for the camera."

I stepped between them and put a hand on Bray's arm. He jerked it away. "You can't seriously believe I'd turn this company over to you. To *you*?"

"Why not? You've been training me to run the thing for years now. That's what you've said, at any rate, even if you've had a hard time actually letting go of anything. But I'm not waiting anymore.

"Besides, what's your other option — Kyle? For chrissakes, do you think anything you said on that tape was a surprise to me? Or to anyone who knows Kyle? He can't run anything more complicated than his mouth, and that gets him into trouble on a regular basis."

"I'd burn the business to the ground before giving it to you."

"Which are exactly your choices. But make no mistake, if you don't take graceful retirement, I'll be out there with the good doctor pouring gasoline all over Bray Consolidated. I'll corroborate anything and everything the doctor says, and add some narrative of my own — maybe about our political contributions and the cash that goes astray when it flows through some of our subsidiaries, and where some of it ends up. You think there'd be an audience for that with the media, or the Democrats on the Hill?"

Harris Bray's shoulders slumped again. "You are —"

"Believe it or not, Uncle Harry, I'm trying to save your ass, and this company too. Because there's no way this doesn't explode on you. It's leaking in too many places, and any attempt you make to cover it up will only get you in deeper. The drapes are burning. Time to find the exit."

Bray tried for a laugh, but it came out like a strangled bark. He shook his head some more, walked to the sofa, and dropped on it like a sandbag. "You have lost your mind, girl. Completely. If you think the board —"

"Your board doesn't give orders, it takes

them. You set it up to be irrelevant, and so it is. The people who aren't irrelevant are our bankers. Short-term financing, long-term financing, debt issuance, M-and-A support — without those guys, we've got serious problems. Fatal problems. Now, what do you suppose they'd say if all this shit went public? You think that the boys at Melton-Peck, for example, would still be happy to do business with you if all of this was front-page news?"

Bray whisked her question away with an angry sweep of his hand. "They want our business — they love it. As long as we generate revenue for them, they don't ask questions."

Mandy crossed her arms, and her eyes gleamed. "Don't kid yourself, Uncle. Those guys have actual boards and actual shareholders that they actually answer to. Believe me, they'll do more than ask questions." Bray made another dismissive sweep. Mandy smirked, and took out her phone.

"You disagree?" she said. "Fine — let's take a poll. Let's see, we can call . . ." She studied her phone. "How about Steven Berger, over at Melton-Peck? He's our senior banker there; his view should be instructive. How about we run this by him?"

"Don't waste your time," Bray sneered.

"That dirty Jew would crawl over broken glass for our fees."

Mandy smiled, tucked her phone into her pocket, and strode to Bray's big desk. "Very eloquent, Uncle Harry, but I happen to disagree. I really think we should consult Steve. And — surprise — it won't even cost us a phone call."

Mandy went around Bray's desk, opened the narrow drawer, and tapped a button inside. Bray's ancient map slid silently into a slot in the ceiling. Behind it was a flat-screen monitor, and the head and shoulders of a fair-haired, handsome man, sitting in what I recognized as Mandy's office. The man wore an immaculate pinstriped suit, and his face was pale and taut with barely suppressed rage.

Mandy looked at the screen and smiled sweetly. "Steve, I'm sorry that our lovely lunch had to end like this. And I'm so sorry for my uncle's vile comments. I hope you know those views are his and his alone."

Berger took a deep breath. "I appreciate that, Amanda, but you're not the one with something to apologize for."

Mandy nodded gravely. "I hate to put you on the spot, Steve — more on the spot, I suppose — but I wonder if you heard the discussion my uncle and I were having?"

"I wish I hadn't," Berger said. "But I heard it and saw it, and if you're asking whether I agree with your assessment of things — I'm afraid I do. If a fact pattern of the sort that's been laid out here became public knowledge, and if it included video of the sort I've just been watching, our firm would have no choice but to curtail our business with Bray Consolidated considerably — *quite* considerably — while your uncle was still involved in day-to-day management. And I'm confident that any financial institution comparable to ours would reach the same conclusion."

"And by *quite considerably* you mean . . . ?"

"Entirely."

Mandy nodded again. "I appreciate your candor, Steve. Now, if you'll just sit tight for a little while longer, I'll be back up to discuss future plans, and maybe to buy you a few drinks." Mandy didn't wait for an answer, but pressed a switch in the drawer and watched the map descend.

She turned back to her uncle and smiled tightly. "All those rounds of golf, up in smoke," she said.

There was a gray sheen of sweat on Bray's forehead, and he wiped his hand across it. "You fucking bitch," he said softly. "My lawyers will eat your bones."

"Sure they will, Uncle Harry. While you spend your golden years fighting God knows how many criminal charges, testifying before God knows how many congressional subcommittees, and dealing with a nonstop media feeding frenzy — all while your company goes down in flames — your lawyers will have plenty of time to snack on my bones, and Steve's, and whoever else's. Plenty of time, I'm sure."

Bray shook his head. "You bitch," he said. He went to the windows again and paced before them, head down, like a bull looking for something to charge. Finally, he stopped, returned to the sofa, and massaged his temples.

He looked at Mandy. "I'm supposed to turn things over to you, and then what? What am I supposed to do after that?"

Mandy shrugged. "Whatever you want. The foundation, the think tanks — you can run any or all of them, I don't care. Or go on the speaking circuit, or write a book. Or go play golf."

"And Alex?" Bray asked. "What happens to Alex in your master plan?"

"Alex goes with his mother," I said, "wherever she wants to go, and with enough money to do whatever they want when they get there, for as long as they want to do it. That's the deal."

Bray shook his head. "He's my son."

"Yeah, well, you've got to forget about that, Uncle Harry."

Bray opened his mouth to speak, but the noise interrupted him. It came from the hall beyond the small doorway — a flat cracking sound — and I jumped when I heard it, and felt a cold rock land in my gut. Mandy didn't recognize it, and neither did Bray, but I knew what it was. I was halfway to the door when Kyle staggered through, gunshot and bleeding.

CHAPTER 57

His jeans were dark with blood, from the left thigh down, and he grimaced when Elena screwed the gun barrel into the back of his neck. She grabbed Kyle's shirt collar and kicked the back of his leg, and he whimpered and collapsed to his knees before her. Her tee shirt and her hands were smeared with blood, and so were her sweat pants.

She was still for a moment, panting, as if she'd run a long way to get here, and the sound of her breath was all I could hear. Then Elena looked up at Harris Bray, pointed the gun at him, and smiled.

"Uncle Harry," she said mockingly. "Yeah, you better forget about stealing my kid, Uncle Harry."

Mandy gasped and Bray grunted, and I took a step toward Kyle. And stopped when Elena leveled the gun at me. The stone in my stomach turned.

"Sorry, doctor. You stay there for now."

"He's hurt, Elena."

She nodded. "Oh yeah. He's not good for much now, but he knew where to find his daddy, and how to get us up here without stopping. He was good for that, and just scared enough."

Kyle's shaking hands were pressed over his wound. There was no spurting, but there was a lot of blood, and I wondered if she'd nicked his femoral artery.

"He's bleeding badly, Elena," I said.

Another nod, and a little smile. "Oh yeah."

"He could die if you don't let me look after him."

She shrugged. "Happens to everybody, right?"

"Let me stop the bleeding," I said, but Elena shook her head.

"Christ," Mandy whispered. Bray hauled himself off the sofa, and took a step toward his son.

Elena snarled, and raised the gun. "You think I won't shoot your face, old man? It's not my plan, but it's okay with me."

"Elena, take it easy," I said.

"Doctor, you want to leave now, it's okay. You take the girl cousin and go. Otherwise, you keep quiet and stay out of things. Either way, it won't be long."

Harris Bray looked nearly as bad as his son. He was sweating, and his skin was waxy and beige. He managed to square his shoulders, but his attempt at a fearsome look became something pained and reeling. When he spoke it was to Elena, but he couldn't meet her eyes.

"What do you want? Is it money? If that's what it is, you can have however much you want."

Elena's laugh was acid. "And if I don't want money — then what? What else you got for me, old man?"

"Just tell me what you want, I'll get it for you."

"What I want is easy," Elena said, and she took a step back from Kyle. She reached into a pocket and came out with a cell phone. She tapped at it and held it up and looked at Bray and at the screen. "You just stand there and tell a story to the camera and to your boy — your oldest boy. You tell him about us, about the time we met, and what you did to me that day. You tell it just like it happened, but I warn you — you lie at all, you leave out things or make yourself look better, or say anything not true, I'll kill him right here, right now."

Harris Bray swallowed hard. "I . . . I don't know —"

Elena pointed the gun at Kyle's head. "You tell the fucking story, old man!"

Bray stepped backward, stumbled, and steadied himself against his desk. He wiped sweat from his forehead and looked at Kyle, who was looking at the floor. "I . . . I met her at the Carol Parc Hotel in Bucharest. I had come there to see you and —"

"He doesn't care about this," Elena said, impatient. "He knows all this. Talk about what happened after — when you sent him away. When you sent everyone away, and I am alone with you. Tell him, old man!"

"We . . . we talked."

"Talked!" Elena spit. "Yes, we talked, while I am trying to cover myself in the bed. Tell him what I am saying."

"You . . . you talked about Kyle."

"Tell him what about!"

"You told me that I should . . . You said that he wasn't cut out for this kind of work, and that I should leave him alone."

"And what you say after that? What you call me?"

"I . . . I told you to be quiet. I called you a . . . whore."

Elena nodded, and the gun bobbed up and down. "You said, *Shut up, you dirty whore.* You said, *I'm not going to take advice about my son from a dirty whore.* That's what you said. And what did I say after?"

"You . . . you told me that your advice . . . You said I should listen to your advice, because you knew Kyle better than I did."

She nodded and glanced down at Kyle, whose chin was lolling on his chest. She tapped his cheek lightly with the back of her hand. "Hey, wake up. You better listen to your daddy — he's getting to the good part." She looked at Harris Bray again. "And you said what after that?"

Bray pleaded. "I . . . I don't remember what I said."

She steadied the gun on his chest. "You better remember, old man. But, here, I remind you. You said, *You're a dirty whore, and all you want is my money.* You remember now?" Bray nodded slowly. "And you remember what I say after? No? I ask you if every woman who tells you something you don't like to hear is a whore. You remember what you say then?"

Bray leaned against the desk, and I saw his legs shake. I moved toward him, but Elena glared at me and shook her head.

"You remember what you say?" Elena barked.

"I said . . . I said that . . . I don't remember."

"Bullshit! You remember! Now, say it, old man!"

"I . . . I said that all of the women I knew were whores, one way or another."

Mandy drew a sharp breath, and Elena laughed. "That's a surprise to you, cousin?" she said. Mandy didn't answer. Elena laughed more. "And then what I say, old man?"

"You said . . . you said . . ."

"I said maybe no woman could stand to be in the same room as you unless she was getting paid for it. You remember?" Bray nodded. "And you remember what next?" Bray was silent for a long time, and breath sounds — frightened, rapid, desperate — were all I heard. Then Elena laughed.

"No? You don't remember hitting me? Across the mouth with the back of your hand? You thought it was so funny when I hit my head on the wall and fell out of bed. You laugh when I try to cover myself with the pillow. Remember it?" Bray kept quiet and Elena smacked Kyle in the head with the gun barrel. *"Remember?"*

Bray nodded.

Elena's grim smile faded, and her face stiffened. She looked down again at Kyle, whose eyes were clouded with pain, but who was staring at his father. "You paying attention? That's good — because now is the best part." She looked back to Bray.

"And I know you remember the next part, yes? How could you forget? How could you forget what you did? And if you do, just look at Alex." Bray shrank beneath her gaze and her loathing. "You remember, old man?" she shouted. He nodded. "Then say it! Say it so everybody hears."

Bray shook his head, looked to the window, and saw only himself. His head bent, and his voice came from the bottom of the sea. "I . . . we had . . . sex."

"No!" Elena yelled, and grabbed a handful of Kyle's hair. She jammed the gun into his neck, and my arms and legs quivered with adrenaline.

"No," she shouted, "we did *not* have sex. We did *not* fuck. You say what happened really, or I swear, old man, I'll blow his head off."

"Don't — please!" Bray cried, and stretched out his arms. Then his voice fell to a whisper. "I . . . I'll say it. It was . . . rape. I . . . raped you."

"How many times, old man?"

"I . . . Twice. I raped you twice."

Bray's knees buckled then, and another silence fell over the room. There was relief in it, but also dread at what would come next. Elena was frozen, Kyle's hair and the gun still in her hands, a look of triumph and something else — sadness, disgust, maybe both — on her face.

She let out a long, exhausted breath and let go of Kyle's hair. He moaned and sank lower. Elena looked at me. "Okay, doctor, you and the cousin go now. You don't need more trouble, and you got to look out for Alex. I know you will — you were good to him, to both of us."

I shook my head and managed to speak over the pounding in my chest. "Let's go together," I said. "You got what you came here for, Elena, and so did I. Let me see to Kyle, and then you and I will go. And you'll have everything you need to take care of Alex and yourself forever — new lives for both of you, anywhere you want." I took a step toward her, but she stepped back.

"I got one more thing for the old man."

"You can't kill him, Elena."

"Not him, doctor. I'm going to do to him what he did to me. I'm going to take away his son, and he's going to watch." Elena took a step back from Kyle, and held the gun in two hands and extended her arms.

"Jesus," Mandy hissed again, and gripped my wrist. Her hands were cold and damp and shaking. Bray made a sobbing noise.

I twisted free and stepped forward. "What the hell are you doing? After everything you've been through for Alex, you're going to throw it all away?"

Elena glared and her voice was shrill. "This is *for* Alex — for him, for my Nico, for my *bunica* — this is justice for them."

She took another step back and tightened her grip on the gun. Her arms quivered, and my throat closed as something moved in the darkness behind her. Conti stepped unseen and silent into the hallway and leveled a small black gun at Elena. He looked at me and raised an eyebrow. I shook my head minutely, but his weapon did not move.

I took a deep breath and forced out the words. "You're full of shit, Elena."

She squinted at me. "You think I won't do it?"

"I think your justice talk is a load of crap."

"Then the hell with you, doctor! You know what they did — to my family, to Alex, to *me* — you heard it all. They took everything. Now we're going to get something back."

"I know what they did, and I know they're evil shits — both of them. But don't tell me killing Kyle is justice for your grandmother and your brother. The dead don't care about justice — that's for the living. And don't say that it's for Alex either — he's too young to give a damn about anything but being with you, Elena. So let's be clear: any justice you get by doing this would be for you. And I'm saying it would be selfish."

Her arms stiffened, and shook some more, and her voice was ragged. "You don't know —"

"I know Alex wants his mother. It's all that matters to him — what he needs more than anything — and you're the only one who can give it to him. Or take it away. You told me once that there was nothing you wouldn't do for him. Were you lying to me then?"

Elena's face softened, and went from bone white to red. Her eyes were red and wet. "It's . . . It's too late, doctor — it's already too late. I shot him already."

"It's not, Elena. The Brays can explain away gunshot wounds — am I right, Mandy?" Mandy nodded vigorously. "We can work things out for you and Alex, as long as you don't shoot Kyle any more and you let me take care of him."

Elena was quiet for a long while, and sweat rolled down my back and soaked my shirt. I could feel the pulse throbbing in my neck, and I tried not to look at Conti, who was motionless in the foyer. Then Elena pivoted quickly and pointed the gun at Harris Bray, who flinched and shrank back.

"You can't shoot him either," I said.

Elena looked at me and smiled and let her hands drop down. "I'm not going to shoot him, doctor, but I think I made him piss his pants." She dropped the gun on the floor, and I knelt by Kyle.

EPILOGUE

FIVE MONTHS LATER

Antipsychotics were Ashe's friends. As long as he kept up and got regular blood work, he did okay — no voices, no visions, no sudden bursts of violence. Then all he had to worry about was living in a cardboard box meant originally for a refrigerator, and whether junkies in the alley would steal the plastic bags that contained his earthly possessions, and whether the police would come again with a fire hose, to scour his world from the sidewalk. But maintaining a grip on the day of the week was often more than Ashe could manage, and asking him to keep up with dosages, refills, and blood tests was like asking him to organize the Manhattan Project. Which was why, at five o'clock on Friday afternoon, he was in my exam room, whispering to himself, his big shoulders hunched and twitching, his white count too low, his triglycerides way too high, and the knuckles on both his hands scabbed and swollen from recent blows. It was this last thing that had prompted his friend Cammy to drag him in that day. I'd called her into the exam room after I'd dressed his hands, in the hope she might convince Ashe to make the trip to County, but neither of them was buying it.

Ashe slumped like a punched-out heavyweight on the exam table, and Cammy stood before him, one hand on his shoulder and another on his brown, scarred head. She squinted at me, her eyes like flecks of mica in her ravaged face.

"We'll think hard on it, doc," she said. "I'll take himself over to the mission for sandwiches, and we'll think really hard. He likes the lunch meat."

I sighed and shook my head. "Sandwiches won't do it, Cammy. He needs his meds adjusted, more liver function tests, and his hands are infected. We're going to close up soon. Lucho can run you to the hospital."

Lucho sagged in the doorway, but managed something like an encouraging look. "I can do it now. Muriel can wrap up."

I nodded, and Cammy and Ashe exchanged suspicious glances. Finally, Cammy nodded too, and she and Ashe shambled, arm in arm, down the hall after Lucho. I took a deep breath and washed my hands and face in the sink.

Ashe was it for the day — for the week, in fact. We were closed that weekend, for painting — exterior work this time. The inside had been done two weekends before, and the new-paint smell still lingered in the stairwell and halls. Painting was the last item on a list of repairs and upgrades that we'd been working on for several months. Painting, wiring, plumbing, new security cameras, new chairs and flooring in the waiting room, new tile and a new toilet to make the bathroom less terrifying, and a half-dozen pieces of new medical equipment — all thanks to a donation that had arrived in a black nylon duffel, three weeks to the day after I'd tended to Kyle Bray's gunshot wound and treated him and his father for shock.

Conti had delivered it to my apartment. He'd opened the duffel to show me the banded packs of cash, and taken a beer from my refrigerator and a seat at my kitchen table. He took a long pull on his beer.

"Mandy said to tell you one of her lawyers will be in touch about transferring title on this palace here."

I nodded. "She lets you call her Mandy now?"

"We're still working things out."

"I can imagine."

"She's not bad — even if I don't understand half the shit she talks about. She's smart, and she does what she says. And she knows how to win. She cleaned the Captain's clock damn good, that's for sure. With your help." He raised his beer bottle in mocking toast. "You see the news?"

I nodded. Bray Consolidated's announcement of Harris Bray's retirement, and of his decision to hand the reins to his niece, had filled three slow news days in the business press the week before, and spawned a lot of inane chatter about torches passed and glass ceilings shattered.

"I might've believed it," I said, "if I hadn't known better."

Conti drank some more and showed me the shark teeth. "Told you — she's pretty good." He wiped his hand over his mouth. "You hear anything from crazy Elena?" he asked.

"Do you think I'd say if I had?"

Conti shrugged. "Just asking."

"Haven't heard. Didn't ask. Don't know."

It hadn't been a lie back then, and now, months later, it still wasn't. The last I'd seen or heard of Elena and Alex was in the Bray Consolidated hangar at Van Nuys Airport.

It was ten days after Kyle's shooting, and they were waiting in a glass-walled office that smelled of kerosene while one of the Bray jets was prepped for a flight to Vancouver. Elena wore a white blouse, a navy skirt, and black flats, and her hair was in a ponytail. Alex wore jeans and a green polo shirt and very white sneakers.

There were more new clothes in their new suitcases, and new Romanian passports in Elena's new Coach bag. There was cash in there too: U.S. dollars, Canadian dollars, and euros, and debit cards besides. There was more money still — much, much more — in the several bank accounts and trusts that Mandy's lawyers had established, in accordance with Anne Crane's instructions and under her supervision. Neither Elena nor Alex would want for anything again, except perhaps for a night of untroubled sleep.

We hadn't talked much at the airport. Alex had stared at the plane with huge eyes, and behind her dark glasses Elena had stared at him, and never let him get beyond arm's length. They were restless and self-conscious standing together, like a couple on a first date, and my presence was a relief to them — an antidote to their awkwardness. They glanced back at me occasionally, and nodded.

The flight attendant had smiled and beckoned when it was time, and I'd walked them out to the plane. Alex had looked up at me for a while, hugged me briefly, and run up the steps. Elena looked after him anxiously and then took off her dark glasses. Her eyes were damp.

She laughed through her sniffles. "You finally get rid of us, yes?"

I nodded. "I'll have to figure out what to do with all my extra time."

Elena smiled. "And I got to figure out how to be . . . a mother again."

"You were always a mother."

"But now . . . it's just the two of us."

"You'll be fine. Spend time together. Hang out. Do things with him. Or do nothing together. He's a really nice kid."

She nodded. "Tough kid. Like his mother."

I nodded back. "You are that," I said. "Both of you. But remember what you promised about getting help, about therapy. You've both been through . . . too much."

"I remember, doctor," Elena said. "And I keep my word." Then she smiled wider, and reached up and took my face in her hands. She kissed me, and her lips were warm and soft on mine.

"You tough too, Dr. Knox," she whispered. "And also crazy. Maybe you need some therapy." She went up the stairs then, and the cabin door closed behind her, and they were gone.

I sighed, shut off the light in the exam room, and went down the hall. I saw Lucho heading out the door with Ashe and Cammy in tow, and heard Muriel buzzing through the exam rooms, the file room, the supply closet, leaving order in her wake. My pristine desktop and the new calendar on my wall were testimony to her organizing will, and still took me by surprise whenever I stepped into my office.

My desk wasn't entirely clean today. There was a postcard on it, from Nora Roby — the third she'd sent in the month she'd been away. Bright fish and a coral reef this time. *On Espiritu Santo now. Bad coffee, bad weather, bad hours — the most fun since residency.* She was in Vanuatu, helping to set up pediatric clinics in Port Vila and Luganville, and even if her Internet access had been more reliable, she would still, I thought, have opted for this old-school messaging. The brisk, one-way communiqués suited the current state of our relationship: distant, cool, and wary. Still, I told myself, she'd taken the time to write.

Nora had been surprised when I appeared at her door with a bottle of Merlot the day after Kyle's shooting. She'd squinted at me, looked around nervously, and finally invited me inside. I opened the wine and we drank, and then I told her about Elena and Alex, about the deal I'd made with Amanda Danzig, and all that had transpired in Harris Bray's office.

She was pale when I finished, and quiet. The wine was gone by then, but she'd found another bottle and opened it before she spoke. "Jesus," she said. "Those fucking bastards."

"That's unfair to bastards."

"What they did — he and Kyle — and they got away with it."

"Not entirely."

"They had people killed; they kidnapped that boy; the old man is a rapist, for chrissakes. And neither of them is facing justice."

"Elena and Alex are together, and they'll be taken care of — so that's a good outcome. As for justice . . ." I shrugged. "Harris is losing his company, which is probably the most important thing in the world to him. And Kyle has to live with it all — what he's done, what his father did — all of it. On top of which, I doubt he'll ever walk quite right again. None of which is justice, I know — not for what they did. But it's the closest I could come."

She shook her head, looked at me. "And you — you were goddamn lucky. Things could've played out very differently. Very badly."

"I know that."

She shook her head. "The things Bray threatened to do — to you and Lydia, to Lucho and Artie — you never said anything about those. Not a word."

"You weren't returning my calls at the time."

Nora nodded slowly. "If you had told me, and I knew you still hadn't called the police, I would've thought . . . I'm not sure what I would've thought."

"That I was crazy. Crazier."

She smiled ruefully. "I think that now. To do the things you did, the risks you took . . . Jesus, simply not reporting Kyle's gunshot wound — that alone could've cost your license. And the danger you put Arthur and Lucho and Lydia in: Why was their well-being less important than Elena's? Why weren't they your first priority? I don't know what to make of that kind of judgment."

I swallowed hard and nodded and said nothing.

Nora shook her head some more. "We've got . . . things to work out, Adam. We wandered into this without much thought or discussion — because it was so easy, I guess. But I'm too old for that, and maybe you are too. We need to figure out what we've got here, and what, if anything, we want it to be."

Which is what we'd been doing since that night. Figuring out *what, if anything.* Seeing each other less, but still seeing each other. Seeing other people too, sometimes. Distant, cool, wary. Still, she'd taken the time to write.

I put the postcard alongside the others from Nora, on the bulletin board behind my desk — another of Muriel's improvements. She came in as I was pinning it up, and smiled her approval. Her cheeks were round and brown and shining.

"You need anything before I lock up, doctor?" she asked. She was from New Orleans, and the city was strong in her voice.

I shook my head. "I'm good, Muriel."

"And you remember about the painters tomorrow, yeah?"

"I remember."

She smiled and nodded. "Okay, doctor, then we see you soon." She disappeared from the doorway, only to reappear in an instant. "And you remember the alarm, yeah?"

"Got it." She smiled again and waved.

Arthur had found her in the office of another of his clients — a Botox clinic in the Valley. She was looking for a shorter commute, and something more challenging than paralyzing middle-aged faces all day, and we offered both. She'd started three months back and was working out just fine — better than fine. But I was still getting used to the fact that she wasn't Lydia.

Lydia had quit — moved with Junie to his cabin in the desert. She'd tendered her resignation the night of Kyle's shooting, when I called to tell her that it was over: that the phony lawsuits against us, the threat to Artie, the eviction actions were all gone, that we were safe again. She'd been quiet afterward, and then she asked about Elena and Alex.

"They're fine, Lyd," I'd answered. "Both of them. They're together, and they're going to stay together. They'll be able to go wherever they want to."

There'd been more quiet, and then a sigh. "That's good, doctor," she said softly. "I'm glad of it."

"You and me both. Now we can get back to business as usual. Better than usual, actually. I'm going to be getting the title on the clinic, so we won't have to worry about being homeless anymore, and we'll have some money to spend, to fix the place up."

The silence after that was endless. When Lydia finally broke it, it was to tell me she was quitting. I hadn't believed it at first, had sputtered and stumbled, and finally managed to ask why.

"You need to ask, doctor? After everything that happened? You tell me it's all okay now, that you waved some magic wand and all the danger is gone, and we're going to live happily ever after, and I'm supposed to say *okay*? I'm just supposed to forget what you got us into? The danger you put us in? I'm supposed to pretend it didn't happen?"

"Lyd —"

"I *told* you I want a quiet life. I *told* you we had it good here, and not to mess with that. But that didn't matter to you. *We* didn't matter."

"It mattered, Lyd — you matter."

"Not enough, doctor — not as much as what *you* wanted. It was selfish, doctor. You were selfish."

She'd come in the next day to clear out her things. I had no idea how she was faring out in the heat and sand. I could've asked Lucho, but so far I hadn't.

I set the alarm and went upstairs and took a Stella from the fridge. I drank half of it before I got in the shower. When I'd dried off and wrapped the towel around my waist, I reached for the other half. I'd taken barely a sip when my cell burred. I checked the number. Mandy.

We'd been in touch three times since that afternoon in her uncle's office.

The first time was two days after, in the hushed offices of her lawyers, where I went after hours with Anne Crane to work out the details of Elena's and Alex's money, and of my own. Mandy was all business then, scrupulous in her attention to detail, and in fulfilling the terms we'd agreed on days earlier, but otherwise too absorbed in the stream of messages, e-mails, and calls she received on her many cell phones to do more than wink at me once.

The second time was six weeks later, after Elena and Alex had flown away, after I'd gotten my cash and the title to the clinic building, after Mandy had seized her empire. She'd called from Van Nuys Airport.

"I'm wondering if you want to have another drink," she said.

"It's two in the morning, Mandy."

"I'm in from Hong Kong, so for me it's cocktail time. And besides, it's Saturday, isn't it? Tell me I woke you up."

"You might have."

"But I didn't. So — what do you say, doc, a drink? I could swing by on my way home, and pick you up."

"It's not on your way."

"Everything's on the way when somebody else is driving." Mandy's Mercedes SUV pulled up forty-five minutes later. She mixed two Sazeracs and raised the partition, and her engagement ring was nowhere in sight.

I didn't return to my place until late Sunday afternoon, when a taxi dropped me off in front. I was bleary-eyed, trembling, sore, rubbed raw, and queasy — and not just from the hangover. I went upstairs and spent half an hour in the shower.

The last time we'd spoken was not quite two months ago. It was around ten in the evening, and she'd called to tell me about the stroke.

"It happened three days ago. The chief of neurology said it was a *basilar artery dissection.*" She was calling from Palms-Pacific, and her voice was tired and without emotion. "He said it was a rare kind of bleed."

"Jesus."

"Apparently, it was a big one. Like, huge. The neurologist said it's left him in something called a *pseudocoma*."

I sighed. "Locked-in syndrome."

"Yep — that's the other thing he called it — *L-I-S*. He's paralyzed from the neck down, he's mute, but he's not vegetative. The doctor says he's aware of what's going on, at least to some extent — enough that he can answer yes or no questions by blinking his eyes."

"Have they given you a prognosis?"

"They've given me stats, which I guess is easier than actually talking to me. When I wade through the numbers, the takeaway is pretty grim. Regaining speech or gross motor skills is a highly improbable outcome — like winning-the-lottery improbable. Most likely, he's going to be a paperweight for as long as he lives."

I sighed. "Jesus, Mandy."

"My aunt is in with him now, and my parents, too. I called Kyle down in Mexico the day it happened, and he's been MIA ever since. Which maybe is for the best."

"It's . . . it's a horrible thing to have happen. To anybody."

She laughed bitterly. "Even to him, right? You know, I've been trying to dredge up some warm thoughts about him, some nice memory, but . . ." She sighed. "My corporate communications guy should be here soon, to work on the press release. Maybe he can come up with something. Anyway, I thought you'd want to know."

She hung up after that, and I stood looking at my phone for a long time, thinking of Harris Bray's massive head and brutal face, and hearing Nora's voice saying something about justice.

I stood in my towel, sipping beer, while my phone rang and then stopped ringing. Mandy didn't leave a voice mail. There were five Stellas left in the fridge, and after I pulled on jeans and a tee shirt, I carried them to the roof, along with the joint I'd rolled the night before.

The sky was a supersaturated orange in the west, and still full of heat. The downtown towers were bright, and Friday night traffic was beginning to thicken on the streets. There was a parking lot a block away, where a charred storefront had been a month back, and it was full every weekend night. A gluten-free bakery was opening next to it next week. The tide of progress, still pushing relentlessly eastward, still driving the poor and sick and luckless before it. I stretched out on a lawn chair, and my bones felt suddenly like lead. I sighed, and opened another beer.

I'd been lucky, I knew — to have survived

Siggy and the Brays; to have survived Elena; to have survived with the clinic intact; to have survived at all. Nora had said it, so had Sutter, and I knew they were right. I knew it, but somehow — even at a distance of five months — I didn't feel it. Maybe it was the cost of my luck — the price paid in fear and danger by people I cared for. Maybe it was the price I was still paying, in relationships that were strained or damaged or gone altogether. Or maybe it was the fact that a pile of money — no matter what height — could never undo what had been done to Elena and Alex. That it was all, finally, just another holding action.

I shook my head at my own bullshit, took a sip of beer, and dug in my pocket for my phone. I scanned through my music but couldn't choose, and put it on shuffle. Miles came on, and I hung the joint at the corner of my mouth and patted my pockets for a match. I'd just found one when my phone burred again.

"You have plans tonight, brother," Sutter said, "or are you up for a house call?"

I sighed. "You know, my cash flow is better, right? Without rent to pay, the clinic supports itself."

He laughed. "You remind me every time I call lately, but still you don't say no. The alley, in fifteen?"

"Make it twenty," I said. I tucked the joint behind my ear, and hauled myself upright.

ACKNOWLEDGMENTS

Much gratitude to the many who helped while I was writing this book: Denise Marcil, for her unwavering enthusiasm and support; Drs. Spiegelman, Miller, and Glucksman, for their various consultations with Dr. Knox; Nina Spiegelman, for another early read; Sonny Mehta, for — yet again — vast patience and invaluable feedback; and Alice Wang for . . . well, you know.

ABOUT THE AUTHOR

Peter Spiegelman is the author of *Black Maps,* which won the 2004 Shamus Award for Best First P.I. Novel, *Death's Little Helpers, Red Cat,* and *Thick as Thieves.* Prior to becoming a full-time writer, Mr. Spiegelman spent nearly twenty years in the financial services and software industries, and worked with leading banks and brokerages around the world. He lives in Connecticut.